TWO MEN BEFORE THE STORM

Arba Crane's Recollection of Dred Scott
and the Supreme Court Case That Started the Civil War

Gregory J. Wallance

GREENLEAF
BOOK GROUP PRESS

Published by Greenleaf Book Group Press, Austin, Texas
Copyright ©2006 Gregory J. Wallance

ISBN: 1-929774-36-2

Library of Congress Control Number: 2005928056

Submit all requests for reprinting to:
Greenleaf Book Group LP
4425 Mopac South, Suite 600
Longhorn Bldg., 3rd Floor
Austin, TX 78735
512-891-6100

Printed in the United States of America

Cover design and composition by Greenleaf Book Group LP

Cover Painting: "Last Sale of the Slaves, 1860" by Thomas Satterwhite Noble.
Courtesy Missouri Historical Society, St. Louis.

Printed in the United States of America

10 9 8 7 6 5 4 3 2 1   08 07 06 05

Also by Gregory J. Wallance:

Papa's Game (Edgar Allen Poe Award Finalist)

For Lies, Daniël, Carina, and Lisanna

Acknowledgments

This is a work of historical fiction. The Author's Note and Chapter Historical Notes at the end of this book describe the historical events and background of the *Dred Scott* case. I am grateful for the information and source materials provided by the Kansas State Historical Society, the Vermont Historical Society, the Historical Society of Windham County, the Minnesota Historical Society, and especially the Missouri Historical Society. State and local historical societies such as these are national treasures and deserve our support.

My editor, Ed Stackler, was indispensable to this project. My agents, Jay Acton of Spartan Literary Associates, Inc., and Ken Atchity of AEI, provided unstinting encouragement and sensible suggestions. Others who have been a source of support and assistance include Coralee Paull, Sandy Schlesinger, Christopher Brewster, Mary McHugh, Marcia Horowitz, Robin Wagge, Tom Crane, and Lynda Matulis. Finally, Clint Greenleaf and his staff, especially Lari Bishop, Tanya Hall, and Sheila Parr, have my gratitude for making this book a reality.

"IF THE SUPREME COURT IS EVER COMPOSED OF IMPRUDENT OR BAD MEN, THE UNION MAY BE PLUNGED INTO ANARCHY OR CIVIL WAR."

—Alexis de Tocqueville, *Democracy in America, Volume II* (1840)

July 5, 1863
Gettysburg, Pennsylvania

Dear Father:

I am wounded but receiving good care in a field hospital. Weakness prevented me from writing earlier and relieving your anxiety. By now you will have read of the great battle. No account in the newspapers can bear the slightest resemblance to what happened. Nor can a letter, but I feel I must try.

The vast sepulchral roar of artillery volleys. Thousands of dead sprawled throughout orchards and cornfields. The mewling sound that badly wounded men make when they cry for their mothers or for water or for death. The puddles of blood in the rocks.

Most wounded lay where they fell, but some crawled or hobbled toward the lines. I was stopped dozens of times by staggering men who asked the way to the hospital of their division.

At night under a stricken moon, my party and I sought to remove those who could be helped and comfort those who could not. We found few to be saved and little mortal comfort to be given the others. When I returned I lay down to sleep but could only think of the Confederate corpse that I had stumbled across. It was an officer and not a vestige of his head remained. It had been severed from his body as though with a knife. His briarwood pipe had been forced down his throat.

I took a wound in the leg on the third day and was taken to a field hospital. The music there is the high-pitched singing of the surgical saws against bone. The screams are so wretched and piercing that a blind, deaf man would be moved to tears. A pale surgeon, exhausted, eyes unfocused, absentmindedly wrung blood from his smock while telling me that my wound should not prove fatal.

My wound greatly surprised the men in my regiment. They thought of me as fearless if not reckless, as I had courted death with impunity but never been harmed until now. One fellow officer visited me here and read from a letter he had written to his family:

"Of Crane, little is known beyond his name and that he enlisted as a private. His conspicuous gallantry won him promotion and his kindly but firm discipline won the loyalty of his men. When wounded severely, he smiled as he was struck. I later heard the surgeon remark that he seemed positively happy under the pain of the probing for the bullet."

After allowing me to hear this, the officer waited for an explanation, but I said nothing. I have not been surly with my men, Father, but I have not sought close comradeship either. I would not expect any of them to understand my mind.

Ask a man why he is here, and he will stammer and mutter something about the Union or how his brother was killed at Savage Station. The truth is that none of them knows why he is here. A man who thought he knew will feel less sure after a sleepless night listening to the wails of the wounded, or after a ball rips off a limb and the blood gushes out as though pumped by the Devil himself.

You are one of the few who understand. I am the reason they are here. Indeed, I made it inevitable that they come here to die.

And I know who set the stage, lit the footlamps, told the actors their positions, and readied the curtain to be raised. How vividly I recall it all, especially the beginning, an eternity ago when I was a hopeful pilgrim on a hopeless journey, as much fleeing what lay behind me as seeking what I thought lay ahead.

I grow weak. I must rest for a time. I will finish this when I am stronger.

—Arba Crane, written in a Gettysburg field hospital

Chapter 1

A girl stood on the platform, the man beside her, in a top hat and formal coat, waving a piece of paper. She kept her head lowered, but her stance could not hide an attitude of exalted grace and sorrow. A simple frock draped her bosom and hips like that of a goddess. Her skin was almost indistinguishable in color from my own, but tight curls of coal-black hair cradled her head.

The man in the top hat gestured at her, but she remained motionless. He spoke angrily and she lifted her arms. In response to another command, repeated twice before it was obeyed, she turned her head in my direction and looked up. Her face held no expression. She was not looking at me or, for that matter, at anything in St. Louis.

"Octoroon," said Samuel O'Fallon. "Possible quadroon but I think not."

A buyer spoke to the girl, but she gave no reply. The man in the top hat raised his hand as though to strike her. She slowly shook her head.

"She's worth $2,000, maybe more," said Samuel. "I know men in New Orleans who would pay $5,000 rather than not get her."

The courthouse stood directly across the street from our carriage. The three story building was only partly finished, with a scaffolding still on the rotunda and one wing yet to be built. Steps led up from the street to a portico supported by Greek columns. To one side of the courthouse steps a German band, its members dressed in frock coats and striped pants, thumped away at a waltz. On the other side stood the low wooden platform and a small group of less nattily dressed men who inspected the girl with the bored, skeptical looks of experienced buyers.

"No one's bidding," I said.

"I'll bet she's lived in a free state. Come back to Lynch's next week and you'll see a real auction. It's an estate sale. Almost a hundred slaves. Hasn't been an auction that big in years."

Samuel took my silence as an indication of interest in the octoroon girl. "Maybe you could get that nigger cheap, Crane. Even if she did live in a free state, that'd be no problem for a good lawyer like you. She'd keep a man warm at night, now, wouldn't she?"

When I was a small boy, I once visited a relative's farm in Shelburne, Vermont. Wandering through a barn I came upon a magnificent dapple gray with arching neck, long silken mane and tail, eyes full of spirit, and hoofs that seemed to disdain the ground. I so desperately desired to ride the gray that I somehow managed to fit the towering horse with a saddle and bridle, lead her from the barn, and mount her. My feet did not even reach the stirrups. Of course, my father roughly pulled me from the gray before I could ride her back to Newfane. The pain at watching the horse led back into the barn and out of my grasp forever was infinitely greater than the pain of my father's caning after we returned home.

Now, God help me, I was possessed by an equally overwhelming temptation, except that this time nothing stood between me and my desire but mere dollars and my conscience. How easy to buy a human being and how gratifying to command satisfaction of every whim, especially carnal ones. A fine horse, a fine musical instrument, a fine house—why not a fine human being? Do not our possessions give

6

us satisfaction? If so, what could be more satisfying than to possess a young girl in the prime of life, one of Nature's finest creations, so striking in physique that, had all eight of her great-grandparents been white instead of just seven, dashing young men would have been hers to command, and not the other way around?

The man on the platform, responding to a question from one buyer, gave another order to the girl, who did not obey. This time the auctioneer did not repeat his instruction but instead yanked the girl's frock to her waist, then spun her around.

I winced at the intricate embroidery. The bounty Nature had conferred on her, so proud and firm from the front, man had taken away from her back. The remaining buyers assumed an uninterested pose, talking to one another, checking their watches, and making notes on pieces of paper.

"In the North," I said, "young women do not need to be whipped to keep men warm at night."

Samuel scowled and started to reply, but then shook his head as though he had thought better.

The German band played on.

Until that moment, riding in stagecoaches and sighting the hurricane deck of the *Kimball* had been the worst part of my journey west. The staging had involved endless dampness or dust, punctuated by jolting, now across a watercourse, now against a branch of a felled tree. I would fall asleep only to awaken suddenly as I jostled against a fellow passenger. If the coach was full, I rode with five other passengers, all of us confined in too small a space.

The hardships of the journey had been more than worth the exhilarating relief of watching Newfane and my father grow steadily more distant. Scenery was another compensation. When we gained the crest of the Alleghenies, trees filled my vision, broken only by the occasional small, neat house painted white. Columns of smoke rose lazily from chimneys in forests that made Vermont look like a meadow. At the Ohio River, the kalmia, wild rose, and purple phlox grew luxuriantly.

Oh America! Oh Garden of Eden! This was the Biblical land of milk and honey through which a sweet river meandered. Here was innocence and plenty such as I had found only in illustrations in children's books. I was on the edge of Fredrika Bremer's enigmatical land, with its buffaloes and golden hummingbirds and cities growing great in a lifetime. My excitement provoked smiles from my weary and jaded fellow travelers.

I boarded the steamboat *Sarah*, where, because the boat was then only partially filled, I was fortunate to have a cabin to myself. The cabin was adequate, but the boat itself was a marvel. A gallery encircled it, giving each cabin a veranda, and an airy hurricane deck afforded splendid panoramas. A grand salon, complete with luxurious sofas, sold as much liquor as I could afford.

When I wasn't drinking in the salon, I spent my time in the rocking chairs on the gallery, studying Missouri law and watching the landscape drift by. Men on the gallery frequently drew pistols and shot ducks, wagering large sums on their marksmanship. On one occasion I borrowed a pistol and, because I had never killed a duck for the dubious pleasure of seeing it die, bet a fellow passenger five dollars that I could hit a distant branch in a dead tree on the riverbank. I had learned to shoot as a boy. To earn money, I had hunted red foxes, which brought twenty-five cents from the Vermont State Treasurer.

I quickly sighted and fired at the branch, which snapped cleanly from the tree and fell into the river. My shot drew compliments but flushed an unseen flock of ducks, who were promptly shot down by other passengers. As the passenger handed over the money and began firing at the ducks, I commented that the consequences of our actions seem seldom, if ever, to follow from the intentions with which we act. He seemed less interested in philosophy than in killing ducks and winning his next wager.

We landed at various towns and villages to drop off and take on new passengers. I enjoyed the nighttime loading of wood fuel. After rapid exchanges of signals from ship to shore and back, the *Sarah* suddenly heeled toward the riverbank, close to the edge of a forest. Piles of burning logs in iron grates lit up the river, the riverbank, and the boat in a ghostly light. When we swerved to the northern bank of the river, grim Irish laborers threw great logs aboard. When we landed on the opposite bank, a gang of chattier negroes did the work. As we resumed our stately progression, the riverbank fire was doused, the noise died away, and the still night descended.

The steamboat was filled with an assortment of aspiring trappers heading west, rapacious businessmen and bankers talking of land speculation, hawk-eyed gamblers lingering in the salon into the early morning hours, German families planning new lives in Missouri, and a French consul on his way to a new posting. One of the gamblers relieved me of the money I had won because my skill with cards was not nearly equal to that with a pistol. The gambling to which I succumbed was constant, as were discussions of steamboats, liquor, cards, dueling, black-land, red-land, bottom-land, timberland, sugar, cotton, corn, and negroes. In one form or another, all the talk concerned one thing: money.

We left the Ohio at Cairo, and on our first day on the Mississippi, the *Sarah* was approached from the stern by a steamboat. From a distance it appeared to be carrying a load of black cattle on its hurricane deck. The *Sarah*'s passengers crowded to the rail.

We heard the other steamboat's firemen shout as they worked the furnaces. Their passengers cheered them. "Shove her up, boys!" "Shove her up!" "Give her hell!"

On our steamboat, a fellow passenger said, "Hear that whistling? There ain't much water in our boilers when you hear that."

A negro waiter shook his head at the *Sarah*'s speed. "The old lady too heavy."

The other steamboat, named the *Kimball*, drew closer. I realized that the steamboat's hurricane deck wasn't packed with cattle but with female slaves, most sitting with their knees drawn up. Their heads were down but at the sound of the *Sarah*'s engine a few looked up with blank and empty expressions. They were the largest and strongest women I had ever seen together.

Soon the *Kimball* was running head to head with the *Sarah*, so close that one might have jumped easily from our paddle box to her guards.

A man said to me, "That's a good lot."

Another passenger nodded. "Damned good."

He mistook my fascination with the deck of the *Kimball* for envy and added in a sympathetic way, "I bet you wished they belonged to you."

Still stunned by the sight, I ignored his well-meant comment. As the *Kimball* drew ahead, I noticed that, although most of the slaves seemed of childbearing age, no children sat on the *Kimball*'s hurricane deck.

Amid much blowing of whistles, the contest was given up. The *Kimball* soon disappeared, and I was left to wonder exactly where it was I thought I was going.

My first sight of St. Louis was a smudge of smoke hanging in the distance over an equally brown river. As we rounded a bend in the river, the source of the dark cloud, dozens of gingerbread-trimmed steamboats, nestled two and three abreast along the levee, came into view.

The levee, miles long, was piled with crates, hogsheads, and bales of cotton that were whiter than the freshest snowfall. Behind the bales stood a row of brick warehouses and other commercial buildings, none taller than a few stories, and behind them more and more rows of buildings gently rose in terraces up the western bank of the river. Only one tall cathedral broke the monotony of the clustered buildings.

With triumphant excitement I stood on the levee, perhaps in the same spot where Meriwether Lewis had set foot before beginning his journey to the Pacific. My escape from Newfane was complete, but I had no opportunity to savor the moment because I was assaulted immediately by a symphony the likes of which can never be heard in an orchestral hall. The bells and whistles of the steamers mixed with the rasps of fiddlers, the serenades of organ grinders, the musical cries of the apple and orange girls, the cigar and book vendors, the little negro boiler cleaners, and the bootblacks. Draymen richly cursed their overflowing wagons on their way to the landing stages, and through it all rang the lament of the negro town crier, "Lost child! Lost child!," only to be drowned out by the whoops of western cowboys lashing cattle and hogs and mules through the streets.

Bowie knives and pistols seemed to be a part of every white man's wardrobe on the levee. Flocks of urchins mingled with loafers, drunkards, and rowdies from the nearby saloons. Young girls exposed themselves for a few pennies and boys hawked newspapers. An old man begged me to buy a gun cleaner, and a girl offered me a watermelon. Muscular slaves, glistening with sweat, carried cargo from the boats to the levee and waiting dray wagons. A man with a cigar in his mouth whipped a horse into agony while some passers-by averted their faces and others went out of their way to express their sternest disapproval at his mistreatment of one of God's dumb creatures. Drivers of carriages and hacks skillfully threaded their way through the melee to pick up the *Sarah*'s passengers. "Virginia Hotel, gentlemen?" "Baggage for the Monroe! Baggage wagon ready!" "Planters' House, sir?"

Passengers thronged around them, shouting destinations, elbowing each other, and waving money at the drivers.

My excitement faded in the face of mundane practicalities. No one had come to the levee to meet me. I considered the dubious prospects for hailing a hack.

"Crane! I say, Arba Crane!"

In an arriving carriage a well-dressed, blond young man in a finely woven coat and a top hat waved his arms. The carriage pulled to a halt, and he jumped out and pushed his way through the mass of disembarking passengers.

"O'Fallon," he said. "Samuel. Harvard? Don't you remember?"

I recalled a young Southerner who had lasted less than a year at the Law School. Unlike the other mostly gay and charming Southern students, he achieved a certain notoriety for fighting, drinking, and boasting about his family pedigree. Our paths had barely crossed. At the Law School, I had embraced the comforting certainties and logic of the law as an antidote to suspicion and doubt. I could go into the law library and, if every volume were in its place, find any volume in the dark. Samuel O'Fallon, went the joke, could not even find the law library. The man in front of me was somewhat heavier and far better dressed than in our law school days. The blue eyes, aristocratically thin nose, and brightly confident smile were the same.

"Samuel O'Fallon. Of course." We shook hands. "The last I heard you were in New Orleans."

"I was, but the Colonel needed my help here. Mr. Field asked me to meet you and help you get settled. He's in court in Pike County. First thing is to get your luggage. Tom! Ezra!"

Two negroes climbed out of the carriage. "This is Mr. Crane. He'll show you his luggage. Be quick about it."

Rather slowly, Tom and Ezra followed me to the luggage stand, shouldered my valises and trunks, and maneuvered them through the crowds to the carriage. We all got in the carriage, the two negroes in the front, one holding the reins, and Samuel and I in the back.

"The levee is the pride of St. Louis," said Samuel, gesturing at the bustling waterfront as we rolled away from the *Sarah*.

As we journeyed through St. Louis, we passed gangs of negroes working on buildings, digging trenches or repairing sidewalks under the watchful eyes of white men in broadbrim hats. Samuel pointed to an empty lot where more negroes were digging a foundation. "That's going to be the new Customs House. Over there is the Bank of St. Louis. We've got you at Planters' House. Best hotel in St. Louis. It's just across from the courthouse."

"Mr. Field wrote that I would be at Daniel Davies."

"One of the boarders at Daniel Davies has cholera."

I was delighted at the change in accommodation, but said, "That is simply too expensive—"

"You Yankees hate spending money, don't you? Mr. Field handles the Planters' House legal matters and got you quite a decent rate. Why, Crane, you'll build a law practice just at the Planters' bar. It's the nerve center of the entire Valley. The old money in this town never goes to the bar, but the new money—the Blows, the Belchers, the Filley brothers—are regulars. The Germans and most of the Yankees drop by at least once a week."

As we bounced through the streets, my first impressions of St. Louis were not inspiring. The main streets had sidewalks paved with bricks, but the middle of the streets appeared to be a sea of mud. Crossing stones were spaced far enough apart that the wheels of a carriage could pass between them and a pedestrian, with some dexterity, could jump from one to another. I watched as one hapless soul misjudged his leap, plunged one foot into the mire and then, lifting it, left his boot submerged. Much laughter came from the sidewalks and our carriage, although it did not seem nearly as amusing several weeks later when I had the same experience.

"No one has time to build roads or parks or even much of a water system. We're too busy making money. You'll learn not to drink a glass of water unless it's been sitting for at least ten minutes." Samuel waved at a man on the sidewalk, who waved back. "Fortunes are made here every day, Crane. The Colonel bought land when it was four dollars an acre and now we've got 2,000 acres and 120 slaves."

He said to one of the slaves, "The Colonel takes right good care of his slaves, doesn't he?"

"Yes, Master. Ezra ain't the same nigger when the Colonel's away."

He turned to me. "If all the slaves were treated the way the Colonel treats Tom and Ezra, there wouldn't be any cry from Boston-way. I never could convince our classmates of that, could I? Not much fun to be a slave owner's son in Cambridge."

"Perhaps not." The resentment in his eyes caused me to add, with undisguised contempt for the weakness that we both shared, "You didn't do yourself any good by half the time coming drunk to the moot courts."

"Well, I got my law license, no thanks to Harvard, and I have more clients than I can handle." We rode in silence for a time. "In Cambridge, I never really knew where you stood, Arba, but you are in St. Louis now. It's not exactly an abolitionist town. And the New England population is small compared to the Southerners."

I looked at him sharply. Samuel's lips creased in a faint smile. He was trying to provoke me and almost succeeding. I had done my share of fighting in the slyly hidden taverns of southern Vermont, but did not wish to mark my first day in St. Louis with a fight.

Then Samuel said with forced cheerfulness, "When you're not making money, if your puritan soul can stand it, I suggest you get a copy of the *Joker's Budget* and then make the rounds on Green Street. Or you can take my advice and go directly to Ann Simms. She's a free mulatto and runs an establishment for white gentlemen of the upper ten. It's very private and if she knows that I sent you, she'll give you the best choice of whatever color suits your fancy."

I ignored him and devoted my attention to the passing buildings.

We turned onto Fourth Street near the Broadway intersection. The crowds appeared mostly young, male, and almost identically dressed in black morning coat, jacket and trousers, a white shirt, and standing collar with black bow tie or stock.

"That's the hotel. Over there is the New Courthouse." The carriage pulled up in front of the Planters' House, a large, stately four story hotel with a limestone front that filled the block.

It was then that Samuel and I saw the octoroon slave girl on the auction block. When I saw her scarred back I felt physically ill and moved as if to leave the carriage.

"Stupid nigger girl." Samuel stepped down with me. "I guess a man'd have to have a whip between his legs to get that fancy to open hers." He spat. "Tom, Ezra, help Mr. Crane with his luggage. I'll be back in half an hour." He gestured at a street beyond the courthouse and then casually tossed me a key. "Mr. Field's law office is on Chestnut, two blocks down from the courthouse. You'll see his shingle. He left you instructions. I will see you on Friday night at the Blows."

"Pardon?" I barely got the word out. My mouth was dry from a familiar thirst that water could not quench.

"Didn't I tell you? You have an invitation to Taylor Blow's party, courtesy of Mr. Field. The Blow sons married rich. The best butterflies in St. Louis will be there."

His jaunty self again, Samuel climbed onto the front seat of the carriage, grabbed the reins, picked up a whip, which he snapped at the horses, and drove off.

Tom and Ezra, laden with my luggage, followed me into the hotel. I glanced back at the girl on the block as she was led away by the auctioneer. She had pulled her frock to her shoulders, hiding the violence done to her back. Her head remained down and she walked with the slow, helpless gait of the doomed.

Chapter 2

I left my bags unpacked in my room at the Planters' House and, resolutely ignoring the smoke-filled, boisterous hotel bar that beckoned like an oasis, walked the short distance to the building on Chestnut Street. Small, elegant signs next to the entrance listed several lawyers, including "Law Office of Roswell M. Field—Second Floor."

I had come nearly to the end of a long journey. I stood like a paralytic, unable to proceed up the flight of stairs. I stared at the gold-embossed letters. The sight of Field's name unexpectedly breached the wall that I had carefully erected since leaving Newfane—a barrier against thoughts of Roswell Field's former law partner.

Our farewell had been characteristically tense.

"We will walk the Commons before you leave," he had said. An order, not a request.

My luggage stood ready in the carriage. We had already spoken parting words, and the fragile bonds that had tethered me uncertainly to my home were slipping away. I was more than ready to leave Newfane and Vermont for St. Louis.

Reluctantly I turned from the carriage to face my father. Dressed in identical black frock coats, we began a final stroll on the snow-covered Commons. We walked past the Windham County Courthouse, where my father had served as Newfane Town Justice for as long as I could remember. There, he had earned a reputation in southern Vermont as a wise but stern judge.

He was a thin, bearded man of somber countenance, the hair along the sides of his head combed forward in a favored style of the day, framing a pale face whose most prominent features were a hawk-like nose and intelligent gray-green eyes. My earliest memory was of my father poring over his law books, to which he was even more devoted than to the Bible.

I had learned the Latin judicial maxims at our dinner table by the time I was ten. "What is the duty of the good judge?" my father would ask in Latin, to which I would respond, "The duty of the good judge is to do justice." If I answered incorrectly, I was sentenced to write the Latin words 25 times on a piece of paper. *Boni judicis est ampliare justitiam, Boni judicis est ampliare justitiam, Boni judicis est ampliare justitiam.* A correct answer was rewarded with a slight nod of his head.

Father was the first to break the uncomfortable silence.

"Who will meet you upon your arrival?"

"Mr. Field assured me in his letter that I will be met at the levee."

"What did he say about accommodations?"

"Board at Daniel Davies, where there are many New Englanders."

"Is his practice large enough to keep you busy?" These were the same questions my father had asked over and over.

"He would not have given me a position if it were otherwise. Father, I am not going to St. Louis to watch the tambourine girls."

He frowned. "Did his letter mention cholera? I read in the newspaper that there is cholera in St. Louis."

I pitied his inability to let me go, but I had endured enough.

"I would rather die of cholera in St. Louis than boredom in Newfane."

"You are a brilliant lawyer with a fine future, including a judgeship. It will be wasted on litigation over seventeenth-century French land titles." These were the dying embers of our quarrel.

"Roswell Field does not think he is wasting his legal career."

"Do you really think Roswell Field left Vermont because he wanted to build a Mississippi River law practice?"

"Then why did he leave?"

He did not answer, and we continued our unhappy walk on Newfane Commons. When I was a child the town fathers had moved the village from its perch on Newfane Hill overlooking the West River. The higher site had been chosen because it was defensible against attacks by Indians. With the Indians long gone, the town fathers decided that their economic interests would be best served if the town relocated to the Brattleboro Road. The inhabitants took apart the town buildings and most of the houses, loaded them onto ox carts, dragged them off the Hill to the flats around Smith Brook, and put them up again. The only remains of the town on Newfane Hill were crumbling foundations and an overgrown Commons. Late each summer, without discussion or planning, a Newfane resident climbed the Hill and scythed the Commons.

I always suspected that the town moved because it had nothing better to do.

But, if the town fathers had chosen England or France for a new home I still would not have remained. I had seen those places. Although I had graduated from Harvard Law School near the top of my class, my father had not regarded my legal education as complete. He sent me on a tour of Europe's legal institutions, where I might study the rituals of lawgiving at their source. In London, I not only saw the famous monuments and buildings but, through letters of introduction obtained by my father, I sat beside a magistrate who periodically belched during hearings at the Old Bailey and was assigned a guest seat in the Queen's Counsel row at the Queen's Bench. In Paris, I attended law lectures at the Sorbonne, dined with pompous French judges, and was given a chair at the Cour d'Assises. In Italy, fed up with the ossified rituals of the European legal system, I abandoned any interest in pursuing civil law studies. Instead, I immersed myself in its language, art, literature and history, spending half my day reading translations of Dante, Boccaccio, and Machiavelli and the other half examining the great works of art and the skeletons of saints dressed in silk. In the evenings, I savored an amorous and inebriated rebellion against the pleasureless social codes applicable to New Englanders of our standing and class.

My travels abroad left me more certain than ever that, like my father, Vermont was old and tired and rigid. Newfane, despite its relocation, remained a small village of several hundred souls. The population center was still the local cemetery. On the return voyage, I furiously paced the deck of the ship like a condemned man, and as soon as I set foot in our home, I announced that I was going west to grow up with the country.

The snow on the Commons was deep enough to be etched by footpaths, which had been covered with ashes to make them less slippery. Passers-by on the Commons saw a tall, green-eyed, beardless young man, with thick and dark wavy hair parted by a crisp hairline, strolling next to a town patriarch. "Good day, Judge Crane." "Greetings, Judge Crane." "Our best to you, Judge Crane." Most knew of my impending departure by now. My announced relocation to Missouri probably came as less of a surprise to my townsmen than to my father, for many restless young Vermonters were marching to the setting sun. The townspeople who knew us less well might have assumed that our walk on the Commons was an occasion for a final father and son intimacy, the giving of sage advice and the return of filial affection. Those who knew us better likely regarded this as my victory parade and my father's final surrender.

Though successful, from a prominent Vermont family, and well regarded, my father had suffered his losses. Once he had been law partner of the legendary Roswell Field. In the heyday of their partnership, the law office of Field & Crane had been a meeting place for the county's politicians and merchants. But the courthouse gossip and political dealings ended when Field & Crane dissolved for reasons that my father never disclosed. Shortly thereafter, Mr. Field had left Vermont for St. Louis.

Mother was a beautiful woman whose help and sympathy were always sought and never withheld. She had been educated like other young New England women in plain and ornamental needlework, arithmetic, geography, and a little history. She established a circulating library in our house, which brought in a small amount of revenue and led to my becoming a great reader at an age when most boys cared for nothing but sport.

Life, however, was unkind to her. I was the only survivor of five births. The death portraits of my sisters collected on the mantel, and my mother's sanity never completely overcame the deaths of her daughters, none of whom lived past a fourth birthday, or the ordeal of bathing little bodies and then wrapping them in cloth for burial in small coffins built by my father. As one and then another of my sisters fell ill and departed for a better world, my mother had grown ever more unable to acknowledge their absence, and my father had retreated into the haven of his law books.

With each death my parents had clung ever more fiercely to the survivors until only I remained to them. I had done my best to accept their unyielding embrace but, unsurprisingly, I turned into an undisciplined boy, unable to pay attention in church, more interested in hunting than Bible studies, and shockingly prone to question the wisdom of the smug teacher in the schoolhouse, who expected students to silently absorb his lessons like witless sponges. My father inflicted ever increasing punishment, which in turn incited me to rebellion and him to harsher punishment, until neither of us knew just who was punishing whom.

I drank and brawled and made a general nuisance of myself, but somehow I excelled in my legal studies. I promptly disappointed my father again by announcing on the day of my return from Europe that I was going to California. To my father, California might as well have been on the moon, and he was convinced that he would never see me again. He expressed considerable anger at my challenge to his authority and I retreated not an inch in the face of his fury. Finally, in the manner of good lawyers, we reached a compromise. I would go to St. Louis.

Without my father's permission, I had written his former law partner, Roswell Field, who had responded with an offer of employment. My father, even more unhappy than before, grudgingly gave in. But, really, what choice had I left him?

Now, after taking leave of my father's fellow deacon, we continued our slow walk around the Commons. My father spoke distractedly about the slow progress in replacing the cracked granite steps of the Union Church but his expression reminded me of the night that Esther Mary died at age 22 months. My father had come out of the bedroom and walked to the fireplace, sat down heavily on a chair, and stared at the flames. The dancing flames had bathed his face in a late-sunset glow that curiously made him look younger, except for his eyes, whose grief seemed to absorb the firelight rather than reflect it.

"She lies in her mother's arms. I have not the heart or the strength to take her away."

Volumes of thoughts of our shattered family might have passed between us, but neither of us knew how to communicate with the other. Later, I had looked in the bedroom, where my mother, sleeping, lay on her side, cradling my still sister. The innocent expression on my sister's calm face caused me to tremble for the sins that we had committed and had yet to commit.

Father and I approached the Post, a wooden cross with an iron ring hung from a spike at the intersection of transverse and upright. Its presence marred the otherwise tranquil setting of the Commons, to which the horse drawn sleighs gave the appearance of a New England fairy tale.

Years later I found the records of the last use of the Post. Abigail White, age 29, had been indicted by the grand jury for "giving in payment certain false, forged, and counterfeited bank notes, knowing them to be such." She admitted her guilt and was sentenced to be whipped thirty-nine times.

But I was very young when Abigail White was whipped. I knew nothing of what she had done to deserve a whipping. I always believed I remembered the event but it had a dreamlike quality. Before a great crowd, Abigail White was led from the small jail behind the courthouse to the Post. She did not so much walk as drift like a ship under sail in a light wind. A black-robed man, his face hidden under a black hood, presided sternly. Other faceless men tied Abigail White's hands to the iron ring. I can still see the color of her hair, her small stature, the cut of her dress, and even her moist cheeks. All these years I have tried to see her eyes but I cannot. Perhaps she never completely turned her head in my direction, or perhaps I saw her eyes but, like the worst nightmares, mercifully cannot recall them. But with the greatest clarity, as though a harsh white light had descended on the Commons, I can to this day see every detail of what happened next.

She was stripped to the waist, which caused a faint tremble in the crowd; the High Sheriff whipped her seven times; and then each of his seven deputies took turns applying the rest. I remember each rising and descending arm, the curl and snap of each whip stroke, the slow but methodical gathering of crisscrossing red streaks on Abigail's back, her pale skin casting the bloody lacerations into stark relief.

The crowd was as still as a forest at night. Abigail White's sacrifice to the puritan God of justice fully satiated the appetites of normal life denied these good burghers by Newfane's stifling social embrace. I glanced at the nearby homes and saw families watching from the windows with such passionate satisfaction that they were as strangers and no longer the familiar men, women, and children I had known since earliest memory on the streets and paths of the village.

Now, on the cusp of my escape from Newfane, I wanted to ask my father questions he surely could not answer. Why had I not heard any sounds when Abigail White was tied to the Post, not a whip cracking on flesh or—most hauntingly—any screams? Abigail must have screamed or at least moaned or whimpered—how could she not? But strain my memory as I might, I cannot hear her cries, her pleas for mercy and relief. Is it possible that she endured her pain in silence? Most of all, Father, what happened to Abigail White? Is she alive or dead or somewhere in between?

The pent-up questions nearly burst the dam of my lips but I thought better of asking them. I had to flee Newfane, which only meant that I must flee my father, and so I returned to our forced conversation.

"A few years from now," I said with a great effort to be gay, "I will send you a copy of the *Missouri Republican* and you will see my name on the front page."

"I am told that Elijah Lovejoy's name was on the front page of the *Missouri Republican*."

"I seriously doubt that I will be publishing an abolitionist newspaper there."

"Lovejoy published in Illinois." My father was ever precise with facts. "That didn't stop a Missouri mob from burning his press and putting five bullets into his chest." He was working hard to dampen my enthusiasm for the coming journey. "Arba, you have taken very little of my advice but heed me in this one matter. The Crane family is not abolitionist in Vermont and you certainly will not be in Missouri."

"I understand."

As we turned and walked back to my carriage, the chariot that would bear me away from Newfane to a West beckoning like Heaven, we might have expressed parting affection, if not love, but the sun broke through thick clouds and the Post cast its long shadow between us.

Chapter 3

At the top of a dusty stairway I found a door with ground-glass panels on which Mr. Field's name was repeated. On the other side of the door lay my future, so I unlocked and opened it somewhat anxiously, only to find a negro sweeping the floor. I had never been alone in a room with a negro. I stared at him.

The negro stopped sweeping, put down his broom and calmly gazed back at me. The silence grew uncomfortable.

"I'm Arba Crane."

He looked at me as though expecting an order.

"I came down from Vermont to work for Mr. Field."

He seemed unmoved by this information. He said, "They call me Dred Scott."

Dred Scott's voice had a slightly hoarse sound. He was of modest height and his skin wasn't black so much as dusky. His forehead was wrinkled and his eyes were in color a rich brown but in mood opaque, as though dark curtains had been drawn across a window. His hair, sprinkled with gray, was woven in such tight knots that it would resist any comb, and his faded, dirty overalls looked as though they had rarely felt a scrub brush.

Without thought, I reached out my hand, which he warily took. His hand was rough and dry and strange. I shook it, assuming that I was violating slave-state etiquette.

Dred Scott waited to see if I had anything further to say to him. I could not conceive of anything that might be the basis for conversation. He picked up his broom and resumed sweeping. I set out to inspect the office, where I expected to spend most of my waking time. I first examined the shelves of law books, which I was gratified to see included not only the Missouri reporters but also *Peter's Supreme Court Reports, Hall's Digest, Shry's Commentaries, Archibald's Pleadings,* the condensed English reports, and dozens of other volumes. I surveyed the daunting heaps of pleadings and affidavits on a large table, the gleaming copper spittoons, and the somber paintings of Washington and Webster. Past a partly opened ground-glass door, on which was printed "Roswell Field—Private," stood a large oak desk and leather-padded chair. Roswell Field's legal throne waited in patient regality for the return of its ruler.

I sat down in Mr. Field's chair, finding it exceedingly comfortable, and luxuriated in the sensation of presiding over the "Law Office of Arba N. Crane." In a far corner of the great desk, under a large stone paperweight, lay a moldy and yellowing legal document, so neatly aligned with the corner as to suggest it had long occupied a special place among the otherwise haphazard clutter of legal papers. I removed the paperweight to find an opinion of the Vermont Supreme Court. The caption was *Clark v. Field* and the case appeared to concern the enforcement of marriage vows. I picked up the opinion, put my feet up on Mr. Field's desk, leaned back in the grand chair, and began to read. Perhaps I might find somewhere in his office some brandy . . .

The room swung dizzily, there was a great crashing sound, a breathtaking jolt, and I was flat on my back, staring at the ceiling. My legs were above my head and tangled in the chair. I struggled without success to rise. Dred Scott appeared in the doorway of Mr. Field's office, looked at me with curiosity, and then held out his hand which I took for the second time on my first day in St. Louis. I struggled with his help to my feet. We looked at the overturned chair and then at each other.

I could not begin to explain to Dred Scott what I had been doing in Mr. Field's chair. Coloring, I righted the chair and Dred Scott, with the barest hint of a smile, returned to the outer office and resumed his cleaning. I put the Vermont Supreme Court opinion back in its place on the desk and set the paperweight over the caption in its original position. I retired to the unpadded hardwood chair at the only desk in the outer office but not without a last lingering glance at Mr. Field's chair. Someday I would be sitting in such a chair.

Two files lay on the desk. I opened the top file. The first document was a note from Mr. Field.

Arba

I trust that your journey was agreeable and that young Mr. O'Fallon was punctual. I am away on a matter in Pike County and will return on the 27th. There are two cases that require immediate attention. One is Cutter v. Waddingham, *which concerns a large parcel of land at the heart of St. Louis. Acquaint yourself with the file and then prepare a draft of a brief on rehearing to the Missouri Supreme Court. The other is* Cephas v. McConnell, *a slave case. Based on my notes, prepare a plea in abatement. Our client has a difficult legal position but Judge Lawless is well known for his proslavery views.*

You have an invitation to the Blows on Friday. I am sure that St. Louis society's first impression of you will do great credit to our native state and that your first impression of St. Louis society will not be cause for retreat to Newfane.

Roswell Field

With a contented sigh I settled in to study the files and finally be a St. Louis lawyer. The *Cutter* case involved a decade-long battle over a parcel of land in St. Louis. The parcel, known as *Prairie La Grange de Terre,* was dominated by a large mound of earth constructed centuries earlier by the Indians. Our client, Norman Cutter, had lost the lawsuit. The highest court in Missouri decided that his great-grandparents' 1777 marriage contract in St. Louis was governed by Spanish law and not, as Mr. Field had argued, by French law, under which Mr. Cutter would have title to *Prairie La Grange de Terre.*

While I worked on the rehearing brief, Dred Scott slowly cleaned the office around me, littered and stained with cigar ashes, scraps of paper, mud from the street, blotting sand, and spilled ink. Occasionally distracted by his movements, I glanced at him as he variously swept, dusted, and mopped. I had difficulty judging his age, so little experienced was I with the appearance of negroes, but he might have been in his forties or even older. He displayed neither distaste nor enthusiasm, but rather a tired familiarity with his menial tasks. He first swept and mopped Mr. Field's office, removing the carpet stains with a mysterious liquid in a bottle that he carried wherever he went; then he emptied the spittoons, surely an unpleasant task; and finally began repeating the process in the larger, outer office where I sat. His work required him to dust the law book shelves with a rag that he pulled from his pocket. Even stretching to dust a law book on a high shelf, he left the impression of being bent over, as though years of toil had permanently bowed his body. He looked at once beaten and hardened, like an anvil that had taken thousands of blows that long ago removed any metallic sheen and most of its shape and left only dented iron.

I returned to the Missouri Supreme Court's opinion. As I considered various strategies for challenging the ruling, Dred Scott finished cleaning, neatly arranged his cleaning implements in the closet, and walked to the door. I said, "Goodnight."

He half-turned, paused, then said, "Evening, Mr. Crane."

With the zeal of a constable trying to solve a murder, I spent days in the courthouse basement searching for marriage contracts made in 1777. Ultimately I concluded that all marriage contracts made that year had been governed by French law.

By the third night, after a final, furious but exultant bout of writing, I completed a draft of the petition for rehearing in *Cutter v. Waddingham,* which argued that the 19 marriage contracts I had found demonstrated that, in fact, French law applied to the contract between Mr. Cutter's great-grandmother and great-grandfather. Next I turned to *Cephas v. McConnell* and discovered that my adversary was a slave, my client the slave's owner. I was defending a lawsuit brought by his slave for freedom.

The slave, Diana Cephas, claimed to have been born into slavery in Maryland and later taken by her owner to Illinois, a free state, where she lived for several years. She claimed that after her owner abandoned her, our client, Murry McConnell, forced her to go with him to St. Louis. She alleged that her residence in a free state set her free.

Our client wanted to keep his property.

I embarked on a journey through the labyrinth of slave law, a subject not taught at the Harvard Law School. Researching the Missouri Reports, I found an 1824 case called *Winny v. Whitesides,* in which a slave owner had moved to Illinois with his slave and resided there for several years before returning to Missouri. The slave, like Diana Cephas, had found a lawyer who sued for her freedom on the basis that Congress, through the Northwest Ordinance of 1787, had abolished slavery in the Northwest Territory, part of which later became Illinois.

To my amazement, the Missouri Supreme Court had ruled in favor of the slave and rejected the slave owner's argument that his ownership rights revived upon the return of his slave to Missouri. Once Illinois law set the slave free, according to the court, Missouri law must respect it. The court had concluded that when the master who takes a slave to a free state "and by the length of residence there indicates an intention of making that place his residence and that of his slave, and thereby induces a jury to believe that fact, does, by such residence, declare his slave to have become a free man." Moreover, the Missouri Supreme

Court had followed the *Winny* ruling in every similar case presented over the next two and a half decades. Under *Winny,* Diana Cephas was entitled to her freedom.

I sat staring at the *McConnell* case file but thought only of the octoroon girl on the block. I read and reread the *McConnell* file, imagining that her name was of French derivation—Eugenie seemed to fit—that one of her maternal great-grandmothers had been a slave, that her well-to-do parents had never been slaves, but when they died and their will had come to probate without any provision for custody, her ancestry had been discovered and she was sold as a child to a man who had seen in her the promise of the rapturous beauty that I had witnessed on my first day in St. Louis.

With a sigh of frustration, I put down the *McConnell* file and left to purchase office supplies before store closing time. I overcame the surging desire to visit a saloon, but lingered among the happy, excited, chattering crowds on their way to the theater. Upon my return to the office I found Dred Scott, holding a mop, bent over my desk. He was examining the slave's petition in *Cephas v. McConnell,* not so much reading it, which I did not think he could, but more trying to divine its secrets in the manner of an archeologist attempting to translate ancient hieroglyphics. His attention might have been drawn by the final page, which I had been reading and left face up. The slave had signed the page with a peculiar mark, two small but thickly drawn circles connected by a sagging line, cut at the middle, like a pair of broken shackles. I watched until Dred looked up. He calmly stared back.

"Evening, Mr. Crane."

"Good evening." He had found me where I should not have been and now I had done the same with him. "There's no need for you to work tonight. The office is as clean as when you left it."

"Mr. Field, he tell me to clean here twice a week."

I shrugged and went back to work on the *Cephas v. McConnell* petition, making several futile attempts at writing a plea in abatement to dismiss the petition as legally insufficient. Restless and distracted and starting to feel the ache in my forehead that could be cured only by a drink of whisky, I flipped a coin into the air again and again. On the fifth toss, I dropped it. The coin rolled into the path of Dred Scott's broom. He picked it up.

"I remember the first money I ever did see." He handed the coin back and waited to see if I would return to my work, which I did not. "When I was a small one, I find something round and shiny on the road and I don't know what it is." He had a way of smiling as he spoke as though amused by his own words. His smile invited conversation.

"How did you find out?"

"My daddy, he tell me that's money and then he grab for it. I run off with it and buy sweets."

"I'll wager that your daddy was cross."

"Lordy," he said with a grin, "he take after me with the hoe." It did not sound as though his father had frightened him.

"I found a dollar once. I showed it to my father. He told me that if I didn't know who lost it I had to put it in the collection plate at church." He looked uncertain, as though I hadn't finished the story. So I added, "I didn't."

Our conversation died out. I tried to focus on my adversary, the slave Diana Cephas. I looked back at Dred Scott, who had not moved.

"Does Mr. Field keep whisky or brandy in this office?"

He nodded.

I expectantly rose from the chair.

"The bottles, they locked up."

I sat again and stared at the *Cephas v. McConnell* petition.

"Vermont, she a free state?"

I looked up. "Yes."

"There great many colored folk up there in Vermont?"

"Almost none. I was ten years old before I saw a negro man. It was quite a surprise."

He laughed and shook his head as if he could not comprehend a state without negroes. He began dusting and polishing the shelves of law books. I realized that, other than my encounter with Samuel O'Fallon, this had been my longest conversation with anyone in St. Louis.

"In Vermont, we think all slaves work on plantations."

"Down south, mostly they do. Up here we does all kinds of work. We gets hired out. We even gets to live out."

"Hired out?"

"That's where the master, he let the slave work for another white man who pay the master. Sometimes we gets to keep some of what we makes. Mr. Field, he make sure that I get to keep some money."

"What is living out?"

"Some of the white folks, they don't care where we lives so long as we does their work. Some of us, we lives in the free quarter. The rooms, they small but we'd rather live there." He added with more than a little pride, "I live out."

Conversing with a slave evoked the same illicit pleasure as when I had feigned illness as a small boy to avoid Sunday visits to church in order to read a new book.

"Have you always lived in St. Louis?"

Without stopping the rhythmic application of rag to leather-bound volume, he shook his head. "Some folks, they tell me I'm from around Virginia. Others, they say Alabama."

"Don't you know?"

"All I remember is my daddy and the bells and the horns." He examined the law books. "Don't this leather look fine?"

"Bells and horns? Well, you must remember more than that. What about your mother or brothers and sisters?"

He shook his head. "There's just me so far as I know, and my mama, she gone when I little so I don't remember her much. One night, I lie down next to her on the bed and the next morning she not there." He finished the law books and began cleaning a window. "My daddy, he don't say what happen to her. Then he go too."

"What happened to him?"

"Sold."

"I see. That must have been hard, losing your parents like that." He did not reply, so I said, "My sister Esther Mary died when I was young but I can remember her face."

"Can't remember no faces except my daddy's. I sure can remember the bells and the horns," he said from the window. "On the farm there is bells for this and horns for that. All we knows is to go and come by the bells and the horns. I can hear them like they ringing and blowing just now."

"When was that?"

"We goes to the field before the sun come up and comes home after it go down."

"That's what you did when you were a small child?"

He paused to consider my expression and the surprise in my voice and nodded solemnly. "That's about all there was, Mr. Crane. Them bells and horns, they only stop ringing and blowing on Sundays."

"Ours only rang on Sundays." At his puzzled look, I explained, "We had a church bell. On Sundays it rang and my mother used to say, 'That's God, ringing our doorbell. Time to go to church.' I hated to go."

Dred Scott turned away from the window. "Your sister, she a little one when she die?"

"I had four sisters. None lived past the age of four."

"Nothing worse I know of than a child dying little. Don't seem fair."

"It's not."

Later, as he was leaving, I said, "Goodnight, Dred."

I heard him say from the hallway, "Evening, Mr. Crane. You sure do work hard."

After a while, I turned to Mr. Field's notes on the *McConnell* case. For a time I was still unable to concentrate. What had led Mr. Field to accept this case? I bent to my unhappy work, a slave catcher who used law books instead of bloodhounds.

Chapter 4

A negro in swallow-tailed coat, white shirt, white gloves, and a black bow tie opened the carriage door and directed me to the etched glass doors of the entranceway to the Blow mansion. Inside, another similarly dressed negro took my coat and escorted me to the large room where guests had already assembled and where yet a third negro handed me a glass of wine from a tray, which I drank efficiently. The greased faces of the negroes shone like polished black diamonds.

The immaculate room glowed from the candle lamps and the flickering light of three huge fireplaces with marble mantels. Most of the men stood while the women were seated. I had never before seen such a large assembly of hoop skirts or such prodigious hoops. Each woman seemed partially enclosed in her own separate cocoon, her natural figure well-concealed, efficient movement all but impossible.

A pleasant-looking fellow in his mid-thirties with straw-colored hair and pale complexion shook my hand. "You must be Arba. I'm

Taylor Blow. Come along and I'll introduce you to some of our finest citizens."

There followed a bewildering round of introductions to an endless succession of Chouteaus, Blows, and other prominent St. Louisians. I inquired why most of the Blows had Taylor in their name.

"My father, Peter Blow, married Elizabeth Taylor," said Taylor Blow with a faint smile, "but mother was so proud of the Taylor name that she inserted her family name in most of ours and, in my case, as my first name." He began a complicated explanation of the Blow family history. I only half listened because near a fireplace I saw a beautiful young woman talking with several other guests. Only a year or two younger than myself, she had come to the Blow party in a white evening dress caught up on each side with a garland of autumn leaves. She wore her red hair in intricate ringlets around a face I found exquisitely smooth and delicate. She glanced up and our eyes met. She smiled and turned back to her guests.

I wanted another look into those green eyes, a darker shade than my own, but someone roughly grabbed my arm and instead I stared into the drunken face of Samuel O'Fallon. We did not shake hands.

"You needn't introduce us," he told Taylor. "I know Mr. Crane from Harvard. Colonel, Mr. Arba Crane of Vermont. He will be working for Roswell Field."

Colonel O'Fallon wore a black jacket with black satin trim and held a gold-knobbed walking stick in one hand. His snow-white hair perfectly matched a white, flowing stock.

"I am most grateful for the skills of your employer, Mr. Crane," said the Colonel. "If you are even one-half the lawyer that he is, then you have a very fine future with us, and I am sure the state of Vermont will mourn the loss of another fine legal mind."

"Colonel, Vermont long ago gave up mourning the fact that people are its number one export."

After more pleasantries with Colonel O'Fallon, who was superior to his son in manners if not many other respects, Taylor guided me to a group of standing men and seated women.

"My pleasure is to introduce Arba Crane of the Crane family of Vermont. He has come to St. Louis to practice law with Roswell Field. I hear that he is one of Harvard Law School's most brilliant graduates. This is Mr. Thomas Cobb, one of the South's most distinguished attorneys. And I'd like you to meet Alfred Fox of New Orleans and his daughter Kate."

For a second time that evening Kate Fox smiled at me, gazing with an intensity of interest at once flattering and disconcerting. More than her smile, I was drawn to dark green eyes that held secrets any man would want to know.

"They are my guests until the Senatorial election. Then Mr. Fox goes on to Washington City to take up a position in President Fillmore's administration with, of course,"—Taylor smiled—"Kate's assistance. May I also introduce you to my good friend Irene Emerson."

Irene Emerson was a somewhat plump, heavily rouged woman in her thirties who wore what might have been the largest hoop in the room and seemed distracted by movement and comments from nearby guests. "Tell us, Mr. Crane," she managed, "how do you find St. Louis?"

"More interesting than I ever imagined."

"Why are all the good schools in the North, Mr. Fox?" asked Irene, turning considerably more charm on him. "The best families in the South send their children to the Northern schools. Why can't we educate them here instead of Yankeefying them?"

Before Alfred Fox could answer, Thomas Cobb, a chubby and genial man at first appearance, broke in. "I attended a commencement at Harvard, Mr. Crane. The speeches were poorly written and worse spoken. Any school that fails to teach oratory is worthless."

"Perhaps not all the best schools are in the North," said Alfred Fox. He smiled at me, awaiting my response. He was a younger and heartier version of Colonel O'Fallon. His aristocratic manner commanded the rapt attention of all in our circle, save that of his daughter.

"I am sure that not all the best schools are in the North," I said, more from courtesy than conviction.

"Oh rubbish," said Kate Fox. "You are just being polite. Have you ever tried to buy a book in New Orleans, Mr. Crane? I can't fault Southern families who don't want their children to be ignorant for sending them north."

"Miss Fox," I said, "too many great men have climbed out of ignorance on their own to ever make me think that Northern schools are the only answer."

"Well put," said Taylor Blow. "Kate perhaps wishes that she could have gone to Harvard and become a lawyer."

"Not a lawyer, Taylor. A writer. Tell me, Mr. Crane, what have you read lately? The literature of the North is to me what the Biblical fleshpots of Egypt were to the wandering Israelites. We long for it."

Amused but uncomfortable laughter came from the men. Her father looked as though he had not entirely grown used to his daughter's conversational manners. Irene Emerson smiled primly.

"While traveling here," I said, "I read a work by Mr. Hawthorne. *Ethan Brand.* Do you know it?"

"'What is the Unpardonable Sin?' asked the limeburner," quoted Kate Fox.

I responded, "'It is a sin that grew within my own breast,' replied Ethan Brand. 'The sin of an intellect that triumphed over the sense of brotherhood with man and reverence for God.'"

The gathering applauded as though we had performed a duet.

"Well done," said Taylor Blow. "May none of us suffer from unpardonable sins."

"Let us all drink to that," said Alfred Fox.

We raised our glasses. I finished mine and almost instantly another servant appeared from nowhere to hand me a full glass, which I took with growing appreciation of Southern comforts. "So, Mr. Crane," asked Irene, glancing at Alfred Fox, "what do you think of our peculiar institution?"

I hesitated, aware how keenly I was being watched, especially by Kate Fox, who leaned slightly forward.

"Surely you don't expect me to have an opinion after only a week."

"Come, now. There are plenty of opinions in the North. Surely you have one of your own."

I did not like Irene Emerson and did not enjoy being her foil to impress Alfred Fox, who I guessed was a widower. Resisting an impulse to ask why Southerners found manual labor so abhorrent that they must own other human beings to do it for them, I said only, "Well, Mrs. Emerson, I am a lawyer. That means I must respect the law wherever I may be." Irene Emerson, at a loss for a response, looked at Kate for assistance, which caused Kate to put a hand to her face as though hiding a smile.

"You are also a diplomat, sir," said Alfred Fox. "How I wish all our Northern neighbors were so diplomatic. I hope that you will keep an open mind while you are here."

"Do you like trance poetry, Mr. Crane?" asked Kate Fox, deftly leaving slavery behind.

"I have read it but I am not a rapper, Miss Fox, but only because I was raised a Congregationalist. We were taught that those saved in the next life have no need in this one for the comfort of spirits."

"My, but you Yankees are hard on yourselves. Perhaps you didn't know that the Rochester sisters visited St. Louis last year and pronounced it a great town for séances."

"Actually, Miss Fox, I have always doubted whether I have been saved in any life." She smiled and toasted me with her glass. I said, "I read in the newspaper that Madame Blavatsky will shortly arrive on her tour. If I could arrange for us to attend her séance, would you like to go?" Kate's father started to speak, but his daughter cut him off.

"Why, Mr. Crane, I would be delighted."

"If you will excuse us, there are more people I would like Arba to meet," said Taylor Blow, guiding me to another group and looking impressed.

"I'll try for Verandah Row a week from Tuesday evening at eight."

Kate Fox gaily waved her hand in assent as Samuel approached her, disgruntled as usual.

As Taylor and I moved through the crowded room, a negro announced that dinner was being served. A slow procession began toward the dining room and I fell behind Irene Emerson and Taylor, who spoke in near whispers, arguing over something. I overheard part of the discussion.

"Taylor Blow, don't you get started on that again. Your father shouldn't have sold Dred Scott to John in the first place."

I moved closer and tried to listen without attracting their attention.

"That was our mistake. John assured me that after he finished his army service he would manumit Dred."

"John never said any such thing. I won't have people saying I'm slave poor, Taylor. I have no need to sell slaves because I can't afford them."

"He offered fair value."

"Dred only offered credit. I hire him out for good money and I need Harriet as a house slave." Irene Emerson's next words were indistinct other than "children" and "money." With an exasperated gesture around the room, she said, "You more than anyone should know that a woman's happiness depends on having at least one good servant."

"Irene, I have known Dred since I was a boy."

"I won't have people say I've fallen on hard times." She spoke with angry finality, as if to put an end to the argument. "I won't let them go." As we entered the spacious dining room, Taylor glanced at me with an unhappy expression.

Dinner was served by aproned negro girls. The table service was brightly polished silver. I was nearly a full table removed from Kate Fox. I sat next to Thomas Cobb, who somewhat pompously explained to me that his specialty was slave law and that he was engaged in compiling in a single volume the leading slave decisions by Southern appellate courts.

"There are some five thousand cases, so I shall have to be selective. No one has attempted such a feat since Jacob Wheeler in 1837. I am talking to several publishers in the South. Are you acquainted with any in Boston?"

"I am afraid not," I said, adding, "I doubt New England readers would have much interest in such a work."

"Yes," he said with a sigh. "I suppose you are right. Will you be attending the auction?"

"I am just a young lawyer with barely money to purchase a green bag."

"My dear boy, most people who go to a slave auction do not buy slaves. By all means, you must come. There won't be another like it in St. Louis for years. I am here on retainer to the estate to draw up contracts and quitclaims."

"I have already seen one. That was enough."

Despite his legal specialty Cobb appeared an open-minded, erudite man. I described the girl on the block, finding it a relief to do so.

Thomas Cobb shook his head sadly, which was heartening. "The truly cruel physical punishments mostly have been eliminated. Regrettably, that means whipping is the only alternative for the lesser offenses. I drafted a code for Georgia, which set the limit at thirty-nine lashes, not to be inhumanely done. It didn't pass in the last session but I am ever hopeful."

I had not dulled my senses sufficiently to continue this conversation, so I signaled a servant by holding up a glass, which was promptly refilled. I downed it almost at a gulp. "Until just now, I had not conceived it possible to humanely whip a human being."

"I can assure you," he said mildly, as though he had been through many similar conversations with Northerners, "that there are whippings and there are whippings. The engine of slavery runs on the fuel of fear of inflicted pain."

"I saw a man whipping a horse at the levee." My voice sounded slurred. "All who passed by looked uncomfortable. One even cursed him."

"You are new to the South, Mr. Crane. Were you ever afraid that your horse would murder you in your bed? I wish your Northern philanthropists would contrive some satisfactory plan to relieve us of slavery. The trouble and responsibility of taking care of our slaves is anything but enviable." He paused to eat the delicious venison set before us. His mouth still full of food, he went on, "But lest you judge us too harshly, Mr. Crane, tell me: wife beating with a reasonable instrument is legal in the North, is it not? I recently read a New York case that upheld a Methodist minister's right to beat his wife with a horsewhip once a month to ensure proper obedience. Can we not beat our slaves as much as your ministers beat their wives?"

I signaled for another glass, drank it, and then, for lack of any other conversational subject, disjointedly mentioned my struggle with *Cephas v. McConnell.*

Cobb was blunt. "I am sorry, my boy, but you haven't a prayer. That's settled law in this state. Once free, forever free. The wonder of it is that the poor brutes only realize they are free after they have left the free state." He added, "The *Winny* court should have applied the doctrine of reattachment. When the slave returns to the slave state, the law of slavery should reattach."

He warmed to his subject. "The judges on the Missouri Supreme Court made a mistake in *Winny,* God bless them, and then repeated it more than a half dozen times since and haven't the courage to admit it. But, they are in good company. Every other Southern court has ruled the same way."

"I would not have expected that Southern courts would extend such courtesies to free-state law."

"Oh, they'll come to their senses sooner or later."

After dinner, the men gathered in the Blow library to smoke cigars and drink brandy. Servants carried in shiny silver spittoons and set them in each corner of the library. Much of the talk was of the coming auction, from how far away bidders had come, the quality of the slaves, expected prices, and the like. A wager was made whether the auction would bring in more than $100,000. Then the conversation turned to politics. Most of the men in the room were seated, if not slouched in their chairs, with their feet resting on stools.

Some grumbled about an antislavery speech given by the aging Missouri Senator Thomas Benton the previous week in Jefferson City. Many made predictions of his defeat in the coming election. I listened politely while drinking Taylor Blow's excellent brandy. Samuel, who had been watching me, spoke in a loud voice that silenced all others.

"I hear that the Vermont papers praised his speech. Since the North seeks to abolish slavery, I'm hardly surprised."

Most of the eyes in the room turned to me. My rising anger dispelled the pleasant brandy-induced fog. I got unsteadily to my feet.

"I am sure the New England newspapers complimented his speech," I said. "But so did some newspapers here. What is not true is that the North seeks abolition." I paused, trying to focus on blurry faces whose expressions varied from outright hostility to simply suspicious, and aimed my words in Samuel's general direction. "Where I am from, we associate that charge with the advocates of disunion."

More than a few nodded. I did not have to look at Samuel to feel his wrath. Later, I said goodnight to Taylor Blow. He warmly shook my hand, looking impressed for a second time that evening. "I am glad you have come to St. Louis. We need smart young men. But beware of Samuel O'Fallon. After tonight, he will be looking for an excuse to hand you his card."

Chapter 5

Itried to finish the plea in abatement in *Cephas v. McConnell,* but my heart was not in it. I looked up to find Dred staring at me. Unembarrassed, he resumed his chores.

I stared at the plea without comprehending the words. My head was pounding. I had never been this thirsty in Vermont.

"Where's the key?"

Dred kept sweeping.

"You know where it is."

He stopped. "Mr. Crane, I can't do that."

"I need a drink."

"Mr. Field, he see that he have less to drink, that's for sure."

"You let me worry about that."

He hesitated for a moment because there was no way for him to know if he could trust me. Whatever his concern about Mr. Field's wrath it was overcome by his desire to demonstrate that he did trust me. He put down his broom and went into Mr. Field's office, where he opened a small drawer at the bottom of the desk. He reached in and handed me a key, nodding at a large cabinet. I opened the cabinet and found a tray with a brandy decanter and small glasses. Carrying the tray, I went back to my desk. I offered Dred a drink. He declined it but did not go back to his cleaning.

The brandy was an elixir, cool and aromatic.

Dred looked doubtfully at me and then at the brandy. "Mr. Crane, how come a young man like you need to drink so bad?"

"It's a way to forget."

"Forget what, Mr. Crane?"

I glanced at the plea in abatement. "Well, St. Louis. At least, some things in St. Louis. I didn't expect it to be like this."

"Vermont, she a much better place?"

"I drank there too."

Dred looked surprised and started to ask me a question. I did not want to answer it so I asked him a question first. "You are owned by Irene Emerson, aren't you?"

He nodded.

"I was at a party at Taylor Blow's. Taylor and Irene Emerson had a row about you."

He offered no explanation.

"How long has she owned you?"

"Her husband, he buy me from Mr. Blow's father. Then he die. He an army doctor but it don't help him none."

"What did he die from?"

"Lot of things. Dr. Emerson, he a man with a lot of ailments."

"John Emerson promised to set you free, didn't he? I heard Taylor say that."

"He surely do that, Mr. Crane. But it don't set well with Mrs. Emerson."

"She broke her husband's promise. Is that it?"

"That's what she do, Mr. Crane." Dred said it in a way that left no doubt as to the truth, or his bitterness. "I tell her if she let us go, I gonna earn the money to pay her, but Mrs. Emerson, she get angry."

"Who is Harriet?"

"Harriet, she my wife. The two girls, they's Eliza and Lizzie."

"Slaves can't get married."

"We do it. No doubt about that. We jumps over the broom."

At my puzzled look, he said, "After the man that marry us say the last words over me and Harriet, they hold up the broomstick and then we jumps over the broomstick backwards. The one that jump over it and never touch the handle going to boss the house. Harriet, she go right over the broomstick same as a cricket. I done had a big dram, and I get all tangle up in that broom." He added, "I give Harriet a wedding ring that I carve with a pocket knife from a big red button."

"I would think it hard enough with one master, but it sounds like you've got two."

He chuckled. "Just Harriet, Mr. Crane, just Harriet." The laughter faded. "That Mrs. Emerson, she never going to let us go."

I filled a glass, handed it to him, and offered a toast. "Here's to you and your family's freedom."

He acknowledged my toast by raising his glass without conviction, and drank slowly. When he finished I refilled my glass and then his.

"Mr. Crane, here's hoping that you find what you looking for."

We drank and then together contemplated the even lower level in the decanter. The brandy had worked its wonder because my headache by now had subsided to a vague throb. Dred was smiling, perhaps at the fact that he was drinking Mr. Field's liquor or perhaps because I was slightly drunk.

"Mr. Crane, how come you ain't got your own family up there in Vermont?"

"I suppose I'll have a family some day. But we young lawyers aren't supposed to have time for such things. Too many cases."

"Mr. Field, he like to tell me about his cases." He looked at the *McConnell* papers. Mr. Field must have told Dred about the slave who had sued our client for her freedom. I avoided looking at Dred's eyes.

After a while, Dred said, "I guess we both got to get back to our work."

"Yes, we do, I suppose." I picked up a water pitcher and shakily filled the decanter and shook it. I held the decanter up to show Dred that, through the dark glass, it looked as though it were still full of brandy. I put the decanter and the glasses back in the cabinet.

"It's not as strong, but Mr. Field will never notice or care. Congregationalists like their liquor weak, if they like it all."

All that week finely dressed plantation owners in plush silk top hats, velvet capes, and knitted-silk gloves, and less elegant slave speculators wearing broadbrim hats and squaretoed boots, had been checking into St. Louis hotels. The owners went off to dinner with St. Louis politicians and merchants, while the speculators congregated at the Planters' House bar, drinking heavily, talking of nothing but the slave auction.

On the day of the auction, I rose at sunup, resolved to spend the day preparing for my Missouri license examination, but an event such as a slave auction has an irresistible magnetic field, and I felt helplessly drawn. On the way to Mr. Field's office, I walked by Lynch's block at the steps of the courthouse. It was empty but the newly constructed sheds drew my attention once more. Mercifully, unlike the night before, when I had passed by after leaving the office, the sheds were quiet. Then, I had lingered to listen to the soft whispers about the killing fields further south.

With the whispers of the night before still an echo, I put aside any thought of the license examination and went in the sheds. A few early-rising speculators were already making last-minute notes on their catalogues. The negroes sat on the floor with their bundles, having apparently eaten rice and beans and slept on bare boards covered with hay. Bodily functions had to be taken care of in a stall adjacent to the sleeping stalls.

I stood with the owners and speculators, looking at the negroes like spectators at a zoo. Some appeared to be resigned to the hard stroke of fate that had torn them from their home, others sat brooding moodily over their sorrows, and a few occasionally turned aside to hide quiet tears. Most were young, but I spotted in a corner, out of sight of the spectators, an older negro man. He stood patiently with his head bowed, while a young slave woman, under the direction of an overseer, plucked gray hairs from his head.

The women had made some attempt at finery. All wore beautiful turbans, manufactured with a graceful twist of a colored kerchief and decorated with a few beads or bright bits of ribbon. Their dresses were mostly coarse. A few had earrings and one possessed a string of yellow and blue beads.

According to the auction catalogue, the youngest child was 14 days old. The babies were generally good-natured, but when one started crying, a chorus joined in. The younger children were more carefully dressed than the older ones. One mother with obvious parental pride had dressed her son, about age three, in a jacket with a strip of gay red broadcloth around the bottom. He was a boisterous little boy, running in fleet steps through the stalls, jumping into a pile of hay and completely disappearing only to emerge with a huge smile on his face. His young mother, with an expression on her face of delight and annoyance, brushed off the squirming child and straightened out his jacket, only to watch in dismay as he then gleefully dived back into the hay.

More speculators arrived to examine the negroes. They pulled open mouths to inspect teeth, pinched limbs to check musculature, and made the negroes stoop and bend and jump to be certain they had no concealed injuries or diseases.

A familiar voice explained the merits and demerits of the negroes to a group of English tourists, who seemed to regard the whole event as yet another of America's quaint customs.

"The skills are worth nearly as much as the man," Samuel O'Fallon said. "A slave without a trade might bring $900 but he'll fetch $1,600 or $1,700 if he's a passable blacksmith or cooper."

The Englishmen and women nodded their heads as though Samuel had made a shrewd point.

"Why, here's my good friend Arba Crane of Vermont." Samuel made a show of exaggerated friendship and turned back to the English tourists. "I wouldn't expect a Yankee like Mr. Crane to know it, but this is valuable stock even without skills because they are pure as the best blood of Spain."

I asked, "Is that because the negroes have been so little defiled by degenerate Anglo-Saxon blood?"

The English tourists laughed and Samuel looked annoyed. He considered his alternatives and then led his entourage out of the sheds, but not before glancing back at me with malice.

By ten the sale was ready to begin. A huge crowd, perhaps a thousand, had gathered around the block. Younger children, excited expressions on their faces, perched at the top of the courthouse steps. Patrons of the Planters' House bar sat on the hotel porch, drinks and cigars in hand, rocking back and forth on the rocking chairs. Faces filled every window along the street. Inside the dense circle of onlookers stood dozens of bidders.

Motioning to the entry clerks to ready their pencils, the florid-faced auctioneer announced the terms of the sale: "One third cash, the remainder payable in two equal annual installments, bearing interest from the day of sale, to be secured by approved mortgage and personal security or approved acceptances." As he spoke, the buyers lit cigars and readied their catalogues and pencils. The first lot, Primus and Daphney and their two children, one an infant, were led onto the block by a mulatto.

In the crowd of bidders were fast young men with orange and ochre pantaloons tucked into boots, velvet caps jauntily tilted to one side, cheeks full of tobacco, and revolvers or knives sheathed but ready for convenient use. Gold-spectacled, sapling-thin, silver-haired old men, indistinguishable from the long line of deacons of the Newfane Congregationalist Church, giddily pointed their canes at slaves as they were led onto the block and excitedly swiveled their heads from bidder to bidder as they shouted out their bids.

Unable to decide which was most unbearable, the block, the bidders, or the spectators, I watched Daphney, who glanced anxiously from one bidder to another. She had a large shawl, which she tried to keep wrapped around her infant and herself, but it slipped from her shoulders. Primus, a muscular slave with an impassive face, gently reached over and pulled the shawl up around his wife and child. This attracted much attention from the bidders.

"What do you keep that nigger covered up for? Pull off her blanket."

"What's the matter with the girl. Has she got a headache?"

"Ain't she sound? Pull off her rags and let us see her."

The auctioneer said that there was no deception. Daphney, he explained, had given birth two weeks earlier and therefore he thought she was entitled to a blanket. I did a quick calculation based on what I had heard in the Planters' House bar. Five days after giving birth, Daphney and her newborn had traveled for two days by horse-drawn cart, spent five days in the horse barn at the race track, and then spent two days in the sheds. The family sold for $2,500. I vainly looked here and there for any sign that even one spectator thought something was wrong with it all.

Some twenty babies and young children were brought to the hammer that day. A speculator explained to me that the babies were worth a hundred dollars on the day they were born and increased in value at a rate of up to one hundred dollars a year until about age 16 or 17. He poked my side and nodded at a middle-aged woman a few yards away who was following the proceedings with keen interest. The woman wore clothes of drab appearance, other than a large hat with a blue feather, and had a knowledgeable and experienced attitude. Occasionally, she exchanged words with other bidders, who would nod or point to their catalogues.

"That Lucy Buck," said my temporary confidant, "never misses an auction. She lives at the corner of Morgan and Garrison streets."

"Why does she come?"

With an envious look at the woman, he said, "She buys up the children from speculators and raises them to sell, and makes damned good money doing it."

The octoroon girl on the block, I now understood, had only been a morsel, an appetizer, a dainty little treat from the St. Louis cupboard, which now emptied its cornucopia of the damned. I had no business standing there. I should have studied Missouri law that day or worked on Mr. Field's briefs or gotten drunk until I could not stand up or wandered aimlessly through the rest of the city like a stunned traveler in a primitive land who has decided that he can no longer believe his own eyes and ears. I should have become a hermit in Italy or a stevedore in New York or gone to sea. I should never have come to St. Louis. Dear God, I should have stayed in Newfane. But I was no more able to leave than to stop breathing.

Late in the bidding, Jeffrey, marked in the catalogue as a "prime hand," was put up. The first bid was $1,100. He went for $1,410. He was sold alone, and shortly, I saw him, hat in hand, talking to his new owner with a desperate, calculating look in his eyes. I moved closer and learned that he was in love with Dorcas, and Dorcas was in love with him. His voice was trembling because a great deal depended on his wild throw of the dice.

"I love Dorcas, Master, I love her well and true. She say she love me. Please buy Dorcas, Master. We be good servants as long as we lives."

His new owner seemed unmoved, but the slave persisted. "Dorcas a prime woman. Do a heap of work in a day, worth $1,200 easy, Master, a bargain at that."

At these remarks, the owner, a baby-faced man no older than myself, told Jeffrey to fetch Dorcas, who was still an hour away from the block, from the sheds. He quickly returned with Dorcas, who made the accustomed curtsy and stood meekly with her hands clasped across her bosom. The owner regarded her with a critical eye. He turned her around, made her stoop and walk, took off her turban to inspect for wounds or diseases on her head, of which there were none, looked at her teeth, and felt her arms.

"She has her good points," he conceded.

For the first time Jeffrey smiled.

"If the price ain't run up too high," said Jeffrey's owner, "I'll buy her."

The two lovers briefly touched hands and whispered to each other.

An hour later, Dorcas stepped up on the block.

Then the auctioneer announced that Dorcas would not be sold alone but with a family of four.

Despair on his face, Jeffrey looked to his new owner, who shook his head. Whatever his inclination to bid for Dorcas alone, he had no use for an entire family. Jeffrey looked away as Dorcas was told by the auctioneer, in response to a question from a bidder, to squat, bend over and then to jump.

"Make her dance," someone called out.

A merry fiddle struck up a tune and Dorcas danced on the block. She was young and lithe and she danced and danced and danced to the fiddle, never looking in Jeffrey's direction, her face expressionless, her eyes rimmed with tears.

Dorcas was shortly sold with a family to a cotton plantation in South Carolina. Jeffrey's owner would be taking him to a plantation in Louisiana. I saw Jeffrey and Dorcas once more in the sheds. Dorcas sat on the floor, as motionless as a statue, her head covered with a shawl. A few feet away, Jeffrey pulled off his hat and spoke to his new owner, "Thank you, Master, for trying to help me. I know you could have done it if you could . . ." He covered his face with his battered hat. A group of his friends surrounded him, standing quietly.

In the end the auction's proceeds exceeded $110,000. Buyers sipped champagne from glasses set out on the block. Pierce Bradford moved among his father's former slaves, handing each a dollar. In the sheds, Bradford's driver whipped a young mulatto girl. A laughing onlooker called out, "Spare the rod and spoil the child, Jethro. She sure got her father's eyes," while the young girl pleaded for him to stop.

Some of the English tourists looked ill, the airy observers of the eccentricities of American life no more, while Samuel O'Fallon lectured on the various types of whips and paddles used by drivers.

Lucy Buck, hat with blue feather perched comfortably on her head, pulled out of the sheds a wildly sobbing and struggling three-year-old boy, wearing a jacket with a strip of red broadcloth. I heard muffled, weeping sounds in the sheds, where the mother and her son had been torn apart. As one might at the scene of a vicious assault on a helpless person, I walked urgently towards Lucy Buck and the thrashing child, shouting at her to stop, but several drivers, alert to any attempt by a slave to escape, heard and moved menacingly in front of me, making intervention impossible. I did not want to listen helplessly to the heartrending sounds in the sheds or look at the terrified child as he was dragged away by Lucy Buck to God knew what cruel fate. I turned and walked away, marveling at the anger that had lodged itself beneath my breast.

It was a most inopportune time to come across my newly made acquaintance. Kate Fox had been watching with her father from an elegant carriage that looked as though they owned a dozen like it. She waved to me and, as I approached and grimly bid her and her father hello, her expression dimmed to match my own.

"Well, Mr. Crane, if you can stand that, then you can handle anything the South has to offer."

Chapter 6

That afternoon I fled St. Louis by horse.

Following the directions given by the stable owner, I crossed a river on a ferry and rode west, deep into the country. At dusk, I halted the exhausted horse at a farmhouse. For a small payment, I was given a bed and dinner by the farmer's wife, who said that her husband had left for California just a few days earlier and that she and the children would be following in a few months. She said she was temperance when I asked whether she had any spirits in the house, having earlier that day depleted the whisky bottle that I purchased as my only provision before leaving the city.

I rose at sunrise and after a few hours riding reached the prairie. The sun shone more brightly here, the sky was a deeper blue than on any other day of my life. In front of me a grassy sea rose and fell, broken occasionally by copses of trees and carpeted with sunflowers often twelve feet high, asters, and gentians. The land had long since been tamed, the Indians and wild animals driven ever further west, but nothing in my imagination could make the eternity of that space any less fearful or compelling. The great expanse unfolded around me; the horse seemed not so much to gallop as to be pulled forward, and I grew smaller and smaller. I was a speck on a vast land ocean; its timeless, stately rhythms for a while doused the fires of my memory, which the bottle of whisky had only fueled.

With only a rented horse and no provisions other than the empty bottle, I decided to ride until I reached California. I might even catch up with the farmer along the way. I planned to ask him in the most calm manner, not why he had left Missouri, but why he had come in the first place and exactly when he had first realized that he had made the mistake of his life.

I never stopped believing that I could reach California, but in the afternoon I turned the horse in a slow, despairing arc on the prairie from west to north to east and started on the long ride back to St. Louis. Bitterly I asked myself, why had I turned the horse? I cursed myself for having the courage to return to St. Louis, because a coward might have ridden across fearsome plains and scaled wicked mountains and braved Indians in order to escape it.

What use was courage in St. Louis? I wrestled with that question for hours as the sun beat down relentlessly, scorching my already fevered mind, until I had the preposterous idea that I was going back to St. Louis to do something about what I had seen at the auction, even if I did not know what that might be. After all, I was a young man and young men can do anything. At last I found comfort only in the certainty that if I at least did not try, I would be damned or become mad or both. In the midst of these deliriums floated the faces first of Dred Scott and then of Kate Fox, both of whom, it seemed, were friendly and smiling, but each barely concealed their desperation.

The sight of a slave coffle, apparently heading west, but now setting up camp, interrupted my demented musings. Some of the female slaves were sitting, others were standing, and a great many little negro children were warming themselves by a fire just springing to life. Dozens of male slaves, shackled and chained by the neck to each other, faces exhausted, stood in double file. Their masters had a caravan of nine wagons and single-horse carriages. Where were they going in that vastness? By now blessedly numb, I rode past without stopping to ask or acknowledging the friendly greetings of the weather-worn white men lounging around the wagons and carriages.

After a sleepless night, I left Planters' House for Mr. Field's office. The drum roll sounded across the city. Carts and drays soon moved noisily through the streets, a negro crossed in front of me carrying bread and milk for his early-rising owner, and other negroes, some in a hurry, others more lazily, moved in the opposite direction towards the markets. At this hour, just before sunrise, the slaves of St. Louis were beginning their chores.

I trudged up the stairs to Mr. Field's office. Mr. Field had arrived even earlier, but since the inner office door was closed, I did not disturb him.

Shortly, his door opened and there Mr. Field stood, tall and stern in lawyerly broadcloth. His black silk bow tie was immaculately knotted, his ruffled shirt, embroidered with the initials RMF, gleamed white, and a stiff and graying beard that flowed from thick sideburns framed his face. An air of sadness hung over him like a fine mist, instantly dispelling my recollection of his lighthearted manner.

"Come in," he said, as though I had been in his employ for years and had not just arrived on a journey across half the country. I sat down in the chair before his desk and he seated himself in his grand chair, one of whose leather arms had a faint abrasion from my mishap.

He held up my *Cutter v. Waddingham* brief.

"You show symptoms of being a lawyer."

I accepted the gruff praise with a slight nod. The French marriage contracts, which I had borrowed from the municipal archives, had been arranged on his desk as if for close and careful study. The paperweight was still on the desk but the moldering Vermont Supreme Court opinion was gone. I gave him news of my parents,

Newfane, and my journey to St. Louis, about none of which he appeared interested. I wanted to talk about the slave auction but he turned to practical matters.

"We will have to get you a Missouri law license if you are to appear in court. That means a personal examination by one of the state Supreme Court judges. Have you been studying your law?"

"On the trip out, and last week—some."

"I will send you packing to Vermont if you fail and insist on repayment of your salary. You say you have been studying, do you? Tell me whether Blackstone wore his hair long or short."

I was incredulous at first because he was so serious. I observed not a trace of a smile on his face or humor in his eyes. He might easily have asked me in the same tone to state the statute of limitations for commencing an action of ejectment under Missouri law.

"He had no hair. He was as bald as a slab of Vermont marble and wore a wig."

Mr. Field nodded. "I was actually asked that on my own examination." He did not say whether he had answered it correctly. "It's early, but we should commemorate your arrival."

Pulling out a key from a desk drawer, Mr. Field went to the cabinet and returned with the brandy decanter and glasses. He half filled our glasses and offered a polite toast to my success as a Missouri lawyer. We drank in silence. I held out my glass. After a disapproving hesitation, he again partly filled it. I drank it quickly, disappointed to find that the brandy only slightly dulled the senses. Then I remembered that I had diluted the decanter's contents several nights earlier. Mr. Field, who drank his brandy without comment, glanced darkly at the marriage contracts and then handed the *Cutter* brief to me.

"I made some notes. I want a revision on my desk tomorrow morning. You'll be here late. I assume you have met Dred."

"Oh, yes, he's been here several times." I paused. "I've heard about his difficulties with Irene Emerson. I think Taylor Blow is trying to help him."

"Taylor's known Dred since childhood. Taylor asked me to hire him out. Part of what Dred earns from me he keeps. He is trying to buy freedom for himself and his family."

"She's not going to give them up."

"That's what I told Taylor."

Mr. Field appeared to have nothing to add on this subject, but I wanted to know more.

"Why does she keep them?"

"Buying slaves is the mark of wealth, but in wealthy circles a stigma is attached to selling the adults. And she needs the money from hiring Dred out—and the help. Irene couldn't go to even the few parties to which she is invited without Harriet to get her ready." He shook his head. "Some Northern men actually think women are just naturally more elegant here."

Mr. Field shifted in his chair. "So, you've met some Southerners by now. How do you find them?"

"I liked some. Others were not nearly so likeable." I described my exchange with Samuel. "They take politics more seriously than Vermonters."

"Indeed they do. When I arrived in St. Louis the city was the topic. Now, it's . . . other things. The state cannot decide if it's in the South or the North or whether it faces east or west. St. Louis cannot decide which side of the Mississippi it should be on." He looked at me thoughtfully. "We practice law on the national divide, so watch where you walk."

He handed me a new case file and turned to the papers on his desk, signaling the end of our conversation. "I will read the *McConnell* draft later this morning," he said as I left. "Our client will be here at six. He insisted on seeing me immediately on my return."

Promptly at six o'clock, a man with muttonchop whiskers entered without knocking. Murry McConnell had seated himself on the sofa in Mr. Field's office before we had even invited him to do so. Without hesitation, he lit up a cigar and boasted about the good bargains he had made at the auction. "Always buy at estate sales, Roswell. The stock is unsullied and the prices are cheap." Then he began an angry tirade, punctuated by frequent and well-aimed use of the spittoon, about the slow progress in his effort to reclaim his slave Diana Cephas, who had been allowed by the court to live in the free negro part of St. Louis until resolution of her claim.

"As I explained when you first came to me," said Mr. Field, "your case is a hard one. The doctrine of reattachment simply is not recognized in this state. Even a proslavery judge like Luke Lawless will find it difficult to distinguish the *Winny* case. But Arba has drafted a plea in abatement which gives Judge Lawless the best possible argument for dismissing the lawsuit. You have as good a chance as any in a case like this."

Murry McConnell looked at me appreciatively. I found it difficult to conceal my overwhelming distaste for our client.

"Our strategy, Murry," continued Mr. Field, "must be to convince the court that Delahay did not intend to reside in Illinois with her but was only sojourning. This will present a fact issue instead of a legal one." He went on for a few minutes, until McConnell interrupted him.

"I'll leave the legal strategy to you lawyers. Just make sure you win. When I get her back, I'll give her a lesson she'll never forget."

I was chilled and even Mr. Field looked uncomfortable. On the way out, Murry McConnell bumped into Dred Scott, who was standing near the door to Mr. Field's office.

"Get out of my way, boy."

For the briefest moment, Dred did not move. Murry drew back his hand as though to cuff Dred. Without appearing in a hurry, Dred took a step back. Murry put down his hand, irritably looked at Mr. Field, and left. After the echo of the slammed door died, Dred went to the closet to get his cleaning tools.

Mr. Field and I faced each other for a few moments, each waiting for the other to speak, which he finally did. "My arguments on his behalf are within the law, which is all that should matter."

"Is it? Is that all that should matter?" I was new to his employment and to St. Louis, but we were both Vermont men and I had seen more than enough.

Mr. Field hesitated and then said, "No, I suppose it isn't."

"I don't like him or his case." I expected an angry reaction from Mr. Field, but was surprised.

"I am not very fond of Murry either." He drummed his fingers on the desk. "Well, we have only been retained to do the plea in abatement. Someone else can do the trial." He added, "It will save me the trouble of defending a lost cause and having Murry fail to pay even more bills."

"I never would have imagined," I said, "that a slave owner could lose a case to a slave before a proslavery judge in a slave state."

"It's a little different than you expected, isn't it?"

"I was at the auction last Saturday. I hadn't expected anything like that."

Mr. Field nodded absentmindedly and I left his office. Dred barely looked at me while he dusted the law books.

"Hello, Dred."

"Evening, Mr. Crane."

Mr. Field dropped on my desk the next day's work—three more case files filled with his notes—and left. I went into Mr. Field's office to find a law book and noticed that the French marriage contracts were still on his desk.

At my desk I opened the law book, stared mindlessly at its pages, attempted unsuccessfully to put pen to paper, and imagined what Murry McConnell would do to Diana Cephas if he ever won his case. After ten minutes I gave up.

Dred was cleaning the leather sofa in the outer office.

"Have you ever been whipped?"

Dred looked over his shoulder at me and then turned his attention back to the sofa. After a while, he said, "They whip me when old Mr. Blow, he sell me to Dr. Emerson and I run away."

"Taylor said he'd known you since he was a boy. You must have been friends. How could his family sell you?"

He stopped working. The look in his eyes told me that I had raised a painful subject.

"Dr. Emerson, he need a slave because he going to the fort at Rock Island." He paused as though expecting me to say something. "Mrs. Blow, she die and old Mr. Blow, he need the money. He say, 'Dred, I got to put you in my pocket.'" He waited for a question but I had none. "You been to Rock Island, Mr. Crane?"

"No. I knew a man in Vermont who lived on Rock Island. At least, I think he did because he was always talking about this island in the Mississippi where he worked as a gunsmith. He said Rock Island is just off the Illinois bank. Is that right?"

Dred nodded and moved to the window, where he sat wearily on the sill, eyes downcast. "Sure don't want to go with Dr. Emerson to Rock Island. I run away. Had no family yet. But the patrollers, they get me in the Lucas Swamps, where the slaves they meet to play cards. So, I go with Dr. Emerson to Rock Island. We live there two years." He looked up, as though waiting to see what I had to say.

"What was done to you?"

As if it were the most natural thing in the world to disrobe in front of a white man, Dred stood up, pulled down the straps of his overalls, casually undid the buttons at the top of his shirt, turned, and shook his shirt from his shoulders, revealing a chaotic crisscross of long, snaking reptilian welts. They were as rough as sandpaper but still tender, as though his back might bleed at the slightest touch. I in turn saw only Abigail White, her soft, white skin, and the bright lines of red that slowly lost their sharp contours as the blood ran down her back, staining her dress bright scarlet.

"Before this happen, I hit one of them, and the man he fall down, yelling to beat the Devil, and the blood coming out of his mouth. So the others, they tie me to the tree and start piling up the brush. They going to set me on fire but then they start talking about how I belong to Dr. Emerson and so they untie me, turn me around, and tie me to the tree again. Then they come at me with the whip until, Lord, I start wishing that they start that fire. Next thing I know, I tied to the back of this mule and they taking me to Dr. Emerson."

Dred pulled up his shirt and overalls, turned, and wiped beads of sweat from his forehead with his shirt sleeve. "Mr. Emerson, he pretty angry about my whipping. He promise that he free me when he done with the army. Then he put something on my back that hurt almost as much as that whip but then it get better. But some folks, when they see my back, they get all white like you."

"Dr. Emerson was angry—weren't you angry?"

"Don't hardly think about it no more."

"That can't be."

"It happen to a lot of folks."

"Yes, but—"

"Mr. Crane, how we going to get by if we think all the time about the whippings we had or the whippings we gonna get?" He spoke impatiently, his face shiny with sweat, a trace of annoyance in his eyes. "We get by 'cause we think about being free. Our master, he giving us our freedom, or we buying our freedom, or finding a way to get to the free state. That day I run away and get that whipping? I ain't angry about that day 'cause that day, it the best day of my life. Before they catch me in the Lucas Swamps, just for that morning, I a free man, I say when I want to go and I say where I want to go and I do it. You always been free, Mr. Crane, so you don't know what freedom feels like. You don't know what it feels like to be a slave all your life and then be free. I feel like a bird that day, up there in the clouds, and I look down on everything, all those white folks like little ants, and they can't touch me or tell me what to do or even see me, and me up there in Heaven. Free, Mr. Crane. Free."

His shirt dark with sweat, Dred sat back down on the sill. "Mr. Crane, ain't this something you know about before you come here? Don't the folks in Vermont they know about all this?"

"Yes, we do," I stammered, "at least I did. I mean, I thought I did. I heard freed slaves speak about what happened to them. But it never seemed real, it was another place, far away. We knew about it but we didn't have slaves so it was easy not to know." I added, "I don't know what difference it would have made, anyway, even if we did know. We whipped people too."

He slowly buttoned his shirt. "I thought Vermont a free state."

"We whipped white people."

Dred shook his head. "Never heard of white folks whipping other white folks before."

"A young woman. Her name was Abigail White. I saw her whipped on Newfane Hill when I was a child."

"She get whipped this bad?"

"Yes."

"Who done the whipping?"

"I don't know."

"That girl she must have done something terrible."

"I guess so."

"Or someone, he do something terrible to that girl."

I was lost in thoughts that were troubling because I could not express them, they lurked at the recesses of my mind, daring me to reveal them to Dred but darting away into blackness whenever it seemed that I might.

"I really don't know, Dred."

For a brief moment, it seemed that he had been studying me with such intensity that his very life depended on it, but when I looked at him there was only Dred, a maimed slave who was friendly and easy to talk with. I had never thought about it but I realized that I liked him.

"How long did you say you lived with Dr. Emerson in the fort at Rock Island?"

"Like I said, two years."

"Maybe you met the man I knew. If you did you would never forget him. He was deranged, with bulging eyes and could never finish a sentence without crying." I listened to my voice as though I was hearing it from a great distance.

Dred shook his head. "I never meet a man like that but lots of folks I know, they feel like crying when they speak."

"Where did you go after Rock Island?"

"Dr. Emerson, he told to go to Fort Snelling and I go with him. That's where I meet Harriet."

"Fort Snelling? Where's that?"

"It's in the place the folks call Wisconsin Territory." He again seemed to expect me to say something. "We live there another two years. Dr. Emerson, he buy Harriet from this major and that's where we jump the broom. Then Dr. Emerson, he marry Mrs. Emerson. Then we come back to St. Louis. Eliza, she born on the steamboat." His face brightened and momentarily lost its weariness. "That sure is a sight. Harriet and Eliza on that white cotton bale."

My thoughts still flashed intermittently on Abigail White. "Dr. Emerson could not possibly have needed two slaves at an army fort."

"Most of the time, I not in the fort. Dr. Emerson, he hire me out. Done the same with Harriet after he buy her from this major."

Dred's voice died away because I was looking at the *McConnell* file instead of at him. I heard him say with some disappointment, "I best be getting back to work, Mr. Crane."

I thought of the girl on the block and her scarred back, the hurricane deck of the *Kimball,* and Kate Fox telling me that I could stand anything that the South had to offer. The images kept coming: Newfane Commons, the Post, the whipping of Abigail White, my ride to the prairie, and the best day of Dred Scott's life.

Dred had risen and was almost at the door to Mr. Field's office when it came to me. How clear and simple the idea seemed.

"You have a claim."

Dred stopped and slowly turned to look at me.

A burst of laughter came from the street, a hearty, booming male laugh joined in by a shrill and high-pitched woman's giggle. Their amusement faded to animated but indistinct conversation.

Dred seemed not to notice but I hesitated because the laughter seemed to mock my words. Dred waited expectantly and I continued, not wanting to stop no matter who was laughing or what might happen.

"You have a claim to be free."

I expected a happy reaction but he simply nodded, eyes warily alert.

"You lived in Illinois and the Wisconsin Territory. If a master takes his slave to a free state or territory and lives there, the slave is freed. You've been free for years."

This caused an amused look. "That's news to me, Mr. Crane."

"Well, you have to go to court. The court will set you free. One slave who lived in Illinois just went to court. She is going to be set free." I listened to the passion and urgency in my voice. I might have been pleading my own case.

"They sell the slaves at the court. They don't set them free there."

"Inside it's different."

"I ain't been inside."

"Inside you have a trial. A jury of twelve men will let you go free."

"Why they want to set me free?"

"It's the law. The jury has to follow the law."

"Don't Mrs. Emerson have something to say about this?" The questions came so fast that it appeared he had already been thinking about a case which, of course, was impossible.

"She'll have her own lawyer. She'll try to make it difficult, I'm sure." I was uncertain whether he understood. "The law in Missouri is pretty clear about this, Dred. Once free, forever free."

I felt giddy. It was just the two of us, in the law office of my father's former law partner, in a city stranger than my wildest expectations.

"Why you telling me this, Mr. Crane?" He seemed even more interested in my answer to this question than the others.

The prairie lay before me but I wheeled the horse through half the points on the compass. "I can free you and your family."

I began plotting how to persuade Mr. Field to take his case and to let me try it.

After a while he said, "I got to talk to Harriet about this then, don't I?"

"Yes, I think you do." He seemed satisfied with our talk and returned to his work. Dred hummed softly to himself while he worked, the rhythms of his cheerful melody matching his movements.

I set aside the *McConnell* case, and completed the last bits of work on the *Waddingham* brief and started on the new case files. That evening I finished before Dred did. I said goodnight to Dred, no longer needing a drink and thinking that, when I left Vermont, the last thing I expected was that my first friend in St. Louis would be a slave.

Chapter 7

"I want speak in English."

Madame Blavatsky, a young, colorfully dressed Russian, gazed at the expectant St. Louis citizens seated around a large table covered with a white cloth. A round Slavic face, wildly unkempt hair, and large, dark eyes gave Madame Blavatsky a hypnotic air.

Gradually, soft rustlings and indistinct murmurs faded and the room became as quiet as a funeral. Someone noisily scraped a chair and it sounded like a shriek. To my right sat a veiled woman dressed head to toe in black, who seemed on the verge of tears. To my left Kate Fox waited expectantly.

I whispered to Kate, "She looks like a gypsy at her own wedding."

Kate shushed me with a smile.

The sound of a harp could be heard somewhere in the air above Madame Blavatsky's head. To the accompaniment of its sad and sweet rhythms the woman in black whispered, "I shall go to him but he shall not return to me."

Crystalline bells tinkled and Madame Blavatsky said, "I become transparent eye. I am nothing. I see all." A hand appeared from the edge of the table, clothed in muslin white as snow, moved about, and then vanished. Something patted my knee, a cat mewed, and a silver pen rolled freely across the white table cloth, only to vanish. All this made little impression because my thoughts had drifted to the arguments that I would use to persuade Mr. Field to take Dred's case, and to Kate Fox, seated close enough that a slight move of my arm would brush her sleeve.

Madame Blavatsky summoned up the dead. "No miracle. All is result of law. All is eternal." We heard a sound as though a great wind were rushing through the room and in a dark recess we dimly saw robed figures.

Madame Blavatsky spoke to the woman in black, who stiffened and glanced longingly at the dark corners of the room and then asked Madame Blavatsky if it were Robert. Madame Blavatsky said it was. The woman in black said to Robert that there would never be another, that she could not manage the slaves because she was afraid of them, and had dreamed last night that her wedding band had broken in two. Interrupting her, Madame Blavatsky mournfully said that Robert was telling her that he would always love her but that he must go now. The woman in black looked frantically around the room, and then rested her head on one hand as though trying to quiet a sharp pain. The harp began to play.

Madame Blavatsky went around the room in this fashion. She conveyed messages from departed husbands, wives, lovers, children, friends, and acquaintances. Amid the tears and outbursts of anguish were also smiles and laughter. Madame Blavatsky never hesitated or faltered in conveying the words of the dead. Most with whom she spoke seemed satisfied.

At last Madame Blavatsky came to me. She appeared tired, as though drained by great exertion.

"There is presence," she said. "It is young woman. Beautiful. In pain."

I heard a shattering sound, as though someone had broken a large mirror.

"You cause pain." She watched me carefully. "*Nyet*—no, I not understand her. Is my fault. Someone cause pain."

"I must know her name. You must tell me her name." I wanted to see just how clever Madame Blavatsky really was.

"She saying always you know her name." Madame Blavatsky paused but I provided no assistance. "She saying name but is not clear. Wait." After an even longer pause, Madame Blavatsky said, "Is 'A.'"

"Oh? I have known many women whose first name began with that letter. Well, then, is it Anne? Or Alice? Or Abigail? Perhaps it's Augusta or Angeline or Ariel or Ariadne."

Madame Blavatsky was so still that she might have hypnotized herself.

"Madame Blavatsky," I said, after a minute had passed, "you are a charlatan." Shocked gasps came from around the table. The woman in black looked no less angry than if I had desecrated her husband's grave. Kate Fox, surprised and concerned, put her hand on my arm as though to restrain further remarks. I softened at her touch, then looked back to the medium. Kate's hand seemed to linger for a moment before she withdrew it.

The only unperturbed person in the room was Madame Blavatsky. The annoyed murmurs died down and Madame Blavatsky and I stared at each other. Her eyes, deep and inviting and strangely soothing, brought forth memories of happy times and long-forgotten faces.

"It is Abigail," she said with the certainty of truth.

My face colored and I drew in a quick, panicky breath. With effort, I broke the iron grip of her eyes, only to be met by smug looks from around the table. Madame Blavatsky's expression remained unchanged. "Abigail is asking what want you from her."

"I don't want anything from her."

"Abigail saying always she forgive what happened to her. Saying always you forgive yourself."

Is it possible to believe and disbelieve at the same time?

"Abigail saying you find her some day and learn forgive yourself. Is saying goodbye."

I said nothing, aware of how fast my heart was beating.

Madame Blavatsky turned to Kate Fox.

"So pretty. But body is prison of soul. There is presence. Is young child."

Kate looked surprised, as though she had expected someone else.

"Is playmate always when you were child."

"Jewel?" Kate spoke the name with reverence. "Is that you?"

"Yes, is Jewel. Jewel saying always you love each other."

"You were my dearest friend when I was small. What happened to you? Oh, Jewel, Jewel, I didn't know that you had died."

"She saying always you not want to know. She saying always she has much pain."

"But I was only a little girl."

Madame Blavatsky was silent, staring at Kate Fox, whose eyes were rimmed with tears.

"*Shto khochesh ot menya?*" Madame Blavatsky, uncharacteristically upset, looked at the wall behind Kate as she spoke. "There. Is standing behind you, putting hand on your shoulder. *Chyornaya.* Black. Is slave."

Kate Fox nodded only slightly, afraid to move.

Madame Blavatsky stared into space with a distant, dreamy look and swayed gently. "Your father own always slaves. Jewel is daughter of slave owned by father. You and Jewel—"

"We played together," whispered Kate. "You and I were so happy together."

"Jewel think always she not slave. Then—"

"I was cruel," whispered Kate. "You didn't understand. But neither did I."

"Is saying—"

"No—"

"Is gone," said Madame Blavatsky simply.

"Please take me outside, Arba."

It was the first time that Kate had called me Arba. Leaving Madame Blavatsky's presence was like removing a heavy weight that bowed the back and shoulders.

On the street, Kate took my arm as we walked towards her carriage. The driver, a negro in a black coat and top hat, opened the door.

"Take us to the river, Ben."

"Miss Kate, that's a dangerous place at night."

"Mr. Crane will keep me safe." I hesitated at the choice between temptation and prudence and then followed Kate Fox into the carriage. Ben closed the carriage door as though sealing our fate. Madame Blavatsky's eyes haunted the night. As the carriage moved off, Kate leaned back in the seat, delicately touched the fingers of one hand to her forehead in a charming manner, and smiled at me.

"My, my. Perhaps that wasn't such a good idea."

"Madame Blavatsky knows her transcendentalists. 'I become transparent eye.' Emerson."

"A most amusing thought. A transcendental rapper. I had hoped to speak to my mother."

"I'm sorry. When did she die?"

"It was eight years ago. How much longer ago it seems. I was thirteen. She was giving birth." She added, "I am the oldest."

"I am the only one left of five. My mother survived. How many did—?"

"She bore eight children. Now there's only brother Robert and I." We shared a silent moment.

"My mother was so terrified of childbearing." An unhappy look in her eyes came and went. "Now, you must tell me. Who is Abigail?"

By now, I had recovered my skepticism. Some slight movement or expression, picked up by Madame Blavatsky's alert eyes as I spoke Abigail's name, had given her the clue. The rest was good guesswork and a judicious use of neither too much nor too little detail. "You actually took Madame Blavatsky seriously?"

"Why, of course I did."

"Madame Blavatsky was very clever. That's all she was."

"Madame Blavatsky was clever enough to know about my Jewel and your Abigail. Come now, I am so curious. Was Abigail in love with you? Did you break her heart?"

"Are all women in the South as direct as you?"

"Hardly any are ever direct with a man. I think Father has never gotten used to me. But sometimes I do feel like a pent-up volcano. I hate the life of visiting, dressing, and tattling. I need a field for my energies. *Les occupations sont . . . un grand reméde.* So, I must be direct." She lightly put her hand on mine for encouragement. "Do tell."

Again conscious of her soft touch, I said, "When I was a child Abigail White was lashed for forgery. That's all I know about her."

"Really?" She was puzzled. "How strange. Madame Blavatsky seemed to know more about her than you do." I started to ask about Jewel, but she interrupted, "Oh, my, isn't the river beautiful in the moonlight?"

The carriage had arrived at the levee. The river glinted and gleamed under a full moon, a broad flowing stream of silver. We left the carriage and walked to the edge of the levee, where the water made gentle lapping sounds.

I gazed across the river to the Illinois side which, after only a few weeks in Missouri, seemed like a foreign country. "If your mother had . . . appeared, what would you have said?"

She shook her head. "If I told you, you would think me melancholy."

A rowboat floated by on the river with one man rowing and another standing and holding a fishing line. We both turned to watch this tranquil scene and, because we were so close, her bosom brushed my arm and we glanced at each other, curious about the other's reaction. She seemed unembarrassed and I suddenly wanted to know how it would feel to stroke her hair and whether her waist was actually so thin that I might put my hands around it. But Ben was there, so I said, "I have always believed that it is much easier to be an ordinary man than—"

"—a privileged woman?" Both of us smiled at how she had completed my sentence. "Men have adventures and conquer strange lands. How I should like to float down that river and out to sea. Instead,

I go with Father to Washington City where I shall spend the days in parlors entertaining the likes of Mr. Douglas. I plotted to make Father the Ambassador to France, but at the last minute he decided it was more important to go to Washington and keep the Yankee politicians from doing too much mischief." She gestured theatrically. "'All my pretty chickens at one fell swoop!'" Despite her words, she did not sound unhappy at the prospect of Washington City.

"Miss Kate, I best be getting you home," called out Ben from the carriage. "Master Alfred be blaming me if you not back."

"Oh, all right, Ben, we're coming." She spoke to Ben as though she were not a master but a relative, perhaps a grandchild. "Well, Mr. Crane, this was certainly a memorable evening."

"Perhaps we can have another. Without Madame Blavatsky."

"I would be delighted. But I'm most disappointed in you."

"I am sorry to hear that. How did I disappoint you?"

"You have forgotten your Shakespeare. Surely you knew I was quoting Lady Macbeth. Yet you said nothing."

"I was being polite. Actually, you quoted Macduff."

That drew a smile.

Ben drove to the Planters' House, where Kate accepted my invitation to a lecture at Wyman's Hall on Hawthorne's latest book.

Late at night I was tidying up Mr. Field's office before leaving when Dred unexpectedly appeared, followed by a negro woman young enough to be his daughter and two small negro girls. "Evening, Mr. Crane, this here's Harriet and these are my girls. This is Eliza and this is Lizzie."

The appearance of the Scott family in Mr. Field's office so took me aback that I could only stare. Harriet was as black as any slave I had seen in St. Louis. Her hair was cropped short and she wore a plain dress. Her only adornments were earrings and the red wedding band made from a button. The skin under her right eye was swollen and creased as though a blow had failed to heal properly. She looked at

71

me with an expression of distrust but nodded politely. I read carefully concealed defiance in her erect posture.

Eliza, who had been born on a steamboat, curtsied when her father spoke her and her sister's names. She looked about twelve years old. The smaller girl, Lizzie, who appeared a few years younger than her sister, did not curtsy until her mother gave her a shove. Dressed up by their parents for the visit, they wore blue gingham dresses embroidered with flowers and tied at the waist with white sashes. Their skin was dark brown and smooth as polished walnut and their black hair was as closely cropped as their mother's, whom they resembled more than the father. Like their mother, they stood their ground, except that their eyes darted here and there, and then, settling down, at their mother, whom they watched as though they were tied to her by an invisible cord that made independent movement impossible.

"Mrs. Emerson," Harriet said, "she don't know we here."

"She will certainly not learn of it from me." I invited them to sit down, which they did, uncomfortably, in chairs facing my desk. It appeared that they had not spent much time sitting in chairs. Eliza and Lizzie went to a corner of the office, sat cross-legged on the floor, and watched us. Harriet looked around the office and then darkly at me.

"What you telling my husband about us being free?"

"I tell Harriet what you say about living in the free state," said Dred.

"That true?" Harriet asked.

"It's the law in Missouri. If an owner takes his slave to a free state and lives there for long enough, the slave is free."

"How long that got to be?"

"You were there long enough."

"Eliza and Lizzie, they don't live in the free state." At the mention of their names, the girls, who had been staring at the Webster painting, looked at us.

"If you are free, your children are free."

Harriet scowled at the word "free." She said, "It the other way around. Every time I hear that word, I know I never going to be free but that maybe, just maybe, my children they get their freedom. And if they free, then no matter what happen to me, I be free." She lapsed into the sullen silence of one who has spoken her piece and assumes without asking that it fell on deaf ears.

"Mr. Crane," Dred said, "Harriet, she here without the pass."

"Then you shouldn't stay much longer."

Harriet was not inclined to leave. "What we got to do to be free?"

"You need a lawyer to sue Mrs. Emerson."

"Sue Mrs. Emerson? What's that mean?"

"You take her to the courthouse and ask the people there to set you free."

Harriet was startled by the thought of taking Irene Emerson anywhere. "She ain't going to like that."

"She won't."

Harriet's nostrils flared as she spoke. "Worse thing in the world if she give up me and Dred. That woman she don't feel good about herself unless she got someone to boss. She can't get out of the bed unless she got someone she can tell, 'Girl, you go sweep the house, then go to the market, after that cook the meal, then you wash and iron the dresses, and when all that is done, you gonna brush my hair.' And she can't stand the idea that her lady friends, they clucking about her giving up her slaves, like she need the money more."

"She will hire a lawyer and fight you," I said, impressed by her near-perfect imitation of Irene's haughty manner. "But she will lose."

Harriet stared at the shelves of brightly polished law books behind my desk. Dred said, "Mr. Crane, me and Harriet, we talk about this last night, the whole night. Harriet, she say she come here and talk with you. Now we need a lawyer."

"I think you know, Dred, that I want to be your—"

At that moment, Eliza yelled at some indignity inflicted by Lizzie, whom she pushed away. Lizzie fell backwards and began kicking her bigger sister, who kicked back. Soon Lizzie was crying. They had quickly grown weary with this exotic world and had begun to pinch and push and tease in the manner of all restless children.

"You hush up," said their father. "You stop that."

"I have something to quiet them." I stood and gathered up a piece of paper, a pen, and the inkwell and sander that my father had given me as a parting gift, and set them in front of the girls, who instantly quieted down. They watched as I dipped the nib in the inkwell and made ink marks on the paper. They appeared to regard me as some kind of magician and huddled over the paper as if it were about to speak to them. I offered the writing implements to Eliza, who tentatively dipped the nib and slowly drew a long, lonely line across the paper. Her sister looked on with a mischievous look in her eyes, as though waiting for an opportunity to grab the pen.

Returning to their parents, who had watched uncertainly, I continued, "I must first speak with my employer, Mr. Field." Dred nodded solemnly. "I am sure he will agree."

Harriet's suspicions were unaffected by my gesture to her children. "Why you want to help us?"

"Woman," said Dred, "I already tell you why."

What, I wondered, *did you tell her?*

"And if he going to help us, what difference it make why he doing it? Any fool see that we need the help."

Harriet nodded, leaned forward, and lowered her voice. "That Mrs. Emerson, I see her talking to Lucy Buck." She leaned back as though no further identification was needed.

Indeed none was. I well-remembered the woman at the slave auction with the large hat and blue feather.

"Mrs. Emerson," Harriet whispered, "she going to sell Eliza and Lizzie to Lucy Buck. They bring Mrs. Emerson money for the dresses. She say she don't have enough dresses." She looked quickly at her children, who were taking turns with my pen. Lizzie, with an impish grin, barely avoided spilling ink on her dress.

I managed not to look at the two slave children. I tried with less success not to recall the sobbing sounds in the auction shed.

Dred interpreted my silence as uncertainty. "We ain't got that much choice. We talking about our children."

Harriet nodded as though that was all that needed to be said, and started to rise. Dred remained in his chair. Unlike Harriet, he did not keep his voice down or appear concerned that his children might hear. He plainly thought that I still did not understand what he had been trying to tell me almost since the day we had met, or perhaps he thought that, in speaking to me, he was also speaking to Mr. Field.

"I tell you that my daddy, he sold." His daughters stopped drawing and stared at their father with large, round eyes. "For a time, he live in the next plantation. He often come to see me, and I crawl up in his lap. That tickle him slap to death. He have this laugh, like it come from somewhere deep inside him, and he laugh when I sit on his lap. He sing me these soft songs, too. He say that my mama sing them to me, and I just lie there like a little cat, purring when he stroke my back with his big hands, all cut up from the day's picking. But he give me this at a painful price. When his master miss him, he find him and beat him with the bullwhip all the way home. I could track him the next day by the blood on the ground.

"But my daddy," Dred's eyes became distant, "he keep a-coming to see me and he keep taking the beatings."

I glanced at Eliza and Lizzie, whose expressions were a mixture of curiosity and fear. "And then what—?"

"One day he don't come anymore."

Lizzie carefully put down the pen and both daughters stood and went to their mother. Dred and I shook hands and the family left.

Chapter 8

"So I cannot imagine a better claim to emancipation under *Winny*. Dred lived for two years in Illinois. Both lived in a territory where slavery was illegal under the Missouri Compromise. The marriage was on free soil and one of the children was born on a steamboat on the free part of the Mississippi."

Mr. Field was impatient. "Your argument fails because you overlooked a key fact. Emerson was ordered to go into free territory. What choice did he have but to bring his slave along?"

I handed Mr. Field a volume of Missouri Supreme Court cases, open to a slave case. As Mr. Field put on his reading glasses, I said, "The plaintiff in *Rachael v. Walker* had been held in slavery by an officer at Fort Snelling. The court acknowledged that the defendant had been ordered to those posts. It freed the slave anyway because no one had ordered him to bring her."

With the overconfidence of a young lawyer, I added, "This is the law of Missouri as spoken by the state's highest court."

"That was fourteen years ago."

"Mr. Field, it's still the law."

Mr. Field snapped the book shut. It sounded like a rifle shot. He removed his glasses. "All right. They've got a case. Why should you take it?"

"Taylor Blow wants Dred freed."

"I've already done right by Taylor by hiring Dred."

"Dred and Harriet are entitled to the benefit of the law, just like Murry McConnell."

"Send them to David Hall. He takes these kinds of cases. His fees come from recovery of unpaid wages."

"Dred wants me to represent him." Unmoved and uninterested in further discussion, he handed me the case volume and picked up a file, which meant that I had been dismissed.

I stood, started to leave, and then turned back. Mr. Field was absorbed in a draft of a brief I had written in a case involving a dispute over fifteen barrels of flour.

"God in Heaven," I said loudly, "Irene Emerson is going to sell Dred's children. To buy dresses." Mr. Field continued to read the brief. "How can we not use the law to help this family stay together?"

He looked up at me with a strange expression in his eyes. After a long silence, he only said, "Do not raise your voice to me again."

At midday Mr. Field went for a walk. I saw him through the window, taking long strides up Chestnut Street, hands clasped behind his back and head down. He returned briefly to the office and then left again. Late in the day, I heard the sound of Mr. Field's footsteps on the staircase. As he hung up his coat, he said, "I saw Taylor. He said he would post the Scotts' bond."

At first I felt more dumbfounded than elated. His attitude in the morning had left little doubt that I could not take the case. I could not begin to guess what had gone through Mr. Field's mind while he walked on Chestnut Street.

Trying not to show my excitement, I said, "I will prepare two sets of petitions, one for Dred and one for his wife. If I include an order keeping Dred and his family in St. Louis, it will keep the speculators away from the children."

Uninterested in my legal strategy, Mr. Field said only, "Do not neglect our paying clients or preparation for your examination. And do not use more ink and paper on this case than is absolutely necessary. I have been spending too much lately on office supplies."

I returned to my desk and briefly thought of Mr. Field's secret past. Was he helping Dred and Harriet or himself? I was anxious to finish my work on the real estate litigations before Dred's next appearance and therefore did not ask myself whom I thought I was helping.

The next evening, I cleared my desk and laid out several sheets of blank legal paper. Dred came into the office, his face posing the anxious question.

"I spoke to Mr. Field. I can take your case."

"Lord."

"We are going to win this, Dred. The law is on your side."

"Mr. Crane, I expect I owe you and Mr. Field a heap of thanks. But that's all I got to pay you with."

"That's enough. We're not charging a fee."

The gratitude was genuine but he could never forget who he was. "How can the law be on the side of the slave? Seem like it just the other way around."

"Well, the free states and the slave states have to get along. This is how they worked it out. The first thing I have to do is prepare petitions for you and Harriet. So I have some questions to ask you. You won't be doing any cleaning tonight."

That evening I traveled with Dred into the past, joining Dr. Emerson and his slave at the United States Army garrisons at Rock Island and then at Fort Snelling in the Wisconsin Territory. Dred had a sharp eye for the foibles of his owner. As he told it, Dr. John Emerson had to be the sickest doctor ever kept on the active duty roster of the United States Army, but his ailments always seemed to be accompanied by a request for a transfer or leave of absence. The diversity of his illnesses would have been amusing but for the man's death at forty.

At Fort Armstrong on Rock Island, a bleak outpost well north of St. Louis, Dr. Emerson variously complained to Dred about an ailment that sounded suspiciously like syphilis, a disease in his left foot that kept him from wearing a shoe, and about his company commander. He used these as excuses for a transfer, but instead of going south, he and Dred were sent farther north to Fort Snelling on the western side of the upper Mississippi, an outpost in what was then the frontier. As I made notes, I explained to Dred that he had been taken into an area where slavery had been forbidden by the Missouri Compromise of 1820.

"What's that?"

"Well, that was when Missouri was just a territory. New states were coming into the Union. The people in Washington City drew a line on the map along the southern border of Missouri. South of that line slavery was allowed. North of that line it wasn't, except in Missouri, which became a slave state. The other territories north of the line became free states." I added, "Fort Snelling is above that line."

"The free state just like the slave state except for the snow."

"In the eyes of the law, there's a big difference."

Fort Snelling had a small garrison, whose soldiers half the time were drunk, and an ever-shifting population of tough French fur traders, quarreling Chippewa and Sioux Indians, and dour Scotch settlers. There Dred met Harriet Robinson, a slave girl perhaps half his age, who belonged to Major Taliaferro, the resident Indian agent.

"That Major, he like the people to marry. He want the fur traders to marry their Indian women and he give Harriet to Dr. Emerson, so we could get married. The Major, he like to do the marrying too and he say the words for me and Harriet."

Dred did not say why the Major had thought of marrying his slave to Dr. Emerson's. I sensed that he was not telling me everything about the circumstances of his marriage to Harriet, but I was impressed by his ability to acquire first a wife and now a lawyer.

At the ceremony, Dr. Emerson repeated his promise to Dred.

"He put his hand on my shoulder and again say that I going to be free just as soon as he leave the army. He say that he also free Harriet. We be good servants to him and so we going to get our freedom. Then something happen that make me believe him."

Dred and Harriet were reasonably content with their lives at Fort Snelling, where Major Taliaferro ruled with impartiality and the Indians thought much of negroes. "They call us the black Frenchmen. They like to put their hands on my head and feel my hair. Then they laugh until the tears come."

After one winter at Fort Snelling, Dr. Emerson began complaining of rheumatism. This time his request for a transfer south was successful and he was ordered to Jefferson Barracks outside St. Louis. The elated doctor left his two slaves behind him at Fort Snelling, planning to send for them later.

Disappointing news, however, waited for Dr. Emerson at Jefferson Barracks in the form of orders to report at once for duty at Fort Jessup in Louisiana. Two days after reaching Fort Jessup, Dr. Emerson requested a transfer back to Fort Snelling. As he later told Dred, the damp Louisiana weather revived an old liver disorder, and his rheumatism was worse. Although proclaiming himself in constant pain, while waiting for a transfer Dr. Emerson found the energy in Fort Jessup to court and marry Irene Sanford, the daughter of Colonel Alexander Sanford, a Virginia manufacturer who now lived in St. Louis.

Several months later, the couple were on their way to Fort Snelling, where Irene had use for the two slaves. At the approach of winter, the fort's quartermaster told Dr. Emerson that there were not enough stoves for his personal servants. Dr. Emerson called him a liar. The quartermaster hit Dr. Emerson between the eyes, bruising his nose and breaking his glasses. Dr. Emerson returned with a brace of pistols, causing the quartermaster to flee across the parade grounds and the commanding officer to place Dr. Emerson under arrest.

"Couldn't believe he do that. Make me think maybe he gonna keep his word about setting us free."

By spring, Dr. Emerson, his new wife, and their two slaves were on their way back to St. Louis by steamboat. During the journey, somewhere north of the Missouri border, Eliza was born.

Dr. Emerson, following his latest orders, continued down the Mississippi to take up a new post in Florida, where he promptly began complaining of intermittent fevers and requesting a transfer back to St. Louis, Fort Snelling, or anywhere else with a cold climate. By now, the United States Army had apparently had enough and awarded Dr. Emerson an honorable dismissal from the service. Dr. Emerson returned to his wife and slaves in St. Louis, where they lived with Colonel Sanford. Dr. Emerson tried unsuccessfully to build a private practice and, within a few months, began writing letters asking to get back into the Army. When Dred reminded Dr. Emerson about his promise, Dr. Emerson said nothing.

While waiting for word from Washington City, Dr. Emerson's health really failed and, after a month in bed, he signed a will that made no mention of freeing his slaves and died during the night. He left his wife property, including land in Iowa and the Scott family. He left Dred a broken promise.

"I know I shouldn't trust Dr. Emerson. Harriet, she say, 'Dred Scott, you dumb nigger, you trusting these white folks and look what happen. Now what we gonna do?'"

Until I arrived in St. Louis there was nothing for Dred to do except endure his mistress. But life for Dred and Harriet with the widow Emerson in St. Louis was far more trying than with Dr. Emerson at Fort Snelling. Dred was hired out to do janitorial work for a succession of employers while Harriet tended to the house and Irene's many vanities and tantrums. Perhaps if the roles been reversed and Dred had stayed at home, matters might have turned out differently. But Irene was never satisfied with Harriet's work and Harriet could not completely conceal her dislike of Irene.

Irene had not remarried, but not for lack of trying. "That woman, she just want a man, but the men, they don't want her," observed Dred.

Her whole life, it seemed, had been devoted to landing a husband. She was considered something of a beauty when she married Dr. Emerson, but by the time I arrived in St. Louis, the widow Emerson was competing with much younger belles. Harriet's labors were supposed to make up the disadvantage and when they did not, Irene blamed Harriet and had her whipped.

Most of Irene's day, and therefore Harriet's, was devoted to Irene's appearance. Irene rarely woke before eleven. Harriet served Irene breakfast while she was still in bed, helped her dress for afternoon tea with lady friends and then, on the occasions—which were less and less frequent—when she was invited to a society function, Harriet did Irene's hair, helped her into a hoop skirt, and otherwise readied her for the evening. The rest of Harriet's duties—cleaning, washing, shopping, and cooking—were performed when Irene was asleep or away from the house.

Irene's only secure social connection, as I later learned from Taylor, was her brother, John Sanford. He had married into the Chouteau family, the wealthiest—if wealth is measured in numbers of slaves—and the most prominent in St. Louis by any measure, since Auguste Chouteau had built the city. Although John Sanford's wife died in childbirth four years after their well-attended wedding in the Cathedral of St. Louis, he became an active partner in the Chouteau business ventures. He spent time as a fur trader in the West and then relocated to New York as the eastern representative for the American Fur Trading Company, a Chouteau family business acquired from John Jacob Astor.

Dred remembered John Sanford's visits to St. Louis principally because they were accompanied by a round of social events attended by Irene, which meant that Harriet worked especially hard. At the end of the evening, John brought Irene home in a lavish carriage and then went off to the Chouteau residence to entertain friends, returning at dawn in a drunken stupor. He bestowed gifts on almost everyone in St. Louis but his sister. One morning, not long after Colonel Sanford's death had brought John back to St. Louis, Dred heard Irene and her brother discussing their father's will, which named John as executor and left nothing to Irene.

"Mrs. Emerson, she just get madder and madder. She saying that old Mr. Sanford he don't like her one bit. Then she start a-crying and a-wailing and her brother, he say that he take care of her, that he got lots of money. But it don't much make her feel better. Seems like she mad at her brother, too. But she careful not to be too mad." Dred shook his head at the recollection of John Sanford. "The brother, he a man always with this angry look in his eyes like a cat that got its tail stepped on. I come upon him once in the dark, and I hear him talking to himself, like he arguing with himself about something, he angry with himself it seem like, and then he see me. That surprise him pretty bad." Dred again shook his head at the memory. "He stay so still that I think maybe I staring at a dead man except that his eyes, they glowing in the dark like coals on the fire, they burning through me, and I back out of there as fast as I could 'cause it seem like he getting ready to jump. After that, I take care not to get too close to him."

The Colonel's death, his comparably good fortune, and his sister's distress at being left out of the will perhaps moved John Sanford to help Irene. He gave Irene a comfortable, although much smaller, residence on the edge of the city. Dred and his family, which now included Lizzie, were sent to live out in a single room in the small, confined negro quarter, which meant a long daily walk for Harriet to and from Irene's new home. Dred was hired out to a variety of small businesses and to Mr. Field, but had enough time to raise Eliza and Lizzie.

Dred finished his story and I put down my pen. My hand was stiff from writing.

"You keep telling me that you are not angry about . . . all this. I don't believe you."

"I been telling you, Mr. Crane, it don't do no good. Dr. Emerson, he gone, and Mrs. Emerson, she ain't no different than most white folks."

"Look at all the white people that you trusted. All the broken promises. Why, you have as much right to be angry as I do to breathe."

"Maybe I do," Dred said after a while. "But that don't do no good."

Looking into his eyes was like peering into a deep well at night.

How did he keep his bitterness at the bottom of the well? But I did not ask and instead requested that he have Harriet come to the office. That night, we left the office together and walked silently through the dark streets until we parted, he in the direction of the negro quarter and I to the Planters' House.

Chapter 9

"Why, he missed the point," declared Kate. The city outside the carriage was shrouded in misty night. "Hawthorne didn't write from guilt but from passion. Pearl was the result of Hester's passion." She added with bitterness, "The townsmen branded Hester for a sin of the flesh that's a sin only because a woman committed it."

For the lecture on *The Scarlet Letter,* Kate had worn a walking dress and a green velvet cloak with buttoned sleeves. I did not ask how many slaves she and her father had brought with them just to manage her wardrobe. Afterward, we had gone for a carriage ride.

"Not at all. Hester shielded Dimmesdale because his fate would have been the same, or worse, if the town had known."

"That certainly would not have happened to Dimmesdale in the South. I doubt New England is any different."

I had never met a woman who argued back to a man. I found it invigorating. "In New England we live by codes and woe to those who break them, man or woman. Hester made her choice and, to her credit, bore the consequences nobly."

Kate looked out the carriage window. "Hester had no acceptable choices except to become multiplying flesh. Hester had spirit, which men have no use for. How strange that the first good novel by a man should point that out."

In the dim light from the coachman's lantern, Kate's face glowed with imprisoned vitality. I took her hands and said, "I have use for Hester's spirit." I kissed her and she did not draw back at first but then leaned away, a faint smile on her lips, which I longed to feel against mine again, at once yielding and urging and resisting. She considered the situation for a moment but then, putting out one hand for balance, moved over to my side of the carriage. She rested her head on my shoulder, her soft, fragrant hair caressing my cheek.

Before the ride ended, almost drowsily, she asked me, "What did you do to make Samuel O'Fallon so angry at you?"

"I think he was born that way. I would not have suspected that you and he were acquaintances."

She was vague. "He comes from a very distinguished family. They are helping Father defeat Benton in the Senatorial election. Samuel said that you were in law school together. Did you quarrel then?"

"He was thrown out of Harvard for drunkenness and I graduated with honors. He still has a grudge." I described my encounter with Samuel at the levee and the exchange at the Blow party. "Is he a beau of yours?"

"Why, Mr. Crane, do you think you are my only beau?"

"I guess not. But I would be disappointed to learn that he was one."

She laughed. "I don't think I will tell you whether he is or not. Samuel told me that I had no business with a Yankee, to which I said that my business was none of his. The same is true for you."

"You should stay away from Samuel."

"I do not think you understand Southern men, Arba. They are all temperament. I don't suppose there is much temperament in Vermont."

We rode in silence until we reached the Planters' House. I asked to see her again, but she merely nodded and told Ben to take her home.

My preparation for the Missouri bar examination could only be done at night since my days were devoted to the endless stream of case files. As I settled in one evening to study the Missouri penal code, there was a knock at the door and Harriet appeared with Eliza and Lizzie. I set aside the statute book without much concern over the little time left before the examination.

Eliza and Lizzie, who seemed delighted to be back in Mr. Field's office, both curtsied with smiles and looked at me straightaway for the writing implements, which I gave them.

"Thank you, Mr. Crane," said Eliza, with a broad, charming smile, momentarily turning her back to her younger sister, who grabbed the pen and began making bold, confident strokes on the paper.

"They been practicing with sticks," said Harriet.

I took another piece of paper and wrote their names in large capital letters, and then pointed at each and then to the name on the paper, which I repeated slowly. They tried to copy their names with poor results. I guided each girl's hand, showing them how to apply just the right pressure to the nib. "You see, if you press too hard, there's too much ink." Eliza quickly picked up the knack, but Lizzie seemed to think the more ink on the paper the better.

"Lizzie," said Harriet, "you listen good to Mr. Crane here and don't make no messes."

"Yes, mama." Lizzie sounded unfazed by her mother's stern voice as she continued to pour ink onto the paper. I made a mental note to check whether it was a criminal offense in Missouri to teach a slave to read and write, in case the question were asked at the examination.

Briefly thinking of my sisters, I lingered for a moment and then returned to my desk. I explained to Harriet that I needed to know the details of her travels in free states and territories in order to draft the petition and start the lawsuit. I picked up a pen and asked question after question but she simply sat without speaking. I contemplated the dwindling number of nights left before the bar examination. Then she told me in a low voice so that her children could not hear, the story that Dred had not told me, how Major Taliaferro, who ruled like a god over the affairs of Fort Snelling, had married her to the slave Dred Scott.

Major Taliaferro had acquired Harriet in Prairie du Chien from an agent of the American Fur Company, who had offered her to Major Taliaferro as a gift. Major Taliaferro, a resolutely moral man, had declined the gift on suspicion that it was a bribe, but nonetheless, having need of a slave girl, paid full value for Harriet, then aged fourteen. She accompanied Major Taliaferro as he keelboated up the Mississippi to his new post at Fort Snelling.

Harriet mended clothes and prepared meals for Major Taliaferro, a tall, burly, and bearded military man with kind eyes and a pronounced sensitivity to criticism. It was Major Taliaferro's habit to refer to himself in the third person when he reflected at the end of the day in his quarters with only Harriet for an audience. He told her, "The agent has neutralized British influence and given efficient organization to the fur trade."

His enemies were legion, the American Fur Company and the British in Canada chief among them. At times it seemed that Major Taliaferro was besieged and embattled from dawn until dusk as he tried to do his duty to God and to his fellow man.

The summers at Fort Snelling were torments of heat, river inundations, and locusts, and Harriet recalled the winters as Dred had described them—long and dreary and unbearably cold. Then she told me about the occasion that a band of thirty Sioux lodges had been trapped by a snowstorm on the prairie. The Indians had encamped in the belief that the storm would not last more than a day, but it raged for several, until the snow was more than three feet deep. The seventy-five men, women, and children, seven pairs of snowshoes among them, soon ran out of food and wood for fires. The strongest men left for the nearest trading post, one hundred miles away. The traders sent four Canadians with what supplies they and the Indians could carry. By the time the rescue party reached the encampment, most of the Indians were dead, and the living were subsisting on their remains.

Among the very few rescued was a young mother who had eaten her deceased offspring and a part of her dead father. After the rescue she made her way to Fort Snelling, where she encountered Harriet, who took her to Major Taliaferro. During the young Indian woman's lucid moments, Major Taliaferro delicately tried to get what information he could about the disaster. Harriet was present when the young and lovely Tash-u-no-ta took Major Taliaferro by the collar of his coat and asked him if he knew which was the best portion of a man to eat.

"The Major, he don't speak for a time. Then he say he don't know. She tell him the arms, they the best." Harriet fell silent and I listened to the familiar sound from the street below of elegant men and women on their way to engagements.

"What happened to the Indian woman?"

"A few days after that they find her in the river. She drown herself. The Major, he give her a good burial. That about the time that Dred, he come to the Fort with Dr. Emerson."

Her encounter with Tash-u-no-ta caused Harriet to consider her future for the first time. She concluded that her chances at Fort Snelling for eventually gaining her freedom and a family were bleak. She did not like Dred when she first met him, thinking him too friendly towards Major Taliaferro, whose favors Harriet jealously guarded from the Post's other slaves. She resentfully spent time in Dred's company while they split logs for the stoves and, after winter ended, when they worked together in the Fort's vegetable garden. She gradually grew impressed at how much Dred knew about the workings of the Fort, such as which fur traders were allies of Major Taliaferro and which were his enemies, or the sentence that the old Sioux, Hole-in-the-Day, would receive for killing a Chippewa even before it was imposed. She was even more impressed when Dred told her that Dr. Emerson had promised that, when his army service ended, he would set Dred free. Although she thought Dred too old to make a husband when he first suggested the idea of marriage, she weighed the alternatives and realized there were none and that her poor prospects would greatly improve if she became

Dred's wife. She told Dred she would marry him but that she did not think Major Taliaferro would give her up.

"Then the next thing I know, the Major, he give me to Dred."

"Dred said that Major Taliaferro sold you to Dr. Emerson."

"The way Dred work it, it seem more like the Major, he give me to Dred even if Dr. Emerson, he pay the Major."

As the highest-ranking officer at the Fort, Major Taliaferro conceived it as his role to enforce morality. He persuaded the fur traders, who had the use of Indian women as long as it suited their convenience, to legitimize their children and then officiated as a justice of the peace. He had once told Harriet as she helped him dress for a wedding ceremony, "The agent has been accused of great mystery in his management of Indian affairs, but in him an all-wise Creator has reposed his powers of control over the hearts of the children in his care."

Major Taliaferro liked presiding at marriages because they afforded an opportunity to reaffirm his moral authority to all within his domains. Harriet never knew whether Dred suggested the idea to Dr. Emerson or to Major Taliaferro or both, but one evening the Major announced while she knelt before the fireplace nursing a fire, "The agent has decided to marry his slave girl to Dr. Emerson's slave, Dred Scott."

He looked at her for a reaction but none was evident.

Major Taliaferro married Dred and Harriet in a ceremony attended by Dr. Emerson, assorted Indians, French fur traders, a few bored soldiers, and the other slaves at the Fort. The Major, regal in dress uniform and beaming with moral triumph, pronounced Dred and Harriet to be man and wife, and then gazed lovingly upon his assembly, his flock of wayward and surly children in all manner of dress, shape, and color. Even though Major Taliaferro had given them a civil ceremony, Harriet insisted on jumping over the broom because her mother, whom she had last seen when she was nine, had told her that was how Harriet's father had married her. At the end of the ceremony, Dr. Emerson repeated his promise to Dred.

"We be married for a time, but then Dr. Emerson, he get the orders and he go away and we stay in the fort."

The rest of the story matched Dred's, focusing on Dr. Emerson's broken promise.

"I guess you were unhappy with Dred."

Harriet's nostrils flared. "I tell Dred at the fort that we can't trust the white folks, but he say, no, Dr. Emerson, he watching out for us. Dred, he think he smart, but I tell him that ain't so. Dred say he think of something, but in the meantime I got to work for that woman. That's all I got to tell."

Harriet turned to her children, "Lizzie, Eliza, we going now."

Eliza reluctantly put down the pen and both girls stood and went to their mother, longingly glancing at the writing implements.

I picked up the ink and sander and gathered up a few pieces of blank paper and a pen.

"Here, take them."

All three looked astonished. Harriet said, "Mr. Crane, we can't take these—"

"Well, you can."

Eliza and Lizzie excitedly stammered out heartfelt thanks and Harriet gave me an appreciative look.

They left and I set out fresh paper to begin drafting the petitions, but my thoughts were of Major Taliaferro. Harriet had last seen him many years ago on the day when, achingly pregnant, she and Dred left Fort Snelling. The Major had watched as Dred and Harriet and the Emersons boarded a steamboat. He held up a benevolent hand, the ruler saluting the departing subjects. Harriet told me that she had said goodbye to Major Taliaferro with great unhappiness because she preferred the hardships of a slave in the fort to those of a slave in St. Louis under Irene Emerson's yoke. She did not know what thoughts of Major Taliaferro had passed through Dred's mind as he watched the lonely figure on the riverbank dwindle in size and then disappear. They never spoke of Major Taliaferro after setting foot on the steamboat.

The Major clearly had liked Dred, just as I did. Had Dred spent time studying Major Taliaferro, I wondered, before offering a suggestion about what to do with the slave girl, Harriet? Had he instinctively appreciated that Major Taliaferro welcomed, if not desperately needed, any excuse to display his moral authority—such as a wedding? And what of my role in this? Perhaps it was only a coincidence that Irene Emerson had hired Dred out to a lawyer. Perhaps. But Dred had been listening when Mr. Field and I met with Murry McConnell to discuss his case against a slave who claimed to be free because she had lived in a free state. Come to think of it, I could not recall exactly why Dred told me that he had lived in both Illinois and the free territories. I seemed to recall that I hadn't asked him, yet he had told me anyway.

I looked at the paper on which Eliza and Lizzie had written their names over and over. The initial efforts were illegible but by the end Eliza had managed to nearly write her name in legible form. Even some of Lizzie's letters were distinct. I was haunted by the dusky beauty of the children, the eagerness with which they had practiced writing their names, and a nightmarish vision of their fate if I lost the lawsuit.

I put aside troubling thoughts and began drafting the petitions, which was easy enough to do, as I was a good pleader. I finished after midnight. Wide awake, as though I had just woken from a long and refreshing dreamless sleep, I felt at peace with the world. I no longer thirsted for brandy or whisky; Abigail White and the man wearing a black robe and hood faded into the apparitions they'd once been.

I lingered over Dred's petition before finally leaving the office.

Dred Scott, a man of color, respectfully states that he is claimed as a slave by one Irene Emerson, widow of the late Dr. John Emerson. That the said John Emerson purchased your petitioner in the city of St. Louis, he then being a slave, from one Peter Blow, now deceased, and took petitioner to Rock Island in the State of Illinois and there kept petitioner to labor and service. That said Emerson was removed from the garrison at Rock Island to Fort Snelling in the territory of Wisconsin. That said Emerson is now dead and his widow, the said Irene, claims petitioner's services as a slave and as his owner, but believing that under this state of facts that he is entitled to his freedom, he prays your Honor to allow him to sue said Irene Emerson in said court, in order to establish his right to freedom.

Chapter 10

"Don't think we've got enough free niggers in this city, do you?"

The nearsighted clerk in the file-strewn room at the courthouse muttered to himself as he prepared the summons for Harriet's petition. His head close to his pen, he first wrote "Harriet" and then started to write "Scott." He got no further than the capital "S" when, realizing his mistake, he cursed, drew slash marks through the "S," and wrote in its place "a woman of color."

"That's right," I said, "I don't think we have enough free negroes in St. Louis." The clerk suggested that the next time Mr. Field wanted a legal document filed he should damn well send someone else.

I returned from the Law Library the next day to find, sitting in the outer office, Dred, an anxious-looking Harriet, and a well-dressed negro man whose head was as bald as Blackstone's. Eliza and Lizzie sat quietly on the floor near the corner jog. Hearing my entrance, Mr. Field, holding legal papers, came out of his office with a disapproving look and took a seat in the corner. I greeted the Scotts and their children, and turned to the stranger, who stood up, filling the room.

"I am Reverend John Richard Anderson." He stood towering over me, and we shook hands. He smiled but there was no joy in his face. His skin was coal black and smooth except for an area on his neck just above the white collar, which was mottled as though it had melted and then fused together again. "I told Dred and Harriet that I wanted to meet you."

"The Reverend, he know all about this," said Dred. "Harriet tell him about Irene and the court."

Dred seemed at pains to emphasize that his wife, and not he, had informed the Reverend. Eliza and Lizzie looked at me expectantly. I gave them some writing materials and candies that I now kept in my desk. Mr. Field watched with a concerned look as the two girls began applying pen and ink to expensive legal paper.

"I have a congregation of slaves, Mr. Crane," said the Reverend. Listening to his deep voice was like hearing the distant rumble of thunder. "People who own nothing, not even themselves. On Sundays, I tell them, 'You belong to your masters and you have no money, but you can have as much religion as anybody else.' Harriet asked me if she and Dred can have as much law as anybody else. You see, I know that the law doesn't come from God. It's the white folks' law, nobody else's. But they say that you are their lawyer. I told them to listen to you and not to me. But now they've started something and I decided to come see for myself."

"Henry Belt rode out to the Sanford place to serve the summons," Mr. Field explained to me. "Irene didn't waste any time. She retained Samuel O'Fallon."

Startled, I said, "O'Fallon? He's not a real lawyer."

"Well, his family is as proslavery as they come and very powerful politically. And Samuel is not bad in the courtroom." He handed me the legal papers. "Samuel had Sheriff Milburn serve the Scotts with a motion for dismissal."

I quickly read the Emerson papers, which Samuel had signed with a flourish. "This says that no bond was put up. Our summons stated clearly that Taylor posted a bond. Judge Hamilton will not grant this motion. Harriet, you needn't worry. This is part of every lawsuit."

"That Mrs. Emerson," said Dred, "she going to fight this pretty bad."

His words were intended for his wife, who said with irritation, "That's what I been saying."

"Mr. Crane," asked the Reverend, "can you get these poor folk justice in a white man's courthouse?"

Before I could respond, Mr. Field asked, "Did you say that Judge Hamilton has the case?" It was the first time that Mr. Field had shown any interest in the lawsuit's progress. "I thought it was assigned to Judge Krum."

"It was reassigned today, which is a blow for Samuel. Dred, Harriet, I am glad you are here because this is good news. Judge Hamilton is an antislavery man. He came to St. Louis from Philadelphia. Yes, Reverend, I can get Dred and Harriet justice."

The Reverend looked skeptical.

"We ain't got no choice in this," said Dred to the Reverend. "God ain't going to help us unless we help ourselves. That's what you telling us all the time."

"Indeed." The Reverend nodded. He turned to me. "You see, Mr. Crane, the white preachers tell black folks that if they be good and work hard, they will go to Heaven. 'Obey your earthly masters with fear and trembling.' But they never tell them they gonna be free in Heaven. You see, they don't want slaves to start thinking about freedom, even in Heaven. But you got Dred and Harriet thinking about freedom and so they are in your good hands."

"And Judge Hamilton's," I reminded him. "He will do right by them."

"We been thinking about freedom since before I can remember," said Dred. "Reverend, I trust this man. He do the best he can. We got to do more than just pray, we ain't got time to wait for God to answer us. The slaves, they been praying for a long while and He ain't answered them yet." He lowered his voice to a whisper. "Eliza and Lizzie, they don't got time." He stood up and said more loudly. "Children, it's time for us to be going."

Eliza got to her feet. "See, Mr. Crane, what I done." She held up a piece of paper on which was painstakingly written "Laws" over and over. Even the Reverend and Mr. Field smiled because she had copied the word from the spine of a statute book.

"Whose name be it?" she asked.

Before anyone could answer, her mother took the children by their arms and marched them out the door, followed by the Reverend Anderson and Dred.

At the end of each week, Mr. Field invited me to share his brandy and cigars, more out of courtesy than affection. After Mr. Field agreed to Dred's lawsuit, in a fit of remorse I had replaced the contents of Mr. Field's brandy decanter with undiluted brandy I had purchased with my meager funds.

Alternately sipping brandy and savoring his cigar, in a more talkative mood than on other occasions, Mr. Field said, "Reverend Anderson taught himself to read from a spelling book. He was Elijah Lovejoy's typesetter. The mob almost killed him when they burned the print shop."

He surprised me by offering to refill my glass but I shook my head. I had found the brandy tasteless.

"Did you assure the Scotts that they would win this case?"

"Yes, I did." At his reproachful look, I said, "They cannot lose. The law is on their side and now we have Judge Hamilton."

His outburst was so unexpected that I almost dropped the empty glass. His face twisted in bitterness, he shouted at me, "The law? What do you know of the law? Do you think it comes from law books?" Calming himself by an act of will, he said dejectedly, "For your sake, let us hope that Judge Hamilton makes an honest man of you."

At an afternoon tea at Taylor Blow's home on a lazy Saturday afternoon, Kate was friendly but distant. I knew she had been seeing other young men, who took her to the St. Louis society balls and elegant parties. Perhaps one was Samuel, about whom she continued to be maddeningly vague. I apparently was her literary beau, to be picked up and put down like a lengthy book that, no matter how interesting, can only be read for so long at a single sitting.

We discussed an issue of *Harper's New Monthly Magazine,* which was serializing the work of contemporary English authors, and played backgammon. In the middle of the game, Kate unexpectedly began to read out loud her brother's letter, which told of the death of their Louisiana neighbor at the hands of four of her female slaves.

> *. . . One of the slaves who confessed said that Mrs. Middlespoon had begged them hard for her life. That innocent lady and her pleas moved them not a jot.*

Kate folded the letter with trembling hands.

"Why did they do it?" I asked.

She did not answer my question.

"I wonder how we can ever sleep soundly," said Taylor.

"At least you are honest about it, Taylor. To hear people, everyone is ready to trust their own yard."

Kate's father walked into the sitting room just as Taylor said, "I don't believe there is anything you are afraid of, Kate."

"My Kate, afraid?" asked Alfred Fox, who warmly shook hands with Taylor and, more stiffly, with me.

"Of course I'm afraid. No one likes to say it but we are all afraid of being murdered in our beds like Mrs. Middlespoon." She glanced at me. "How I envy those saintly Yankees in their clear, cool New England homes writing books to make their fortunes and shame us, while we sit in perfect fear."

I found Kate's sarcasm irritating. "Then why don't you free them and be done with it?"

"Oh, but Kate would if she could," said her father. "I have only met one or two women who were not abolitionists in their hearts."

"These Yankee writers do not hit the sorest spots," said Kate. "They should write of the mothers and daughters who never dream of what is plain before their eyes."

A shocked silence followed. Her father's face reddened. Finally Taylor spoke up. "Those are old world stories. The condition of Southern women is improving."

"Yes, Taylor, we should not judge our fathers or our husbands and take them as the Lord provided. We play our parts as unsuspecting angels to the letter."

Kate's undisguised bitterness surprised me.

"Enough, Kate." Her father's anger made no visible impression on her. "Northern agitation choked the breath from that great lady. Never forget that."

Taylor glanced briefly at me. "Well, Alfred, what news from the Senate contest?" The tension abated.

"Old Bullion Benton may yet live to fight another day." He turned to Kate, obviously grateful for the change in subject and an opportunity to reconcile. "You were right and I was wrong. I have traveled the state bestowing the good blessings of Mr. Fillmore. I had no idea that Missouri has so many post offices." He chuckled. "And so many vacancies that need to be filled. But it will go to a ballot in the Assembly."

"Of course it will. Many ballots." Kate's voice was calmer. She offered a precise analysis of the sentiments of the various competing Whig factions and the political impact of the growing community of antislavery German immigrants. It occurred to me that Senator Benton would be in more trouble if Kate, instead of her father, were managing the campaign of the proslavery St. Louis lawyer, Henry Geyer. The sober talk of politics ended when Taylor's wife, Eliza, and his sister, Charlotte, joined us to exclaim over the latest issue of *Godey's Lady's Book*.

The three women sat side by side leafing through the magazine. They debated the demise of bloomers, laughed at the advice to clean black lace with skim milk, and collectively approved gilets lined with white silk.

I said, "I am never certain whether women dress to please themselves or to please men."

"Why, they dress to please men," said Charlotte.

"They dress to worry other women," said Kate, which provoked laughter from us all.

As the afternoon drew to a happier close than had seemed possible just a few minutes earlier, Kate and I went for a stroll. Kate still held her brother's letter.

"Mrs. Middlespoon made green peach tarts and pound cake. She always made an odd number of tarts. My brother and I would name state capitals or spell long words until one of us made a mistake. The other ate the extra tart."

"And Mr. Middlespoon?" I asked.

"He was a horrible man. He did unspeakable things with his female slaves. Mrs. Middlespoon could not stand it but she dared not speak back to him. Some women would have blamed the slaves but she was a saint." We walked in silence until she said, "Of course, I did not know all that when I was a child."

"I'm sure you could not have known." I hesitated and then asked the question that had been on my mind since Kate's quarrel with her father, "Did Mrs. Middlespoon really play her part as unsuspecting angel?"

For a moment I thought she might cry but instead, more to herself than to me, she said, "No. She didn't." I took her hand, wondering whether the slaves had decided to murder Mrs. Middlespoon because her behavior in punishing them was even more inexplicable than the sins of her husband for which she blamed them. Or, perhaps she was just easier to kill. We walked together without speaking until we reached a moss-covered stone wall that separated the Blow family grave site from the rest of the estate.

Kate let go of my hand and ran her fingers along the ancient and all-knowing stones. Once more in Kate's presence, I was overcome by a longing for sweet melodies I could never hear.

"We never spent a Saturday afternoon like this in Newfane. We did chores or went to meetings."

"I imagine that Northerners enjoy life less than any other civilized people."

"I suppose you think that all there is to life is Taylor's idle amusements and your father's political gossip."

"Father is going to be Secretary to Mr. Fillmore's cabinet. All of Washington will be at our feet. Besides, of the two of us, I am the better politician."

"To what end?"

She did not answer my question. "We are loyal, we Southern women, to a fault, I suppose. Or else we do what we must because there is so little choice in the matter. I'm not sure which. Perhaps it doesn't matter why we do things, only that we do them."

"It does matter, especially when you have a choice. Make your way in the world." I added, "Be yourself."

She looked at me thoughtfully, the way she had on the night I kissed her. "I cannot leave my father, even if I were fond of you," she teased. The gloomy Kate had disappeared and in its place was the spirited young woman who had captured my heart.

"You are fond of me. What binds you to him?" She did not answer. "You are afraid to leave him."

"So you may think. I love intrigue and great gleaming marble buildings."

"You do love carriages and cloaks but you were not born to be some blueblood's plaything."

"True, so true," she sighed and took my hand with an affectionate clasp and then let go. "I am so fond of you. You know more than just soirees and fox hunts. Perhaps if I had been born in the North I would have made my way in the world and then met you."

"It shouldn't matter where you were born."

She put a hand to my face and I felt the warmth of her fingers on my cheek. Then she turned away. "Oh, but it does."

We left the stone wall and the eternal resting place of Captain and Mrs. Blow and walked silently together back to Taylor's mansion, where I got in a carriage and left. I was so absorbed in delicious confusion over her simultaneous declaration of love and separation that in almost an instant, it seemed, I was back at the boardinghouse to which I had recently moved from the Planters' House. But mixed with elation and disappointment was an uncomfortable vision of the little girl who loved Mrs. Middlespoon's tarts so much that she memorized all the state capitals, but who could not see what was plain before her eyes.

I sat for my examination in Jefferson City on the thirteenth and final day of the state Assembly vote on whether to re-elect Thomas Hart Benton as United States Senator from Missouri. The state capital was a sleepy village of homes and garden plots with a skyline dominated by the domed capitol building, where the badly divided Assembly was meeting. As each inconclusive vote had been taken on the previous twelve days, just as Kate had predicted, the antislavery Benton steadily lost ground to the proslavery Henry Geyer.

I shared a hotel bed with one of the beefy, cigar-smoking politicians who had descended by horse and carriage for the vote. I caught glimpses of Alfred Fox, always in the company of two or three or four politicians, plotting, no doubt, how to find the last handful of votes to push Henry Geyer to victory and deal a blow to the antislavery faction in Missouri.

It was thus in the midst of great political tension that I arrived at the Missouri Supreme Court to be examined by Judge William Scott. Perhaps Madame Blavatsky knew more of the cosmos than I dreamed possible. Mere coincidence cannot explain why the Missouri Supreme Court Judge who examined me for the bar had the same last name as my then obscure client, both of whom were destined to meet on a legal battlefield that shaped so many destinies, not least my own.

I waited in the courtroom with only Billy Hart, the janitor, for company. Billy was a mulatto who was a universal favorite with the bar and bench and, so it was rumored, even was consulted by the judges when they had any doubt as to the law.

"Judge Scott has a book of legal maxims in Latin." He paused for effect. "You best know your Latin." Billy Hart's English spoke of self-education from a quarter century of listening to lawyers argue cases and judges read opinions.

It was cold in the courtroom. I shuddered slightly but not because of the temperature. Billy smiled at his well-aimed blow to my self-confidence because I had not spent much preparation time on the Latin maxims or, for that matter, on the law.

Judge Scott appeared in the doorway and I stood. He gestured to follow him. He was a heavyset man who walked with great difficulty, like a walrus with short legs. He was breathing hard when we entered his chambers, a large comfortable room with worn sofas, shelves of law books, and a desk piled high with legal briefs.

The judge sat down heavily in the chair behind his desk with a great sigh. I took the facing chair.

"Are you afraid of drowning?" he asked, lighting up a cigar. With each draw and puff his great jowls ebbed and flowed.

"No more than any man, Your Honor."

"Good. Then you can ride circuit. I rode the Ninth Judicial Circuit, which has more rivers than Mesopotamia. I had to cross the Meremac in winter with several lawyers, your Mr. Field included. That river was colder than a snowstorm on a black night. Now pay attention. *Boni judicis est ampliare justitiam.*"

I let myself breathe and gave silent thanks to my father for his dinner-table drills. "It is the duty of the good judge to do justice."

"*Bonus judex secundum aequum et bonum judicat, et aequitatem stricto juri praefert.*"

"A good judge decides according to what is just and good, and prefers equity to strict law."

"Good. The Latin maxims are still true. Missouri has abolished some of the distinctions between law and equity. But I never forget that I am still a chancellor and wield the law to maintain right and justice. That is our job, Mr. Crane, to do justice."

He then fired at me question after question about the law of Missouri, rulings by the United States Supreme Court, federal procedure, English common law, and the Napoleonic Code. "What are the grounds for an attachment?" "What is the Statute of Frauds?" "What was the holding in *Marbury v. Madison*?" "What is the Rule against Perpetuities?" "What are the exceptions to the hearsay rule?"

Judge Scott used no notes or law books but seemed to draw his questions from some bottomless well of legal knowledge. Occasionally, he supplemented my answer with an observation or qualification, but for the most part my answer was followed by a question, answer, question, answer, question, answer, until I grew desperate for a glass of water or an excuse to stand up or a short rest but dared not break the rhythm for fear that I would prolong this misery. My existence was a small circle in which the two of us sat and my vision seemed filled by Judge Scott's enormous, flabby face, his puffing cigar, and his hard gaze, which only increased my tension. I was too slow to answer one question and he pounced like a fox on a chicken.

"No hesitation, Mr. Crane! A lawyer cannot hesitate in a courtroom. Quickly now, what is the basis for diversity jurisdiction in the federal courts?"

I thought desperately back to my constitutional law studies. "The Constitution says that the judicial power of the United States shall extend to lawsuits between . . ." But I faltered because I was unsure if the answer was residents of different states or citizens of different states. Was it worse to guess and make an error or to admit ignorance?

"Residents of different states."

Judge Scott blew out a voluminous cloud of blue smoke.

"Citizens, Mr. Crane, citizens of different states. Citizens of different states can sue each other in the federal courts. A resident may be a citizen but the Framers wrote down citizen, which is what you forgot."

This was the only such interruption and therefore, I prayed, my only serious mistake. The questioning resumed and I lost track of time and everything else, so powerfully was I concentrating on the volley of questions. Had he suddenly asked me what state we were in, I'm not sure I could have answered correctly. Finally, and most mercifully, he asked the question that signaled an end to the ordeal.

"Are you an honest man and of good character?"

"That I am."

"Keep it that way." He asked me to raise my right hand and swear to God to faithfully respect and promote the law as a member of the Missouri bar, which I gladly did. "Respect that oath, sir. Little charity is felt these days for the legal fraternity because of dishonest lawyers. Hand me your license."

I gave him my license and, to my relief, thrill and pride, he signed it.

"This is a great day," said Judge Scott as he handed back the license.

"I am indeed honored—" I stopped because I realized he was not talking about me but the balloting at the Assembly.

"A great verdict is about to be rendered. A long agony is over. The charm of the tyrant Benton is broken. Good day, Mr. Crane."

I decided that no purpose or good would be served by a response and so I said simply, "Thank you, Your Honor," and left his chambers.

Billy Hart, court jester to the high court, was sweeping the courtroom as I left. "This is a great day," he said in a perfect imitation of Judge Scott, and then giggled.

As I left the courthouse, gunshots broke out and men streamed through the streets cheering and shouting wildly and firing pistols.

"Benton is beaten!" they cried, "Free Soil is dead!" Here and there I saw downcast, weary men whom I took to be Benton supporters, collars askew and unshaven, wandering amidst the celebrants. Benton's defeat tempered my own elation. Although new to Missouri, I had come to think of Benton as a great, aging oak tree, as much a part of the landscape as the river, except that while the river flowed eternally the oak had toppled over. It felt lonelier to be in Missouri without a Senator who opposed the expansion of slavery. But there was another reason for my change in spirits. While Judge Scott's years of agony had this day ended, I feared that mine were just beginning. The election meant that Kate and her father would be leaving for Washington City.

Chapter 11

Dressed in my best broadcloth, I strode down the sidewalk along muddy streets to the courthouse, carrying a green bag filled with depositions, pleadings and our jury instructions. I met Dred and Harriet, and their children, outside the courthouse. The parents wore their finest, Harriet in a gingham dress with long sleeves and Dred in an ill-fitting, worn and fraying blue suit. Somewhere he had found a black bow tie, which gave him a jaunty look, although the mood of the Scotts that rainy morning was anything but cheerful. Eliza and Lizzie were dressed as they had been on the occasion of their first visit to my office. They clung to their mother, looking warily at the bustling scene on the courthouse steps as lawyers and litigants hurried past them, and managed a faint smile as I approached. Mr. Field arrived shortly.

I led my clients up the courthouse steps, where Dred and Harriet briefly glanced at the empty slave block. Inside, the rotunda was crowded with dozens of immigrants waiting to take their oaths as new citizens of the United States of America. We pushed through the crowd and into Judge Hamilton's courtroom, where Irene and Samuel had already arrived. Irene never once looked at Dred and Harriet, who averted their eyes. Irene chatted gaily with Samuel O'Fallon, smiling and nodding, as though she had come to the courthouse only on a social visit to see an old friend. She wore a flounced dress with a white bonnet and collar. I wondered if Harriet had to help Irene dress for her court appearance. I was certain that Irene could not appreciate the irony of using Harriet to get her ready to appear as the defendant in Harriet's suit for freedom. On reflection, I decided that, even if she did, Irene still would have insisted that Harriet dress her for the occasion.

As the two sides seated themselves at different tables, Samuel looked at me with cold contempt. "Well, Crane, we'll find out if a Harvard law degree does any good in a Missouri courtroom."

Ignoring him, I took Eliza and Lizzie to the public seats closest to our table, where the two slave girls sat for the rest of the day with hardly any restless movement, except for their eyes, which never seemed to stop moving as events unfolded here and there in the courtroom. Several tough-looking young men walked into the courtroom and sat down behind Samuel's table and were soon joking with Samuel and Irene Emerson, and glancing our way with disdainful expressions.

The court clerk cried out, waking a sleeping dog next to the judge's bench, "Hear ye, hear ye, draw near and the cases of Dred Scott, a man of color, versus Irene Emerson, and Harriet, a woman of color, versus Irene Emerson, shall be heard." Judge Hamilton, a tall judge with long white hair and eyebrows, glowering eyes and a commanding demeanor that instantly silenced the courtroom, entered and, as we all began to stand, motioned for us to remain seated. The dog went back to sleep.

"Gentlemen," he said to the lawyers, ignoring their clients, "we are going to try *Scott v. Emerson*. However it goes, so goes the other."

I whispered to Dred and Harriet, "He doesn't want to try two cases. He doesn't see the need since the facts are pretty much the same."

There was a brief, angry look in Harriet's eyes. She whispered back, "I lives in the free place for the most time."

Dred quietly watched the judge and, as they filed into the courtroom, the jury venire. Once again, he had found a way to fit his surroundings, appearing neither cowed nor afraid, with not the slightest hint of anything in his face or posture other than respectful attention.

Samuel stood. "Your Honor, I would like to point out that representatives of the Anti-Abolitionist Society are present today in the capacity, let's say, as a friend of the court. George, why don't you stand up?" One of the toughs, apparently the leader of the group, got to his feet with a smirk.

"They have come to the court today because the Society has a strong interest—"

"Mr. O'Fallon, I don't give a damn why they have come to this courtroom. We are here to try a case." Judge Hamilton looked at George, who was no longer smirking. "Sit down, sir." George sat down abruptly.

We spent the morning picking a jury of twelve white men. All maintained they could decide the issues impartially. Most were bearded and all wore dark coats and white shirts. In the manner of all juries, they looked curiously at the litigants and obediently at the judge. Several fidgeted or played with their fob chains and one lit a cigar.

"Gentlemen, there will be no smoking, spitting, cursing, or sleeping in this courtroom," said the judge. "Frederick, remove that man's cigar." The clerk went to the surprised juror, who handed over the offending cigar, which was thrown out the window.

The clerk swore in the jury and the judge said, "You will learn the facts from the witnesses and the law from me." Then he turned to the lawyers. "We will conclude this case today. Mr. Crane, present your first witness."

This was my third trial since admittance to the Missouri bar. I had won the first two without a word of praise from Mr. Field, who told me that he would attend my first three trials and then I would be on my own.

This trial appeared easier than the others. As I had explained to Dred and Harriet, we had to prove that Dred had been taken to live on free soil and, since John Emerson was dead and our lawsuit was against his widow, that Irene Emerson had then and now owned him. The peculiarity of the law, however, was that while Dred could sue for his freedom he could not testify on his own behalf since slaves were forbidden from giving testimony. Neither Dred nor Harriet expressed puzzlement over this state of affairs. Perhaps the whole business of appearing in a lawsuit against their owner to win their freedom in a courthouse on whose steps they could be bought and sold had already proved puzzling enough.

My first witness was Taylor Blow's older brother, Henry T. Blow, who had been an adult when Dred was sold. I questioned Henry, who sat calmly in the witness chair while Taylor watched from the spectator pews.

Henry testified how his father had sold Dred Scott to Dr. John Emerson.

Samuel stood to cross-examine, looking like a man spoiling for a fight. "I knew your father, Mr. Blow. He was a credit to our city. Now, how long ago did you say it was that your father sold this slave here to Dr. Emerson?"

"Your Honor," I objected, "I respectfully request that Mr. O'Fallon refer to the plaintiff by his name."

"Why, Mr. Crane," said Samuel, grinning at the jury, "I am always willing to accommodate a colleague, especially one as new to Missouri as yourself." Samuel chuckled and bowed to the jury, who laughed, joined in loudly by the Anti-Abolitionist Society, until Judge Hamilton silenced them with the crack of his gavel. "How long ago did your father sell Dred Scott here to Dr. Emerson, sir?"

"Oh, I guess, about fifteen years, maybe more."

"Sir, do you know for a fact that Dr. Emerson's wife was the owner of Dred Scott at Fort Armstrong or Fort Snelling?"

"No, I do not."

"No more questions."

Henry left the witness stand and, as he passed by Dred, reached out and patted him on the shoulder. Dred nodded but otherwise remained impassive. The slave-owning jurors watched keenly and exchanged whispers.

My next witness was a United States Army officer, Miles H. Clark. He sat stiffly in the witness chair. He answered my questions in crisp, soldierly fashion. He testified that he had been stationed at Fort Armstrong on Rock Island in Illinois, where he knew Dred Scott as Dr. Emerson's slave. On cross-examination, he admitted that he did not know if Irene Emerson had owned Dred.

My last witness was Samuel Russell, a farmer from north of St. Louis with whom I had corresponded. I had planned to offer his testimony by deposition, but he wrote of his plans to be in St. Louis on business the week of the trial. Russell was a weathered man with dirty hands who spoke in short, dry bursts.

"I lived in Fort Snelling."

"I knew Dr. and Mrs. Emerson."

"I knew the slaves Dred Scott and Harriet Scott."

"It was my money that paid their hire to work my farm."

This time, with a slight bow to the jury, Samuel came from behind the defense table and walked up to the witness.

"Did you actually hire the plaintiff, Mr. Russell?"

"I didn't hire 'em. My wife did."

I was incredulous. Mr. Field leaned forward, listening closely to the testimony and watching the judge. Irene Emerson was smiling.

"What do you personally know of the hiring?"

"What my wife said."

"Did you make payment to Mrs. Emerson?"

"Gave the money to my wife. I supposed it was for Mrs. Emerson but don't know for sure."

"Where is your wife?"

"Home."

"Nothing further."

I asked for an opportunity to re-question, for which the judge gave permission. Heart pounding, I reached into the green bag and pulled out two letters, one of which I put in front of the witness.

"Mr. Russell, do you recall receiving that letter from me?"

"Yes, I do."

"The letter asks you to furnish the date upon which you hired the plaintiff, from whom you hired him, whether Mrs. Emerson or anyone else, and to whom you paid your wages."

"That it says."

I then showed him the second letter.

"Is that your response?"

"Yes."

"What does it say?"

He read from the letter. "'Dear Sir: I hired Dred and his wife from Mrs. Emerson. I paid the hire of the servants to Mrs. Emerson.' That's what it says. But my wife hired 'em. Wasn't me."

Before I could ask another question, Samuel stood up.

"Your Honor, I have an application."

"That's no surprise." Judge Hamilton looked quite unhappy.

"With all due respect to Mr. Crane, his case has failed for lack of evidence. The plaintiff has no evidence that my client owned him at either fort. Mr. Russell's testimony about his wife is hearsay. All of the witnesses hired the plaintiff from Dr. Emerson, now deceased. I request a directed verdict in favor of the defendant, who has suffered much from the bringing of this lawsuit."

"Well, Mr. Crane, what do you have to say?"

My father had once told me that the hardest part of trying a case was acting as if nothing was wrong when matters could not be worse. I understood what he meant as I tried to keep the tone of my voice at a casual, conversational level.

"The testimony was as much a surprise to me as anyone. Based on his letter, I expected the witness to testify that he hired the plaintiff directly from Mrs. Emerson. I request an adjournment to allow the plaintiff to depose Mrs. Russell."

"We object to any adjournment," Samuel fairly shouted. "The slave has had his day in court. His case fails for lack of evidence." The jurors watched with amusement over the legal wrangling, Irene kept smiling, and Dred and Harriet looked confused and anxious.

"A directed verdict in favor of the defendant would be unjust and oppressive." I exerted all available willpower to speak calmly and precisely despite the sickening sensation that my case, and Dred and his family's freedom, teetered on the edge of a precipice. "The defendant's absurd argument is that Dred Scott must remain her slave because he cannot prove that he was her slave. My client is entitled to prove that he was unjustly held in slavery by the defendant."

Samuel tried to interrupt but Judge Hamilton cut him off.

"All right, Mr. Crane, I'll give you three days to call Mrs. Russell or produce her deposition. Otherwise, the case is dismissed."

"Your Honor, I object—"

"Sit down, Mr. O'Fallon, and be quiet." Now Judge Hamilton was shouting. "I'll hear nothing further from you. Members of the jury, I'll expect you back here on Friday at 9:30. Good day."

Outside the courthouse, Irene, Samuel, and the Anti-Abolitionist Society toughs joked and laughed. Our unhappy group gathered on the steps. Lizzie and Eliza huddled behind their mother. I said, still feeling relief that Judge Hamilton had given me a second chance, "I will get a deposition from Mrs. Russell."

"Irene, she know we her slaves at the fort," said Dred.

"Yes, she does. But she does not have to testify. Take heart, Judge Hamilton wants to help you. Most judges would not have given us the adjournment."

"She sure look pleased with herself," said Harriet. "That smile it never come off her face the whole time."

Samuel walked by. "I thought Harvard Law School fitted a man to practice law, Crane."

"Case isn't over, Samuel," I said with a forced smile.

On the way back to the office, Mr. Field, for the first time, offered encouraging words. "There is enough time for you to obtain Mrs. Russell's deposition. I will send a notice to Samuel."

I said "thank you" over my shoulder because I had already begun running to the stabler.

Three days later, I rode back into St. Louis. I was covered with mud and soaked to the skin. I had gone with Lyman Norris, one of Samuel's law partners, found Mrs. Russell's farmhouse after a day's ride, taken her deposition the next day, and then dashed back.

A plain but hospitable woman, with braided hair, rough hands, and skin darkened and wrinkled by the sun, Mrs. Russell had served us coffee in her kitchen. She seemed to enjoy reminiscing about her days at Fort Snelling as the young bride of Samuel Russell, who had worked in a saddlery on the army post. She missed Dred and Harriet, whom she recalled as hard workers. When she and her husband moved from Fort Snelling to Missouri and bought a farm, they struggled through their first year because they had no mule to pull the plow. Now, they had a mule and enough money to buy their first slave.

"Samuel wanted a girl. Oh, maybe eight or nine years of age. I could be a proper white lady with a slave to help in the house. Then we decided that if we could buy a boy for the same price, he could work outdoors when he got older. We changed our minds again and decided to buy a girl, which is why Samuel went to St. Louis." She added, "She'll have children."

Pouring more coffee, she said with some embarrassment, "You likely think we don't know our own minds."

"Hard decisions require time and effort," I said. She smiled.

Mrs. Russell was quite willing to give a deposition, although I was not certain she understood which side she was helping. The deposition did not take long to prepare. As she signed it, I thanked her for her time and soon I was on my horse with, not only her deposition, but a letter to give her husband, who was still in St. Louis, asking whether, if it was not too late, it might make better sense to buy a boy. Since Lyman Norris had business further north, I rode back to St. Louis alone.

As I neared the city, it began to rain steadily and soon the horse was stumbling through thick mud. I had to dismount and walk, which required effort because my boots sank deep into mud with each step. The light, dim from the overcast skies, grew even fainter as evening neared. It was almost impossible to see the road, which for long stretches consisted merely of blazes and notches on the trees made with an axe. Using one hand to feel along the trees for a notch and the other to tug at the horse, I lost my balance, slipped and sprawled headlong in the mud.

As I wiped off mud, I heard a sound in the brush. An animal was just yards away but I was unable to see it in the fading light and rain. It circled to my left and stopped. Keenly aware that I had no weapon, not even a knife, I crouched and slowly turned as the animal began moving even further to my left. It stopped moving again, and I remained motionless, facing the direction where I thought the animal was waiting. I heard snorting and then the soft thud of hoof on ground. I leaped into the saddle and spurred my horse, crashing through the thick brush into a small clearing, where I surprised a horse and rider.

"Who are you?" I shouted but the rider turned his horse and galloped away. I followed and the rider, who wore a slouching hat that obscured his face, turned in his saddle, pulled out a pistol and fired, the sound of which brought my horse up short as the bullet flew past my face. The rider cursed and barely ducked in time to avoid a branch, which knocked off his hat. Before he disappeared I briefly glimpsed his face in the gloom. It could have been anyone: a robber, a lonely rider surprised at my appearance just as I had been surprised at his, or one of the toughs from the Anti-Abolitionist Society.

The rain slackened, the skies cleared and the moon appeared. I did not pursue my mysterious assailant, but instead continued to St. Louis, finally finding the plank road. Applying the whip, I galloped down the plank road, reaching St. Louis at sunrise. I left the shivering horse with an angry stabler, went to my boardinghouse, changed, and met Mr. Field and our clients at the courthouse.

I was in high spirits despite the encounter in the gloomy wilds, smiling at the Scotts and Eliza and Lizzie. I triumphantly pulled the deposition from my green bag and handed it to Mr. Field, who read it, merely nodded, and gave it back. We went into the courtroom, where the jurors were already waiting. Irene and Samuel arrived and, seeing me, looked less cheerful than at the previous appearance. The young toughs also were more subdued, especially the one with fresh scratches on his face. I walked over to him, pulled a damp hat from my green bag, and tossed it in his lap. He started to rise, but Samuel barked at him to stay seated.

The clerk announced Judge Hamilton, who entered the courtroom and motioned for everyone to sit down. He looked expectantly at me.

"Your Honor, the plaintiff offers the deposition of Adeline Russell."

"You may proceed, Mr. Crane."

I read the deposition. "'I am the wife of Samuel Russell. I did not know Dr. Emerson at Fort Snelling, but I was acquainted with Mrs. Emerson. I know the plaintiffs in these suits. They were in my service for almost a year. They were under the control of Mrs. Emerson. I engaged them from Mrs. Emerson while she was in Fort Snelling. Mr. Russell paid for their services.'"

I turned to Samuel. "Perhaps Mr. O'Fallon wants to read the cross-examination by his colleague, Mr. Norris."

Less than enthusiastically, Samuel read the part of the deposition taken by Lyman Norris. "'The only way I know these negroes belonged to Mrs. Emerson is that she hired them out to me. I did not hear Mrs. Emerson say they were her slaves.'"

When Samuel finished, I said, "The plaintiff rests."

Judge Hamilton looked expectantly at Samuel, who turned and whispered to Irene, who nodded her head. He stood and said, "The defendant rests."

"Very well," said Judge Hamilton, who slammed his gavel so suddenly and sharply that he woke a dozing juror. "Mr. O'Fallon, I have refused your instructions and will give the instructions requested by the plaintiff. You have asked me to repeal the Missouri Compromise and to ignore the *Winny* case. The first is beyond the power of any court in this state and the second is a matter best addressed to my brethren in Jefferson City."

He turned to the jury. "Gentlemen, here is the law. You are obligated by your oaths to follow this law. If you believe from the evidence that the plaintiff was taken in slavery by the defendant to Fort Armstrong in Illinois or any free state or, at any time after the sixth day of March 1820, to Fort Snelling or any other place in the territory ceded by France to the United States under the name of Louisiana above thirty-six degrees thirty minutes not included within the State of Missouri, other than for the purpose of sojourning, then the plaintiff is entitled to his freedom."

I had requested these instructions and was gratified both that they were given and that the jurors appeared to listen carefully.

"You are now going to hear the lawyers' closing arguments," the judge said to the jury. "Mr. O'Fallon."

Samuel stood, walked up to the jury box, and put his hands on the rail. He was no more than a handshake from the nearest juror. All twelve men leaned forward to hear his words. He spoke without notes but more like an orator than a conversationalist. Harriet watched Samuel as though he had a whip.

"Gentlemen of the jury, the history of the Missouri Compromise is well known to all of us and of which we may say, *magna pars quorum fuimus.* With an earnest desire to calm the storm, Missouri, under protest, accepted the Compromise."

Gesturing at the Scotts, Samuel said, "But suppose Congress should now pass a law declaring that the keeping of black horses, a species of property existing in Missouri and protected by the law, is hereby prohibited in the territory of Utah. The same government that passes the law through the executive department orders you, an officer who unfortunately owns a black horse that you can neither sell, lose, nor give away, to the territory of Utah, and you take with you this horse. I admit that the horse, if there were horse abolitionists there, would get his freedom in Utah. But when the horse comes back here and asks you to give him up, would you do it?"

Samuel paused for emphasis and several jurors leaned forward. "The law should not encourage in a slave-holding state the multiplication of a race whose condition could be neither freemen nor slaves. Their existence and increase will only dissatisfy and corrupt those of their own race and color remaining in a state of servitude."

Samuel sat down and I rose.

"The law in this state could not be more clear. Judge Hamilton instructed you that if Dred Scott was taken as a slave to the fort at Rock Island and to Fort Snelling and there remained, he is entitled to his freedom. The evidence that this happened is equally clear."

I gestured toward Dred. "The fact that they were military posts does not affect my client's rights. No one ordered Dr. Emerson to remove Dred Scott to those posts or to leave him there to be hired out when he was transferred. Dred Scott, no less than you or I, is entitled to his rights under the law, whatever they may be, regardless of who he may be."

The jurors filed out of the courtroom to deliberate. All of us— Mr. Field, the Scotts, their children, who seemed uncharacteristically subdued, and I—huddled in the Rotunda to await the verdict.

"Whatever the verdict," said Mr. Field, looking both at the Scotts and myself, "I want no displays of emotion. Especially a plaintiff's verdict."

We then waited in that timeless state of suspense endured by lawyers and their clients while a jury deliberates. The Scotts stood with their children against one wall of the Rotunda without talking. Harriet looked at me with a mixture of hope, anger, and despair, while Dred, catching my eye, offered a sober smile, which I returned. Nothing resembling what I understood to be affection had passed between Dred and Harriet in my presence but I sensed that without Dred's quiet presence Harriet would not have dared show emotion.

"Mr. Crane," he said, "whatever happen today, I be glad that you my lawyer."

"Dred, this is going to be the best day of your life."

Eliza anxiously watched her mother, while Lizzie peered around the Rotunda at the colorful murals, and then settled her eyes on me, as though expecting a game or piece of candy. I idly considered what to do if we lost, and decided that I would ask Judge Hamilton for a stay of judgment and file an immediate appeal, but my thoughts wandered to Kate Fox.

After two minutes or two hours, I cannot to this day say which, the court clerk called us back into the courtroom. Both sides assembled at their tables and the jury filed in and stood by their seats. The jurors did not look at either table. Judge Hamilton appeared.

"Members of the jury," asked Judge Hamilton after everyone had sat down, "have you reached a verdict?"

The foreman, a slave owner, stood. "We have, Your Honor."

"Very well. What is your verdict?"

He unenthusiastically glanced at the other jurors.

"We find for the plaintiff, Dred Scott."

For a moment, the courtroom was still. The foreman remained standing as if waiting for further instructions, the parties and their lawyers did not move, and Judge Hamilton stayed on the bench, still looking at the jurors. Then the courtroom came back to life as Samuel, who avoided looking at me, whispered to Irene. Dred and Harriet turned slightly in their chairs to look at me. They appeared not to understand what had happened.

"You won the trial," I whispered, mindful of Mr. Field's caution. I thought briefly of my father and imagined his stern disapproval, and then turned to look at Eliza and Lizzie, whose expressions brightened when they saw my smile.

Judge Hamilton said, "The jury is dismissed. The State of Missouri thanks you for your service." The jurors filed out, several glancing at Dred and Harriet, expecting perhaps to find triumphant faces and apparently surprised that the Scotts looked anything but triumphant.

Mr. Field had worried unnecessarily that Dred and Harriet would display satisfaction or in some way draw attention to a slave victory over a white woman. I was sure that their happiness was even greater than my own but I could not tell that from their faces, which showed only disbelief, as they looked at each other, at the departing jury, at Mr. Field, and then at me. Soon though, after the jury had left, their disbelief gave way to an expression that made me glad that on the prairie I had turned my horse back to St. Louis.

Dred whispered, "Mr. Crane, do you remember when you said that I have this claim? I thought it just words then. But look what you done." He started to reach out his hand but then, glancing around the courtroom, pulled it back, even as I had begun to extend my hand to his. My hand remained suspended in mid-air, a few inches from his and then I withdrew it. Dred only said, "Now I got to do the same for you."

After a few more words with an unhappy Irene Emerson, Samuel O'Fallon rose and walked to the judge's bench. As he passed me, without even glancing down, he said in a low voice, "Well done, Arba, before a Yankee judge. See how you do in Jefferson City."

I said to Dred, "Irene has the right to appeal, to ask another court to review the jury's verdict. That will happen in Jefferson City. Don't worry, she will be no more successful on the appeal than she was here."

Dred had even less reason to doubt me now and so he simply nodded. The Anti-Abolitionist Society noisily stormed out of the courtroom.

Addressing the judge, Samuel said, "Your Honor, no man pays tribute to our juries more often than I. But even the wisest and most judicious jury has little choice but to follow an erroneous statement of the law." Judge Hamilton looked impatient at yet another speech but Samuel persisted. "When Missouri accepted the Compromise it did not waive her just views of the constitutional powers of Congress or recognize the right of any created being to control or weaken in any manner her state rights. I call for a new trial."

"Denied."

"Your Honor, my client intends to appeal this highly unjust verdict to the Missouri Supreme Court. I request 30 days to file a bill of exceptions."

"Granted. Gentlemen, this court is adjourned."

Chapter 12

I ce floes filled the Mississippi. Steamboats that ventured onto the river returned to the levee to wait for warmer temperatures. I resumed my real estate and other mundane litigations. Samuel obtained a stay of judgment and then filed a notice of appeal, but too late for that term of the Missouri Supreme Court, which meant that the appeal would not be argued for months. Since the judgment had been stayed, Dred and Harriet continued their lives in much the fashion as before the trial, except that Irene promptly hired Harriet out.

Kate and her father waited for the ice to melt. First the bar examination and then the trial had kept me from seeing Kate until what was to have been a farewell dinner at the Blow home, but which instead became an interlude in their wait for a more hospitable river.

"You won," I said.

"So did you." She was cordial but distant. "Taylor was quite complimentary. Father, of course, disapproves. Samuel is, well . . ." Her voice trailed off.

"I am sure he is." I was still basking in the glow of my victory.

The dinner was tedious. Taylor had invited two rising stars of Missouri politics to the dinner, the proslavery Senator-elect Henry Geyer and the antislavery Heinrich Boernstein, a German immigrant and the publisher of the *Anzeiger des Westens,* the most influential German-American publication west of the Mississippi. After desultory conversation about the revolutions in Europe, the two Henrys briefly argued over slavery in such a bitter manner as to dash Taylor's hopes of finding a common ground between two foes. The rest of the evening was spent in strained conversation about the cold weather, living arrangements in Washington City, and Senator-elect Geyer's plans for giving up most of his law practice.

"I still hope to take an occasional case in the Supreme Court." Missouri's new Senator seemed shrunken and ill at ease. The man had little warmth and it was impossible to tell just what his supporters saw in him other than support for slavery.

Kate appeared thoroughly bored throughout the evening and left the table when Taylor signaled to a servant to bring dessert.

Falsely pleading the need to prepare for an upcoming trial, I excused myself to avoid the inevitable after-dinner brandies and cigars. I found Kate with Charlotte Blow, Taylor's sister, who had missed the dinner because of a broken carriage wheel.

"I will see you to the door," said Kate. Charlotte looked at me with a gleam in her eyes.

At the door, thinking of ice melting on the river, I whispered to Kate, "I must see you."

"In front of the theater tomorrow evening at seven."

I left the office at six for a walk before going to the theater. From the street I could see the floating chunks of ice that clogged the river from bank to bank. The levee was crowded with steamboats. Men sat in skiffs with small barrels of gunpowder ready for use against any larger floes that chose to drift in the direction of the steamboats.

I reached the theater at seven but Kate was nowhere to be seen. The bill announced a performance of *Richard III*. I paced back and forth as laughing and chatting couples walked in the front entrance while prostitutes, eyes straight ahead, went in through the side door, where stairs led to the balcony. I was restless and impatient when her carriage arrived.

"Hello, Ben," I said.

"Evening, Mr. Crane."

Kate leaned out the window. "I am ravenous for Shakespeare."

I had little interest in spending what might be my last hours with Kate in a dark theater. I opened the door, gave her my hand, and she stepped to the ground, wearing a long cloak of rich brown satin over a moss-green dress. As she took my arm, my impatience subsided and I could not imagine that anything else in life might be as satisfying as having her at my side.

During the play, Kate made pungent and sometimes devastating comments on the actors. "Oh, brilliant," she whispered in my ear, to be followed a few minutes later by "too loud and bombastic." Each time she leaned over to whisper, her hair brushed my cheek like a soft breeze carrying the fragrance of rose water. The play ended to enthusiastic applause from the audience and many curtain calls. An exhilarated crowd swept into the street, carrying us along.

We walked arm in arm. She held my arm in an intimate but polite way, as if to declare confidence and affection but not love, companionship but not more.

Neither of us mentioned her imminent departure, and instead we argued over whether the real Richard III had been a hunchback.

"Richard was not a hunchback and he did not murder his nephews," I said. "Shakespeare murdered history."

"Do you doubt that he was ambitious?"

"No more than I doubt you are." The air was warmer than the night before. "Or that your conscience also afflicts you."

"'O coward conscience, how dost thou afflict me!'" Kate was warily amused. "What does a Yankee lawyer know of my conscience?"

We stopped a short distance from the carriage. Ben sat high above us, dressed formally like the servants of other rich Southerners. He was tall, and when he smiled his teeth flashed whiter than his ruffled shirt. I knew only that Kate and her father had brought him along when they left Louisiana.

The streets had emptied of the theatergoers. She let go of my arm, which allowed me to face her.

"You cannot leave St. Louis with your father," I said simply, not caring if Ben heard or whom he might tell.

"I most certainly can and I will."

"You think that ambition will bring you happiness. It will not."

"And no doubt you think you can, Mr. Crane."

"I do."

Staring at each other, we listened to drunken, happy shouts from a party of men and women in a carriage. They cheered us and each other and their driver and his horses. Their laughter faded.

"Make your own way, Kate."

Her face was in shadows.

"You have every right. I know what your father did."

"You know nothing of my family."

"You read the letter about Mrs. Middlespoon. You wanted me to know that Jewel—"

"Stop."

"—was not just a little slave girl who grew up with you."

"Please, Arba."

"That she was—"

She put her fingers against my lips. Then she was in my arms. I felt the tears on her cheeks. Were they for herself or her mother or her half sister, the slave girl Jewel?

After a while, she said, "How wretched a world this is." I offered her a handkerchief, which she took with a halfhearted smile. She dabbed at her eyes and then looked around.

"We must go somewhere." She was composed and spoke practically. "Charlotte and I have become very close. She said there is a side entrance that no one ever uses. You can come and go without being noticed. Ben is discreet."

Without further words, we got in the carriage. Ben snapped his whip and the carriage rolled off. We sat tightly clasping hands, listening to Ben singing softly to the night, just as he had done when she was a child. He sang of blackbirds and magpies, willow trees and whippoorwills, and the smell of newly cut hay borne on a soft breeze on a warm sunny morning.

In her bedroom, to which we had crept like excited children, I had no patience for her elegant dress with its infuriating buttons and clasps and belts and neither did she so we half removed it, half tore it off, until she stood before me in glowing nakedness, everything that my impassioned dreams had foretold. When I embraced her, no matter where I touched her, her breasts, which felt like soft, gentle doves, or the glorious curves of her waist or the bounty of her hips, it felt as though one or the other or both of us might burst into flame. Her impatient desire also knew no limits as she helped me, with less difficulty, remove my clothes and we embraced and kissed and caressed and ultimately joined together with such cries of ecstasy on both our parts that we should have woken the dead, let alone the others sleeping in the house, but for the thick walls with which the Blow family had constructed their great mansion. As impassioned as I was, Kate was even more so, frantically urging me on, at times pleading and beseeching, but once she grabbed my hair and pulled back my head so that her eyes might meet mine. She asked me quietly in the midst of our desperate passion to please lead her not just to love but to salvation and forgetfulness even though I scarcely knew where I might find them for myself.

Much later that night, just before the dawn, after our passions had finally cooled, Kate talked of the long rows of cabins facing each other across a broad sweep of thick Bermuda grass, great trees draped in moss, little doorways that led to a crooked white path, beaten smooth by the march of many feet in the early dawn, under a hot noonday sun, and through the welcome dusk. In the mornings, the little girl watched

the seamstresses with huge shears working on the great bolts of white
woolen jeans, linseys, and red flannels and, in the afternoons, on mist-
and fog-shrouded days, sat on the back porch listening to the singing
of an invisible gang of negroes cutting timber.

A cold frosty morning
The niggers mighty good
Take your axe upon your shoulder
Nigger, TALK to the wood.

They sang to mark the blows. On the word "Talk," they all chopped
together. When the tree was about to fall, someone shouted "Hi" to
warn everyone out of the way.

Her earliest recollection was pity for the negroes and her mother's
sobbing. Kate accompanied her father on his visits to the cabins. She
remembered his gleaming knee-length leather boots and easy talk and
laughter with them.

Her father was a sheltering tower. Their lives revolved around his
comings and goings. Kate ran after his horse when he left for New
Orleans and into his arms on his return. He gave her a spirited pony
and beautiful dresses and, as she grew into a woman, took her on his
visits to the neighbors and showed her off at the lavish parties. He was
handsome and strong and powerful, like the knights in her children's
books who wore armor that even sharp swords could not dent.

As she grew older, she noticed one, then two, and then more
brownish-yellow faces among the scampering negro children by the
cabins. When her mother argued with her father, begging him to sell
the female slaves, "I'll work with my hands, as hard as I can, but my
mind will rest," Kate went quietly to her bedroom and read a book
until she fell asleep, still wearing her dress.

Kate played with one of the yellow-faced children, named Jewel,
a beautiful little girl with greenish-brown eyes and russet hair. They
embraced each other and laughed joyously, until the day Kate's
mother slapped Jewel's pregnant mother on the face and then made
the overseer apply the lash until the blood ran down her back. Jewel

watched with big, fearful eyes as her mother pleaded, "It's not my doing, please, please." Kate, who had trailed after her mother and stopped at a distance from the cabins but close enough to hear the cries, put her hands over her ears but did not look away.

Afterwards, her mother lay on the bed with a cold compress on her forehead. With Kate standing next to her, she said, "I wish to die or to be a man. I would give them up but for one good negro to wait on me."

The next time Kate and Jewel played together, they quarreled over Jewel's rag doll. In the past, their fights ended in laughter but this time Kate did not smile. They were in the barn and Kate slapped Jewel, grabbed a piece of split hickory and began hitting the doll with it until the cloth shredded. Jewel solemnly knelt before what had been her doll and looked up at Kate, who expected to see tears or anger or fear but saw only a beautiful brownish-yellow mask.

"You are a slave. Don't you know that? You're my slave. I can do what I want," Kate yelled at her and fled the barn.

A faint flicker of light crept into the room. "My father heeded my mother's wishes and sold her and her mother to a speculator," murmured Kate, "I tried to find out what happened to her. I dream of her often."

It was that time when everything outside of Kate's bedroom was not just quiet but in a state of suspension. It was a time when we should have existed only for each other. But all night I had felt the presence of others. Even in our moments of bliss, the invisible bonds that stretched over generations and spoke of warm hearths and long verandas and baskets of peaches sent with affectionate notes pulled Kate back from wherever she thought I was taking her.

She stretched lazily. "What is Vermont like?" The room grew brighter. She lay on her side, facing me. Her red hair glowed incandescently against the white cotton sheets, which had draped themselves over her hips but left her breasts uncovered.

"Bleak in the winter and green in the summer and upright and hardworking all year. I left because I was bored. You would not like it."

"Ben said he would like to see Vermont. He heard that every negro in Vermont owns a farm."

I laughed. "The few negroes we have do not own farms. Are you taking Ben to Washington City?"

She seemed surprised at my question. "Ben goes where we go." She spoke so casually that she could have been referring to a valise. I could not help but look away. She noticed and, pulling the sheets up to her neck, said, "Why don't you talk about Abigail White."

"She's a mystery. I don't know much about her."

"Was she beautiful? Madame Blavatsky thought she was."

"Unlike Madame Blavatsky, I didn't see her very clearly."

"I imagine she did something most awful. Have you asked your father?"

Something about the way she asked the question made me uncomfortable. "I don't think he knows. No one has been whipped in Newfane for many years. Or Vermont."

"You must think we are cruel, then. Ben asked me if he'll be free like Dred Scott once he lives in Washington City, but I told him that it was a slave city in a slave state."

I murmured agreement.

"If we don't free him, will you hate me?"

"Of course not."

"How can you hate slavery and not the slave owner?"

"How can I ever hate you?"

Kate turned away, crying softly. I cannot remember whether we fell asleep or just lay in the near dark waiting for the sun to fully bathe us in light or how I left the Blow mansion and returned to the boardinghouse or even what I said to Kate before I left. I can only remember her words as she turned from me.

"Oh, my sweet, how can you not?"

Two days after our night of dark passion, without a spoken or written word to me, Kate boarded a steamboat with her father. Warmer air had finally freed the river and her father, long overdue in Washington and perhaps concerned over his daughter's possible infatuation with a Yankee, took the earliest opportunity to leave St.

Louis. I did not see Kate again until years later when, through an unforeseen and improbable course of legal events, I found myself in Washington City.

Her memory haunted my days and nights. Lovesick, I mourned her loss, but intimacy brings knowledge which, in its turn, like the taste of the forbidden apple, lifts the veil of ignorance. Gradually, as though my mind were clearing, I came to the painful understanding that Kate had not considered remaining in St. Louis. The ice on the river had melted and she had left.

We had not stolen that night from a splintered world but only borrowed it. It took me a long time to understand this, but Kate had known it since the dawn. The act of honestly sharing her unhappy secrets revealed to her then, but not for some while to the infatuated young man who had spent the night in her bed, that the poets were wrong about the power of love, that other, overwhelming forces swirled around us, and that, no more than any man, I could not vanquish the darkness that lay on her soul like a shroud.

Chapter 13

I was on my way to the boardinghouse when I saw the burning steamboat. It had broken free of its moorings and was now drifting south in the current as the hurricane deck burned. I was awestruck by the beauty of the fiery river chariot, whose flames leaped higher and lit up the dark river. Shouting men ran down to the levee but there was nothing they could do. Slowly, ever so gracefully, the *White Cloud* gently drifted into its sister steamboats and soon one, then four, then twelve and finally some two dozen steamboats were aflame. A northwest wind fanned the flames, which jumped from the burning vessels to the warehouses on the levee.

With a shock, I realized that Mr. Field's law office was in the path of the fire. I ran to Chestnut Street, where the smoke made breathing difficult. I dashed up the stairs to find Dred Scott in the inner office hastily gathering files. His face was shiny with sweat from his exertions and the heat of the fire.

"I know you need your papers but I don't know which they is." He looked around the office in frustration. "I need these papers, Mr. Crane."

From outside came the shouts of running men, the clanging bell of a fire wagon, and a roaring sound as the fire swept closer.

"Your family?" I gasped from lack of breath and the smoke.

"They all right. The wind, it keep the fire away from us."

We worked frantically to gather files from the desks and cabinets, including the *Scott* case files, bind them with rope, and carry them downstairs where I vainly tried to get terrified men in carriages or pushing carts filled with personal possessions to take Mr. Field's files. The fire was now just a block away, a towering wall of orange and red violence whose heat almost knocked me down. I left the files on the sidewalk and went back up the stairs.

I was carrying more files down the stairway when Mr. Field pulled up in a single-horse carriage and ran into the building.

"Arba, do you have all the files?"

"Most of them. Dred has the rest." Dred came down the stairs with the last of the files and the Webster and Washington paintings.

"Dred was here before me," I said, but Mr. Field appeared not to hear.

I heaved files into the carriage, which shook as the terrified horse jerked madly against the rope that tied it to a post.

"This is all we can do," I shouted to Mr. Field, whose face was bathed in harsh orange light. The fire's roar made normal speech impossible. Dred tried to control the horse while Mr. Field got in the carriage.

I recalled scattered papers left on a desk and began frantically searching through the heaps of documents in the back of the carriage. "Not all of the *Scott* files are here," I shouted to both Mr. Field and Dred. "I forgot Mrs. Russell's deposition. I think I left it on my desk."

"Mr. Crane," said Dred, struggling with the terrified horse, "there ain't time."

"We may need the deposition for the appeal." I started towards the doorway.

"No, Arba!" shouted Mr. Field.

Dred let go of the horse and grabbed my arm, leaving Mr. Field to pull on the reins with all his strength to keep the bucking horse under control.

"I'll get it, Mr. Crane."

"Let go of my arm, Dred." I had practically dragged him into the doorway.

"Mr. Crane, my family, they need you more than me."

"I am the one who has to go in there."

"Mr. Crane—"

"Damn it, Dred, I have to go." He looked startled and let go of my arm. "You can't read."

I ran into the building, which was now on fire, and put an arm across my face to ward off the heat as I went up the stairs. Smoke poured out of Mr. Field's inner office, where his chair and the shelves of law books were ablaze. I rummaged through the discarded papers on my desk, found the Russell deposition and, gagging from smoke, sparks flying onto my clothes, dashed out of the office, racing the flames now spreading along the ceiling. The stairway wall was on fire so I leaped three stairs at a time. Halfway down, clutching the deposition in one hand, I lost my balance and put the other hand against the stairway wall to keep from falling but my sleeve caught fire. I beat at my arm and managed to put out the flames, less concerned about my singed skin than about the clouds of black smoke that kept me from drawing a breath. I reached the bottom of the stairs disoriented, unable to breathe or see in the thick smoke, and without any sense of direction.

Dred Scott, holding a rag to his face, burst through the smoke, grabbed my burned arm, which caused such pain that I screamed, and pulled me into the street. He helped me into the wagon, where I lay in the back, coughing uncontrollably and clutching the deposition. Dred untied the horse and climbed onto the seat next to Mr. Field who snapped his whip but the horse needed no urging and we raced up Chestnut Street alongside the looming fire and then turned away at the next intersection. The air was more breathable and cooler but it took some time before I stopped coughing. My arm hurt, but the *Scott* documents were safe.

Dred looked at me. At first, I thought he was concerned for my arm.

"I am all right, Dred. It's not that bad a burn."

"It ain't that, Mr. Crane. It's your face—" and he started laughing.

I touched a finger to my forehead and looked at it in the fire's glare. It was black. I rubbed my palm against my cheek and saw that it was smeared with black soot. My face must have been almost as dark as Dred's. I looked at Dred's dark face and burst out laughing so hard that tears came to my eyes, which caused Dred to laugh even harder, and soon we were gasping for breath even though the air was free of smoke. Mr. Field looked at the two of us as though we were madmen.

The carriage came to a stop, and from a safe distance we watched the spectacle below. Dred and I stopped laughing.

Mr. Field and I said in unison, "My God."

Dred murmured, "Lord."

The center of the city was a mass of writhing flames. The warehouses, the banks, the newspapers, and the lawyers' offices, much of the commercial center of St, Louis, were an inferno. Firemen vainly tried to contain the blaze. At midnight, buildings as yet untouched by the flames suddenly exploded one after another. The explosions tossed up debris and rubble so brightly illuminated by the fire that I could see chairs and desks and polished spittoons fly through the air.

"Gunpowder," said Mr. Field. "They're trying to save the Cathedral."

I found the spectacle both terrifying and sublime. Slowly, the dust settled and where once was a city block lay only a pile of bricks, as though a whimsical giant had slapped his hand. The explosions went on and on until a swathe of flattened buildings encircled the fire which, raging at its imprisonment, grew ever higher as it feasted on what had been the heart of the city. "We can do no more tonight," said Mr. Field, snapping the reins. As we drove off, he did not thank Dred and only said to me, "Your arm must be tended to."

The next morning, my arm bandaged, occasionally holding a handkerchief to my face where the smoke was still thick, I walked through the smoldering, charred ruins. Only a single blackened wall was left from the building that had housed Mr. Field's law office. The law books that we had left behind, and the furniture, supplies, and personal items, were gone. Similarly ruined and scorched buildings could be seen for half a mile in the direction of the St. Louis Cathedral. The firemen and their gunpowder had saved the Cathedral, the courthouse, and the Planters' House, and the wind had saved the Field home and the negro quarter.

I was shocked and appalled at the loss of the law office and the destruction of so much of the city. But even so, I felt better than in some time. For all its destruction, the fire seemed to offer the promise of a fresh beginning. Since yesterday evening, I had not thought once of Kate Fox.

Before the day ended, wagons had begun hauling away rubble. Building owners, businessmen, insurance agents, and builders could be seen throughout the ruins, pointing, talking animatedly, making notes, and sketching diagrams of new buildings that would be taller and grander than the old. Whatever their immediate grief at their loss, these were surprisingly cheerful men, excited at the challenge of rebuilding and the prospects for creating an even better city. Old St. Louis, the narrow streets and historic buildings, had been swept away in a great blazing pyre and new St. Louis would arise phoenix-like from the ashes.

Everywhere, strangers were helping strangers dig out belongings. Emissaries from churches and charities streamed through the ruins with baskets of food and clothes for the homeless. Women stood in the ruins of the homes where their children had been born and raised, wiped away tears, and then began sifting through the rubble for whatever possessions might be salvaged. Slaves brought in to help clear the streets chatted amiably with the exhausted firemen, whose skin, as soot-blackened as mine had been, made the two groups nearly indistinguishable in appearance. I spent some time standing on the ruins of Mr. Field's law office, watching this bustling scene, and experiencing an overwhelming surge of pride as it dawned on me that they all were Americans and so was I.

I wandered the city that day. The farther I walked from the business district the more normal life became, until I found myself in the freed-slave quarter, which I had never visited and which upset all expectation. Here, unlike white St. Louis, were more women than men. I was jarred to see negro men wearing broadcloth suits, ironed shirts, white Marseilles vests, and polished boots, or women wearing fine French muslin dresses and holding umbrellas for sunshades. They mingled with poorly dressed negro men in overalls and women wearing roughly sewn cotton dresses and turbans. Negroes, poor and well-to-do, gathered in small groups to chat. I overheard talk of the fire, a public whipping, and an upcoming wedding. A few whites, dressed in the manner of overseers, gathered around them negroes seeking work. I attracted little obvious attention as I walked by but behind me I could feel careful stares.

Some of the houses could have fit inconspicuously into the richer white neighborhoods, but there were also run-down shanties and long, plain red brick buildings with thick walls and narrow balconies. Clotheslines were strung everywhere, sagging under the weight of expensive-looking, freshly-washed shirts, pantaloons, and undergarments, drying in the dying daylight so that they might be returned the next morning to their owners, most of whom likely had never seen this neighborhood. From the windows came cooking smells and occasional cries of babies. Leaving the street, not entirely certain what I was looking for, I walked down an alley and found myself lost in a maze of red walls and small courtyards, some with vegetable gardens. It was late afternoon and the sunlight had begun to fade.

In the gloom of the shadows cast by the austere buildings, I was looked at with less disguised suspicion by passing adults. I grew uneasy, but the presence of children was reassuring. Most seemed to be on their way from one chore to another. One carried a box with bootblacking utensils, another passed by with a broom, and a familiar-looking young girl walked briskly along while expertly balancing with one hand a large wrapped package on her head.

"Eliza," I called out.

She turned and looked at me uncertainly. She wore a plain frock and red turban. When she realized who I was, she looked surprised.

"Do you live around here?" She nodded and gestured to a ground level window in a building at the end of the alley. She gracefully knelt to the ground, still balancing the package, and with her free hand traced her name in the sandy dirt.

"Well done."

With a proud look, Eliza rose, the package as firmly on her head as though it were a well-fitting hat, and went on her way.

Dred, who had been making dinner, was more than a little surprised at my appearance in his tiny room. The furniture was a few narrow boards for beds, a stove with a pipe that went through a hole in the wall, a rough table with scattered bowls and spoons and a cutting knife jammed point first into a table plank, and hooks on the wall for clothes. I had worn casual clothes and old boots because of the fire, but even so I could not have been a greater contrast with my client and his surroundings.

He invited me to share his dinner, looking doubtfully at the bandages on my arm. "Mr. Crane, no white man ever help me the way you doing. But you can't keep running into buildings that are on fire. Don't know where I'd be if something happen to you."

"I guess that's all you care about." I affected to be hurt.

"I care about a lot more."

We sat on the bed boards and ate bacon and cornmeal.

"I saw Eliza. She had a big package on her head."

"That's white folks' clothes. There's a big barrel where they keeps the water hot and Eliza she go there to do the washing, and then she dry the clothes and when they ready she bring them. She'll be back soon. But Harriet, she and Lizzie, they taking care of this white woman who be sick to die. Harriet and Lizzie, they sleep on the floor of her bedroom and feed her and keep her clean. Thought she'd be dead by now, but she hanging on, so Harriet and Lizzie, they got to stay there."

"Do these white people pay much for all this work?"

He shook his head. "But we get by. Since the trial we keeping it all now instead of giving most of it to Mrs. Emerson. I guess that mean we free, excepting that Mrs. Emerson, she going to another court and try to make us slaves again."

"Well, she'll try, but—"

Eliza came in, looking drawn and tired but better fed than on her visits to my office. "Hello, Mr. Crane." She curtsied gracefully, the way she had done on the first visit. "Papa, seem like everyone in the quarter know my name." She went to the table, picked up a spoon and plate, helped herself to the contents of the pan on the stove, and sat down on one of the bed boards to eat.

"The folks here they all know about my case," said Dred, not at all shy about acknowledging his celebrity. "They ask me what they can do to be free and I tell them that they got to have lived in a free state and they got to have a good lawyer. So then they ask me how come I still living here and I explain that we still in the courts."

"They know about it because you always telling them," said Eliza.

"You sound like your mother. They find out about it anyway."

Eliza had been sneaking glances at me. "Mr. Crane, why you come all the way to St. Louis?"

"Well, I wanted to be a lawyer and live in the West." She glanced at her father. "Where would you like to live?"

"The free state."

"What would you like to do there?"

"Do?"

"Women do all kinds of things in the free states. Marry and have children, teach school, write. What would you like to do?"

She put down her plate, and pulled her knees up, encircling them with her arms. The red turban, her smooth walnut skin, and dark eyes created an exotic appearance. She furrowed her brow, then looked at her father, who gave her unseen encouragement. "Once I go to this white woman's house to bring the laundry. I come in the door and this woman, she making music. Another woman, she standing there singing. I just listen and listen and forget why I come there. Then they see me so I give them the laundry and go. But I never forget the way that woman sing, like nothing could stop her and they could hear her in Heaven. That's what I want to do. I want to sing." She picked up her plate and resumed eating.

"Eliza, she know how to sing real well," said Dred with evident pride. "Girl, sing something for Mr. Crane."

"Yes," I said, "I'd like that."

Eliza put her plate aside again, stood and sang, in a low, soothing voice, a song that told a melancholy tale of a life with no past, no future, only a voyage over which the voyager had no control as he was swept helplessly from one place to another. The song ended,

This time tomorrow night,
Where will I be?
I'll be gone, gone, gone,
Gone to Tennessee.

Eliza looked first at her father, who beamed with pride, and then at me. I clapped softly and she looked happy.

The door opened and Harriet and Lizzie came in and stopped abruptly when they saw me.

"Don't just stare at Mr. Crane," said Dred.

"Good evening, Mr. Crane," said Harriet, recovering from her surprise.

"Hey, Mr. Crane," said Lizzie. "You got any sweets?"

I shook my head in mock sadness, and she made certain I knew that she was genuinely disappointed.

Harriet looked wearily at Dred. "That woman. She die. She sure not quiet about her going."

Mother and daughter helped themselves to food. We all sat together eating dinner, Dred, Harriet and myself on one set of bed boards and the children on the other.

"Mr. Crane," Harriet asked, "when this case going to be over so we can stop being slaves?"

"We have to go to one more court. But you really aren't slaves."

"Don't feel like we free either. This woman, she got a sister who think we her slaves and got to do all the chores for the house. I tell her that the court say I a free woman and the only thing we have to do is care for her sister. She just laugh at me and tell me to do my work or she make certain I get a whipping. 'Girl, unless you got emancipation papers, you a slave and you do what I say.' I say we done with the court, we getting out of this state."

"Mr. Crane," said Dred, glancing at his wife, "Harriet, she keep asking me if we be free why we can't leave the state before we done with the court."

Eliza and Lizzie had finished their dinner and fallen asleep in their clothes. Harriet removed her sleeping daughters' shoes and put them under their heads.

"You have to wait until the Missouri Supreme Court rules. It's just the way the law works."

"The law," said Harriet as though the word would always sound strange to her. She was having trouble keeping her eyes open.

"It's getting late," I said.

Dred walked part of the way home with me. He was stopped frequently by negroes who asked him in a half-serious, half-joking way if he had won his case yet. He shook his head and then proudly introduced me as his lawyer, which caused much uncovering of heads by the men wearing hats and curtsies by the women. As we left the negro quarter, he avoided eye contact with whites, fell a step or two behind me, and, as on the evening of Murry McConnell's visit to Mr. Field's office, somehow became less visible.

For the next several days, I worked out of the Law Library and my room at the boardinghouse. The offices of many St. Louis lawyers had been on or near Chestnut Street. We consoled one another and exchanged information about available leases in other parts of the city. Mr. Field and I managed to meet all our filing deadlines without seeking any adjournments, even though the judges made plain their willingness to grant them. Within a few weeks we had leased a new office and set about finding furniture and law books. Our new accommodation was large enough for me to have the luxury of a private office. We also had several new clients, fire insurance companies who had insufficient capital and assets to cover the tidal wave of claims and needed advice on bankruptcy law. As our professional lives returned to normal, I began preparation of the Scotts' brief on appeal. Samuel O'Fallon, after several adjournments, had finally filed a brief to the three judge Missouri Supreme Court.

Carrying a nearly finished cigar, Mr. Field came into my new office, sat down, and stretched his legs. He puffed at the cigar. He looked tired. The fire had been a strain on both of us and our case load was unusually heavy. Besides the Scotts' appeal, Mr. Field had six other cases before the Missouri Supreme Court. He asked me to argue three of them in addition to the Scotts' appeal, and then said, "I read the Emerson brief."

"Fire and brimstone," I said. "Nothing resembling a legal argument. Not even a reference to *Winny* or *Rachael v. Walker*."

Mr. Field seemed distracted for a moment by other thoughts that briefly brought a look of such desolation that I considered excusing myself from my own office. Mr. Field shook his head as if to clear it and, with impressive self-discipline, talked a bit about other cases. But the desolate look returned and he took his watch out of a vest pocket. "I will leave a little early."

"Goodnight, Mr. Field."

He spoke distractedly as though reminding himself of something that he preferred not to remember. "I must buy some salt and mustard before closing hour at Comstock's. Little William Bradley is not feeling well."

It felt as though the blood had rushed out of my face. "But the fire—?"

"It may not have been as purifying as we had hoped. But I'm sure my son just has an upset stomach. Nothing to worry about. You can lock up."

Chapter 14

The doorway of the Field home was draped in black cloth. Several carriages and a hearse waited outside. Mr. Field stood in the parlor receiving visitors. Only the black rings under his eyes testified to the torment that he had experienced since William Bradley had taken ill. Mr. Field's wife, Frances, a slight woman who had always worn a shawl whenever I saw her, sat by his side, her grief hidden by a black veil, but even so it was unbearable to look at her for more than a few moments. She sat with her head bowed in agony, lifting her hand to grasp that of a friend. Every so often her body shook with silent sobs, causing her husband to put his hand gently to her shoulder. The few hushed and mournful friends who had dared come, among them Taylor and Henry Blow, stood talking in muted voices. The small casket sat by itself at the other end of the living room.

I approached Mr. Field, who had been speaking with Taylor Blow. I looked into his expressionless eyes and fought the tears that welled up in my own, not just at the tragic death of a small child but because the father's self-control was so unfaltering even in the midst of unimaginable sorrow.

"Thank you for coming," he said in a voice without emotion.

Frances raised her hand and I took it, feeling how thin it was, and then left them. I talked with Taylor and Henry but none of us really listened to each other.

After an eternity, the casket was carried out to the hearse and the procession to Bellefontaine Cemetery began. Mr. Field and Frances and their children followed the hearse in their carriage. The rest of us came after in three other carriages. Now out of the Fields' presence, we talked of the cholera that had struck the city.

"The steamboats brought the cholera," a woman said.

"Yes," said another woman, "the immigrants on the steamboats."

"No," offered someone else, "it was the vegetables."

As we drove through the city, the smell of burning tar and sulphur forced us to put handkerchiefs to our faces. Despite the devastation of the Great Fire and its proven inability as a purifier, at each crossroad the population had dragged old crates, tar barrels and other incendiary materials and set them on fire. Youths jumped and danced around the fires. As we passed one such fire, an overexcited boy suddenly turned pale as death and dragged himself away. Here and there sparks blown by the wind had started fires on the shingle roofs.

At Bellefontaine Cemetery, near where the Missouri and the Mississippi meet, coffins lay scattered everywhere. The graves of the dead who had been interred were visible as rectangular mounds of newly turned earth. The overwhelmed gravediggers had not dug deep enough to bury the caskets. They had finished the job by piling the caskets with clumps of dirt and clay. The mounds all pointed with military-like precision in the same direction.

We gathered in a copse of woods on a hill. Mr. Field had purchased a gravesite here when their first child, Theodore French, died in an earlier outbreak of cholera a year before I came to St. Louis. Frances wept inconsolably and the expression on Mr. Field's face was heartbreaking for being so forcibly disciplined against tears. For a while I clung to the soothing words of Pastor Post, who called our attention to the love that the Field family had given little William Bradley. In their hour of grief, he said, Roswell, Frances, and their children can draw comfort that God's love for William Bradley is just as great because otherwise He would not have wanted William Bradley at His side at so young an age.

As the small casket of William Bradley was lowered into the shallow grave beside his brother's, I looked away and thought of my dead sisters and wondered why God demanded the presence of so many small children. Listening to the shovels of dirt splash onto the coffin, I gazed in the direction of the stately river, flowing through the mists of time, a landscape of plains and farms snug in their plentiful fields, and smelled the sorrowful sweet fragrance of eternity.

As we walked away from the gravesite, Dred Scott, hat in hand, appeared as if from nowhere. Eyes downcast, Dred waited patiently until Mr. Field saw him and then tentatively approached the grieving parents. I was close enough to hear his brief words. "Harriet and me, we be praying for this child."

Mr. Field, supporting his wife, only nodded. Dred stepped aside and we exchanged sad glances. I asked if his family was all right and he said that they were.

I prevailed on Taylor to find room for Dred in one of the carriages. He was given a space next to a driver. No one spoke on the ride back to St. Louis.

Cholera raged in the city. The Committee of Public Health, a body of private citizens, took control of the city government to reassure fear-crazed citizens in near rebellion over the city's ineffectual measures. The Committee placed two twelve-pound cannons near Montesano House, which overlooked the river. Whenever a boat approached the city, a signal shot was fired, giving notice to receive the quarantine officer, who turned away any vessels with sick passengers; but the citizens of St. Louis continued to die. The Committee ordered more tar and sulphur fires, which had no effect other than to burn down row after row of buildings. In desperation, the Committee set aside a day for prayer.

Only after the cholera had done its worst did the Committee make an effort to clean the streets and clear the alleys into which all manner of filth and trash had been thrown because, as Samuel O'Fallon had boasted on my first day in St. Louis, the citizenry was too busy making money to build a decent water system, including sewers. Of the latter, there were none.

Slight diarrhea, for which the prescription was salt and mustard, gave way to fever, vomiting, cramps, and discharges. The cholera patient complained of enormous thirst and a cold tongue; then the skin wrinkled and turned blue, and the eyes, surrounded by a livid hue, seemed to sink into the skull. The final stage was loss of strength followed by a painless death.

The newspapers filled with advertisements for cures. "Davis Pain Killer. At the commencement of the disease take two teaspoonfuls in sugar and water, repeat every fifteen minutes. BEWARE OF COUNTERFEITS!! Buy none without the likeness of Perry Davis on each bottle."

The doctors had not much more success than Perry Davis and his ilk. The doctors applied dry cups to the spine and wet cups to the abdomen, tried warm baths, resorted to frictions with capsicum, and, in desperation, ordered hot bricks, which were used to burn the soles of the patients' feet to a crisp. When the external remedies failed to work, they tried injections of acetate of lead and laudanum. When none of this worked, the doctors even prescribed brandy, which was already being imbibed in great quantity by the negro teamsters who hauled away the dead but themselves were falling ill. When their patients and the negro teamsters continued to die, the doctors still living turned to the lancet. The blood first came drop by drop, and was of dark molasses color, but gradually began to flow freely in a brighter hue, at which point the bleeding was stopped. It proved as useless as the other remedies.

Funeral processions such as ours soon became rare. The dead were simply taken to the cemeteries as quickly as possible, where they often waited for days in coffins because the diggers were dying as fast as everyone else, which was at a citywide rate of hundreds a week, one third of them children. The coffins ran short and so the brandy-drinking negro teamsters came by night with wagons, hauled the dead by their feet out of their beds and dragged them down the stairs, thumping from step to step. The bodies were thrown on the wagon which, when filled with corpses, was pulled to the cemetery, where its contents were emptied into a common trench.

A week after William Bradley's funeral, I accompanied Mr. Field and Frances back to Bellefontaine Cemetery to bury their son, Charles James, and their only daughter, Frances Victoria. We needed only a single carriage because, like most St. Louisians with means, the Blows and other friends had left the city or were busy with plans to flee with their families. Mr. Field had sent his two oldest children, Eugene and Roswell, to an aunt in Vermont but he and Frances had been unable to leave because first one and then another and then a third small child had grown sick. Before he fled, Taylor pleaded with me to leave, but I felt certain that death happened only to others.

The human spirit can absorb only so much grief before it becomes numb. Whether Frances was still capable of grief, I could not tell. She looked like a ghost, pale and weak from lack of sleep, no longer crying, and tending to burial arrangements in a dazed, lifeless state. Occasionally, Mr. Field came to the office. He worked at his desk for a few hours with unbroken concentration, and then left with only a formal, "Good day, Arba."

I managed our legal affairs alone, including the filing of several briefs in the Missouri Supreme Court. My memory of those days may have been affected by the fact that I also became ill. Concerned about Dred, whom I had not seen for several days, and his family, I had been on my way to the negro quarter when I suddenly felt weak and nauseated. I had returned to my boardinghouse in a feverish state, half-crawled up the stairs to my room, and lay on the bed wondering who would even know that I was sick.

I was fortunate. Dred had come looking for me, just as I had with him. He knew a German physician who had successfully treated many cholera-stricken Germans and some of the free negroes, and persuaded him to visit me. The German physician gave me strong doses of calomel and quinine, which British doctors had used in India in similar circumstances. Gradually the cramps and vomiting stopped and my body temperature returned to normal. The physician then prescribed an effervescent powder, and a hydropathic treatment for Dred to administer: strong rubbing with wet linen cloths, followed by aggressive toweling with a woolen blanket.

I was in bed for a week, much of the time delirious. When I finally woke, Dred was at my bedside.

"I'm thirsty."

Dred picked up a glass, cradled my head with his other arm, and raised my head so that I could sip from the glass. "You doing much better."

"How is your family?"

"They's fine. Some folks get sick and some don't. You been real sick."

I felt dizzy and the room darkened. Suddenly afraid, I reached out for his hand, which clasped mine firmly and affectionately. It was comforting to hold his hand and gradually I calmed down. In a dim recess of my feverish mind, I tried to imagine how I once might have felt about holding the hand of a negro. I could not recall how I might have felt. It was so very long ago.

"You sorry that you come to St. Louis?" Dred sounded genuinely curious.

I shook my head but then the room started to turn. Unable to stop it, I closed my eyes.

"How come you stay in the city, Mr. Crane? Most folks who have a choice, they go. How come you don't?"

"My father warned me about cholera . . ." My voice trailed away in weakness.

"While you sleeping you sure talk about your daddy."

I opened my eyes and found that the room had steadied. "What did I say?" Asking even a simple question was exhausting.

He was about to answer, and then halted. I stared at him. "You also asking a lot of questions about this girl, Abigail White. Seem like you can't get her out of your head."

"Dred, what did I say . . . about her?"

"Mr. Crane, you got to save your strength, you still a sick man."

"Yes. I have to get better. File your brief. Win your case." I tried to sit up.

With a look of both concern and exasperation, he gently stopped me from moving. "Mr. Crane, sometimes it seem like I gonna be free but only so long as I can keep you alive."

I asked him another question. I thought I had spoken loud enough for him to hear but he did not answer. Using all my strength, I tried again.

"Mr. Field, he having a hard time."

As parched as I was, tears still managed to form. Mercifully, I fell asleep and dreamed of pine forests in bright sunshine where brooks with clear, icy water bubbled over smooth rocks, a doorway draped with black cloth, and burial mounds that stretched to the far horizon on a grassy plain. I awoke feeling much improved in strength, fell asleep again, dreamed of Kate Fox, and in that manner recovered my health.

After a few days, I was able to read the newspaper, whose lengthy obituaries reported, "Died—on Tuesday, Mrs. Frances M. Field, wife of R.M. Field, Esq., funeral on Friday, 9 o'clock." I asked Dred to bring me paper and a pen. I wrote two letters. The first was to Mr. Field conveying my sorrow at his inexpressible losses. The second letter was to my father, informing him of Mr. Field's tragedy and assuring him that, although briefly ill, I was well and in no danger. I worked on the letter to my father until I grew weak, slept, and then wrote more. Since arriving in St. Louis I had written him only occasionally and without much detail. This time I filled page after page with an account of Mr. Field, our cases, St. Louis, Kate Fox, the Blows, and Dred, but nothing about Abigail White.

Three days later, barely recovered, I sat with Dred in a carriage at Bellefontaine Cemetery. Walking was still tiring and so, bundled in a blanket, I watched from the carriage the burial of Mr. Field's wife beside the graves of her children. When the shovels were still, Mr. Field stood before the graves, head down, alone in unimaginable bereavement.

The cemetery had grown vastly larger since my last visit. Throughout the endless mounds mourning fathers, mothers, widowers, widows, and orphans, all dressed in black, gathered to lay flowers, kneel in prayer or simply stand silent in remembrance. I experienced a premonitory shudder.

Mr. Field turned away from the graves and walked to the carriage. He got in and directed the driver to leave. The only sign of what must have been excruciating pain at the core of his being was a distant look in his eyes. Mr. Field stared at the passing landscape as though he had never seen it before. When we finally reached his home, he perfunctorily thanked Dred for having nursed me back to health. Without looking at the black cloth over his doorway, he went inside.

Chapter 15

Dear Arba:

I was much relieved by your letter. The cholera in St. Louis had been reported and, until your letter, I experienced considerable anxiety. I wish that you had heeded my advice and stayed in the East, but somehow you have managed to survive. Thank God the worst of our fears did not come true.

A severe disappointment in reading your letter is to find that you have not kept your promise to me. In this I hold Roswell responsible. He has a thriving practice and more than enough clients to keep you busy, yet he agreed to your impetuous proposal to represent a slave in a suit against a white woman of some social prominence. I do not see what good will come of this, especially if you are successful on *appeal. It certainly is not a promising way to build a law practice in a slave state.*

The agitation over slavery here grows daily with enforcement of the Fugitive Slave Law which, I might remind you, was the North's part of the recent bargain struck by Senator Webster, about whom, in the past, you have spoken fondly. The newspapers report that when a fugitive slave was apprehended in New York City, an angry crowd gathered and several lawyers, to much applause, stepped forward to offer their services to the poor wretch without fee. Such lawyers may be celebrated in New York City, but in a slave state they are the Devil's mercenaries.

Even with the agitation over fugitive slaves, abolitionists are barely tolerated in Vermont. When the Reverend Tyler spoke in Brattleboro, one justice of the peace advocated the application of tar and feathers, and a mob fired cannons near the windows of the lecture room to drown out his words. Why should they come here to lecture us on slavery where we have no slaves?

Your father

Mr. Field returned to the law office the day after his wife's funeral and applied himself to his work as though he had not just buried most of his family. I resumed my activities with the Law Library Association, visited with the Blows, and spent time in the company of young women who always seemed to lack a certain charm or intellectual interest. They talked of balls and parties, gossiped about their friends, and attended an opera without so much as speaking a word about it afterward. An attempt at conversation about the latest news from Europe or Benton's campaign for election to the House of Representatives invariably was met with a blank stare and a polite response, "That's all very interesting, I'm sure."

The fire and the cholera, the loss of our office, the deaths of Mr. Field's wife and children, and my own illness had created a divide.

Everything on the other side of the divide—my arrival in St. Louis, the Scott trial, and my affair with Kate Fox—seemed to be from another lifetime. Life on this side of the divide was not nearly as exciting as in those days, which was fine with me because I'd had enough excitement.

>⌒~

I began work on Dred's brief. The Emerson brief argued the hypocrisy of the North. Before the Missouri Supreme Court should recognize any rights of freedom under the Missouri Compromise, it said, "those rights should first be enforced and perfected by the tribunals of that country north of the line thirty-six degrees thirty minutes."

I resisted the temptation to match the Emerson brief's oratory. Instead, I pointed out that the brief nowhere explained how Northern states had failed to enforce the Missouri Compromise, and reminded the Missouri Supreme Court of its ruling in *Winny v. Whitesides* that a slave owner, by residing with his slave in a free state or territory, "declares his slave to have become a freed man." I devoted considerable space to *Rachael (a woman of color) v. Walker,* where the court on the basis of *Winny* had declared free a slave whose owner was an army officer ordered to a post at Fort Snelling. The brief cited the other decisions of the Missouri Supreme Court that reaffirmed these principles: *Milly (a woman of color) v. Smith; Vincent (a man of color) v. Duncan; Ralph (a man of color) v. Duncan; Julia (a woman of color) v. McKinney; Nat (a man of color) v. Ruddle;* and *Wilson (a colored man) v. Melvin.*

I finished the draft and read and reread it. It was a strong brief because the Missouri law of slavery was as clear as any law I had studied. Everything I had been taught in law school and all that I had learned as a lawyer convinced me that the Missouri Supreme Court, on reading our brief, must conclude that, under the law as spoken by that same court again and again, Dred Scott was a free man.

I then copied the brief and enclosed the copy in a letter to my father.

Dear Father:

Mr. Field appears well enough. He comes to the office from sun to sun, as do I. You must not be concerned about the Scott case because such cases are not uncommon here and the rulings of the juries or courts little remarked upon other than by the affected litigants.

But you cannot hold Mr. Field responsible. I explained the law to Dred Scott and convinced him to bring the suit and I then prevailed on Mr. Field to let me take the case. The fault, if there be such, is mine and mine alone. Dred is an appealing fellow, the law is on his side, and I have felt the better for helping him. I have seen many things in Missouri that disquiet the conscience.

Please convey my love to Mother.

Your devoted son

Arba

Mr. Field and I did not discuss the draft until the day before the last mail pickup for delivery to Jefferson City in time to file the brief. Mr. Field had taken all of my briefs into his office. One by one they had been returned to me but the Scotts' brief remained in his office and I grew concerned as the filing date neared. On the evening of our last day to post the brief, I knocked on his door. There was no answer and I knocked again.

Mr. Field opened the door. "I have not forgotten the brief." I could see a brandy decanter and a glass on his desk but the decanter was full. I tried to, but could not, recall my ancient thirsts.

"At the end of each day when I was your father's law partner we discussed each other's cases, most often with good result." Abruptly, he shook his head as if to ward off a troubling memory. "Those were my happiest days as a lawyer." It was the first time since my arrival in St. Louis that Mr. Field had spoken of my father.

He handed me the Scotts' brief, put on his coat, and left the office to return to a cold and empty house.

I stayed in the office to write the final brief, which was simple enough to do because Mr. Field had made few changes to my draft. As I was shaking the black blotting sand from the brief, the door opened.

"Evening, Mr. Crane."

"Hello, Dred." He had not been to the office to clean for two weeks. "We haven't seen you for a while."

He studied my face and seemed satisfied with my recovery. "It's just not a good time for me to be walking in the streets. They been catching the free folks and putting them in jail."

The Anti-Abolitionist Society had grown more boisterous, holding rallies, handing out leaflets, and harassing free negroes.

"Those are free blacks charged with failure to show a pass. You've got one."

"Seems like I ain't a slave and I ain't free, neither. So I've been waiting for all this to die down a bit before I come here." He asked, "Your daddy, he write you?"

Dred still had not disclosed my delirious words about my father.

"He wrote a letter. Here, look at this." I handed him the freshly-written brief. He held it by the edges, examined it, and then handed it back.

"It's your brief to the highest court in this state." I explained to Dred that it was our argument to the court why the jury had made the right decision. I read him the brief from beginning to end.

He smiled when I finished. "You spoke words that I ain't heard before. I just got to trust you and Mr. Field. Can't do nothing else."

"All those names you heard were cases like yours brought by slaves. In each the court ruled that the slave was free because he had been living in a free state or territory. Our best case is the one where the army officer was sent to Fort Snelling and took his slave along. The court said the slave was free. It's no different from your case. The court must rule in your favor."

"What's the name of that slave?"

"Her name was Rachael."

"That ain't a name I hear at the fort."

"She was there many years before you."

"What she do when the judges, they set her free?"

"I have no idea. Perhaps she returned to the Wisconsin territory or she might have gone to Illinois. What would you like to do?"

Dred took some time to answer. "Can't remember anyone asking me that before. Sometimes I think about staying. But it seems like the times, they getting harder for the free blacks even. Harriet, she raring to go to the free state just as soon as we can." He shook his head thinking of Harriet. "She don't care which state so long as it's free and far from this one. I tell her that maybe you help us go all the way up there to Vermont."

"Why, you might even go to Newfane." We both laughed because Dred knew how desperate I had been to leave Newfane. "Are you sure you can live in another cold weather state?"

"Well, Mr. Crane, I think you know that I'd rather be cold and free than warm and a slave."

"I think I do. Dred, Fort Snelling was free territory surrounded by free states. Why didn't you leave then?"

He again hesitated before answering. "We talk about running away. Harriet, she want to leave, but she be with the child." He seemed to recall an uncomfortable memory. "That a pretty bad time for me and Harriet when Dr. Emerson, he die, and then Irene, she don't let us go. Seems like Harriet ain't ever going to forget that I make her stay at the fort. She think we be living now in the free state or in Canada like the other runaways."

"I can understand that."

"But I never look behind me when I'm walking. That's the best way I know to cross my legs." Dred surveyed the office. "This place it sure need a cleaning. I best be getting to it."

I left before he did and as I closed the door, I noticed that he had gone to my desk, picked up the brief, and slowly begun to turn the pages and stare at the words he could not read.

Chapter 16

D ear Father:

　　A strange incident occurred a few weeks after Mr. Field and I returned from the Missouri Supreme Court in Jefferson City. I found it so unusual that I feel compelled to share it in this letter. Before I do, in answer to your last letter, the argument in the Scotts' case was surprisingly uneventful. The judges asked many questions in our other cases but none when I argued the Scotts' appeal. All three judges listened carefully to both sides but, no more than the great Sphinx of Egypt, did they reveal their secrets. Many cases were argued while we were in Jefferson City and therefore it will be some months before we have a decision. But I have every confidence as to the ruling.

　　As to the strange incident, there was a knock on the door one afternoon while Mr. Field was in his office with his door closed. I opened the door to find a handsome, elegantly dressed woman *standing in the hallway. She asked in a hushed voice if I might announce her to Mr. Field. "You may tell him that Mary Almira Phelps is here and desires an audience."*

She declined a seat in the office and I went to get Mr. Field. At my knock, he told me to come in, although in a tone, now quite familiar, suggesting a preference not to be disturbed. I announced the visitor by name.

He looked up, quite startled, removed his reading glasses, and asked me to repeat it. I did so.

Mr. Field did not reply. He seemed quite disturbed. I asked, "Shall I tell her to come in?"

"No!" he said. "No. I will not see her. Tell her that I have urgent matters that require my attention."

I returned to the hallway. I must have been troubled by Mr. Field's reaction to her presence because when she saw my face, she raised a hand as if to keep me from uttering words she did not wish to hear. "Mr. Field is unable to see you," I said. "He is engaged in pressing matters for his clients."

"Did he say whether I might have an appointment at a later date?"

"No, he did not."

She nodded slowly as if my words were not entirely unexpected. "Please advise Mr. Field that I shall be in St. Louis for the next week. You may tell him that I am staying at the National Hotel and would be pleased to receive him."

As she turned to leave, I thought I saw tears in her eyes, but it may only have been a trick of the reflection of the dim light in the hallway.

Later, I conveyed her words to Mr. Field, who had no response. As far as I know, he never called on Mrs. Phelps (or is it Miss?) and I assume she has left St. Louis. I have not discussed this woman with him. Perhaps you know something of her? If Mr. Field knew her from his Vermont days, I would guess that she was then quite a beautiful young woman.

Your affectionate son,

Arba

My father did not respond for some time. Then a thick package arrived, which I opened late one night in my room at the boardinghouse. It contained a letter and a separate note from my father, several yellowing legal documents, and an opinion of the Vermont Supreme Court.

Dear Arba:

> *Your letter called forth many disturbing memories about which you are ignorant. By now, Mary Almira Phelps has departed St. Louis, and, I can state with certainty, Roswell did not see her. Even her name has not passed from his lips. I was convinced that the past should stay in the past.*
>
> *I changed my mind after rereading the enclosed opinion of the Vermont Supreme Court, which I last looked at many years ago. It is my only copy and the very thought of sealing it in this letter and leaving it at the Newfane Post Office helps relieve the strain of the recollections that your letter brought forth. The opinion and the other documents will tell you a great deal about Roswell Field which I would never have thought to share with you but for this* Scott *case. Despite your protestations, I believe that you have embarked on a perilous course. When Roswell and I practiced law together, in every case but one—*

He had written a different word than "one," but then scratched it out—

> *our shared wisdom and experience enabled one or the other to steer a true legal course to the best possible outcome. Clark v. Field convinced me that I never really knew the man whom I practiced law with. I decided that you must have this advantage.*

I stopped reading my father's letter and picked up the opinion, *Clark v. Field*, the same one that I had seen on Mr. Field's desk on my first day in St. Louis. By the dim light of a camphene lamp, alternately reading the opinion and my father's letter, I learned the unhappy tale of Mary Almira Phelps, the 18-year-old beauty who broke Mr. Field's heart, destroyed the partnership of Field & Crane, and drove my employer from Vermont.

They had met on a late summer day in Newfane, when warm afternoons turn slightly chilly as sunlight fades. Mary Almira, accompanied by my mother, had pulled up in a chaise at the entrance gate to Mr. Field's home. They had taken a drive along the West River from Brattleboro and now stopped to visit Mr. Field, the law partner of the man whom my mother had just married.

Mary Almira received Mr. Field with a nod and a gay smile. Judging by the questions Mr. Field later asked my mother, he had found her to be of "very pleasing face and form and agreeable manners," which were the words from Mr. Field's pleading.

According to the Vermont Supreme Court opinion, Mary Almira was the daughter of a widow, Susanna Phelps, who had recently remarried under the name Susanna Torrey. Mary Almira had been raised in Windsor, some thirty miles north, but was then attending the Leicester Academy in Massachusetts. There, she had met and become engaged to a young man named Jeremiah Clark who, in his pleading, claimed that they had formed a "natural and virtuous" attachment.

In these circumstances, Mr. Field might have lost interest, although he could not have so easily forgotten Mary Almira, regarded as one of the most beautiful young women in southern Vermont. Her high spirits, attractive figure, and large, enchantingly dark and flirtatious eyes charmed all who met her. Young men flocked to her side, vying for her attention, jostling one another to have a word, and sending invitations to this or that picnic or tea or social. Her father, a doctor, had left his family a substantial estate, and she dressed in expensive clothes that enhanced her natural beauty. In the South she would have found more competition, but in Vermont Mary Almira had few peers and unlimited choices among her suitors. On these, she lavished regal but temporary affection that left many young men shaking their heads at how quickly her attention, after such a promising start, wandered elsewhere, until, finally, she had settled on Jeremiah Clark.

> *Roswell, like every other man who met her, including myself, was struck by Mary Almira's feminine allure. Had I been wiser, I might have questioned whether the male world had properly educated such a young woman to use prudently this potent combination of restless spirit and beguiling feminine power.*

The last thing that Mr. Field might therefore have expected was Mary Almira's appearance at his house two weeks later. At her request, my father had driven her from Windsor, where he had been on business, to Newfane. In his letter, my father recalled the look on Mr. Field's face as he approached the carriage and saw Mary Almira.

> *They both began talking with much animation, but at the time I did not regard Roswell as expressing anything more than natural delight at receiving such a vivacious visitor. Over the next eight days the friendly affection between the young woman and a much older man turned into something else, I am afraid.*

According to his pleadings, on the third evening of Mary Almira's stay with my parents, Mr. Field passed "beyond the bounds of formal civility in his relations with the young woman." As Mr. Field informed several courts, as he was saying goodnight to Mary Almira, he plucked a leaf from a rosebush, kissed it, and gave it to her. The next day, she took from her bosom a paper, unfolded it, and showed Mr. Field the same leaf neatly stitched on the paper. She carefully folded the paper and replaced it in her bosom. That evening, while playing chess, Mr. Field named her chess queen "Miss Phelps" and sacrificed most of his pieces to capture her queen. They played a second game, during which they named one of her bishops Jeremiah. Mary Almira soon sacrificed the Bishop Jeremiah for a pawn. He then asked permission of Mary Almira to hold her hand and to kiss her cheeks and lips, which she gave.

> *I have no doubt that Roswell knew of our disapproval of his behavior towards a young girl then engaged to marry another man. I tried several times to discuss the matter with him but on each occasion he contrived a reason to turn to a different matter. Word finally reached her mother of the daughter's possible infatuation with an older man. Susanna Torrey immediately dispatched a letter demanding the daughter's return, which only sent Mary Almira into Roswell's arms. Both came to me and, as I had just taken up the post of Town Justice, announced that they had resolved to wed immediately and asked me to perform the ceremony then and there. To Roswell's dismay, I declined. I do not remember my excuse but I may have suggested that I required the consent of Mary Almira's mother. Matters were never quite the same between us as they had been before Mary Almira arrived in Roswell's life as suddenly as a midday mountain storm.*

The couple decided to marry in Putney and left immediately in Roswell's carriage. My father, who declined to accompany them, wrote only that the few witnesses to the ceremony later testified that it was solemn and serious in manner. Immediately after the ceremony, Mary Almira returned to her mother's residence in Windsor and Mr. Field to Newfane.

> *Sometime in the next few weeks, Mary Almira's family learned of the ceremony. Her fiancé, Jeremiah Clark, was immediately summoned from Massachusetts and there followed a series of family conferences. The family lawyer forwarded a letter to Roswell from Mary Almira, which you will find printed in full in the opinion of the Vermont Supreme Court.*

I leafed through the opinion, part of which was devoted to the court's jurisdiction over the enforceability of marriage vows, and found the letter.

To Mr. Roswell F.

Sir,—Moments of consideration and much reflection have at length caused me to see in its proper light the whole of my late visit. I have been led by you in a course of conduct which my own reason, sense, and feelings entirely disapprove. I am not willing, on any account, to see you again.

Mary A.P.

My eyes grew tired in the dim light and I stopped reading to rest them. Memories of a hand lightly touching my arm, soft hair against my cheek, and sunlight creeping into a bedroom as my unattainable lover turned away from me with a question that I was afraid to answer, mixed with admiration at Mr. Field's bold flouting of the sensibilities of neighbors and friends.

Roswell read me the letter and then denounced it as a forgery. He wrote an immediate answer urging that the Putney marriage be made public and that Mary Almira announce the end of her engagement to Jeremiah Clark. No reply was forthcoming and so he left immediately for Windsor. He was not expecting, and did not receive, a friendly reception. As he told me later, he went into the parlor and there extended his hand to Mary Almira, who first looked for guidance from her mother and then declined it. He asked to be left alone with his wife and the family retired to the hallway but kept the door open.

"I received a most awful letter. I know it is a lie."

"Be assured that I wrote that letter."

"Then your hand wrote some other person's thoughts. I know that in my heart."

"Since returning to my home, I have devoted much reflection to my own heart. I do love Jeremiah, he has been kind and loving to me, and I will marry him."

"I cannot conceive how you could do such a thing since you are already married."

"Why, you can give up the certificate. Let it all go and nobody will know anything about it."

On seeing his face, she pleaded, *"Come, now, I'm sure you've got the certificate in your pocket. You can give it up just as well as not and let me marry Jeremiah."*

As Roswell was about to reply with, I have no doubt, a refusal, Mary Almira's mother, in great distress, came into the room and begged Roswell to hand over the marriage certificate.

"Let things be as if they had never been," she beseeched him.

Mary Almira's stepfather also entered the parlor and made the same demand, adding that his stepdaughter had affection for the whole of the other sex, often without discrimination since she was young and inexperienced.

"If that be true," asked Mr. Field, *"why are you in such anxiety as to her choice of husband?"*

"Why, damn it, sir," said the stepfather, *"we have our preferences."*

At this, Roswell concluded that the family had demanded return of the marriage certificate because Jeremiah Clark's wealth and social standing was greater than his own. He said to the stepfather, *"And I have mine. I will not give up the certificate. If you attempt to marry Mary Almira to another I will publish the Putney marriage in every newspaper in New England."* Roswell left the house, waited in Windsor for three days with no word from Mary Almira or her family, and returned to Newfane. A week later Mary Almira and Jeremiah Clark were married and sailed for a long honeymoon in Europe. When she returned she was several months pregnant with Jeremiah Clark's child.

There was no more writing on this page of my father's letter, as though he had broken off with no intention of completing the letter or sending it. But the letter resumed on the next page, although the writing was somewhat shakier, which was uncharacteristic of my father's precise, even penmanship.

I too urged Roswell to tear up the marriage certificate or at least to have the Putney marriage formally annulled. I argued with him that he was well rid of an unprincipled young girl who had been raised by a greedy and selfish mother without government or discipline. But he had turned to stone. He insisted that their marriage was legal and binding. I reminded him that the marriage had never been consummated but he was unyielding. I pointed out that if the marriage was binding then, in the eyes of the law, Mary Almira was a bigamist and her child a bastard. It mattered not in the slightest. The only thing that did matter to him was the law, the law, the law. It was on his side, he claimed, and made their contract sacred. His firm view was that Mary Almira's family was asking him to, as he put it, "acquiesce and consent to the prostitution and adultery of his wife."

How well I remember that wrenching argument in our small office. Before, our arguments had been conducted in the spirit of a critical but friendly challenge to one or another's interpretation of a case or draft of a brief. Now he sat at his desk, furiously writing the first of many pleadings involving this unpleasant matter, and answering me over his shoulder. He was so deeply wounded that I found it painful to look in his eyes. His humiliation had hardened into an iron resolve to seek vindication in the temples of justice, in which he so profoundly believed. I now see that he was never the same man after meeting that woman and, I suppose, neither am I. What I also failed to see at the time was that Roswell may have been driven mad by her.

The letter went on for several more pages. It was a history of the decade of litigations between Roswell Field and the family and husband of Mary Almira. The history began with presentments by Mr. Field to grand juries against Mary Almira's two brothers for her abduction and prostitution, against one brother for opening a letter Mr. Field had sent to Mary Almira, and against Jeremiah for adultery. None resulted in a conviction.

Susannah filed a suit for libel, which came to trial first. A Woodstock jury found for Mr. Field, and the Vermont Supreme Court, in the first of several opinions arising from the ill-fated marriage, upheld the jury's verdict. Then Jeremiah Clark and Mary Almira filed a lawsuit seeking an injunction to prevent Mr. Field from obtaining any of her property. For the first time after years of litigation, the validity of their marriage was directly at issue.

Clark v. Field went to trial in Woodstock before a Chancery Judge. Mary Almira testified that Mr. Field had used various artifices and persuasions to induce her to break her engagement with Jeremiah Clark. She claimed that Mr. Field took advantage of her youth and inexperience.

Mr. Field, his sister, my father, and others testified at the trial, which was followed by many newspapers. In a bitter blow for Mr. Field, the Chancery Judge ruled that the marriage was void. Mr. Field appealed to the Vermont Supreme Court.

I was as much in awe at the legal skills that Mr. Field applied to his relentless quest as at the passion that had driven this now passionless man. His special pleadings were masterpieces. He conceived ingenious legal devices and resourcefully responded to defeat with new arguments or lawsuits. But after so many years, his affection and desire for Mary Almira could not have been what it was and surely he did not dream that some day he would find marital harmony with her. Certainly, he desired vindication of his reputation, but that would never have been in doubt if he had given back the marriage certificate on his visit to Susannah Torrey's parlor. The litigation burned its own coal. Once started, it was no longer entirely in the control of its creator but had a life and logic of its own. Its needs triumphed over Mr. Field's.

The Vermont Supreme Court reached a decision, which caused Mr. Field to immediately leave Vermont for St. Louis. By then, Jeremiah Clark had died.

The court unanimously affirmed the Chancery Judge and declared that there had been no valid marriage between Mr. Field and Mary Almira. The court, in the one part of the opinion that may have given Mr. Field some comfort, noted that Mary Almira "was pleased with the society of Mr. Field and not reluctant to receive his attentions" and that her attachment to Jeremiah Clark was greatly weakened, "if not effaced."

The court took pity on the then eighteen-year-old Mary Almira, who "did not appear fully acquainted with the legal consequences of a solemnization of marriage." The court then stated firmly that the "evidence is satisfactory to us that the parties did not, by the ceremony at Putney, intend a marriage, as far as we can learn their intentions." The court concluded:

> The immediate parties may find some excuse or palliation in the thoughtlessness of youth, the strength of affection, the pangs of disappointment and blighted hopes, in the versatility of feelings to which all are subject. We say nothing about the parties before us, except what has been thought necessary in deciding the case.

I had been reading my father's letter and studying the opinions and pleadings for much of the night and now it was just a few hours before dawn. In a short while I would appear at the law office of Roswell M. Field and greet a stranger whom I liked more than the man I had thought I knew. I read last my father's separate note:

Arba

> *I have decided to send this letter after all.*
>
> *Do not judge Roswell harshly nor think ill of him, as I did during those long and painful years when Roswell thought the law would soothe and heal his wounds, which, of course, it could not. We do what we must and only the Creator truly knows why, and therefore only He is fit to pronounce judgment. Roswell bore his*

final defeat and shame with a dignity that had escaped him since the day he met that woman, who ended our law partnership.

My father had first begun another sentence but then, as in the first letter, scratched it out. I could make out the words " . . . two women . . . law partnership . . ." The letter continued.

That ill-advised visit—I cannot guess at what passed through Roswell's mind upon your announcing her presence—has awakened painful recollections. Since receiving your letter, I have asked myself again and again, why did she come? What had she intended to say to him? I have no answer and now we shall never know.

I leave to you whether these matters should ever be the subject of conversation between you and Roswell. I think not but I have committed the story of this unhappy incident to your safekeeping, to use as you see fit. Oh, what a pity it happened! Had Roswell remained in Vermont he would have gone down as one of the state's greatest lawyers and, I know as a matter of faith, found happiness instead of tragedy.

Your father

Chapter 17

"Since you were late, I took the mail." Mr. Field stood in the doorway of his office as stern and as stiff as ever. He could not possibly be the same man who had kissed a rosebud leaf and then handed it to the beautiful Mary Almira.

"Why are you smiling?" Mr. Field asked impatiently.

I stopped but continued to stare at him.

"This is no time for daydreaming. You have a decision."

"The *Scott* case?"

"The opinion arrived this morning."

I followed him into his office, no longer thinking of *Clark v. Field*, and seated myself expectantly in front of his desk.

He hesitated at first.

"They reversed."

"Pardon me, Mr. Field. What did you just say?"

"I said they reversed." He reached across his desk to hand me the opinion and then looked up. "Did you hear me? They reversed. Two to one. Judge Scott wrote the majority opinion."

"You are not . . . serious, Mr. Field."

"I am indeed serious. You lost. What is the matter with you?"

At that moment, there was a great deal the matter with me. I sat rigidly in the chair, my face red. Mr. Field grew concerned as I just sat there and even more so when I stood up and violently kicked the chair over. He relaxed slightly when I picked up a Missouri case reporter, as though to look up a fine point of law regarding the ruling, but then I threw the heavy volume against a wall, damaging the wallpaper and breaking the spine of the book.

I expected him to discharge me from his employment, the prospect of which troubled me not in the least, since, among the many thoughts flying through my fevered mind was the notion that I should find a different profession, but instead he said with surprising sympathy, "It is a very bad opinion, which you did not deserve."

Judge Scott's face mocked me. I righted the chair, picked up the broken book, and sat down heavily, clumsily trying to keep the pages from the maimed volume from slipping to the floor. "My God. *Winny* and *Rachael*. Those were their own rulings."

Mr. Field put on his glasses and began reading from the middle of the opinion where he had made notes in the margins and underlined some passages.

Times now are not as they were when the former decisions on this subject were made. Since then not only individuals, but States, have been possessed with a dark and fell spirit in relation to slavery, whose gratification is sought in the pursuit of measures, whose inevitable consequence must be the overthrow and destruction of our government. Under such circumstances it does not behoove the State of Missouri to show the least countenance to any measure which might gratify this spirit. She is willing to assume her full responsibility for the existence of slavery within her limits, nor does she seek to share or divide it with others. Although we may, for our own sakes, regret that the avarice and hard-heartedness of the progenitors of those who are now so sensitive on the subject, ever introduced the institution among us, yet we will not go to them to learn law, morality, or religion on the subject.

I was rigid with welling pain and anger. Mr. Field removed his reading glasses and rubbed his eyes. "Judge Scott wrote for the majority, Judge Ryland concurring. The majority held that each state has the right to determine"—he put on his reading glasses again—"'how far, in a spirit of comity, it will respect the laws of other states.'" He peered at me and strained for something lighthearted to say. "Apparently, there is not much comity in Missouri." I did not smile and he quickly said, "The opinion adopts the doctrine of reattachment and on that basis ruled that Dred had no legal claim based on residence in a free state or territory."

Mr. Field handed the opinion to me. "I have never read a more intemperate judicial document. It is one long outburst of resentment."

I picked up the opinion gingerly, afraid that by holding it I might be even more wounded, and silently read the most heavily marked passage, in which the court suggested that Dred should be grateful to be a slave.

As to the consequences of slavery, they are much more hurtful to the master than the slave. There is no comparison between the slave of the United States and the cruel, uncivilized negro in Africa. When the condition of our slaves is contrasted with the state of their miserable race in Africa, we are almost persuaded that the introduction of slavery amongst us was, in the providences of God, who makes the evil passions of men subservient to His own glory, a means of placing that unhappy race within the pale of civilized nations. The judgment will be reversed and the cause remanded.

"I'm sure Dred will feel better for hearing that." It took a moment to recall when I had last been as angry and then I remembered the day I attended the Bradford estate auction.

"It is more political tract than legal opinion," Mr. Field observed. "You might want to read the dissent."

I read Judge Gamble's dissent, which reviewed the many decisions by the Missouri Supreme Court and other Southern states' highest courts enforcing a slave's right to freedom on the basis of voluntary removal by his master to a free state or territory.

> The cases here referred to are cases decided when the public mind was tranquil, and when the tribunals maintained in their decisions the principles which had always received the approbation of an enlightened public opinion. Times may have changed, public feeling may have changed, but principles have not and do not change; and, in my judgment, there can be no safe basis for judicial decisions but in those principles which are immutable.

I put down the opinion, uncomforted by Judge Gamble. "I raised Dred and Harriet's hopes. I was so sure."

Wisely, Mr. Field said nothing.

"How do I explain it to them? The highest court in Missouri refused to follow three decades of its own decisions. Dear God, three decades. How do I explain that?"

But I had no way to explain it other than that Dred and Harriet were slaves. I stood but did not leave. "I will petition for reconsideration."

"If Moses, Hammurabi, and Blackstone all signed the petition, Judge Scott still would not change one line of this opinion."

"Then I will seek a writ to the United States Supreme Court."

"The opinion presents no obvious federal issue for direct Supreme Court review. Judge Scott stayed away from the Missouri Compromise."

"I will start another lawsuit in federal circuit court."

"What on earth would be the basis for federal jurisdiction?"

"I cannot leave these people to the whims of Irene Emerson."

He shook his head. "Arba, you have bad news to give your clients."

We heard footsteps in the hallway and a legal document fell from the mail slot to the floor. I picked it up and, after quickly reading the document, I walked back to Mr. Field's office.

"We have an appearance tomorrow before Judge Hamilton. Samuel O'Fallon has moved for an order reclaiming Dred and Harriet and the wages they have earned from hiring out." I added, "And their children."

"Samuel didn't waste time, did he? Well, you will have to tell Taylor that his bond may be called."

I studied the papers. "The order seeks restoration to Irene Emerson Chaffee." On any other occasion I might have smiled. "Irene remarried."

I arranged for delivery of a message to Taylor Blow and Dred and Harriet to come to the office at the end of the day. I spent the day in a state of grief, as though the opinion had delivered news of great personal loss and not simply the outcome of a lawsuit, forcing myself to read and reread the Missouri Supreme Court's opinion as though I might detect some as yet unrevealed flaw that even the judges themselves must acknowledge, reviewing a treatise on appeals to the United States Supreme Court, and wondering how to break the news to Dred and Harriet.

As the sun's dying rays flushed the office with soft crimson light, Taylor Blow appeared. We sat in Mr. Field's office, where we drank brandy. Ignoring Mr. Field's disapproving glances, I consumed several glasses of his expensive brandy while he and Taylor talked politics. Taylor casually mentioned that Alfred Fox had accepted a position in the Pierce Administration.

"I hear that Kate presides over one of the most exclusive salons in Washington City." Both he and Mr. Field glanced at me. My heart stirred from not entirely faded memories, only worsening the stupor of pain and remorse over the decision, which the brandies did little to temper, despite my not having tasted liquor in a long time.

Mr. Field and Taylor exchanged information about the recent municipal elections in St. Louis and prospects for trouble along Missouri's western border if the Kansas-Nebraska Act passed Congress. Taylor was concerned about rumors of New England abolitionists making plans to come to Kansas—and of proslavery men from Missouri preparing to stop them.

"The resentment is not to be underestimated."

"I underestimated it," I said, staring into my glass.

"They are angry and they are afraid," said Taylor, "Almost hysterical. Not a day goes by without a report of a slave murdering a white. Most of it is rumor but that hardly matters."

Taylor finished his drink. "This is very fine brandy, Roswell. I'll wager it cost you a pretty penny." Mr. Field glanced darkly at me as I finished my fourth brandy. "Well, I have some news. Irene Emerson, that is, Mrs. Chaffee, has left the state and married a Massachusetts man. A physician, no less."

"Let us hope she at least married an abolitionist," I said.

"I don't think," said Taylor, "that she would give up Dred and Harriet even if she had married Senator Charles Sumner."

The laughter that followed helped relieve the gloom that filled the room like dank mist.

"But seriously, Taylor," I asked, feeling a faint glimmer of hope, "what are her intentions?"

"She is selling the family to her brother, John Sanford. The transaction should be complete in a matter of days. He is paying more than the Scott family is worth. I imagine it's his way of giving a wedding gift to his sister."

"I never made Mr. Sanford's acquaintance," said Mr. Field.

"I attended John's wedding but I have not seen John for some years. I always thought him a bit, well, erratic, but he married Pierre Chouteau's daughter, which gave him his place in life. He lives in New York and only infrequently visits St. Louis."

"Perhaps this is good news for Dred and Harriet," I said. "Why would a resident of New York fight a legal battle over slaves in St. Louis?"

"Arba, this is bad news for Dred and Harriet. John is part of the Chouteau empire, which was built on fur and slaves. John will fight hard to protect Judge Scott's opinion."

"Which is why he should be willing to settle," I said without much conviction, "instead of risking more litigation."

"I thought about that possibility, Arba, but I cannot offer much hope. After such a victory, Irene—John has no reason to settle. By keeping Dred and Harriet in bondage, and perhaps breaking up the family, he discourages more slave suits, which serves Chouteau interests."

Before I could answer, there was a knock and I went to the door and opened it. Dred and Harriet politely stared at me as if to learn from my expression the reason that they were there, and then, when they did, looked stricken. Eliza and Lizzie at first greeted me happily, peering past me to see if I had already set out pen and paper, but grew solemn after studying my face.

I took Dred and Harriet into Mr. Field's office and left the children in the outer office. I lingered for a moment as they settled on a sofa. To judge by their faces, no one had to tell them that their parents were about to hear bad news. It was not an occasion for playing with pen and paper. They were sitting quietly, looking straight ahead, as I closed the door.

Dred and Harriet sat on the edge of Mr. Field's couch, Dred leaning forward slightly and Harriet sitting stiff and upright.

"I have such disappointing news." It required an effort to look at Dred. "The Missouri Supreme Court has reversed the jury's verdict. That means . . . you are no longer free."

Dred and Harriet's already shaken expressions did not change other than the briefest flicker of fear. Dred must have had the same look when Captain Blow told him that he would be sold even though his young playmate, Taylor Blow, had assured him that they would never be apart, or when Dr. Emerson broke his word. Taylor avoided looking at Dred and instead stared blankly at Mr. Field's law license, which hung on the wall over the couch.

"What about them other folks that won? That girl Rachael, she be free."

"The court changed the law, Dred." The anger slowly rose in my voice. "They shouldn't have but they did. It's like someone who made a promise and then decided not to keep it." Dred looked startled at hearing the word "promise."

I added bitterly, "What they did is shameful."

Taylor, his attention drawn by my emotion, looked at me curiously.

"How come they didn't keep their word?" asked Dred.

"The judges are filled with hate at the abolitionists."

"But what's that got to do with us?" asked Harriet.

"It's just that your case happened to come up at the wrong time," offered Mr. Field. "A few years ago, you would have won."

"That don't do us much good," said Harriet, looking at Dred, who was staring at me.

"There were three judges," I said, uncomfortable under his gaze. "Two voted against you and one voted for you. That gives us some hope."

"The law," said Harriet as though she were spitting out an unpleasant taste. "You told us we going to win this. But, the law it ain't for the slave, that's for sure."

"What's going to happen to us?" Dred asked.

"Irene has moved the court to return you to her and to recover the wages you have earned since we filed your lawsuit. We have an appearance in court tomorrow before Judge Hamilton." Taylor explained what he had learned about Irene's intention to sell them to her brother.

"Mr. Sanford, he going to own us?" Dred for the first time looked openly surprised.

"Irene has finally remarried," said Taylor, relieved to talk about Irene Emerson instead of Dred's misfortune. "I am told that she moved to Massachusetts." He added, "She married a doctor."

Despite the bad news and its dire implications, Dred shook his head and smiled, as though his expectations of white people, for once, had been confounded. "Don't that beat all. That woman getting married after all. And to a doctor."

"Husband," said Harriet, "why you smiling? She get the last laugh. She going to get the money. Where you going to get the money to pay the wages?"

"My bond will cover the wages," said Taylor.

"For that I give a heap of thanks." As always, Dred's face was empty of feeling when he spoke to Taylor. He turned to me. "But what you going to do now?"

"I will think of something," I said without the slightest idea of what it might be.

"You already done thought of something, and look where it gets us." Harriet began to say, "The Reverend Anderson—"

For the first time since I had met them, Dred angrily silenced his wife. "Hush, woman. Mr. Crane, he my friend. I trust these lawyers. And we ain't no worse off than if we ain't been to the court."

"We going to be a lot worse off. What you think Irene's brother going to do with slaves in St. Louis when the brother, he live in the other state? He going to sell us, that's what he going to do."

How out of place they looked in Mr. Field's office. Most of our clients were well-dressed and educated men who, as I had come to appreciate, regarded lawyers as tools, extremely well-machined ones, to be sure, but tools nonetheless in their pursuit or defense of money and power. Dred and Harriet's simple, worn clothes were a contrast to the finery of the three white men who had taken up their cause, and until now, I had never thought of ourselves as tools of their ambitions but more like lifelines to which they clung with varying degrees of hope. But Dred's question—"But what you going to do now?"—suggested that he had much in common with our other willful clients. Harriet also seemed more like our other clients to whom we delivered bad news, because she, at least, blamed her lawyers.

A long silence followed in which each of us appeared lost in thought since everything there was to say had been said.

I stood up and so did everyone else. "We cannot accomplish anything more tonight. You must both be at the courthouse tomorrow afternoon. Come here after the noon bell. And . . . you must bring your children."

They both blanched when I mentioned their children. After a pause, Dred nodded.

Silently, like a friend of the bereaved at the end of a funeral, I escorted Dred and Harriet from Mr. Field's office. Eliza and Lizzie were sitting on the couch just as I had left them. They seemed more anxious than before, despite, or perhaps because of, the forced smiles on the adults' faces. Dred tenderly took Lizzie's hand while Harriet went to Eliza.

Comfort the little children, for they face a hideous future.

"Eliza and Lizzie, they's everything to me," said Dred and then he left with his family.

I engaged in distracted talk with Taylor, who said, "I fear that all that can be done, has been done." I walked him to the door. He seemed reluctant to leave. "I was very attached to Dred when I was a child. Mother died and then Father had financial difficulties. Against my wishes, he sold Dred to John Emerson." He had a guilty look in his eyes. "You see, we never purchased to sell. All we bought we expected to hold."

I said nothing and he left.

After the door closed, I turned to Mr. Field. "It is the job of the good judge to do justice."

"Pardon?"

"When I sat for my examination, Judge Scott asked me to translate *boni judicis est ampliare justitiam.* This wasn't justice. This wasn't what Father taught me judges are supposed to do."

"Your father?" Mr. Field looked startled at my last words. "Your father taught you about justice?" He started to say something else and then stopped himself. "You worked hard on their case and I can see this is a bitter blow." With a sad and distant expression, he said, "It is painful to lose a case you should have won. Indeed, your father once tried to console me after such a loss by saying that you win some cases you should lose and lose some that you should win. He was right but I did not find much consolation at the time. This is most clearly one that should have been won."

And, I asked him silently, *do you feel any better now about* Clark v. Field?

As he put on his coat, I said, "I am going to stay and research the federal jurisdiction issue."

He nodded, gathered some papers, and left. I went into Mr. Field's office, sat down in his chair, and began drinking brandy, at first downing glass after glass, then pouring the contents of the decanter directly down my throat. When the decanter was empty I rummaged through the cabinets and found a half-filled bottle, which I drank in gulps, not even noticing or caring what I was drinking. Whatever it was, the bottle's contents finally worked their wonders. I passed out on the floor and came to only because Dred was shaking me and calling my name.

"Mr. Crane, you got to wake up."

"Let me be, Dred. Why did you come back? Go home."

"Can't do that, Mr. Crane."

"I lost your case."

"You say you think of something, Mr. Crane." His face could not have looked more serious. "Now you got to think of it."

"I am drunk. At least, I hope I am. How can I think of anything?"

"Lord, Lord. I afraid something like this might happen."

"You should get drunk too." I groped around for the bottle, which took time because my eyes at first would not focus. I held it up to the lamp. "I think there's some left. Help yourself." I started laughing. "You'd better because I certainly can't."

"Mr. Crane, you tell me I had a claim."

"Judge Scott made a liar out of me. He took all that law, Dred, and just threw it away, like so many scraps of useless paper no one wants anymore. There is no justice for slaves in Missouri. Go home, Dred."

"I ain't going home, Mr. Crane, not until you start acting like a lawyer instead of a drunk."

His tone sobered me slightly. "It was me acting like a lawyer that got you into this mess. Go home to your family. While you still have one."

"I ain't going to lose my family, not while there is a breath in me. Or you."

"I can't save your family, Dred."

"How you know that if you don't even try? Mr. Crane, you got to listen to me."

I began drinking again from the bottle.

A stinging blow to my cheek jerked my head to one side. I nearly dropped the bottle.

"Mr. Crane, I sorry I got to do that, but I need you to save my family. Without you, I got no hope."

I gingerly put a hand to my stinging cheek which, together with rising anger, began to clear my head. "Goddamn you, Dred Scott. I said, I can't save you."

"It ain't just me, Mr. Crane. How you going to save yourself if you don't save me?"

"What are you talking about?"

"When you is sick, you never stop talking about that Abigail girl back in Vermont. How you been looking for her in the woods on this hill, how once you find her you going to put dressings on her back. Still can't figure it, 'cause you was just a child. But there it is."

"You have nothing to do with Abigail White."

"I know I don't. But I don't think you see it that way, Mr. Crane. You save me, you saving yourself."

"Save myself from what? From what?" I was begging him to tell me.

"Only you know that. All I know's, you my only hope. And I'm the only hope that you got."

I looked at him uncertainly, sat up and then with some difficulty rose to my feet, putting a hand on the chair to hold myself upright. Dred's expression was a volatile mixture of hope, desperation, and fear. I was not drunk anymore, or at least not so drunk that I had failed to understand Dred. I looked around the office as though seeing it for the first time. I stared at the volumes of the Supreme Court case reports that lined the wall behind Mr. Field's desk. The volumes beckoned me to plunge into their depths and immerse myself in their wisdom.

"I thought you knew the penalty for striking a white man."

He grinned with relief. "Mr. Crane, I sure do."

"Didn't have a choice then, and don't now, is that it?"

"If you ain't got nothing to lose, Mr. Crane, then, well—you ain't got nothing to lose."

"Yes, I think that's right. Dred, go home." He was not entirely satisfied so I said, "No, no, I'm all right. Go home to your family and come back with them tomorrow. I'll be staying here to do some work." I picked up the bottle, went to an open window, and emptied what was left onto the street. "Doesn't that satisfy you?"

He still did not move.

"Dred, I have work to do. Remember, you can't read."

An even bigger grin lit his face. "Goodnight, Mr. Crane."

I was very tired and feeling hung over but I managed to clean up the office after he left. I sat in Mr. Field's chair and, fighting an urge to rest my aching head on the desk and fall asleep, began reading jurisdictional treatises, which proved fruitless. Then I picked up *Scott v. Emerson* but I was unable to finish the majority opinion. After each hateful sentence, my mind conjured up Judge Scott's shimmering jowls and glowing cigar. "*Boni judicis est ampliare justitiam.*" "What are the grounds for an attachment?" "What is the Statute of Frauds?" "What is the basis for diversity jurisdiction? . . . No hesitation, Mr. Crane. A lawyer cannot hesitate in a courtroom."

And then, I had the answer. The obvious idea simply formed itself. I sat thinking it over and then, smiling to myself, picked up legal paper and a pen, locked up the office, went to the law library and let myself in with the key that was a privilege of being a member of the Law Library Association. I lit a lamp and stood for a while in the silence, smelling the civilized aroma of leather-bound law books. I felt peace here, such as one experiences upon entering an empty church—and hope, for both Dred and myself. I retrieved several books from the shelves and a copy of the United States Constitution.

I did not leave until sunrise.

Chapter 18

Mr. Field put down the draft of Dred's declaration, which I had captioned *Scott v. Sanford*. He looked thoughtfully at the Webster painting.

"It is an ingenious, audacious idea for which you have no authority whatsoever."

"It has never been addressed by a federal court," I conceded, "but five state courts have recognized that free blacks residing there were citizens."

He gave me an irritated look. "All in the North undoubtedly. What good will—"

"One was North Carolina. *State v. Manuel.* Judge Gaston wrote that emancipation is the removal of the incapacity of slavery and that slaves manumitted there become freemen and therefore are citizens of North Carolina."

"If free blacks can be citizens in North Carolina, they can be citizens in Missouri. That's your premise?"

I nodded vigorously.

"All right." He leaned back in his chair. "Let me see if I have grasped your point. Dred is not free, but for purposes of whether the federal circuit court has diversity jurisdiction under the Constitution, the court must assume the truth of his allegations that he is free. Therefore, Dred, as a free negro, is assumed to be a citizen of Missouri. As a Missouri citizen, he sues John Sanford, a citizen of New York, Dred's new owner. The federal court has diversity jurisdiction inasmuch as it is a suit between citizens of different states. Is that what you are saying?"

I nodded again.

"Where did you get this idea?"

"From Judge Scott." At his surprised look, I said, "At my examination, Judge Scott asked me to state the basis for diversity jurisdiction in the federal courts. I answered residency and he blew a cloud of cigar smoke in my face." I imitated Judge Scott's grumpy rumble. "'Citizens, Mr. Crane, citizens of different states. Citizens of different states can sue each other in the federal courts.' It was the one question I answered wrong. God bless Judge Scott after all."

"I believe Judge Scott would be rather annoyed if you argued to him that a free black, no, a slave claiming to be free, is a citizen."

"But we will bring the case before Judge Wells in the federal circuit court. He's a Virginia man who has said more than once that slavery is a barrier to progress."

Mr. Field nodded his agreement. "I have been in Judge Wells's court many times. He is a cold fish but he is not filled with bile." He studied the declaration and shook his head. "Didn't they teach you at the Harvard Law School about the Privileges and Immunities Clause of the Constitution?"

I recited, "'The Citizens of each State shall be entitled to all Privileges and Immunities of Citizens in the several States.'"

"Samuel O'Fallon couldn't recite it but he'll find it soon enough. He will call us—you—a dirty abolitionist or worse." Mr. Field did a remarkable imitation of Samuel's snide voice. "'Arba Crane thinks that Dred Scott is a citizen of Missouri. Arba Crane thinks that Dred Scott is entitled to all of the privileges of his fellow white citizens in any state. Arba Crane thinks Dred Scott, or any free negro, can marry a white woman. Well, gentlemen of the jury, is that what you think?' Samuel will have a lot of fun with that before a Missouri jury, even in federal court."

"Citizenship under the Diversity Clause is not necessarily the same as under the Privileges and Immunities Clause. That's true of corporations, which can be citizens only for diversity jurisdiction."

Mr. Field shook his head. "It's a nice lawyers' argument, but try explaining that distinction to our slaveholding brethren. They won't argue the finer points of constitutional jurisprudence. They'll simply take up their pistols and bowie knives before allowing the word 'negro' to be linked to the word 'citizen.' For that matter, some of our fellow Vermonters would join them with enthusiasm."

"I would tell them that unless a free negro can sue as a citizen, he will have the special privilege of being immune from diversity suits, which whites do not have. I would point out the cases in which whites have sued free negroes under the Diversity Clause. As we say in Vermont—"

"—if it's good for the goose, it's good for the gander. I haven't forgotten."

"One of the cases was *LeGrand v. Darnall*. The attorney who brought the case against the free negro under the Diversity Clause was Roger Taney."

"Who, rumor has it, is currently the Chief Justice of our majestic United States Supreme Court." Mr. Field leaned back in his chair and put up his feet on a stool. "Well, you certainly have been working hard. You look quite tired, in fact."

It was midmorning and I had not slept for two nights. Anticipating his questions, I had spent hours in the Law Library preparing to answer them. Staring at the ceiling, Mr. Field said, "Even if you limit the argument to the Diversity Clause, they'll still say that you are opening the door for the dog to run out. Even if you win the jurisdictional point, you then have to persuade the federal circuit court to reject an interpretation of Missouri conflicts law issued by no less an authority than the highest court in Missouri. Can't you think of easier things to do?"

Neither of us spoke for a time.

I asked, "Don't they make you angry?"

"Not when I first came here. But . . ." His voice trailed away. "You can't solve all this with a lawsuit."

"We can help a man who asked his state's highest court for justice and was told there is none."

At the phrase "state's highest court," Mr. Field sat up, redfaced.

"Do you think Dred Scott is the first litigant to lose a case in a high court that he should have won? Is that what you think?" His voice was so harsh and bitter that it appeared we were reenacting an argument that had taken place many years before, except that I was playing the role of Mr. Field and he was playing that of my father.

"No, but I think that is why he is entitled to every inch that the federal courts will give him."

"An inch is all he may get." He calmed down. "Judge Wells is not the last word in the federal courts. However he rules, this case could very well go to the Supreme Court."

"Where there are four free-state Justices and Chief Justice Taney, who freed his own slaves and voted to free the *Amistad* slaves. Dred could win his freedom in the Supreme Court."

He was lost in thought.

"Mr. Field, you know what will happen if we do nothing."

He stared at the declaration.

"The family will be sold, probably apart," I said, as ruthless with him as Dred had been with me. "Dred will lose them."

His eyes were vague and distant. "Yes, Dred will lose his wife and children." Mr. Field rubbed his eyes and sighed. "I can no longer hear mine. For a time there were echoes in the rooms. The worst time was when I would close my eyes to try to sleep. At first, I drank. It helped but only a little. I have never believed in spirits, you see, and this was a contest between rational thought and superstition aided and abetted by fatigue." He smiled and shook his head. "Not much of a contest.

I tried to make out what they were saying but there were no sounds because it was all in my head, as I always knew. Gradually, the echoes faded away and then I began to wish I could hear them. That was the most painful part, when I couldn't hear them anymore. You see, Arba, I am haunted by spirits I can't see or hear."

He stood, put on his coat, and walked past me. I was so surprised that Mr. Field had revealed his feelings that I did not rise.

As he opened the door, he said, "I will meet you at the courthouse."

"You have an appointment? Now?"

"I plan to have lunch with an old friend."

With that, he closed the door and I was alone.

Exhausted, I fell asleep in the chair in Mr. Field's office and dreamed. I was a boy on Newfane Hill, hunting foxes and listening to the sound of thunder roll over the mist-shrouded mountain. Something drew me ever higher and higher until I reached the top of Newfane Hill, where I found Abigail White, who was trying to tell me that—

I awoke to the sound of someone knocking loudly at the door.

Opening it, I faced the imposing frame of Reverend Anderson and, behind him, Dred and Harriet and their children. The Reverend Anderson looked at me suspiciously.

They all crowded into my office. Dred rejected my suggestion that the children again wait in the outer room. He and Harriet sat in the hard-backed chairs in my office, while Eliza and Lizzie sat on the floor in front of them. Dred looked weary and Harriet seemed especially anxious. Standing, the Reverend Anderson said, "These poor people they come to me—"

"Harriet, she go to you, Reverend," said Dred quietly. Harriet turned on him with an angry look.

"And they say, 'Reverend, we are in trouble. You were right. The white folks' law ain't for us. Just like you told us.' And they asked me to come with them to hear what you got to say to them."

"Reverend, please have a seat. I do have something to tell you."

"I will stand, thank you." He moved next to Dred and Harriet.

I explained that Mr. Field and I would bring a new lawsuit on behalf of Dred and Harriet against John Sanford in the federal circuit court. When I had finished describing our plan for Dred and Harriet to sue as citizens of Missouri, they looked at each other and then at me.

The Reverend took a step toward me. "You are going to call a slave a citizen? These white judges, just like that, they are going to agree with you?"

"We have good arguments."

The Reverend Anderson moved even closer, looming over me and blocking my view of Dred and Harriet. "That's what you told these poor people the last time. And while you making these arguments, what's going to stop this family from being sold?"

"That's why we come here to see Mr. Crane," Dred said quickly to his daughters, who looked anxiously at their parents.

"That's right," said the Reverend. "We ain't going to let that happen."

Eliza and Lizzie stared at me as though I were about to perform a mighty feat, such as heroes do in fairy tales.

"That's the purpose of the new lawsuit. To stop you from being sold and set you free."

"And if you lose this lawsuit like you lost the last one," asked the Reverend, "what's going to happen? Mr. Crane, what's—?"

"We do what you and Mr. Field think is for the best," said Dred, cutting him off. "You say you think of something and you do. And if you say we citizens, then we be citizens. But how is being citizens going to help our children? I been thinking last night after we talk"—he did not mention my condition at the time we talked (and my cheek still stung from the slap of his callused palm)—"that I got faith in you, Mr. Crane, but not in the courts. We's sick to death about Eliza and Lizzie being sold by Mr. Sanford. Maybe you win this after all but it don't do no good if our children, they been sold in the meanwhile." Lizzie trembled and turned to her father. Dred put his hand on her shoulder.

"That's right, it don't do no good, no good at all," said the Reverend.

"Harriet and me," Dred said, "we start something with this here court. We ain't going to quit and run. We going to see it to the end, even if we lose. Maybe it do some good for the slave. And maybe it don't. If we gets sold, well, we been sold before. But Lizzie and Eliza, they too small, they just too small." He drew both daughters closer to him. They peered at me with large, fearful eyes from their temporary sanctuary in their father's arms.

The Crane family is not abolitionist in Vermont, my father had said, and you certainly will not be one in Missouri.

"We been hearing a lot about conflicts of law, Mr. Crane. Well, maybe God's law conflicts with the white man's law that you said would help Harriet and Dred." The Reverend Anderson appeared to have read my mind. "How you going to resolve that conflict, Mr. Crane?"

Are you an honest man and of good character? Judge Scott had asked me, as I raised my hand and swore to God faithfully to respect and promote the law as a member of the Missouri bar.

"How will I resolve it, Reverend? I will tell you. So please sit down."

The Reverend sat down and Harriet lost her angry look.

"I am going to get Eliza and Lizzie to a free state. And I'll file this case in federal court and take it to the Supreme Court of the United States if necessary. I can still win this family's freedom."

The children were wide-eyed and the adults looked at me with varying expressions of surprise and doubt. The Reverend, after recovering from his initial surprise, said, "Young man, since the day I put on this collar I been helping slaves cross into the promised land." The Reverend's voice was full of pride, and condescension. "I helped young men and women cross the Mississippi on cold dark nights lying in a rowboat under a blanket. I've hidden families in hay bales in the back of an ox cart, in potato holes, behind fireplaces, and in caves so black that a scratch of charcoal on the wall looks like chalk. What I have never done, you see, is send young children to freedom on their own and I am not going to start now. They get stopped by the bounty hunters, why, two young children on their own, well, I can take a chance with the grownups, but these children, no sir, we ain't taking that chance."

"Reverend, *I* will take them to Iowa. They will have emancipation papers so good that the sharpest slave lawyer won't even ask them a question."

"You will take them?" The Reverend was openly skeptical. "And where you going to get these papers, Mr. Crane?"

"I will take them." I added with a smile, "As to legal papers, Reverend, that's what we do here."

The Reverend looked at the shelves of law books, the heaps of affidavits and pleadings, the writing utensils, and all the other paraphernalia of a law office. His eyes fell on my law license, mounted on the wall and bearing Judge Scott's signature, which I had also stared at frequently since reading the *Scott* opinion.

"You would take this risk for these children?"

"I am familiar with the penalty under Missouri law for helping slaves escape."

He studied my face and then bowed his great, scorched head slightly. "I am most appreciative, Mr. Crane, and most impressed."

I looked at Dred, his eyes met mine, and he nodded ever so slightly. Eliza and Lizzie looked back and forth from Dred's face to mine and seemed reassured by what they saw.

"Now, we have to be in court."

Judge Hamilton's clerk called the matter, "Hear ye, hear ye, draw near and the cases of Dred Scott, a man of color, versus Irene Emerson, and Harriet, a woman of color, versus Irene Emerson, shall be heard."

We were all standing, Samuel and his law partner Lyman Norris, Mr. Field, Dred, Harriet, Taylor Blow, and myself, waiting for Judge Hamilton. Samuel gave me triumphant glances, the smirk never leaving his face. The Reverend Anderson sat in the back of the public seats with Eliza and Lizzie, who had grown ever more frightened on the walk to the courthouse. They huddled next to the Reverend, who had his huge arms around them, as though he might shield them from danger by his size alone.

Mr. Field whispered, "Make no arguments." I started to object, but he held up his hand. "Trust me, Arba."

Judge Hamilton appeared and took his seat at the bench, looming over us.

"Do you have an application, Mr. O'Fallon?"

Samuel was as smug as I had ever seen him. "Has your Honor received the mandate of that august body, the Missouri Supreme Court?" He solemnly drew out the words "Missouri Supreme Court" as though he were speaking of higher beings.

Judge Hamilton seemed reluctant to answer. Then he said in a low voice, "I have."

Samuel spoke crisply. "Pursuant to that mandate, the defendant moves for a return of her property, to wit, the slaves Dred Scott, Harriet, a woman of color, and the darky children, Eliza and Lizzie." A faint stir came from the back of the courtroom where the Reverend and the children sat. "The defendant also moves for restitution of the wages earned by the plaintiffs since the commencement of the lawsuit, with interest. Alternatively, we would accept payment under the bond posted by Mr. Taylor Blow. I have prepared an order for you to sign. With the court's permission, I will hand it to the clerk."

"You may."

Samuel, strutting like a peacock, walked up to the clerk and, with a flourish, handed him the order. The clerk then handed it to the judge, who took it and, leaning back in his chair, read it and then looked up.

"Mr. Crane, have you been served with this order?"

"Your Honor, I have received it."

Judge Hamilton stared at Dred and Harriet with a grim expression and then looked at Eliza and Lizzie even more grimly. The Reverend protectively tightened his embrace of the Scott children.

"Very well." Judge Hamilton picked up a pen and carefully wrote on the order. He handed it back to his clerk who handed it to Samuel, who examined it. His smile instantly disappeared and his face turned crimson with anger.

In a barely controlled fury, he said, "With all due respect, the court made a mistake."

"I made no mistake."

Samuel held up the order. I could see, in bold, clear letters, the words "Said motion be overruled. A. Hamilton."

"The Missouri Supreme Court gave you a mandate. You are bound to follow that mandate. This is illegal."

"This court is adjourned," said Judge Hamilton.

"Sir, you have no authority to do anything other than grant this application." He ripped up the order and threw the pieces on the floor.

"I said, Mr. O'Fallon, court is adjourned." Judge Hamilton left the courtroom and the sputtering Samuel O'Fallon.

"That goddamned abolitionist Yankee. I'll have him removed from office and run out of this state. Damn him, Arba, he knows better than that. That is an illegal order."

"I think, Samuel, that your legal option is to file an appeal to the Missouri Supreme Court."

He turned on me in a fury. "You'd like that, wouldn't you, Arba? Give your clients time to hightail it out of the state."

"My clients, Samuel, have had plenty of time to do that but they are still here." I gathered up my papers. I was filled with awe at Judge Hamilton's act. "Unlike your client."

We began filing out. As Dred and his family walked by Samuel O'Fallon, Samuel snarled at them, "Before I'm done the free niggers will wish they were slaves." The children drew closer to their parents.

"Don't talk to them that way." I motioned to Dred and Harriet to take Eliza and Lizzie out of the courtroom.

"Don't you talk to me like that. Quite the abolitionist nigger lover, aren't you? I had you figured exactly right."

"I've nothing to say to the likes of you."

Samuel seemed startled, not so much by my words but by the contempt in my face that had welled up from some fathomless depth of my soul, and took a step back. Perhaps if I had slept more in the last two days I might have held my tongue further. But, as I walked past him, I did have something to say to him.

"Samuel, you have the manners of a boor."

Now there was a tight but triumphant smile on his face. He put his hand out to stop me from walking away. "That, sir, is an insult. I demand that you apologize."

Mr. Field and Dred stared at me.

"Not only will I not apologize but I will repeat it. You are an ill-mannered boor."

Mr. Field, looking concerned, walked over.

"You shall not insult me. We shall soon settle this."

I started at him, but Mr. Field moved between us. "Arba, our business here is over." Lyman Norris came over to Samuel, took him by the arm and began marching him out of the courtroom, but Samuel broke free, reached into his pocket, and handed me a card. "I demand satisfaction by way of an apology. If not, sir, then you may choose your weapons."

I took the card, ripped it in two, and let the pieces fall to the floor. I did not fully appreciate that I had been challenged to a duel until I saw the alarmed expression on the faces of Mr. Field and Dred Scott.

"We will deal with this later," Mr Field said and led me outside and down the courthouse steps.

I said to Dred and Harriet, "You have a friend on the bench. That took courage on Judge Hamilton's part. Do I have your permission to proceed?"

"Mr. Crane," said Dred, "Harriet and me, we be wanting to go to the other court. But that man in there—" He stopped speaking, stared at me, and just shook his head.

I held up a hand. "Don't worry about him. Taylor, how soon will the sale to John Sanford be complete?"

"Word is that John Sanford will be in St. Louis in two weeks," said Taylor. "Likely he'll sign the papers then."

"When he arrives we will serve him with the new lawsuit in federal court."

The Scott family and the Reverend left more cheerfully than when they had come to Mr. Field's office that morning, although Dred gave me a last lingering look of concern and exasperation. I returned to the office with Mr. Field, who walked briskly and with a jaunty high step. I had not seen him like this in some time.

"Did you expect Judge Hamilton to deny Samuel's application?"

He did not reply.

"Is that whom you had lunch with?"

"Yes, it was a most pleasant lunch."

"Did you discuss the case?"

"That would have been inappropriate. We did not discuss the case before him. But"—I saw a faint smile—"I did mention that we would be filing a new one shortly in the federal circuit court that might have some prospect of reaching the United States Supreme Court. He simply said that was none of his concern. We then turned to reminiscing about our days as young lawyers new to Missouri."

"I see. I'm sure you were as surprised as the rest of us when he denied Samuel's motion."

He did not comment but instead said, "I regret the day I asked Samuel to meet you at the levee. I shall arrange for a suitable settlement."

"I have no intention of apologizing. I would rather accept his ridiculous challenge."

"I cannot afford the loss of your services. Besides, your parents would hardly forgive me if I allowed you to fight a duel, let alone lose one."

His lightheartedness was unconvincing. It was starting to dawn on me that, even by my standards, I had acted intemperately. "I am a good shot."

"Only a fool would fight a hothead like Samuel O'Fallon. Don't you become one either. The art of the duel is to avoid it gracefully and with reputation intact." Lowering his voice, he said, "I did not understand that principle when I was young and hotheaded. I did things too painful to recall. They were nearly my undoing."

I had made no vows of silence. "Father once told me that passion can be forgiven when it is driven by love."

He slowed his pace as though surprised by my words. His expression reminded me of his reaction to the unexpected appearance of Mary Almira Clark outside his law office. He looked at me so intently that it seemed he was trying to read my thoughts. "I am sure your father told you many things. He knows even better than I that too much passion can sometimes never be forgiven, whatever the justification."

I did not have the courage to ask him what he was trying to tell me. I was not certain that Mr. Field would have explained, in any event. His manner suggested that I ask my father.

We walked the rest of the way to the law office without speaking. In the office, Mr. Field, glancing at the shredded wallpaper, picked up my draft of Dred's declaration. "Go home and get some sleep. I will complete the declaration. We will serve and file it as soon as Taylor gives word of the sale. And we will discuss the matter of Mr. O'Fallon when you are rested."

I started to protest but he silenced me. "You have done brilliant work. I will finish it. Tell me, do you like a hard fight?"

"If it's in a good cause."

"Well, you are in for a hard fight." He studied my draft and then looked at the caption I had written for Harriet's declaration. "I have some ideas, but first, that caption needs changing."

"It's the same caption as her summons in *Scott v. Emerson*."

"Yes, 'Harriet, a woman of color.' It should be 'Harriet Scott, then and still the wife of the plaintiff.'"

"The clerk of the St. Louis Circuit Court started to write it that way on the summons when I filed *Scott v. Emerson* but then struck it out."

"In the federal circuit court, we write the caption. Harriet will be identified properly. This is a man and woman bound by the sacred bond of marriage." His next words seemed to bring to a close the distant, unhappy past.

"We may not win the case." He looked directly at me. "But at least we can make this court honor Dred's marriage. At least we can do that."

He sat at the desk to work on the petition and, just before I was out the door, said over his shoulder, "Your salary this week will be reduced to cover the cost of repair to the wall and the purchase of a new case reporter."

I glimpsed a gratifying trace of a smile on his face as he bent his head to his work.

That was the only day that Roswell Field and I ever acknowledged to each other the case of *Clark v. Field*. That night I slept the sound, dreamless sleep of the utterly spent, awoke refreshed at least in spirit, if not in body, and left early for the office. It was a bright, sunny morning and the idea of a duel with a former Harvard Law School classmate seemed less probable than the day before.

Mr. Field had apparently worked until early in the morning because he had finished Dred's declaration and had begun working on Harriet's. The documents were on his desk covered with black blotting sand. I shook off the sand and read the first page of Dred's redrafted declaration with the long forgotten sensation of what it was like to be a child on a narrow path leading to a forbidding forest. The forest warned, "Here there be dragons," but I took the path nonetheless, fully aware it would lead both the Scotts and me to our respective fates.

Dred Scott, of St. Louis, in the State of Missouri, and a citizen of the United States, complains of John F. A. Sanford, of the city of New York, and a citizen of New York, in a plea of trespass, for that the defendant heretofore at St. Louis, in the county of St. Louis and State of Missouri, without law or right held him as a slave and restrained him of his liberty . . .

Chapter 19

D ear Arba:

  I have shown the ruling by the Missouri Supreme Court to several friends, including Judge Watkins from Townshend, who, by the way, now sits on the Superior Court. All remarked at its intemperate nature and lack of respect for precedent. However, more than one pointed out that, precedent aside, each state has the right to decide for itself what recognition to give the laws of another state.

  I certainly respect your loyalty to your clients. Your idea of suing under the Diversity Clause is original and clever. It may even carry the day in federal court. But to what end? I, like many Vermonters, thought sectionalism was a sleeping tiger, but the beast is stirring again. If Congress passes the Kansas-Nebraska Act, as seems likely, Senator Douglas will be able to travel from Chicago to Boston by the light of his *burning effigies. He chants popular sovereignty like a religious catechism, but it can mean only that mob rule decides whether Kansas is to be a free or slave state. I even hear talk of New England men, abolitionists all I am sure, moving to Kansas. No good will come of it.*

I therefore ask you, will a ruling by a federal court in Missouri that slaves have the right to sue as citizens calm the angry animal? I hardly think so, and more likely, it will only further enrage it. The Crane family should keep its distance. I remind you that the Constitution enshrines slavery. While some may debate both peacefully and otherwise whether slavery should be extended to the vastness of the West, no one save the most radical abolitionist advocates tampering with slavery in the states where it already exists, which includes the one in which you have chosen to practice law, at least for the time being.

Your father

My father's letter did not reach me until after we had served John Sanford with the new lawsuit and Taylor Blow had agreed to act as my second. Sanford's attorneys, of whom Samuel O'Fallon was not one, promptly filed a plea in abatement to dismiss the lawsuit on the ground that Dred was not, and could never be, a citizen because "he is a negro of African descent, his ancestors being of pure African blood and were brought into this country and sold as negro slaves." The Sanford plea cited rulings under the Privileges and Immunities Clause that free negroes were not citizens.

By day I worked on a demurrer to the Sanford plea in abatement and by night secretly forged the manumission documents for Eliza and Lizzie. Mr. Field and I were delighted that the Sanford plea in abatement was so broadly and ineptly drawn. Our demurrer argued forcefully that Dred Scott's African descent alone did not bar him either from citizenship or from the right to sue. Citizenship under the Diversity Clause, unlike the Privileges and Immunities Clause, we contended, required nothing more than residence. We cited the states that allowed free negroes to vote on the basis of residence and pointed out that a negro could sue in the United States courts if he was a citizen of another country. Why should a native-born American negro not have the same right?

"I regret to report that compromise is not in the nature of young Mr. O'Fallon," said Taylor at a meeting in Mr. Field's office to discuss the duel. "He still demands, as his second explained to me, 'the satisfaction which is due one gentleman to another for such an indignity.'"

"Colonel O'Fallon said pretty much the same thing to me." Mr. Field had grown increasingly somber as his efforts to avoid a duel had met with no success.

"Arba," said Taylor, "terms are requested. It was suggested that Bloody Island would be a suitable venue."

"Arba, you shall have to apologize." Mr. Field spoke as if there were no room for argument.

"For speaking the truth? I shall do no such thing."

"You do not want to kill him, and if he were to kill you, then you would die a fool's death."

Taylor, to Mr. Field's annoyance, did not entirely agree. "Some say that death is preferable to certain indignities."

"Dueling is a barbarous practice," said Mr. Field. "Men keep their reputations by throwing away their lives."

I remembered the look in Samuel O'Fallon's eyes and the rage that had simmered in me. "It is an asinine custom. But I cannot choose between my life and my reputation."

"That, I am afraid, is the point of an affair of honor," said Taylor. "But, we have delayed as long as we could. They insist on terms."

"I am not ready." My abruptness took them by surprise. "I will fight him but I am not ready yet." I went to my desk, pulled out a piece of paper, and wrote for a few minutes. I came back and handed the paper to Taylor, who read it and, an amused look on his face, handed it to Mr. Field, who appeared dubious about its contents.

Dear Sir:

My principal's articles of combat are as follows. The weapons shall be broadswords of equal length. The parties shall fight until either be so much injured as to prevent the combat from being continued with swords, when immediate resort shall be had to rifles, which neither of the principals shall have seen until they are to be used.

Respectfully,

Taylor Blow

Mr. Field shook his head. "Arba—"

I politely interrupted. "I must have some time. Taylor, please deliver these terms today."

Taylor reread my terms. "I don't know whether to hope he accepts or rejects."

Feeling the same nervous excitement as on the day I left Newfane, I set out on foot for the white clapboard building near the free negro quarter. By the time I arrived, the Second African Baptist Church was already in session. Through the open doors I could see packed, backless pews and, facing them from the pulpit, the huge figure of the Reverend Anderson. The women wore their colorful turbans and the men were dressed in tattered coats. A few whites sat among them, and to my dismay, standing in the back, a well-dressed white man with an official air watched the Reverend closely.

I waited by the doorway, out of the man's sight, and listened to the reverberating voice of the Reverend Anderson ask his congregation, "I know you wondering if you ever going to get to Canaan. Well, the Lord knows when, doesn't He?"

They responded in unison. "Yes He does, yes He does."

"The Good Lord has given us hope and He knows that we ain't ever going to lose that hope. So now we going to sing to the Good Lord. We going to sing loud. We going to rock the gates of Heaven."

They sang. The church seemed too small and frail to contain the singing and not burst apart. Members of the congregation shouted and moaned and swayed. The singing ended with a hymn that faded away.

A few more beatings of the wind and rain,
Ere the winter will be over—
Glory, Hallelujah!
Some friends has gone before me.
I must try to go and meet them—
Glory, Hallelujah!

The Reverend Anderson said a few words I could not hear and then the congregation began filing out. Those in the front waited until the scowling white man, whom I took to be a member of the Anti-Abolitionist Society, had left the church. After he had climbed into a carriage and driven away, I went inside the church, squeezing past the departing worshipers, who squinted and shaded their eyes as they came into the sunlight. They spoke in soft whispers, like the rustle of leaves in a mild breeze, and their tired faces hinted at the week of labor that awaited them before they could listen again to the Reverend tell them that the Land of Canaan was only a matter of time and God's will.

The Reverend stood inside the entrance talking to lingering members of his congregation. Seeing me, the Reverend bade goodbye to the last of his flock.

"You should have joined us this morning, Mr. Crane. Our voices were heard in the rafters of Heaven. Only the courageous sing like that."

I showed him the papers, including a quitclaim deed and a license for Eliza and Lizzie Hill to live in Iowa as free blacks, conditioned on their "good behavior."

He examined them thoughtfully, as I explained the purpose of each. "These look mighty good, mighty good. You see, Mr. Crane, as hard as it is to get them to the free state, it's even harder keeping them there once the bounty hunters come looking. But these will keep them there." He added, "I expect that Roswell doesn't know about this."

"Mr. Field," I spoke with some emphasis, "has no knowledge of these papers or anything else. You will keep it that way." I said, "For his sake, not mine."

"I think I know Roswell Field better than you do, Mr. Crane. You needn't worry about him. But the secret is safe with me."

Dred and Eliza and Lizzie sat in the front pew. Dred had dressed cheerfully for the occasion, wearing the same jaunty suit that he had worn to his trial. Eliza and Lizzie wore plain blue frocks and bonnets. Dred held on his lap a multicolored quilt. Two neatly wrapped and tied bundles sat on the pew next to him.

"Dred, Mr. Crane has brought your children's tickets to the road to freedom," said the Reverend.

Dred slowly stood and handed the quilt to Eliza, who arranged it on her lap. Eliza and Lizzie held each other's hands and watched their father walk over to me. His face was a study in contained grief. It was as hard to look him in the eyes now as when I had to tell him about the decision by the Missouri Supreme Court. Moved by his agony, I embraced him, which startled the Reverend Anderson, since this was a sight he had not seen before.

"Dred," said the Reverend, "we need to be about this business."

Dred stepped back. "Harriet, she can't come 'cause she got to take care of another sick white woman." He looked at Eliza and Lizzie as though fixing their appearance in his mind. "Children, stand up. Mr. Crane is here."

Eliza tucked the quilt carefully under her arm and, still clutching her younger sister's hand, came over to me. I knelt and hugged each child.

The Reverend looked impatiently at his watch. "Dred, it's time."

"Just once more." Dred turned to his children. Eliza handed him the quilt. Dred unfolded it to reveal a variety of patterns.

"After Mr. Crane, when he have to leave you, then you got to remember the map on the quilt and watch for the signs. Now, last time, Eliza, what do this one mean?" He pointed at a pattern in one corner of the quilt. It looked like a row of log cabins overlaid with jagged streaks of black lightning.

"If we see that on the quilt hanging from the house, then we can knock on the door."

"That's right. That's a safe place for you. And this one?" Dred gestured at a pattern of small circles.

"Don't stop."

"What else, girl?"

"We puts on our bonnets and keeps our eyes on the ground."

Dred waved his hand in front of a pattern of boxes. "Them tumbling boxes, what you do if you see that?"

"We gets going."

The Reverend nodded. "They'll be fine, Dred. They'll do just fine." He gently took the quilt from Dred, who did not let go at first, folded it, placed it inside a white box, and slid the box under a pew where it was hidden from view.

"Don't you go falling in the mud again," Dred said to Lizzie, adjusting her bonnet. "Your mother ain't going to be there to clean you up." Dred took the legal papers from the Reverend, untied one bundle, and tucked the papers inside. In the bundle was the inkwell and sander that I had given his daughters. Dred tied and retied the strings, and then handed the bundles to his daughters, who clutched them to their bosoms. "Eliza, if the white man say, where the papers, then you get out them papers. Don't look scared, you just hand them papers over like you a free woman. And you got to look like a woman. Don't go acting like you a child."

"Yes, papa." There was no fear in Eliza's face, only studied obedience to her father.

"What them papers say?"

"Dred—" said the Reverend.

"One last time, that's all."

"I'm Henry Cooper's emancipated slave Eliza Hill and this here's my sister Lizzie." Eliza carefully repeated the rest of the information on the documents. Her father nodded his approval and then turned to his youngest child.

"What's your name?"

His younger daughter smiled mischievously as though this were only a game. "My name is Lizzie Hill."

"Good, child," said Dred, relieved. He put a hand on his youngest daughter's shoulder.

"Reverend," I said, "Let's go outside."

We left Dred and his daughters to their parting sorrows and walked outside. Before coming into the harsh sunlight, I glanced back. Dred sat down on a pew and arranged his daughters on either side of him. Putting an arm around each, Dred drew them closer. Eliza and Lizzie rested their heads on his shoulders. Dred sang a soft and soothing hymn whose words I could not hear but which I guessed was the hymn that Dred's father had sung to him when he crawled into his lap like a kitten.

We waited by the wagon, which was filled with piles of old clothes for the children to hide under. It was a hot day to be wearing a collar and the Reverend's face was shiny with sweat. We both looked around but no one was in sight.

"We use to go across the river," said the Reverend, "but Illinois is a harder place for the runaways than it use to be. Lord, how I hated that river."

I climbed onto the wagon and picked up the reins.

"Keep the children under those clothes until you get to Iowa." He added, "Bless you, Mr. Crane."

"Give your blessings to the Scotts, for they need it more than I."

"Don't you know your *Psalms*, Mr. Crane? 'Blessed is the man that walketh not in the counsel of the ungodly.'"

"Jesus taught that the slaves should be treated kindly but not freed. Do you bless Him?"

The Reverend laughed deeply. "I have done so every day since I put on this collar because at least He knew that He wasn't perfect and, like the rest of us, needed forgiveness."

He looked around. "Are you afraid, Mr. Crane?"

"Should I be?"

"I was afraid, the first time I rowed across that river. My only passenger was a pretty girl who looked as scared as I felt. It seemed like I rowed all night but it was short, too, because when I reached the other side the girl would be gone. They told me to row to a tall light. When I finally reached it, men were waiting. Two of them reached down and grabbed the girl. Another man took my arm. I was trembling, thought the Maker was ready for me. 'You hungry, boy?' he asked me. If he hadn't been holding my arm I would have fallen backwards into the river. Never did see that girl again."

He again looked around to be sure that no one was watching and then called to the church, "Dred, we can't wait longer."

Dred appeared with his daughters, holding their hands.

With an effort that appeared to cause physical pain, Dred let go. "You go now." His voice was strained. He looked at me. "Take care of my children, Arba." It was the only time he ever called me by my first name.

Breaking away from their father, Eliza and Lizzie, carrying their bundles, walked quickly to the wagon and climbed in the back, sitting on each side half-turned toward their father. I had seen tears at the slave auction my first days in St. Louis when hope was lost completely, but Dred and his children shed no tears. I snapped the reins at the horses and the wagon rolled away. I glanced back at Dred, who squinted and shaded his face with one hand and watched as the wagon drew away his daughters, who stared with large brown eyes and expressionless faces as their father grew more distant. Then they crawled under the mounds of clothes like small gentle creatures burrowing into a safe den in a forest. Every time I looked back, until he grew too distant for me to see him, Dred was standing motionless in front of the church, still holding his hand over his eyes.

><del></del>~

We journeyed in peace through the wilds north of St. Louis, where I had ridden madly on the way back to Dred's trial. To confuse any pursuers, I took a route west before heading north again. Each night we pulled off the road and Eliza and Lizzie came out from under the clothes, gratefully breathing fresh air. While I hunted for rabbit or squirrel, they wandered through the woods to gather sticks for a cooking fire. After we ate, I told them fairy tales. They listened with enchantment, bright eyes gleaming in the firelight. We slept each night in the wagon, the heaps of clothes our bedding, each child nestling close as though I would keep them safe from evil spirits. I lay staring at the bountiful, blinking stars, hearing the soft breathing of the two sleeping slave children, and thinking how long it had been since I had last seen my sisters' graves.

I drifted off to sleep only to be awakened when Lizzie or Eliza cried out in their sleep, which one or both did every night of our journey together. At first I listened helplessly to their demons and then reached out and gently rocked the tormented child until her anguish had subsided and she fell into dreamless sleep.

Two days before we reached Iowa I stopped in a small town to buy provisions and encountered a band of men on their way west who had paused to rest their horses. They were mostly unshaven and uncombed, wearing rickety straw hats, torn shirts, buttonless corduroys, and mud-covered boots. All were armed with squirrel rifles, pistols, knives, or daggers, many with two or more weapons. They swore a lot and boasted about how many abolitionists they were going to kill once they got to Kansas.

I attracted the attention of one rough-looking fellow who wore a slouched hat adorned with a turkey feather. The handles of large bowie knives projected from both boot tops, revolvers were fastened to both sides of his leather belt, and a carbine was swung over his shoulder. He walked up to me, grimaced, and spat.

"You one of them psalm-singing button makers from New England?"

"I am a lawyer from St. Louis."

"What's a lawyer doing with a wagon full of old clothes?" I glanced casually at the wagon where Eliza and Lizzie lay under the clothes.

"Relief, sir, Christian relief. I may be a lawyer but I am also a Christian."

He spat again. "I'll bet you've got slaves under them clothes. I have a mind to look."

I went to the wagon, grabbed a pistol and pointed it at him. "Look all you like but, sir, if you find no slaves then I will have to shoot you for having so grossly insulted me. I am no abolitionist."

He laughed, revealing broken and dirty teeth, and unslung his carbine. "Lawyers can't shoot."

With no hesitation I sighted and fired at a sign across the street, neatly putting a bullet hole in the "o" in the word "apothecary." An aproned man came out of the doorway below the sign with an angry expression on his face, but after looking at the two of us, he turned abruptly and went back inside.

The ruffian stared at the sign. "Nice shot, lawyer."

"Do you still wish to search that wagon?"

"I'll bet if I did I'd find slaves in there." There was less certainty in his voice.

"Then look. But I still have bullets in this pistol."

He seemed tempted and I feared for a moment that all might be lost but then he laughed. "I never met no lawyer worth a damn. I didn't ride this far to kill lawyers in Iowa. I'm going to Kansas to kill abolitionists." He slung the carbine over his shoulder and walked off. My shirt was wet with perspiration.

After we had put some distance between us and the town, a small voice from under the clothes asked, "Mr. Crane, why do white folks hate us so much if we try to be free?"

I supposed there were many answers. "I wish I knew, Eliza."

The countryside was peaceful, filled with neat, trim farms that looked as though there were no cares in this world.

"My daddy, he says you different than most white folks."

"Did he say why I am different?"

She answered my question with one of her own. "Mr. Crane, don't you know?"

Having no answer, I snapped hard on the reins and the wagon picked up speed and Iowa drew so close that I thought I might reach out and touch it.

Chapter 20

My dear Mr. Blow:

    I hereby inform you that I have refused to allow my principal to fight with the uncivilized weapons selected by your principal inasmuch as they are not usual on such occasions. Dueling is a custom whose usage depends entirely on custom. The weapons are established by custom and that custom excludes the use of the broadsword. It also excludes the use of the tomahawk. We await further terms on the basis of customary weapons.

Your obedient servant

W.C. Richards

The time consumed by this pointless exchange and the succeeding lengthy negotiation of date and time, place, and appropriate weapons had allowed me to get Dred's children out of Missouri and win the jurisdictional argument before Judge Wells in the United States Circuit Court. To my considerable satisfaction and relief, Judge Wells agreed that if Dred is a free negro then he is entitled to sue in the federal courts. He accepted all of our arguments and held that "every person born in the United States and capable of holding property was a citizen having the right to sue in the United States courts."

We then met with John Sanford's lawyer, Hugh Garland, who rejected out of hand any settlement. Garland was no Samuel O'Fallon and therefore was quite businesslike. We managed to agree on two points that made the proceedings more efficient. The first was that Garland could file a new answer because his original answer, that persons of African descent can never be citizens, had been overruled. Since he was not appealing Judge Wells's jurisdictional ruling, a new answer conceded jurisdiction. I felt this meant the jurisdictional issue would not arise again and therefore we had won a significant victory. Second, we agreed on a statement of facts which would be read to the jury at trial, instead of presenting evidence through witnesses. The statement conceded all the essential facts that we had argued before Judge Hamilton in *Scott v. Emerson,* including Dred's residence in Illinois and at Fort Snelling. Garland even agreed that John Sanford was the new owner of Dred and Harriet, something that Taylor Blow admitted he had not been able to confirm.

The trial, if that is the right word for it, was held in a courtroom that was a poor cousin to the Circuit Court of St. Louis County where we had tried *Scott v. Emerson* before Judge Hamilton. The courtroom was stuffy and noise from the street sometimes made it difficult to hear Judge Wells, even though his voice was sharp and shrill.

Neither side called any witnesses and the only issue at trial was whether Dred was free. The only task for the jury was to apply Judge Wells's charge to the agreed facts. Mr. Field requested that Judge Wells instruct the jury that Dred was free by operation of the laws of Illinois and the Missouri Compromise. He refused, with the explanation that he was obligated to follow the law of Missouri as stated in *Scott v. Emerson.* As he told us, "The United States courts follow the state courts in regard to the interpretation of their own law. I am bound in this case to take the interpretation of the law of Missouri from the Supreme Court of the state. The authorities you have cited to me, rightly or wrongly, are no longer the law of this state."

Then, with an awkward, jerky manner of speaking, in which gestures were unrelated to words, Judge Wells told the jury that the removal of a slave by his master to a free state or territory freed the slave, but on return to Missouri, the master's right to the slave reattached. Although this was only my second day in Judge Wells's courtroom, I had observed him enough to appreciate his discomfort at giving these instructions. Every now and then he glanced at our table, where Dred and Harriet sat quietly, just as they had at the trial of *Scott v. Emerson*. As he read from his charge, the strained look on his face suggested that he had been forced to engage in an unpleasant task. After the trial, he told Mr. Field, "I may say to you that my feelings were deeply interested in favor of these poor people, and I wish the law was in favor of their freedom."

Given these instructions, the jury had little choice but to return a verdict for John Sanford, and so our strange little trial ended. It lacked the drama of *Scott v. Emerson*, and at its close the winner and his lawyer were not greatly elated—in fact, John Sanford was not even there—and our side not highly disappointed. From the outset of the trial, the shared but unexpressed understanding in the courtroom had been that, whatever the outcome in the federal circuit court, the case would go to the supreme judicial body of the land. After the jury had left, we moved to set aside the verdict, which Judge Wells overruled. We then presented a bill of exceptions, which Judge Wells approved, and so Dred and I set foot on the road to the Supreme Court.

Mr. Field drafted a letter to the Washington City lawyer, Montgomery Blair, inquiring whether Blair "should feel interest enough in the case to give it such attention as to bring it to a hearing and decision by the Supreme Court. By such action, the cause of humanity may be served! At all events a much disputed question would be settled by the highest court in the nation."

Mr. Field said, as I dubiously handed back the letter, "I know of no one better than Montgomery Blair. He was United States Attorney in Missouri and comes from one of the most politically influential families in Washington City. His father was an advisor to President Jackson."

"The Blair family keeps slaves on a Maryland estate."

"Their support for the Republican Party should reassure you. His brother, Frank Blair, helped start the Republican party here in St. Louis." Passage of the Kansas-Nebraska bill had provoked a spontaneous uprising in the North and virtually every organization that opposed the extension of slavery had adopted the name Republican.

"Mr. Field, I should argue Dred's case. I have won fifteen cases in the Missouri Supreme Court, all that I argued except *Scott v. Emerson*. I know the case better than Montgomery Blair ever will." I added, "I will survive the duel."

Mr. Field did not reply. His sons had returned from Vermont, which restored some of his vigor, but he had aged far more than his years could explain.

Montgomery Blair not only accepted, but wrote that he would take the case without fee. "The case involves important issues, which might just possibly be engulfed in the great political controversy now emerging in relation to the power of Congress over the territory of the United States."

Even though Montgomery Blair would not charge a fee, we still needed money to pay for brief printing costs and filing fees. I wrote a pamphlet about Dred and the case to help raise the money. I made up Dred's words:

The judge said that according to these laws while I was in Illinois and Wisconsin I was a free man—just as good as my Master—and that I had as much right to make a slave of a white man as a white man to make a slave of me. I was sorry nobody ever told me that while I was there. Yet I was glad to have the judge talk so, for I thought he would set me free. But after a little while the judge said that as soon as my Master got me back on this side of the line of Missouri my right to be free was gone; and that I and my wife and children became nothing but so many pieces of property. I thought it hard that white men should draw a line of their own on the face of the earth and on one side of which a black man was to become no man at all, and never say a word to the black man about it until they got him on that side of the line. My fellow countrymen, can any of you help me in my day of trial?

I read the pamphlet to Dred and Harriet when, just before the duel, they came to the office with gifts for me. When I finished, Dred said, "That's the truth, but I sure don't talk as fine as that."

"It has to be written as though you received the same education I did."

Dred accepted my explanation without comment.

"I have no news of Eliza and Lizzie," I said, even though I hadn't been asked. Only the Reverend Anderson and I knew Eliza and Lizzie's location.

"Long as we don't hear anything they doing fine," said Harriet, who did not appear to have convinced herself that was true anymore than she convinced me. With Irene Emerson gone and her brother in New York, no one in St. Louis had noticed the disappearance of two slave children.

Dred suddenly said, "Mr. Crane, you a smart man. Why you doing this duel? It gonna get you killed. I get you out of that fire and take care of you when you is sick. But I can't fight this man."

"I don't have a choice."

"You got so much to choose it make me dizzy in the head. So why you choosing to die?"

"I am not going to lose this duel."

"He sure don't think he going to lose. He wouldn't be fighting it if he did. Neither of you going to find out which one is right until one of you is dead. I just don't understand white folks."

"I am going to fight."

Harriet had brought me a gift wrapped in plain paper. I unwrapped it and held up a handsome scarf cut from a bolt of jersey. Embroidered on the scarf was a log cabin pattern with black lightning bolts.

"There's a safe place nearby," I managed to say with some effort.

Harriet said quietly, "We be hoping that there's a safe place for you, Mr. Crane."

"And for you," I said, but they did not appear to believe that they would ever be safe. "Dred, if anything does happen your case will still be argued by Mr. Blair in the Supreme Court." My voice did not falter but they both looked startled, as though they never expected me to acknowledge the possibility. "He is a very able Supreme Court advocate."

Dred shook his head, genuinely angry at me. "Mr. Crane, I can't win this case without you. Don't you know that by now?"

I did not answer.

"Well, I do some thinking. If you going to fight it then you got to do it right. You got to wear the right clothes."

Mystified, I asked, "What do you mean?"

"Here, this cost me my wages for a whole week." He handed me his gift, a wrapped bulky package, which I opened to find bright red flannel underwear.

A letter from Montgomery Blair arrived just before I set out for Bloody Island. Mr. Field handed it to me, saying, "Montgomery accepted my suggestion that you do part of the argument. It is a privilege for any lawyer to argue a case in the Supreme Court. I suppose that even so you will not be dissuaded from this foolish enterprise."

"I am afraid I will not be, Mr. Field." He nodded as though expecting my response and abruptly left the room.

Blair also wrote that my pamphlet had secured the services of an eminent lawyer before the Supreme Court—for the defendant, John Sanford. Blair wrote that he had encountered Missouri Senator Henry Geyer, who informed Blair that he had been retained to represent Sanford before the Supreme Court. Blair observed that he had not associated Geyer with slave cases such as this and wondered why Senator Geyer's client was going to such trouble over a slave no one wanted. Senator Geyer mentioned that the pamphlet had stirred up much indignation in Southern circles, and in consequence, he had offered his services without fee. He added, "Mr. Sanford is my client, but he is not the real defendant."

Montgomery Blair inquired as to who the real defendant might be.

"The real defendant, sir, and whom I said I would represent in addition to Mr. Sanford, is slavery itself."

Taylor and I pushed off from the riverbank in a small skiff. We at first did not speak while he strained at the oars. The water lapped against the boat as the oars rose and fell with an inexorable rhythm that drew me ever closer to Bloody Island. I sat facing Taylor, who was perspiring from the exertion of rowing, while I shivered in the cool morning mist that swirled on the river. I wore striped pantaloons, a vest, a newly laundered shirt, a fine coat, and a top hat. On my lap was a mahogany box with two pistols. The leaves of the cottonwoods and willows had begun to yellow. I smelled rotting driftwood.

"Taylor," I finally said, because the morning quiet had grown uncomfortable, "were you afraid when you fought?"

"I only recall cold anger."

"What happened?"

"We both missed and then reached agreement that honor had been satisfied."

"Whose honor had been offended in the first place?"

"Why, it was . . ." He paused and shook his head. "I really cannot remember."

"I do not think that both of us will miss."

"Nor do I." Neither of us spoke as the mists parted and Bloody Island appeared. I looked back but I could barely see the St. Louis side of the river, which was one reason why Bloody Island had been the location for the settlement of so many affairs of honor, illegal for nearly two decades under Missouri law. I idly wondered how many times I had broken the law of Missouri since taking my oath as a lawyer to uphold it.

As the rowboat scraped the bottom, Taylor shipped the oars. After we were on the island bank, I handed him the box of pistols and a letter to my father.

"Taylor."

"Yes?"

"If . . . anything should happen, please try to explain to Dred that I had no choice in this. The last thing he said to me was, 'Mr. Crane, you can say what you want but this here fight, it just don't make any sense to me.'"

Taylor nodded.

"And I want you to get word to Kate. Tell her . . ."

He waited for me to complete the sentence but the words never came.

Together, we walked to a clearing where Samuel O'Fallon waited with his second and two doctors selected by agreement between the seconds. Samuel, who also wore morning dress and top hat, had been joking and laughing with his second and the doctors. As we approached he stopped smiling and fixed me with a glare. I returned his look with a disdainful glance, which seemed only to enrage him even more. Was this our destiny? Had I held my tongue in Judge Hamilton's courtroom, would we sooner or later have taken up arms against each other anyway? Was it his anger over my representation of Dred or jealousy over my brief affair with Kate Fox or lingering bitterness from our days at the Harvard Law School, or did it go even deeper than anything that had taken place between us? "The resentment is not to be underestimated," Taylor had said.

Samuel and I remained apart while our seconds met to confirm the rules of our engagement and check the pistols in Taylor's mahogany box to be sure that each held only one bullet. Each second made a last-minute search of the other's principal to be certain neither was carrying concealed objects that might deflect a shot. After they were done, I followed Dred's suggestion and took off my coat, rolled up my sleeves and undid the top buttons of my shirt, which allowed a sight of Dred's bright flannel underwear, so red that it might have been seen from the riverbank like a beacon. The sun broke through the clouds and the flannel glowed like a fanned fire. Samuel stared first with surprise and then annoyance at my indecorous violation of any gentleman's standard of good taste. His eyes seemed irresistibly drawn to the sight of the bright red flannel. He looked away only to have his gaze again settle on the bright color.

Taylor, who had been selected to do the honors, explained that he would call "Fire-one, Fire-two, Fire-three." Neither of us, he said, could shoot before the first count or after the last. The seconds did not need to state what was understood perfectly by all present: that if one of us should attempt to fire before the "one" count or after the "three" count, the other's second would shoot him.

Taylor offered Samuel's second the choice of pistol. After a moment's hesitation, he selected one. The seconds shook hands and, each carrying a pistol, walked to their principals.

Taylor, a grim look on his face, handed me the pistol, which felt coldly comfortable to hold. "Good luck, Arba," he said, "I will be watching to assure that Mr. O'Fallon obeys the rules."

We shook hands and he walked to the edge of the clearing, shortly joined by Samuel's second. The doctors stood a few paces away from the seconds, their open medicine bags on the ground.

"Gentlemen," called out Taylor, sounding nervous for the first time, "please take your positions."

Samuel and I walked over to the small piles of pebbles that marked the agreed distance of twenty paces. He seemed so impossibly close that I could not conceive how either of us might miss.

We stared at each other, our arms at our sides, each holding a pistol in the right hand. The world had grown so still that I thought I had lost the ability to hear and in a panicky moment feared that I might not know when Taylor had begun the count. A bird suddenly trilled sharply, which relieved my anxiety. Listening to the sweet sound, it dawned on me that surely I had never been in a more absurd situation.

Neither Samuel nor I moved a muscle. He stared at me, his eyes focused slightly below mine, still drawn to the garish red flannel.

An eternity passed.

"One." Taylor in his nervousness failed to say the word "fire." Samuel looked surprised at the omission of the word as though he had depended on hearing it. The bright sunlight dimmed from passing clouds and then burst through again.

I heard Taylor start to speak and saw Samuel jerkily lift his arm, as though in slow motion. I stared down the gaping barrel of his pistol, surprised that my weapon remained at my side and that I had not aimed and fired on the one count just as Samuel lifted his arm, exposing his right side and his vital organs.

The sting of the bullet grazing my left shoulder preceded by a split second the sound of the discharge, which echoed madly in my ears. I felt a spreading wet sensation along my left arm and side and I trembled slightly. Several things seemed to happen at once and I keenly observed them all from a distance as though only a spectator.

I raised my pistol despite the pain and pointed it straight at Samuel's heart. Samuel's face turned white, his outstretched arm holding an empty pistol, his eyes still distracted by Dred's bright red flannel, which the sun had re-ignited just as Samuel had aimed. Taylor tensely cleared his throat to begin the second and, as we all knew, fatal count.

This time Taylor omitted no words. After the word "fire," it was an eternity before the word "two," an eternity in which to shoot Samuel O'Fallon, now so visibly distressed at his fleeting mortality that he had closed his eyes, an eternity in which to kill him as easily I had shot foxes on Newfane Hill, an eternity in which to think of those I loved and those I hated, including the terrified man twenty paces away, who had come to stand for all the loathsome things that I had seen in Missouri.

Before Taylor could say the word "two," I pointed my pistol at a cloud and fired, filling my ears with a thunderclap and the air around me with the acrid smell of gunpowder. Samuel opened his eyes in unbelieving relief, Taylor and Samuel's second looked at me in astonishment, and the doctors appeared slightly disappointed at having made a long journey for no apparent use of their skills other than to put a bandage on the modest wound to my shoulder.

I turned my back on Samuel, threw the pistol on the ground, and walked quickly away from it as though I had never seen it before. Taylor approached me and said respectfully, "Honor has been—"

"None of us has any honor, Taylor. Don't you know that?"

I refused the fawning assistance of the doctors and, blood seeping down the flannel and staining the expensive broadcloth, I walked painfully to the skiff and waited for Taylor to row me across the river.

Chapter 21

My return east was a far more comfortable journey than the trip west years before. A short steamboat ride, and I boarded the Ohio and Mississippi Railroad and traveled by train to Washington City. The train was filled with well-dressed and well-mannered businessmen. They mainly talked of bonds, interest rates, sugar prices, beer sales, the manufacture of dry goods, and the troubles in Kansas, where the free-stater town of Lawrence was under virtual siege by proslavery Missourians. Most of the Kansas conversation was about the Lawrence women. A St. Louis beer merchant read out loud a newspaper article about the refusal of the town's women to flee the city for safer ground. They stayed to make cartridges and bandages and to practice shooting pistols. One nineteen-year-old girl told the newspaper reporter that she dreamed of shooting at least three Missourians. "Breastworks," joked the beer merchant to much laughter from our companions.

I asked, "Isn't anyone on this train disturbed that armed Americans are confronting each other over slavery?"

Several passengers nodded but the beer merchant returned to his newspaper with a sour expression, as though I had spoiled a gay occasion.

My first impression of Washington City from a train was no more favorable than that of St. Louis from a steamboat. The outskirts were a succession of fields with a few scattered, dirty, and dingy frame houses, most with whitewash instead of the dignity of paint. The fields were stagnant pools swarming with geese, pigs, and children. Here and there a few slaves worked in the fields or hung out laundry in the yards, but the impoverished look of the houses suggested that only a few could afford much in the way of possessions, human or otherwise.

The landscape improved with my first sight of the unfinished Capitol, glittering and gleaming in white marble glory, although when I later visited the building I found the floors, the bottoms of the columns and the staircases covered with brown tobacco stains.

The train reached the station, I descended to the platform, passed through a dirty, cheerless hall, and emerged onto a muddy street. A long line of hacks waited while black porters milled about the station entrance. I thought of my conversation with Dred after the duel, a week before I had left for Washington City.

"I don't know any folks got so many lives as you do, Mr. Crane. I don't think cats got so many."

"Well, thanks to your gift he missed his aim."

"Sure don't look that way." The bandages were visible above my shirt. "But one of these days, Mr. Crane, you going to find out you don't got near as many lives as you think you do."

"I will stay out of trouble in Washington City. Writing the briefs to the Supreme Court should keep me busy enough."

"Them judges on that court. How many are there?"

"There are nine of them."

"They own slaves?"

"The Chief Justice, Mr. Taney, once owned slaves but he freed them."

"They any different from the judges in the Missouri court?"

"Well, four are from free states. The question is whether we can get a majority, that is, five votes. If we can persuade Chief Justice Taney, we'll win."

Dred was skeptical by now about the predictability of judges. "Why this judge free the slaves he own?"

"I don't really know."

"They don't free the slaves because they likes them, that for sure." He seemed certain of his insight. "They wouldn't own them in the first place if they did."

I described the merits of his new lawyer, Montgomery Blair. Dred listened carefully but offered no comment. He appeared satisfied with his prospects, uncertain as they might be, and with his attorneys.

His apparently relaxed mood was striking. "If I were in your place," I said, "I don't think I'd be nearly as much at peace as you appear to be."

"I tell Harriet that most the time we got so much to worry about that once we get started it don't stop. She don't listen but I keep saying it. I do all I could in getting this case going and I do the best I could for my children. So what's the use of worrying about things once you can't do nothing about them?"

Then he had picked up a broom, stared at it for a moment as though reminding himself what it was for and why it was in his hand, and slowly begun to sweep the office.

"Metropolitan Hotel, sir, best house in the City, sir." "National, sir, National. Only first-class house in Washington." "Willard's. Whose a-going to Willard's?"

I told a carriage driver that my destination was the Blair home, across from the White House.

"Know where it is," he said grumpily as he loaded my luggage. We splashed along in mud as deep as any I had seen in St. Louis until we reached Pennsylvania Avenue, the only paved road in the city. Along the avenue men walked or clustered in twos or threes, dressed in frock coats and top hats. Women wearing hoop skirts and bonnets were escorted in small groups by older men but there were few couples. Christmas was only a week away and wreaths hung from doorways.

"Where you from, guv'nor?" The driver, a portly and unshaven man, spoke while looking directly ahead.

"St. Louis."

"You here on business or pleasure?" He glanced back at me through squinted eyes.

"Business."

"If it's pleasure you want after you done your business, I know the best houses in the District. Young, beautiful, and accomplished women, guv'nor, like you've never seen."

I thanked him for the information.

The White House loomed ahead, a stately building that did not sparkle like the Capitol because it was merely painted white. I peered at the great windows, where I might sight a young woman with red hair attending a reception.

"It's safe now, guv'nor, but stay away in the spring. Ague and fever. Wouldn't live there myself. Here we are, guv'nor, number 1651, Mr. Blair's home."

I fumbled for coins. "New Hampshire, guv'nor? Maybe Vermont?" I vaguely nodded. "Knew right off you wasn't from St. Louis. They always ask for the addresses. Merry Christmas, guv'nor."

It was a Sunday afternoon and distinguished-looking men and elegant women strolled past the Blair mansion on their way to parade in front of the White House. I carried my valises up the steep stairs and the front door opened. I announced my name to the man in the doorway.

"We have been expecting you. I am Montgomery Blair." He stood at least six feet tall, straight and spare with the erect posture of the West Point cadet that he had once been. He carried himself with the air of a man who could marshal unseen resources. Unlike many of his middle-aged contemporaries, he was clean-shaven and had close-cropped hair. He inspected me with bluish-gray eyes.

Behind him was a hatchet-faced elderly man of medium height dressed in a winter coat that could not hide an impression of such wiry thinness that I would have been unsurprised to find that the coat was draped over a skeleton. The man leaned on a hickory cane with an engraved emblem on its head.

"Father, this is Mr. Arba Crane of Vermont and St. Louis. He works with Roswell Field and will be helping me argue the *Scott* case. The Crane family is prominent in Vermont."

I looked into another set of Blair blue eyes and shook the bony hand of the patriarch of the Blair family.

"Is this your first trip to Washington, Mr. Crane?" Old Blair's voice was mild. Without waiting for an answer, he said, "There are two things always to remember in Washington, young man. When the genteel folk say seven they mean nine. And when the people get wrong, they have to be damned wrong before they get right. Violet, we must be off."

A stern-looking woman of equally advanced years appeared in the doorway. She was dressed in an expensively elegant riding outfit. Unlike her husband, she seemed to be better fed and made of more than just sinew and nerve. She shook my hand with a grip that left an ache in my fingers.

Old Blair readied his cane to walk down the steps. "General Jackson gave me this." He paused for a moment to assess whether I had sufficiently appreciated the reverence with which he spoke the name of the late President and then, apparently satisfied that I had, said, "Enjoyed your acquaintance, Mr. Crane. Merry Christmas. Goodbye Montgomery." With a wave of General Andrew Jackson's cane, he and his wife descended the steps and strolled down the avenue.

Blair watched until his parents were out of sight. "He doesn't need the cane. It's a matter of sentiment. They gallop in from Silver Spring on Sundays and then ride out in the afternoon. The stables are on the other side of Lafayette Park, which gives Father an excuse to walk by Jackson's statue. His happiest days were spent in the White House as an adviser to the General."

Montgomery Blair's voice was as thin and fine as an excited young woman's whisper and as high-pitched as a well-tuned whistle. On occasion, as I was to observe, it cracked as suddenly and sharply as a dry stick. In time I grew accustomed to his voice but never ceased to be amazed at how Montgomery Blair had overcome such a handicap to rise to the zenith of a profession where one's business largely is done with the vocal instrument.

"You are fortunate to have such vigorous parents."

"Actually, Father's health was somewhat delicate when he was young. Grandfather opposed Mother's marriage to him. 'You will be a widow in six months, Violet,' he told her. She answered, 'I would rather be Francis Blair's widow than any other man's wife.'" He smiled nostalgically. "Leave your luggage. The servants will bring them to your room, where you can stay until you find a suitable boardinghouse. I trust that you are not overtired from your journey because there are some people I would like you to meet."

The interior of the mansion was comfortably but not lavishly furnished. We passed a large living room in which men and women sat on sofas or helped themselves to food at a table. I quickly glanced through the room at the faces but did not see her; and the women facing away from me lacked her profile and red hair. Montgomery gestured to a negro servant and rejoined his guests. The servant escorted me to a room on the second floor and another servant appeared with my valises. After changing from my traveling clothes to more fit attire for this company, which took some time because my shoulder was still stiff, I went downstairs. I passed a room in which a tall, handsome, dark-haired man of Montgomery's age, wearing a brown waistcoat and lavender-colored trousers, stood before a mirror muttering to himself.

Montgomery greeted me at the living room entrance. "Did you meet Charles Sumner?"

"Senator Sumner? That was the man talking to the mirror?"

"He's practicing a speech. He'll be down shortly." Blair escorted me to the table, which was laden with canvasback ducks, turkey without bones, quail, oysters and an assortment of custards and jellies. A servant offered me a choice between Rhenish sherry and Flemish champagne but I declined both. While I tried to select from the assorted delicacies, Montgomery began introducing me to his guests, a process that lasted the better part of the afternoon because the Blair guests, principally senators, congressmen, cabinet ministers, and ambassadors, were constantly coming and going.

I chatted with Governor Seward of New York, a slender macaw of a man who had been a senator for many years but still preferred the gubernatorial title.

Montgomery Blair and Senator Sumner joined us.

"Charles, I'd like to introduce Arba Nelson Crane from Vermont by way of St. Louis, where he practices law." Sumner peered at me from his haughty senatorial pinnacle. "Arba comes from an old Vermont family and, like you, is a graduate of the Harvard Law School. We will be arguing a slavery case in the Supreme Court."

At Blair's invitation I described the *Scott* case.

"It sounds like a reversal of the multiplication table," said Sumner. "The slavery question is a matter of morality, not of mortal law."

Senator Sumner and Governor Seward departed and Montgomery Blair introduced me to a newly arrived visitor. To the surprise of both of us, I shook hands with Alfred Fox. Kate was nowhere to be seen.

Fox seemed less than enthusiastic at my presence. "What brings you to Washington, Arba?"

"I am arguing a case in the Supreme Court with Mr. Blair. My client is Dred Scott."

"Scott? Oh yes. Didn't you lose his case in the Missouri Supreme Court?"

"Only because the judges on that court refused to follow their own law. We filed a new case in federal circuit court, which is now before the Supreme Court."

Fox looked amused. "Why on earth does this slave persist?"

"He seems to want his freedom."

"Really? Most don't because they haven't the vaguest idea what to do with it. Why should he be any different? I did hear talk in St. Louis that this slave once lived in the same county as Nat Turner. Perhaps that explains it."

"A coincidence, nothing more," Blair said. "He has not started an uprising or murdered anyone in their beds. His grievance will be settled by the law."

"If I were a Southerner," I said, "I might be more afraid of a slave with a lawyer than a slave with a knife."

Alfred Fox did not smile.

"You must pardon me, Alfred," Blair said, "I see our distinguished Governor Chase, in from Ohio. We will talk later, Arba."

Alfred Fox and I talked stiffly for a while about St. Louis. Neither of us mentioned his daughter, until he said abruptly in answer to my unasked question, "Kate is visiting Ellen Taney, the daughter of the Chief Justice. Ellen's mother and sister died in September. Most tragic."

"I trust Kate is well."

"I will convey your regards. Kate's never been happier." He paused for maximum effect. "She is engaged."

I denied him the satisfaction of a reaction. "I did not know. When was it announced?"

He hesitated. "It hasn't been but will be, soon enough. We are both so busy. An election year is approaching. He's a fine young man from a fine family in Texas."

I was tempted to ask how much time it took to announce an engagement. "I'm sure. Please congratulate her for me on her good fortune. I imagine that Kate is of great assistance to you in Washington and will be sorely missed."

Alfred Fox smiled wanly. "More than anyone can possibly know. But I told Mr. Pierce that I do not plan to stay on regardless of the outcome of the election. I yearn to return to Louisiana and the life of a farmer. There is not much more that I can accomplish here. The South now controls the three branches of government, as I try to explain to certain passionate legislators from the slave states. They insist that the free states have the upper hand, although when I ask for examples, they can think of none. The more battles they win the more they are convinced that their destiny is to lose the last one."

We exchanged holiday salutations and went our separate ways, I painfully to remember the fragrant smell of rose water and he to consolidate further the Southern grip on the national government.

><del></del>

Six weeks later, Montgomery Blair and I walked along a narrow passage with a dim light. We proceeded through a glass door, descended several steps, and entered a gloomy room.

"This feels like a tomb."

"With Mrs. Washington's approval it was to serve as the Founding Father's crypt," Blair said. "The Virginia legislature insisted on a grave site in Mount Vernon."

Even without Washington's body, the Supreme Court, in a basement room directly below the Senate chamber, resembled a mausoleum. An oppressive, vaulted stone ceiling resting on thick columns left the impression of a catacomb like those I had seen on my visit to the Vatican. Busts of the former Chief Justices, like ancient Popes, adorned the room. The thick, dank basement air smelled of decaying paper and cold walls.

"The deaths of some our most talented jurists," said Blair as I looked around, "have been attributed to the location of this room." The faces of lawyers and spectators had a sickly hue because the room was poorly lit by dim light from curtained windows and flickering lamps that spewed a faint yellow glow. The floor was covered with thick red carpets that muffled footsteps and all present spoke in hushed voices. Here, it was always afternoon.

"No matter how many times I come, I always shiver," said Blair. "America's Bible is the Constitution and this is our national church."

I was also shivering. Since leaving St. Louis, I had felt the pull of this courtroom, as though the journey had been an irresistible slide towards this basement chamber. Standing in the historic well of justice where American history had repeatedly come to seek guidance, the case seemed larger than just my clients. I had felt steadier when looking down the barrel of Samuel O'Fallon's pistol.

Blair and I, having arrived early, arranged our papers at one of the lawyers' tables and then chatted with the journalists who reported on the Court. Most seemed bored, but one, James Harvey of the New York *Tribune*, who signed his correspondence "Index," remarked that the case presented some interesting issues and that he was struck by the Sanford lawyers' request for additional time to argue.

Senator Henry Geyer appeared with his newly named co-counsel, Reverdy Johnson, a former Attorney General of the United States and regarded by many as the leading constitutional lawyer in the country. Geyer and Johnson walked with the confidence and authority of barons entering the king's palace. We four lawyers shook hands, Senator Geyer and I exchanged immediately forgettable words about our encounter at Taylor Blow's dinner party, and we took seats at our respective tables.

A few minutes later, at precisely eleven o'clock, the Marshal of the Court walked backwards out of a door behind the bench, which was nine mahogany desks and velvet covered mahogany armchairs on an elevated platform. He cried in a loud voice, "The Honorable, the Justices of the Supreme Court of the United States." Everyone in the courtroom rose to their feet.

The Justices, wearing black silk robes and led by Chief Justice Roger Brooke Taney, filed in. "Oyez! Oyez! Oyez! All persons having business before the Honorable, the Justices of the Supreme Court of the United States, are admonished to draw near and give their attendance, for the Court is now in Session. God save the United States, and this Honorable Court!" The Justices took their seats, followed by the lawyers and spectators.

The Chief Justice was a flat-chested, frail old man, so bent and warped that he resembled a wizard. His skin was like cracked parchment but, even in his late seventies, his hair was still mostly its original dark brown color, his eyes were bright, and his thin face and pursed lips left an impression of such penetrating intelligence that for a moment—an extremely brief one, to be sure—I wished that I had not persuaded Mr. Field to recommend to Montgomery Blair that I argue part of the case. The Chief Justice gave a dour glance at the journalists sitting on the cushioned sofas in the middle of the courtroom. I wrote a note to Blair. "He makes Senator Sumner look like a paragon of mirth and humor."

Blair glanced at the note and nodded but did not smile. We had quarreled over our brief. Blair wanted to devote too much space to defending Judge Wells's ruling on the plea in abatement that Dred was a citizen, which we had won, and not enough to attacking his charge to the jury that followed the ruling in *Scott v. Emerson,* which was the reason why we lost.

"We are wasting space defending ground already won that should not even be before the Court."

He had shrilly replied, "It is certain to come before the Court because the Court cannot decide whether it has jurisdiction in the first instance unless it decides whether the slave is, or is not, a citizen." He even rejected my plea to at least argue that any challenge to jurisdiction had been waived by Sanford's answer to the merits of the lawsuit. Our most severe quarrel had come over his refusal to argue that Dred's residence at Fort Snelling irreversibly freed him. "He resided in a free state, which is sufficient. We need not also contend that he was freed by the Missouri Compromise. Even if the Compromise was then in force, it since has been repealed by the Kansas-Nebraska Act. Why resurrect it and risk extraneous issues?"

In frustration, I had walked out of his office and then, calming down, returned and pointed out that Dred's claim to freedom was more plausible if made under an enactment of Congress instead of a state law, since even the Missouri Supreme Court should have deferred to a national law.

"We must be aggressive and take the initiative before the Court, Montgomery."

He was courteous, complimentary of my research, writing, and persistence, but unyielding.

Behind the Chief Justice came the eight Associate Justices, in the order of seniority. To my eye, they were a collection of aging to aged, pale and graying jurists, but Blair knew them either personally or through his father and his practice before the Court. In my time in his office, I had listened to him analyze their personalities and inclinations the way an enthusiastic geologist might distinguish seemingly identical rocks.

The four Southern Justices first drew my attention, even though we had already lost their votes. The old and lean Peter Vivian Daniel of Virginia, who recently had married a younger woman, had an air of aristocratic superiority that, Blair had said, masked resentment at Northern disapproval of slavery. "His politics are those of a Virginia slaveholder."

The aging but still robust former state judge from Tennessee, John Catron, at the time of his appointment had privately doubted his legal ability. Blair only said of him, with disdain, "A shameless politician with no understanding of judicial decorum."

The handsomest Justice was James M. Wayne, former mayor of Savannah and, according to Blair, socially versatile enough to visit the Blair home on Sunday afternoons. "He would dispute the right of any Northern man to have an opinion on slavery."

Blair had mentioned that the fourth slave-state Justice, John A. Campbell, a middle-aged, middle-sized former Alabama state legislator, had opposed the acquisition of territory from Mexico not because he thought it wrong to take it but because it would not make good slave territory. "On slavery, he is more fanatical than the fanatics."

The four free-state Justices were of greater interest because we could not afford to lose a single one of their votes. As a group they appeared less aristocratic but more serious than their Southern brethren, who smiled and laughed more often. The oldest was the square-jawed and ambitious John McLean, a former Ohio Congressman, who had undisguised ambitions to win the Republican Party's first Presidential nomination. "He will be in our camp from the start and certainly will be joined by Benjamin Curtis, but we will be thankful if McLean's ambition and zeal lose no votes that might otherwise be ours."

The pinched-looking Curtis, a former Boston lawyer and Massachusetts state legislator, said Blair, although not an abolitionist, was constantly aligned against the slave-state Justices on issues touching slavery. Blair had higher regard for Curtis than any other member of the Court. "He respects the law and he has a conscience. If we do our job right, he will not have to choose between the two."

Blair had spoken drily of the two other free-state Justices. "They should be with us but we must be very careful with them." He had mentioned that Justice Robert Grier of Pennsylvania, a blonde-haired, rotund former state judge and descendant of a long line of Presbyterian ministers, had once chastised a minister for reading from the pulpit a notice of an abolition meeting. "His real character conforms to his physiology. He is soft and easily shaped."

The fourth, Samuel Nelson, had been the former Chief Judge of the highest court of New York. His father had remained a slaveholder so long as permitted by New York law. "There is a rumor," Blair had said one night in his spacious law office, in which the most prominent feature was a huge and fierce portrait of General Andrew Jackson, "that Justice Nelson's education was paid for by the sale of his father's slave girl."

Even so, Blair was optimistic. "If we win over Taney, the pliable Justice Grier will follow. Nelson has not the courage to cast the only vote from north of the Mason and Dixon line in favor of the South. If we lose Taney, then it will not matter how they vote."

I finally turned my attention to the Chief Justice. I cannot date the beginning of my obsession with him. It may have been the day in St. Louis that I persuaded Mr. Field to bring the lawsuit in federal circuit court and it dawned on both of us that the case might go to the Supreme Court. Perhaps it was my conversation with Alfred Fox in which he said that Kate was friendly with the Taney family. It may have been the day Montgomery Blair showed me the ancient court papers that recorded the young lawyer Roger Taney's defense of the Pennsylvania minister, Jacob Gruber, charged in Maryland with inciting slaves to insurrection and rebellion.

"A good old-fashioned Methodist," said Blair of Minister Gruber, "who knew how to give a fire-and-brimstone antislavery sermon and make it stick. Taney did not like trying cases. It was too hard on his frail health. But he took the case and won an acquittal from a jury of mostly slave owners."

According to Blair, even as a young man, Taney wore black and ill-fitting clothes, his eyes were gloomy, and his tobacco stained teeth irregular and prominent. He had been in delicate health since birth, and the excitement and mental exertion of a trial always left him exhausted. Even so, his arguments in defense of Minister Gruber were so clear, with such apt illustrations and plain common sense, that he made the issues understandable even to the most illiterate farmer sitting on the jury. He was a man with a moonlit mind, which shines with all the light of day but none of its glare. He told Minister Gruber's jury:

> A hard necessity, indeed, compels us to endure the evil of slavery for a time, and it cannot be easily, or suddenly removed. Yet while it continues it is a blot on our national character. Until the time shall come when we can point without a blush, to the language in the Declaration of Independence, every friend of humanity will seek to lighten the galling chain of slavery and better, to the utmost of his power, the wretched condition of the slave. Such was Mr. Gruber's object in his sermon and those who have complained of him will not find it easy to answer him, unless persecution shall be considered an answer.

"Were those his convictions or his advocacy?" I had asked Blair, who shrugged.

"Perhaps a little of both. He was young and hopeful and so was the country. Now he is old and lately suffered the loss of his wife and a daughter. There is less hope and the choices are much harder than when he defended Minister Gruber. Slavery was supposed to just fade away."

They seated themselves, nine mostly old men balanced in their dispositions as precariously as the country, and peered down at the lawyers, journalists, and the few spectators. The Chief Justice nodded at the Marshal, who called out, "Case Number 61, Dred Scott, a man of color, versus John F. A. Sanford."

I recalled what I had told Dred in Mr. Field's law office on a lonely evening in the distant past. "You have a claim." How unimaginably far we had come and how much Dred would have relished hearing his name called in the highest Court of the land. "Don't that beat all," I was sure he would have said had he been here. "All this fuss in this big court before all these judges over me."

The Justices waited expectantly. Blair awkwardly rose and went to the speaker's lectern, where he fumbled for a moment with his notes. "May it please the Honorable Court. I am Montgomery Blair, counsel for the plaintiff-in-error." His voice began on a high pitch and never retreated, save for an occasional moment when it faltered in midstride. He always recovered quickly and none of the Justices seemed to notice. They gave Blair respectful attention, some Justices leaning forward, others sitting back, some occasionally making notes, and others at times picking up the briefs and leafing to a previously marked page. I scarcely could listen to Blair's argument because I was preoccupied with controlling the pounding in my chest as the time grew nearer for me to take my place at the podium and face nine of the brightest and most experienced legal minds in the nation.

Blair finished his argument and sat down. I walked to the podium, where I set out my notes, and grasped it with both hands. I looked up and the cold, skeptical glares of the Justices dashed me in the face like a slap. My throat was dry but I dared not take a drink from the pitcher at our table for fear that my hands might so shake that I would spill water from it.

"May it please the Court, my name is Arba Nelson Crane, co-counsel with Mr. Blair for the plaintiff-in-error."

But I barely had begun my argument on the defendant's waiver of the jurisdictional issue when the Chief Justice, who had been almost motionless, interrupted me to raise a point that I thought Blair had addressed, although poorly. The Chief Justice's voice, either from frailty or age, was so low that at times it was difficult to hear.

"Mr. Crane, what do you contend the word 'citizen' means?"

"Mr. Chief Justice, it has been used frequently in both state and federal law to mean an inhabitant or free inhabitant. 'Free inhabitant' was the phrase used in the Articles of Confederation and although it was changed to citizen in the Constitution, there was no intention to exclude free negroes—"

Justice Catron interrupted with a Tennessee drawl. "Free negroes have been excluded from voting, office holding, and jury service. Are you saying, sir, that such exclusions are unconstitutional?"

"I am not. But such political disabilities do not deprive free negroes of citizenship anymore than the other excluded classes, such as women. Nor does social discrimination—"

Justice Catron again interrupted. "Haven't some courts excluded free negroes from the protection of the Privileges and Immunities Clause on the ground that they are not citizens?"

"Justice Catron, that exclusion in no way impairs their rights and liabilities under the Diversity Clause, which have been exercised without question, something," I turned to the Chief Justice, "Mr. Chief Justice, that you recognized in *LeGrand v. Darnall* by suing a free negro in federal court under that provision."

Blair had warned me against this argument for fear of giving offense, but the Chief Justice remained impassive, although his eyes narrowed slightly at the mention of his old case.

Surprised at finishing an answer without interruption, I then argued Judge Wells's error in charging the jury on the basis of *Scott v. Emerson* but was immediately interrupted by the Chief Justice, whose question was accompanied by a soft rustling sound as the lawyers and spectators leaned forward to hear him.

"But was that freedom valid in Missouri after the plaintiff returned there?"

"This Court, Mr. Chief Justice, has recognized repeatedly the principle that liberty, once admitted, cannot be recalled. So too have courts in Virginia, Mississippi, Kentucky, and—"

Justice Wayne, in a thick Georgia accent, interrupted. "Mr. Crane, was not the circuit court's charge based on a ruling by the Supreme Court of Missouri that is the final word on how to interpret that state's law?"

"That decision, Justice Wayne, is of no weight at all, beyond what is due to the research, reason, and authority which the accompanying judgment displays or which may be due to the character of the court which pronounces it." I pushed aside a distracting memory of kicking over a chair and hurling a Missouri Supreme Court case reporter against the wall of Mr. Field's office. "The question depends on general principles of law that must be decided by the courts of the United States according to their own judgment—"

Justice McLean, our strongest ally on the Court, broke in with a voice so loud that I thought I saw the Chief Justice, to whose right McLean sat, flinch. "There was a vigorous and eloquent dissent in *Scott v. Emerson* on this very issue, was there not?"

"Yes, Judge Gamble cited the many prior decisions of the Missouri Supreme Court recognizing the emancipation of slaves by the laws of free states or territories—"

Justice Catron once again prevented me from finishing an answer. "Is it your argument, sir, that a sovereign state can put no limits on its obligation to enforce another state's laws?"

"That is not my argument. A state might refuse to enforce another state's laws that it found repugnant. But Missouri has never, until *Scott v. Emerson*, manifested hostility to such suits. To the contrary, its code and decisions made such suits favored actions." I added, "The same is true of all the slaveholding states in the Union. Until the Missouri Supreme Court's decision in *Scott v. Emerson*—"

For the first time, I was cut off by a moderate Northerner, Justice Nelson. "I question whether we even need reach this issue, Mr. Crane, if we decide that the plaintiff is not a citizen and therefore we lack jurisdiction."

"The defendant, by answering the complaint, waived the issues raised by his original plea in abatement, and therefore the Court has jurisdiction to decide whether the lower court erred in denying the plaintiff his freedom—"

Justice Nelson, no more willing to let me finish an argument than any other Justice, persisted. "Well, do you concede, Mr. Crane, that, if we decide that the plea in abatement is properly before the Court and that the plaintiff is not a citizen, then we have no jurisdiction and therefore need not consider the other issues you raise?"

I hesitated, and having no choice, acknowledged that such was the case and with that ended my maiden argument before the highest court in the nation. I sat down, more exhausted and excited than I could remember and nagged by a feeling that the dry, legal exchanges missed the point of the case.

After the Court adjourned for the day, Blair complimented my argument.

Like all lawyers in the heat of battle, I felt elated by the day's events and convinced of progress.

Blair was skeptical. "They approach this case as though it were an animal whose bite is venomous. As well they might."

The next day, Henry Geyer, dressed in black coat and vest, went to the podium. He kept his gestures to a minimum, spoke in an even, conversational voice, and never faltered. "Mr. Chief Justice, Honorable Justices, counsel"—he nodded toward our table—"I am Senator Henry Geyer of Missouri, counsel with Mr. Reverdy Johnson, for the defendant John A. Sanford. I submit that parties in a federal diversity suit must prove their national as well as their state citizenship. Citizens of the United States are either born to that status or they acquire it by naturalization. The plaintiff admittedly was by birth a slave rather than a citizen and he has never been naturalized. Even if his travels with Emerson had made him a free man, which I do not concede and which Mr. Johnson will address shortly, they did not make him a citizen of the United States. A slave who is not a citizen cannot become such by virtue of a deed of manumission or other discharge from bondage."

Chief Justice Taney looked up. "Are you distinguishing between free-born free negroes and slave-born free negroes?"

"I make no such distinction. The latter, however, are more obviously excluded from citizenship."

After Geyer finished his argument, the sharply dressed Reverdy Johnson rose to address the issue we had not raised—whether Dred had been emancipated by residence at Fort Snelling. He was interrupted almost immediately by Justice McLean, who leaned forward to question Johnson about the passage in the Sanford brief that had caused Blair to walk over to my desk after he had read it.

"I have read your brief carefully, Mr. Johnson. Are you asking this Court to rule on the constitutionality of the Missouri Compromise?" He sat back to survey the results of his question, which, possibly to his gratification, had caused a stir among the journalists on the spectator couches. They whispered to each other and rustled the pages of their notepads, while the other Justices leaned forward to hear Reverdy Johnson's response.

Johnson was firm. "We have so raised that issue." He spoke his next words as though they would be chiseled on stone. "Congress does not have the authority under the Constitution to prohibit slavery in the territories."

The pens of the journalists scratched so loudly and furiously on their pads that Chief Justice Taney seemed momentarily distracted. Several Justices began to ask questions.

Justice McLean's oratorical voice prevailed. "Mr. Johnson, the Territory Clause of the Constitution states that Congress has the power to dispose of and make all 'needful rules and regulations' in the territories belonging to the United States. What else could that mean than that Congress has the power to protect or abolish slavery in the regions not yet admitted as states?" McLean's voice was loud enough to address a convention.

Reverdy Johnson, not in the least intimidated, skillfully delivered a response that offered, to my thinking, a preposterously narrow construction of the Territory Clause. "The Territory Clause of the Constitution provides only for the disposal of soil. It does not endow Congress with supreme and universal power over the persons of the territories or their property." McLean, irritated and dissatisfied, began another question only to be interrupted by the Chief Justice. Blair turned to look at me, as if to say, "Perhaps now you see why I did not want to argue the Missouri Compromise." I returned his look with one of my own that I hoped conveyed the message that, "Better we should have raised it first."

Unlike Justice McLean, the Chief Justice spoke without obvious predisposition. "The plaintiff also claims freedom by virtue of residence in Illinois. Are you arguing that the states have no power under the Constitution to forbid slavery within their own borders?"

The courtroom fell silent. I glanced back at the *Tribune*'s James Harvey, who put down his pen and pad and stared at Reverdy Johnson as though he might announce that the Capitol had caught fire.

"That issue presents a closer question. I would say they do not, but I concede that there is an argument that the states might have residual constitutional power to prohibit slavery. However, the Court need not reach that issue in this case." He put special emphasis on the last two words. "The plaintiff's claim in the court below was based in part on residence in a territory where slavery was then forbidden by the Missouri Compromise, a federal, not a state, enactment. Since Congress never had the power to forbid slavery he was never free there in the first instance. Even if he could have been free in Illinois, his return to Missouri plainly remanded him to slavery."

As though a long-held breath had been suddenly expelled, the courtroom came back to life. The journalists, heads bowed over their pads, wrote furiously, and the Justices relaxed in their chairs and began fiddling with their papers. The Chief Justice nodded for Johnson to continue, which he did for the next two hours without interruption by any Justice.

After two more days, the arguments finally ended and the Justices retired. Several Northern journalists requested copies of our brief.

"A most important case," said the *Tribune*'s Harvey, a dapper man with observant, merry eyes. "The Missouri Compromise was in force for thirty years and somehow no one noticed that Congress had never the power to enact it in the first place." He gleefully rubbed his hands together at the heady prospects for Index. "A sharp lawyer like Reverdy Johnson knows where to draw the line, doesn't he? God bless us but for a time I thought he might actually advocate the nationalization of slavery. Do you think McLean will write a dissent or a convention speech?"

"He will not be writing a dissent. We are going to win and McLean will vote in the majority."

He smiled at my confidence. "Oh, what a fascinating muddle this is going to be."

Chapter 22

Arba

As doubtless you now know, people here do not talk about books or even pretend to artistic taste. I would be most grateful if you would escort me to a theatrical event. I miss companionship with a literate man.

Why didn't you write that you would be in Washington City?

Kate

I tore up the note, which had been delivered in a gold-embossed envelope and written with fine and even penmanship, because my ardor had so cooled over the years that I had no interest in seeing her. Then I knelt and painstakingly reassembled the pieces so as to read her address. I wrote a reply proposing that we see *Othello*.

"Evening, Mr. Crane," said Ben, slowing the carriage to a halt in front of Ford's Theater. He spoke as though we had seen each other only last week.

"Good evening, Ben. How do you like Washington City?"

Ben climbed down. "Mighty good place, Mr. Crane, mighty fine folks hereabouts."

Ben opened the carriage door. Kate stepped out. She wore a dress and jacket of pale lavender silk and a white bonnet that framed hair as fiery red as ever. Her face was calmer than I remembered, but hardly less beautiful than I had dreamed. I held out my hand and she took it to steady her descent from the carriage to the ground. Her fingers closed tightly on mine, causing a rush of memory.

She let go of my hand and swung around to look at me.

"Thank you, Arba. Well . . . you look well." Her eyes were friendly and warm.

"As do you."

"I was so delighted to receive your note. I have not seen *Othello* in ages."

"I remembered that you enjoy Shakespeare."

She excitedly looked around to find the notice. "I do hope that Edwin is playing the title role tonight. I last saw him a year ago and he made me promise to come see him the next time he played in Washington City. What luck! He is playing Othello. And what a pity that his brother is not playing Iago. I hear he has nowhere Edwin's talent, which of course is why he is perfect for the role of the envious and resentful Iago. No one is more naturally envious than one brother of another's talent. Don't you agree, Arba?"

I hesitated, remembering my feelings when told by her father of Kate's engagement. "Oh, some might say that. But literature has more examples of men possessed by envy because of women or, especially, power, which I hear that you and your father possess in no small amount."

"Not as much as you hear but in this city what you hear is what matters. Oh, how good to see you after so many years." To my disappointment, she spoke only with friendly affection. "We must talk but, as usual, I was late—sir, I do apologize—so we should take our seats." She took my arm and we went into the theater. Edwin Booth was indeed an accomplished actor. It was more than a little strange to watch one white actor, whose make-up gave him the color of a mulatto, play a powerful Moorish king and the other actor play his resentful white subordinate before a white audience in the capital city of a country that had enslaved most of the colored people who lived within its borders.

During the intermission, we talked about our lives since Kate had left St. Louis. Neither of us mentioned her engagement. Kate's life in Washington City seemed largely to involve social events at the White House, social calls on cabinet members, senators, and representatives, and dinners at the embassies. "An eternal boring stream of rustling silks." She put her hand on my arm. "I was so relieved that neither you nor Samuel were hurt. Why men must engage in such a ridiculous pastime utterly escapes me. Samuel no longer writes. He left St. Louis. Now, you must tell me about your case. I hear talk that the Court may rule on congressional power over slavery in the territories." She watched me with anticipation.

"That issue was raised at the argument," I answered cautiously, "but the newspapers suggest that the Court is divided over procedural issues and may never reach that question."

The *Tribune*'s James Harvey had reported that the Justices had conferred several times on the case and severely disagreed about whether the citizenship issue was properly before the Court. Apparently, a majority were disinclined to address the issue of the constitutionality of the Missouri Compromise.

I added, "But Blair thinks we may win over Roger Taney. So do I."

"I would not expect you to understand Roger Taney, but Montgomery should know better. He's not the same man that he once was."

"Even recently he's sided with Northern interests in important cases."

"He does not wear his robes day and night. He is a man, even if a very old and weak one, and he is of the South."

The bell rang and we returned to our seats. A sense of irony, I decided after the audience applauded appreciatively at the end of the scene in which Othello kills the white Desdemona, is not an American virtue.

When the play ended we went backstage, where Kate introduced me to Edwin Booth, still in costume and brown makeup. Edwin Booth was not much older than I, with dark hair that fell in waving curls and soft and luminous eyes. Booth asked me if I had ever been an actor since, he said, my features were suited to the stage.

"I am a lawyer, although some say that trials are theater."

"I tried the law," Booth said, "but decided I would do less harm acting in a theater."

"Except when you fence," said Kate. "I hear that Laertes has to fight for his life when you are playing Hamlet."

Booth nodded agreement. "My critics often complain but not of boredom."

After we left, Kate said, "The Booths are mad as hatters. But Edwin is the least so. His father died of drink and sorrow and John Wilkes is sober only on the stage. Sometimes, not even then."

We went to dinner at Willard's Hotel. The air was hazy with tobacco smoke, the floor slippery with tobacco juice, and the crowds of politicians noisy and boisterous. Several greeted Kate as we made our way to a table in a room full of men. Others looked at her with undisguised annoyance.

"The first time I came here I was told to go upstairs, where the women hold court. I said that I did not suffer from the blues of Washington wives and therefore had no need of their companionship. They tolerate me now because of Father, but I'm certain that our departure next year will be a great relief."

"Even more so now that you have come here with me." She looked puzzled. "Your father said you are engaged."

"I am sure he did. Father exaggerates because he thinks you will try to steal me away again." Her carefree manner was astonishing. "A marriage proposal is not an engagement. I have not yet answered."

The waiter came, we ordered, he left, and we stared at each other. She spoke first.

"I cannot ask forgiveness. I do not deserve it."

Her eyes were a shade of green that I once had been irresistibly drawn to but which now made me wary. "What possible reason would your father have for concern? We have not seen each other since you left St. Louis."

"He knew, because I told him, that I had been in love with you and nearly stayed."

"That was very long ago." Her words caused me both elation and pain.

"Father could not be sure it was over." She added, "Nor could I. Oh, I have thought of you so often."

"Not enough to write."

"I have written many letters but sent none."

"What did they say?"

"Does it matter?"

"No, I suppose it does not. The fact that you left is what matters."

"What matters is that I could not stay. Do you understand that now?"

"You left because you could not forgive yourself about matters that are unforgivable. What good would my forgiveness do?"

She touched her fingers to her forehead. She looked at me, her eyes glistening. "I should have stayed." We sat silently while the waiter put dishes on the table.

"You don't mean that, Kate. You are loyal to your father and to his cause, which means you are loyal to the South and therefore to slavery. Despite the awful things they did to you. You are incapable of giving them up."

"Would you have given up your cause for me? Could you live on a slave plantation if that was the price of love?"

"I did not expect you to become an abolitionist."

She leaned forward. "You didn't answer my question, Arba. I could not pay the price of your love, but you haven't said whether you could have paid the price of mine."

The answer might not have come so easily several years before. "No. I could not have." We sat silently without talking or eating. A waiter came by to ask if everything was satisfactory and I asked him to bring a bill. He glanced at the uneaten food and nodded. Kate's face was so sad that I could have wept, or perhaps it was the other way around.

To make conversation, I said, "Your father mentioned that you are friendly with one of Chief Justice Taney's daughters."

Relieved at the excuse to talk about other people, she said, "One summer Father and I vacationed at Old Point Comfort. It is near Norfolk in Virginia. The scenery and the walks are beautiful and the sea bathing is safe. I met Ellen and we became close. Her father works extremely hard and is often fatigued. After her sister Alice married, much of the burden of caring for him fell to Ellen, even though she has been in poor health since birth. That was our common bond, loyalty to our fathers."

That, and the fact that neither had married.

"I see Ellen often. She lives with her father over a candy shop on Pennsylvania Avenue." At my surprised look, she said, "When he was a lawyer he had fine homes. It is shameful how little he is paid now. Their apartment is so small that his office is partitioned by a calico curtain from the kitchen. Oh, he is a man of great dignity that no surroundings can diminish, but his home is little better than a garret."

Blair had never mentioned Taney's domestic life. I had vaguely imagined that Roger Taney lived in a mansion like the Blair home. Kate left an indelible image of the Chief Justice drawing a curtain in a tiny apartment to close off the distraction of his daughter's cooking while he drafted an opinion on some great legal issue.

The waiter came with a bill, which I paid, and we left the hotel. "He must be lonely, with his wife and a daughter gone."

"His loneliness is unimaginable because he was the cause of Alice's death. Not that he would or could admit it."

I was stunned by her words. "You are speaking of the Chief Justice of the United States. Your father said his wife and daughter died after illnesses."

"They did but Alice would still be alive but for him. Ellen has said it many times in the privacy of our conversations. She is so bitter."

We stood outside Willard's Hotel and waited for Ben, who had been told by Kate to return at a later time. Smartly dressed men and women walked past, talking, like us, of men and power.

In a strained near-whisper, she continued the story. "Last summer Alice's husband was away. She was invited to Newport in Rhode Island by family friends, who thought it safer than Old Point. Newspapers had reported that a man died of cholera on a steamboat bound for Norfolk. Her father objected and insisted that she accompany the family to Old Point. He pointed out that the Washington City papers had said nothing about the disease. Alice still begged to go."

Kate had been visiting the Taneys when Alice and her father had their final argument. She had been struck by the severity of his words, the harshest she had ever heard him use with any member of his family.

The Chief Justice had been working on an opinion and, at Kate and Ellen's urging, Alice had interrupted him to again plead to go to Newport. He stood and faced her. "His voice is so soft that I had to strain to hear everything he said. He seemed to speak more in sorrow than anger but it was sharp, oh so sharp. 'I have not the slightest confidence in the superior health of Newport over Old Point, and I look upon it as nothing more than that unfortunate feeling of inferiority in the South, which believes everything in the North to be superior to what we have.' He then said that he would permit Alice to leave provided that her mother approved and it would not cost more than a hundred dollars. He said he could spare that much from his salary but not more without injustice to others."

"Then he gave permission."

"He did nothing of the sort. Alice's mother scarcely would have disagreed with her husband and he made clear his disapproval. Ellen stayed in Washington and Alice accompanied her parents to Old Point. Alice fell ill. Her mother died from a stroke. A few hours later, Alice died." Something seemed to catch in her throat. "From cholera."

She fell silent for a time.

"He spent his days with Catholic priests. He said it was his duty to submit to God's chastisement with calmness and resignation. I have often wondered whether in the privacy of those prayers, he has ever asked forgiveness. Ellen doesn't think so. She once said that she was sure he had not because otherwise he would have lost his sanity, even if God had forgiven him, which, in any event, Ellen did not think He ever would."

"I cannot imagine why his daughter would continue to care for the Chief Justice if he did what you say he did."

"I don't imagine you will ever understand Southern women," she said.

Her carriage arrived and Ben climbed down to open the door for her. "I have had a most interesting evening, sir, as I always do in your company. Now, I must take your leave." She hesitated, "Might we see each other again?"

"Yes, we might," I said, trying to push away bittersweet memories. Perhaps the fires of love could only be banked and not doused. "But I leave tomorrow for Vermont."

"What will you do there?"

"I plan to see my parents."

She seemed unable to leave. "After so many years, they will be glad to see you, I'm sure."

"I have unfinished business in Newfane."

"You and your father will have much to talk about." Her words made me vaguely uneasy. In different words, Dred had said the same thing to me when I had told him my plans.

A memory broke through, a night in a room and soft pillows and unspoken fears and the glare of the light of an all-too-early sunrise. The recollection filled me with unbearable sadness.

"Yes, I think we will."

Chapter 23

"There will be a pie supper next Sunday at the Grafton Congregational Church to which all are invited. I've been reminded to announce that the Barrett pew is still for sale, first come first takes it. The congregation is especially pleased to welcome Arba Crane. You may have read in the newspapers that Arba has a very important case in the Supreme Court in Washington City."

All heads turned in my direction, although there were fewer than I remembered and almost all were white-haired. My father, mother, and I sat in the family pew that my grandfather had purchased when the town was still on Newfane Hill. The pew, an uncomfortable wooden bench with a straight back, had left me restless and impatient as a boy. I had distracted myself by concealing a tiny knife in my hand out of my parents' sight and slowly carving my initials, which were still there. I was no longer a boy, but not even halfway through the service the walls of the church closed in, the air seemed harder to breathe, and the same iron bands tightened around my chest that had loosened only after my departure for St. Louis. I smiled at my parents' neighbors, men and women who I had known all my life but who now looked at me with curiosity and suspicion.

"Please remember in your prayers Harry Bartlow, who served faithfully as deacon for 40 years." With that the service ended and we spoke briefly with the minister, who explained that he had called my presence to the attention of his congregation, not all of whom may have realized that one of Newfane's sons was playing a role in the great case.

On the train from Washington City, some passengers had opened their newspapers to read first about the Supreme Court's conferences, which were the subject of such detailed articles in the New York *Tribune,* the Philadelphia *North American* and *The United States Gazette* that the reporters appeared to have been sitting in the conference room. Some papers reported our defeat and others our victory. Several weeks had gone by since these confident assurances, and no decision had been issued. Mr. Field had sent me the articles from the *Missouri Republican,* which noted the St. Louis origins of the case but, like the others, had almost nothing to say about Dred, who was visible to the reading public only as "a slave" who had filed a lawsuit.

Dear Arba:

I read the Republican *to Dred one evening when he came by to clean up. He laughed at hearing me read his name in a newspaper but I think he is concerned that he will be the target of proslavery men. He asked again whether I thought we would win the case, to which I replied, again, that we are always hopeful. I told him that the long delay in issuing an opinion may be a good sign, but the passions of the day forbid a prediction, despite the speculations of the newspaper correspondents. He has not heard from John Sanford or Irene or anyone else. He and Harriet live with a dark cloud of uncertainty always above their heads. I asked him if he had any regrets about bringing the case and he says, quite firmly, that he does not. I'm not certain that Harriet is as sure of their course of action as he is because he mentioned that she cries in the morning before leaving for her various jobs. Dred never speaks of his vanished children but they must be on his mind as well. Somehow, despite all that has happened, Dred still lives his life cheerfully. When I think of my beloved, departed children, I also think of Dred, who seems always able to take his life's misfortunes in stride.*

There is nothing of importance in St. Louis in the way of news that I can tell you. The reports from the border, however, are most distressing. The Missouri River is a dangerous place for a Yankee who fails to remember proper etiquette. One unfortunate passenger on the Polar Star, *the Reverend William Clark, made the mistake of frankly admitting that he favored admission of Kansas as a free state. He was asked by another passenger what he would do if a black man wanted to marry his daughter. He replied, according to an account of a third passenger that appeared in the newspapers, 'I would advise her to reject him, but if she was resolved upon it, and I could not persuade her to the contrary, I suppose I should be compelled to submit to it.' The passenger to whom the Reverend Clark uttered these words then beat him until his face was unrecognizable and another broke a chair over his head.*

Please convey my best wishes to your father. You may assure him of my firm belief that the lawsuit is a worthy one and much to your credit.

Yours,

Roswell Field

The religious calm of a Sunday morning on Newfane Commons was as far from the deck of the *Polar Star* on the Missouri River as

I could imagine. Yet I thought of the *Polar Star* as we made our way slowly from the church, shaking hands and exchanging muted Sunday morning greetings with our fellow worshipers. We emerged into the warm sunshine of a fresh, early spring morning, where the trees had only just shown their fragile green shoots and the air had a moist smell. Like my parents, the good citizens of Newfane were dressed in their severe and unfashionable Sunday clothes, a variation on black or gray, strolling around the Commons or climbing into carriages. This peaceful, tranquil scene was unmarred by strife or anger and, as the worshipers had been told only just minutes ago, blessed by God. Yet I sensed an unbreakable bond between the bloody deck of the *Polar Star* and the green-carpeted Newfane Commons. Despite, or perhaps because of, their mutual lack of comprehension of one another, neither could escape the other.

"Have you been attending church, Arba?" My mother walked slowly. Having acquired Mr. Field's walking habit, I had to shorten my stride. My father looked at me. "As much as I can, Mother."

"Is there a temperance society?"

"There is, but temperance is not as popular in St. Louis as in Vermont. You needn't worry, I have been working much too hard to indulge myself." This was the truth, at least since the night Dred slapped my face.

She patted my arm. "You must come more often. This has been such a short trip, Arba, and you leave tomorrow. It's such a pity that you haven't seen your sisters."

I could not look at my father's face. Even though I thought I had prepared myself, my mother's condition had shocked me. To a stranger, perhaps, she might seem normal but it had not taken much time on the day I arrived in Newfane to realize that she was no longer part of this world. She spoke to me as though I had only been away a few days, casually referred to my long-dead sisters as though they might appear in the living room at any moment, laughing and tumbling like little puppies, and clutched a faded quilt that she had stopped sewing on the day my last surviving sibling, Esther Mary, began to cough blood.

"I will try, Mother." We passed the cemetery, which she barely glanced at. Many Cranes were buried there, but I picked out the four graves as though I had been away for weeks instead of years. A friend of my father had carved into one after another of the gravestones the outline of small, smiling faces surrounded by a halo of willow branches, each with an inscription. "Sweet as the rose that blossoms in the morn, withers at noon, dies at night." I looked away from the cemetery and, as I had done many times since arriving in Newfane, glanced at the spot on the Commons where the Post had once, but no longer, stood.

Later that day, I went upstairs to the room where I had slept since boyhood until I left for college and once again stared at the cherished objects of my childhood. I lingered over the jigsaw puzzle of the United States with the huge swath of land beyond the Mississippi marked as "Indian Territory." The puzzle was unfinished, exactly as I had left it so many years ago on the last occasion of any desire to play with it.

As I was packing, my father appeared in the doorway, still wearing his Sunday broadcloth.

"I read your brief." He handed me the copy of the *Scott* brief that I had given him. "I have no need to keep it." I put it in my valise. "Or these." He handed back the newspaper that Mr. Field had sent me from St. Louis, which had prominently featured the case on the front page. He seemed out of place in a boy's room, a solemn deacon surrounded by the remnants of a childhood.

"Some undisciplined boys confessed to knocking over gravestones on Newfane Hill. I volunteered to right them. Do you care to accompany me?"

Carrying shovels, we climbed Newfane Hill without speaking. It was a warm day and soon my father, still wearing his Sunday church clothes, was perspiring. He took off his coat and loosened his collar. The dirt path was steep and narrow, but hunters and berry-picking children had groomed it enough for us to manage even in our stiff shoes. After an hour, we reached the top of Newfane Hill. We gazed at the crumbling foundations of the town meeting hall, the Union Church and the homes of the Crane and Field families. The Commons, which extended down the hill from the meeting hall to the jail, had been kept clear, but the fields that had surrounded the town, and which had afforded the settlers clear views of approaching Indians, were overgrown with brush.

The cemetery was in a wooded grove. Together, we righted the toppled gravestones, redug their foundations, and reset the stones. One gravestone marked the tomb of a member of the Field family and another was the gravestone of my mother's uncle.

"Why didn't the town take the graves down the Hill?"

"We decided that the souls would rest better here."

My father sat down on a granite block that had been the front step of the church but which no one had bothered to drag down the Hill when the town relocated itself.

The view of the surrounding pale green Vermont hills, despite the overgrowth, was magnificent. "I find it sad to come here," said my father. "The ruins disturb my memories." The faint sound of a gunshot reached our ears. I judged the hunter to be at least a half mile away. My father did not notice. The breeze at the top of Newfane Hill gently rustled the branches.

"Walking on the Commons I could not but recall our conversation the day you left for St. Louis. It brought to mind the prediction you made."

"I remember that day well," I said, "but I do not remember what I predicted. Whatever it was, things did not turn out quite as I had imagined."

"Someday, you said, I would read your name on the front page of the *Missouri Republican*. Your prediction came true."

"Oh, yes. I remember. I was an excited boy, saying silly things."

"As the years passed, I hoped that your excitement would die down and you would return to Newfane for more than just a visit. I have parted with that hope. I have followed this case for some time. Seeing your name in the newspaper and remembering your prediction convinced me for the first time that you will never return. Newfane has nothing to offer you."

"In the church this morning, at times I thought I could not breathe." The wind grew stronger, shaking the trees and drowning out the birds, whose melodies had accompanied us on the climb up the Hill. My father shivered slightly and put on his coat.

"Why do you care so much about this slave?" My father seemed genuinely curious.

I responded as I had whenever that question was asked, which lately had been often. "He lost a case he should have won."

"At Bible reading David Kellogg made a point of raising his voice when he read from Exodus."

"Yes, God permitted the ancient Israelites to hold their fellow creatures in servitude. And even to beat them. If slavery was wrong, God would not have granted the Hebrews permission. Well, do you think God has given us permission to have slaves?"

"Since we have no slaves, we have no need of His permission. If the slave owners do, that must be their concern and not ours. You act as though I am answerable to God for not opposing it."

I stood up and looked around, trying to determine where the Post had been when the town was on Newfane Hill. "I think we all are." I walked a few steps. "Is this where the Post stood?"

He seemed distracted. "I really don't remember, Arba. I suppose it was near the jail, farther down." I walked down the hill to another crumbling foundation and then looked up at him. He nodded, rose stiffly, and joined me.

We both stared at what had once been the Newfane jail.

"Who was she?"

"Who?"

"Abigail White."

He flinched slightly at the name.

"No, I mean, who was she to you? I know who she was. I found the records yesterday in the basement of the courthouse while you and mother were visiting."

I had searched through yellowing, crumbling files that told Newfane's tale from records of the public auction of the original land grants because the first settlers had been unable to pay taxes to the warning-out notices, legally meaningless pieces of paper that the selectmen handed to any newcomer who they suspected was without resources. I found cases handled by the young lawyer, Roswell Field, most so petty and trivial—his defense of William P. Curtis, charged with stealing two pistols from Ezekial Osgood, or his prosecution of a lawsuit over the expiration date of a promissory note in which the issue turned on whether a month under Vermont law was a calendar or a lunar one—that I decided he would have left Vermont even if he had never met Mary Almira Phelps.

I finally found Abigail White. She had come down from the Province of Lower Canada, then notorious for counterfeiting, had been warned out of Dover, and had then joined a counterfeiting ring near Newfane. She and another woman, Converse White, had been arrested and then bailed out of the Newfane jail by a stranger. Converse White had failed to appear for trial but Abigail had appeared and been tried in the Windham County Courthouse in front of Judge Crane, who had sentenced her "to be whipped thirty-nine stripes on the naked back between the hours of four and seven o'clock at the public whipping post at Newfane."

The man who had Abigail White tied to the Post and whipped until her back was red with blood, who had presided over her punishment in black robes and a black hood, had been my father. What had been plain before my eyes I had refused to see, what Dred and Kate had sensed, I had banished from my memory, the recollection of my father, who taught me the meaning of justice, inflicting injustice.

"I have always known," I said to myself in a near-whisper, staring at the spot where the Post once stood.

"Abigail White was tried and found guilty and I imposed a lawful sentence," said my father as though the event had happened only a month before.

"Was she whipped up here?"

"Where you now stand."

"Why was the Post taken down to the flats?"

"We thought we might have need of it to punish criminals. It was never used again." He added, "The town decided to remove it last year."

"When I arrived in St. Louis I saw a slave girl's back, all cut up from whipping."

"Abigail White was a common criminal."

"And the whole town had to watch?"

"Punishment has more purpose if others witness it. Justice must be stern and it must be obeyed." Father lost his patience. "How dare you compare a lawful sentence of a criminal to the whipping of a dumb slave?"

"The slave I saw in St. Louis had violated the law by refusing to submit to her owner's desires. So she was whipped. Abigail White violated the law and you had her tied to the Post. Both were punished within the law." I asked him calmly, "Did they receive justice?"

"If their judgments were within the law, Arba, then justice was done."

My father turned his back on the empty spot where Abigail White had been whipped, picked up his shovel, and began walking away. I lingered for a while because I was intoxicated by ghosts. Then I too tried to turn my back on the ruined memories of Newfane Hill.

I caught up to my father, who was striding down the path. He walked on the trail as though he was alone. "What happened to Abigail White? I would like to know."

His face was grim and he did not look at me. "Perhaps it is best that you are leaving tomorrow."

Carrying my shovel, I stumbled once and nearly fell but he kept walking down the path, sure-footed despite his age, as though he had walked it many times. "At the time I thought the girl on the slave block was the most beautiful woman I had ever seen. She was there only because one of her eight great-grandparents was a negro. I like to think that eventually she escaped and married a Frenchman who took her to Paris where she lived a life of luxury. But Abigail White is dead, isn't she?"

We walked in silence, I behind him, and then he spoke over his shoulder. "I imposed a fine of forty-eight dollars. She was returned to the jail until it was paid. She escaped and that was the last anyone heard of her."

"I can see her in my mind perfectly well, only I cannot hear her screams. Did she scream?"

He kept walking.

"You taught me as a small child what justice is supposed to mean. What you did to Abigail White was no more just than what was done to that girl in St. Louis. Or to Dred Scott."

My father stopped abruptly and turned. He held the shovel like a staff, a righteous lawgiver ready to cast the wicked out of the Kingdom of Newfane Hill, as sure of his past judgments as any Biblical prophet in his prophecies.

We were halfway down, suspended between the past and the present on Newfane Hill. The sun had vanished behind dark clouds and the air now felt chilly.

"She screamed. Horribly."

"I can't remember the sound of her screams."

"Understand, Arba, it was not for me as a judge to decide whether the law was unjust. I was bound by an oath under God to carry out the law and God will judge whether I did an unjust deed. Not you."

"If He does judge you he may damn you for having a poor girl whipped until she bled for stealing a trivial sum of money."

He stared at me for a long time with the same concentration as though he were working through a legal problem, and then made a wry, pained smile.

"He already has." He leaned on the shovel as though he needed it for support. "I looked into her eyes and thought I saw the cold heart of a thief. I had her whipped with supreme satisfaction. Roswell never forgave me and that, as much as Mary Almira Phelps, ended our law partnership. Later, I found myself drawn again and again to this place, even after it fell into ruins. I was haunted by her screams and the memory of her, just as you have been. But my greatest regret, the punishment that God inflicted on me for presuming to act like Him, worse even than what I did to Abigail White, is that my son believes that what I did was so sinful that he has to atone to God for it. That my sins are his."

"The whipping of Abigail White was not my sin before God."

"How I have wished that you truly believed that."

"How can I possibly atone for the whipping of Abigail White?"

He did not answer directly. "I do not doubt that you desire his freedom and sympathize with his cause. But ask yourself, Arba, whether you might also be using this slave for your own purposes."

Stunned and outraged at the suggestion, I stammered for words. "What? What could possibly be my purpose other than to free him?"

"To free him, yes, but in doing so, expiate my sins and, therefore, what you think are your own. To find for this slave the justice that I failed to give Abigail White."

I protested that I was only helping my friend, who had been treated unjustly, but my voice was shrill when it should have been calm. Then my anger drained away and he turned and walked down the path. I watched him until he was no longer in view and I stood alone on Newfane Hill.

Chapter 24

"I could not believe that a thing like this was possible."

The man lying on his back on a bed in the dark room in Francis Blair's home at Silver Spring carefully touched a badly bruised left hand to his bandaged head and involuntarily groaned. The bandages were discolored by blood and pus. He appeared in a greatly weakened state and slowly let his hand fall to the bed, as though anxious not to jar even slightly the rest of his battered body.

The doctor unwrapped the bandages to reveal ugly cuts on both sides of the head several inches long and as deep as the bone. He studied the wounds, nodded, and then applied new bandages, which elicited more groans from his patient. In addition to Montgomery, Francis Blair, and myself, several politicians, including Senator William Seward, observed the examination.

"The crisis has passed and you are safe. It is well that your brother called me in. Massachusetts has produced noble statesmen but its medical profession is not nearly as distinguished. Guncotton and chloroform! Unlike Dr. Boyle, I have let the wound freely suppurate."

"The crisis, doctor, has not passed," said Senator Charles Sumner weakly from the bed. "The crisis is upon us."

The physician gathered up his instruments. "I only minister to the body, Senator, not the body politic, which I leave to your skills and those of your colleagues." He said goodbye to his patient, and the friends of Charles Sumner edged closer to the man whom South Carolina Senator Ben Butler's cousin had beaten senseless on the floor of the United States Senate.

Senator Sumner recounted the event of several days earlier. Those present knew better than to remind him that he had already told them of his ordeal many times.

Sumner's two day "Crime Against Kansas" speech had packed the Senate galleries. On the first day, he had called Senator Butler the Don Quixote of slavery, who "has chosen a mistress to whom he has made his vows and who, though ugly to others, is always lovely to him—the harlot, Slavery."

On the second day, he had charged Butler, who had a slight lisp, with an inability to speak coherently or truthfully on the subject of Kansas. "He utters incoherent phrases and discharges the loose expectoration of speech. He cannot open his mouth but out there flies a blunder. Yet he dares in an imbecility of madness to compare his state of South Carolina with its shameful imbecility from slavery to the free territory of Kansas."

Three days later, after reading the printed speech, Senator Butler's cousin, South Carolina Congressman Preston S. Brooks, walked into the Senate chamber.

"He approached me and said, 'Mr. Sumner.' I looked up but I did not know Congressman Brooks by sight. He said, 'I have read your speech twice over carefully. It is a libel on South Carolina and Mr. Butler, who is a relative of mine.' I started to rise, but first one blow and then another and another rained down on my head. I tried to stand but I had forgotten that my desk was bolted to the floor."

The newspapers reported that, in order to rise, the Senator first would have had to push back his chair, which was on rollers. Instead, he stood and, in twisting away from the blows, tangled his feet under the desk and fell back.

"My eyes were blinded by blood. I tried again to rise. I do not remember what happened after that."

Senator Sumner managed to rip the desk from the floor but succeeded only in offering a better target to Congressman Brooks's gold-handled cane. As Sumner staggered around the Senate chamber, reeling from seat to seat, Brooks beat him until the cane snapped, and then continued beating him with the remaining portion. Knocking over another desk, Sumner was about to fall but Brooks held him up by the lapels with one hand and continued to beat him. Sumner went into convulsions under the blows from Brooks's cane while senators and congressmen watched. One aging Whig senator from a border state warned Brooks, "Don't kill him," which caused a Southern senator, a Democrat, to shout back, "Let them alone, goddamn you." Finally, the cane shattered completely and, his cousin's honor vindicated, Congressman Brooks walked off. He told a reporter, "I gave him about thirty first rate stripes. Towards the last he bellowed like a calf. I wore my cane out but saved the head, which is gold."

On his way out, the doctor was overtaken by Senator Seward, who inquired, "If you are asked by the press, whether the wounds were grievous and nearly mortal, what—"

The doctor interrupted and said sincerely, "The wounds were nearly fatal, of course."

Seward smiled and patted the doctor on the back as he left the room.

Montgomery Blair whispered to his father, "Dr. Boyle reported that they were nothing but flesh wounds and that he might have taken a carriage and driven as far as Baltimore the next day."

His father smiled grimly. "A recovering Sumner is of more use than a recovered one."

Seward walked back to Sumner's bed and picked up a pile of letters lying on the blankets. "These are just a few of hundreds," said Seward. He unfolded one letter. "Here, this is from a young Massachusetts woman. 'The instant Papa told me it seemed as if a great black cloud was spread over the sky. I keep always thinking about it, and no matter what I am doing I have a sort of consciousness of something black and wicked.'" Senator Sumner was unmoved by the letter.

"Virtually every Northern city has held a public meeting to protest," said Montgomery Blair. "The Northern press is in a state of apoplexy." He pulled an editorial from his pocket and began to read, but Sumner waved a hand for him to stop. Blair added, "We have had many requests to display your shirt."

"What of the Senate?" Sumner asked, looking at Seward.

"The investigating committee issued a report and declared the assault a breach of the privileges of the Senate," said Seward, his voice dropping. "But, as Brooks is a member of the House, the committee declared that the matter is not within the Senate's jurisdiction. Not one Republican was on the investigating committee." At Sumner's dismayed look, Seward hastily added, "Massachusetts is united behind you. Your reelection is assured. I hear talk of nominating you for vice president at the Republican convention."

Sounding even weaker, Sumner said, "I care not for the vice presidency. The South? What do the barbarians say?"

Seward cleared his throat uncomfortably. "In the main, they applauded Brooks. A few newspapers questioned his choice of arena but not the principle on which he acted."

Blair said, "Well-wishers are sending Brooks gold-headed canes."

Seward was about to say more but stopped because Sumner suddenly seemed more preoccupied with his pain than with the South's adulation of the man who caused it. The pain subsided and he asked, "What is the news from Kansas?"

Seward gestured in my direction. I had been asked to gather the fragmentary reports still coming in and bring them to Silver Spring. "Lawrence was sacked by several hundred border ruffians," I said, "on the day that you were—encountered Congressman Brooks. They destroyed the offices and presses of the *Kansas Free State* and the *Herald of Freedom* and marched away with books impaled on the points of their bayonets. The New England Aid Society's hotel was blown up, and then the town was looted."

"How many dead?" He raised his head but, in obvious pain, let it fall back to the pillow. "First it is numb and then I feel as though the blows were raining down on it and then it grows numb again."

"A Southerner struck by falling debris from the hotel. Five days later an abolitionist named John Brown led a raid near Pottawatomie Creek, where they dragged five proslavery men out of their homes and killed them."

Several spoke at once.

"Some say Brown went mad over Lawrence."

"Others says he went mad over Brooks."

"Some say he was already mad."

I had returned from Vermont only the day before to find Washington City a different place from when I had left. Men warily looked at me as though judging whether I was from the North or the South, and any man carrying a cane was the object of furtive glances. The hack driver who took me to a hotel offered, "Mr. Sumner got what he asked for, don't you agree, sir?"

Since I had no pressing legal business in Washington City and Kate was away, I had intended to return to St. Louis, but Montgomery Blair had left a note at my hotel. He requested my presence at Silver Spring and that I bring any newspaper accounts of the Lawrence troubles. Attached to the note was an order from the Supreme Court directing

reargument of "*Scott v. Sandford*" in the next term, which meant it
would not be heard, let alone decided, until after the presidential
election. The order instructed counsel to deal "especially" with the
question of whether jurisdiction was properly before the Court and
the citizenship issue. If the Court's misspelling of John Sanford's name
was an omen, I could not imagine what it might mean.

Blair had also left for me newspaper accounts of the order. Some
called the postponement "little more than a convenient evasion."
Others claimed the order "proves that the great tribunal to which the
country looks for the dispensation of justice is not prepared to rush
into the political arena."

In his note, Blair had written, "Political considerations dictated the
postponement. They would rather not rule at all than give McLean a
pulpit in an election year."

Senator Sumner had fallen asleep. Silently, we withdrew from his
bedroom. My departure for St. Louis was still several days away and I
spent the time partly listening to the Blairs and their allies plot strategy
for the Republican convention and the coming presidential election,
and partly wandering the paths of Silver Spring. Montgomery Blair
and I talked occasionally about the *Scott* case, but since our brief would
not be filed for many months, while the Republican convention was
imminent, our conversations never resulted in agreement on legal
strategy. Blair inevitably was interrupted by a servant announcing
that yet another Republican dignitary had arrived; after promising to
return shortly, he would depart and I would not see him until dinner.

Such occasions were more of a relief than a frustration. I left the
house to sit by the spring that Francis Blair had discovered when, during
a ride in the country, he had fallen from his horse, which galloped away
into a valley of pines. He had found the horse caught by its reins on a
bush that grew next to a spring that sparkled from the silvery specks
of mica in the white sand beneath the water. There, Blair had built his
country estate, where the great and petty came to drink the cool spring

water and, as I liked to do, walk the shady, winding paths along the ravine below the spring, protected from warm sunshine by pine trees. At the end of the circuitous path back to the spring, a summer house shaped like an acorn provided seats, a lamp, and refreshment from a nearby wine cellar.

I planned my walks so that they ended at the acorn house, where I sat and thought of Charles Sumner, who would never fear that his motives would be anything other than of the highest morality. If he had ever questioned the purity of his motivation, Brooks's caning surely had removed any doubts. Thinking of Dred and Abigail White and the conversation with my father on Newfane Hill, I envied Senator Sumner.

At least our conversation had accomplished one thing. After we had finally come down from Newfane Hill, my father and I had sat by the fire and talked late into the night. We did not mention the *Scott* case or Abigail White but had talked of trivial things, which I no longer recall. An unspoken but painful bond finally had been broken and we both struggled to find a new one. I found comfort in his presence and in the knowledge of how hard he had tried to understand my letters from St. Louis about the *Scott* case and Roswell Field. He, too, had been searching for Abigail White and found her in my letters about Dred. He showed me the letter he was writing to Mr. Field, the first he had written since Mr. Field left Vermont. I had said goodnight to him with affection, which he returned with a nod of his head and a warm look in his eyes.

Chapter 25

Younger but as frail as in old age, Roger Taney walked in front of an old brick mansion set in the midst of a broad lawn and surrounded by trees and a terraced garden of shrubs. Beyond the lawn was a meadow of waving grass that spread towards a range of low hills curtained by a sunset in clouds of crimson and gold. Taney wore bright red riding clothes with shiny leather boots and held in one hand a riding whip and in the other a sheaf of legal documents. A group of slaves, most in overalls, waited for him in front of the mansion. Eyes averted from Taney, they held their hats in their hands. Taney approached them and announced that, in consideration of their long and faithful service, he had decided to set them free.

One by one, Taney handed each slave a deed of emancipation. The freed slaves humbly bowed their heads, clasped the deeds to their chests, and slowly backed away from Taney, until only one slave remained. Dred Scott, who had no hat, looked directly into Taney's eyes. He waited calmly as though knowing what to expect from Taney.

The effort of speaking to his slaves had exhausted Taney, who turned towards the house as though it were not merely a home but a cherished refuge from the harshness of the outside world. Finally, as though he had no choice but to stay, Taney, shouldering an unwanted burden, wearily turned back to Dred—

As though I had plunged my face into a bowl of cold water, I was wide awake, lying in my bed in a boardinghouse in Washington City. I rose and dressed because sleep was no longer possible. I lingered for a moment over a copy of *Leslie's Illustrated Weekly* and the portrait on the cover of Dred Scott, wearing a white shirt and black bow tie. The story described Dred and Harriet and mentioned the disappearance of their children. I read again the paragraph that identified me as "Dred's lawyer" and quoted Dred as saying that he would do anything I asked because Arba Crane "was his friend."

Leslie's Illustrated Newspaper had been the topic of my meeting with Dred and Harriet in Mr. Field's office while I was in St. Louis awaiting the second argument.

"Has the Reverend Anderson any news of Eliza and Lizzie?" I asked before Mr. Field came out of his office.

Dred shook his head.

Mr. Field joined us and we talked of Washington City and the case. I explained that the Supreme Court had scheduled another argument, for which I would be returning to Washington City, and that the Justices had not wanted to rule before the presidential election. A week earlier, in a surprisingly close election, James Buchanan, the Democratic candidate, had beaten the Republican Party's John Frémont.

Dred said, "This man come to see me and Harriet. He say he come all the way from New York. He say he from the Leslie's newspaper."

"What did you say to him?"

"That I got to speak with my lawyers."

"You should talk to him. The case isn't just about politics. It's also about you."

"I ask this man if he also going to speak with Mr. Sanford. He say he sure would like to but he can't find him."

"Even if he could find John Sanford, I doubt it would be much use to talk to him." Mr. Field's voice had a dry tone. "Taylor said that John Sanford is insane and has been in a mental institution in New York City for several months."

Dred and Harriet contemplated the latest news of their adversary. "That don't surprise me, Mr. Field," said Dred. "There be times this here lawsuit, it make me tired in my head."

Dred's disconsolate tone surprised me.

"If Mr. Sanford, he sick in the head, how come we still got to do this case?" Harriet answered her own question. "It's that Irene, ain't it?"

"We have no information about Irene or her whereabouts or of any suggestion that she's involved," I said. "Even without her and even if John Sanford is insane, the lawsuit can still continue."

Dred was offended. "The folks that say they want to own us, they is crazy or gone. All the other folks, they just can't let us alone."

"Your case is too important to the country," I said. "Congress tried to solve the problem of slavery in the territories. That failed so they decided to let the people try to solve it in Kansas. That hasn't worked very well either and now the Supreme Court will have to resolve it."

"Seem like the lawsuit is about the mess the white folks get themselves into," said Dred. "It ain't about us being free."

"Which is why," I said, "you should speak to the newspaper man."

The lawyers and their clients looked at one another. Dred asked, "When this case finally going to be done with?"

"The second argument before the Supreme Court is in December. We should have a decision by the spring of '57."

"We got to win this," said Dred. "Our children, they . . . " But he stopped and just bowed his head.

I walked with Dred and Harriet part of the way to the negro quarter. Harriet left us to go to her various toils. We continued in silence for a long time until I asked him, "Before we met had you ever been friends with a white man?"

"Seem like a lot of the white men I know, they say a lot of things about being my friend and make a lot of promises. But then I find out that they just using me for something and don't keep the promises if they get in their way."

"What about Taylor Blow and his family?"

"For a time, I think Mr. Blow and his father, they my friends."

"Am I your friend?" It seemed like yesterday that I had unlocked the door to Mr. Field's office and found Dred on the other side.

"Mr. Crane, you the first white man ever be my friend."

"What if it turned out that I am using you just like the others?"

"You use me? You helping me."

"Well, suppose I was helping you because of something else someone did and this was a way to make up for it?"

He peered at me. "This other person, he do something bad?"

"Yes."

"It have to do with this girl you always talking about?"

"Yes."

He shook his head. "Mr. Crane, that girl, she get hold of you and don't let go. But why should you help me because of what happen to that girl? It don't make sense."

"I thought if I helped you, well, that would make up for what happened to her." I struggled to explain. "It's like trying to balance something on the scales. Except that I put you up on the scales so things would even out. I helped you, or at least I have tried to, but all the time it was really to help myself. Taylor needed you as a playmate when he was a boy, his father needed money so he sold you, and Dr. Emerson needed you at Fort Snelling to do his chores. I needed you to help me atone for what someone else did. Why am I any different? We all used you. You are a slave and we all used you for own purposes."

He was quiet. Then he said, "Mr. Crane, it ain't the same what happen with Mr. Blow and Dr. Emerson. You keep the promises you make. So it don't matter if by you helping me you help yourself. Nothing wrong with that." He added, "We still friends."

I had a sudden insight. "Yes," I said, feeling relieved, "we serve each other's needs well. Maybe that's the best kind of friendship."

᠁

Once again, Blair and I descended into the basement of the Capitol building. Unlike the first argument, the Supreme Court was packed with spectators eagerly awaiting the second. Even Blair had been moved by the way that the case had drawn the attention, or so it seemed to us at the center of the storm, of every thinking man in the United States. "There has never been a case like this in the history of the country." From our counsel table, he surveyed the tightly packed spectators, nodding and waving his hand to many of the senators, congressmen and judges and other officials who were in attendance.

The *Tribune*'s James Harvey approached us, gleefully sarcastic over the case's prominence.

"So, Montgomery, can we expect more moderate arguments? Like the ones in the last argument that did such damage to the antislavery cause?"

"You know better than that, James," said Blair. "Moderate arguments make it more likely the case will be decided on legal grounds and not sectional ones."

"Why, what a touching idea. This band of regionalists deciding a case like this on the law."

"The Court has put itself on trial. How else can it vindicate itself other than with an opinion that disappoints the agitators?"

"I assure you that the Court's ruling, whatever it is, is not going to disappoint all of the agitators. Well, I wish you and freedom's cause the best of luck, but I fear that the forces of evil must have their day first."

The black-robed Justices, led by Roger Taney, filed in exactly as they had at the first argument. "Oyez! Oyez! Oyez! All persons having business before the Honorable, the Justices of the Supreme Court of the United States, are admonished to draw near and give their attendance, for the Court is now in Session. God save the United States, and this

Honorable Court!" I heard someone in the audience whisper, "God save this honorable Court, if He can."

As they seated themselves, not one Justice acknowledged the presence of the enormous crowd of onlookers. Nothing distinguished the appearance of the Justices from the first argument except an indefinable sense of alertness to each other that had been more subdued in February. The slave-state Justices seemed joined together by some invisible bond while the free-state Justices appeared as wary of each other as their Southern brethren. In the middle, four Justices on either side, sat Taney in the lonely dignity of age and frail health, remote and detached. He had been born less than a year after the Declaration of Independence and now he sat on the bench of the Court like the visible face of American history, about which he was soon to pronounce.

Blair spoke for an hour on the Territory Clause. "The broad construction of the Territory Clause has been implemented repeatedly by Congress, confirmed by the Supreme Court, and accepted without question by the American people. Under it—"

Justice Wayne appeared less interested in Blair's argument than in making a point to the other Justices. "Why were the Framers concerned about anything other than the disposal of land?"

"The Framers were dealing with both the disposal of soil and the problem of government in the western territories. Even Southerners like John C. Calhoun acknowledged the power of Congress to prohibit slavery in the territories. They accepted the Missouri Compromise line, for example, and later proposed extending it to the Pacific."

Henry Geyer and Reverdy Johnson devoted little argument to the citizenship issue, which might have benefited their client, and spent most of their time arguing the unconstitutionality of the Missouri Compromise.

"Some portion of the press has given the impression that this is not a genuine suit but a feigned issue created to obtain from this Court a ruling on important slavery questions." Henry Geyer was no longer the dignified Supreme Court advocate. He might have been speaking in the Senate chamber over our heads. "I deny the allegation and declare that the case is genuine, brought in the regular manner, and for the same purpose as any other case, to decide upon the facts of that particular suit."

For once I agreed with him, having read these charges with a mixture of amusement and anger.

Geyer briefly disputed Blair on the plea in abatement. "The Court has to review the plea in abatement. Otherwise, how else could it know whether it has jurisdiction?"

He then argued, with evident enthusiasm, the unconstitutionality of the Missouri Compromise. "I acknowledge the power of Congress to institute temporary municipal governments in the territories. But that is an implied power and arises out of necessity. Only such legislation necessary for the establishment of a municipal government can be constitutionally justified and a law prohibiting slavery does not fall within that category. The Missouri Compromise violated the spirit of the Constitution by disparaging the domestic institutions of certain states and by denying their citizens equal access to the western territories."

The Justices listened patiently and asked no questions. Neither side had mentioned their individual clients.

The next day, Reverdy Johnson began his argument with the Missouri Compromise. Once again, Sanford's lawyers had fashioned an unanticipated argument. "The Constitution recognizes the principle that man can have property in man and that, as provided in the Fifth Amendment, no man can be deprived of his property without due process of law. The force of the Union is pledged to protect those property rights, which the Missouri Compromise violates. The Territory Clause is not to the contrary since, absent an express grant by that Clause for Congress to legislate over slavery, Congress has no such power."

He paused and drew himself up. "The Missouri Compromise was unconstitutional and therefore null and void. How and why, then, did Congress pass this unconstitutional measure in the first place? It had been acquiesced in by the Southern states under duress, for only to save the Union had the South been willing to sacrifice principle. The South should be acclaimed for placing patriotism to the Union above self-interest and compromising on such a measure." When he finished, I expected to hear applause but there was only a hushed silence.

I argued on the last day, feeling far less nervous than in the first argument. The Justices seemed more mortal and ordinary, less than the legal Gods that they had appeared on my first sight of them.

I began with a rebuttal on the Territory Clause issue. "Nothing in the Constitution limited Congress from legislating over slavery in the territories, either for or against it. The Missouri Compromise Act was constitutional and—"

Justice Wayne, whom I now perceived as the Justice most adamantly antagonistic to our arguments, asked, "Will you concede that if the Fifth Amendment protects the defendant's property interest, then the Missouri Compromise Act is unconstitutional?"

"Justice Wayne, I concede no such thing. My client is not a piece of property, like a valise or a horse."

"Hasn't that been the condition of that unhappy race since before the founding of this Republic?"

"Only in certain sections. In others they are given a status and rights superior to that of white women."

He so vehemently disputed my point that his long gray hair shook. "That is only because it was discovered that slave labor is unsuited to the climate and productions of those regions. The Constitution guarantees and protects the right of ownership in slaves."

"It doesn't say that, Justice Wayne, it only allows the slave trade for a specified period. And the Declaration of Independence embraces the whole human family—"

He was not listening to me but speaking to the Chief Justice, whose vote he wanted. "It is too clear for dispute that the enslaved African race was not intended to be included in that document. Mustn't this Court conclude that slaves are property within the meaning of the Fifth Amendment and therefore no law of Congress can deprive a slave owner of such property without due process?"

Justice Wayne leaned back, glancing at Chief Justice Taney who impassively waited for my answer. My argument was nearly complete and all that remained was to answer Justice Wayne's question.

I was silent for so long that an impatient expression formed on the Chief Justice's face, the tension behind me grew palpable and Blair shuffled his papers as though to snap me out of my seeming stupor.

Glancing from one end of the bench to the other, I answered Justice Wayne's question.

"This Court must not so conclude. Dred Scott is not mere chattel. He bears the impress of his Maker. He is a man like you and I."

No whispers, rustles of pen and paper, coughs, or any other sounds broke the silence that followed my words. One or two of the Northern Justices nodded, while the Southern Justices scowled almost as one. I looked at Chief Justice Taney, who held Dred's future in his hand, but he alone among the Justices had no visible response.

I sat down, the Court adjourned, and the lawyers mingled with the press and the spectators. I remained alone at the counsel table and struggled to adjust to a desolate feeling. After so many years, the case was no longer mine but theirs. I could do nothing more for Dred and Harriet and Eliza and Lizzie but, like everyone else, wait for the Court's decision. My sense of loss and helplessness was far more deeply felt than after the first argument, which, as I could now see, had only been half-completed.

"It's up to them now." James Harvey seemed to read my thoughts. "Ludicrous, isn't it, that one case concerning this illiterate slave could settle a question that affects the entire country?"

I ignored him.

"You were very eloquent, but the Constitution makes slaves property and why shouldn't it? After all, many of the men who drafted it owned slaves. If that's true then you've lost, haven't you? The sacred document guarantees that no man shall be deprived of his life, liberty, or property without due process. Why, then, the whole American army should be employed, if necessary, to keep anyone from taking away John Sanford's slave."

Utterly drained, I no longer cared what James Harvey thought or wrote. I gathered up my papers and left the courtroom without saying a word.

Chapter 26

Several weeks after the argument Kate sent a note requesting that I meet her at Washington's column.

I arrived on foot and she by carriage driven by the ever reliable and loyal Ben. The day was gray and bleak and a sharp wind chilled us. I wrapped Harriet's scarf more tightly.

She took my arm as we walked around the unfinished monument. For a time, while we walked silently, it was possible to imagine that so many things had not happened and that she had stayed in St. Louis while her father continued to Washington City. Could we have found happiness after all?

"When do you leave?"

"Six weeks ago. We live amid trunks and boxes."

"And your engagement?"

"I said no." I looked at her and she gazed calmly back. Now it was her turn to ask questions. "How soon do you expect the decision?"

"Soon."

She nodded as though I had confirmed what she already knew. "What happened on your trip to Vermont?"

"I enjoyed a reunion with my parents."

She smiled at my evasion. "Come now, Arba, you must tell me all that you learned about Abigail White."

I was silent.

"Please do, I have thought so often of both of you."

"Your memory is truly inexhaustible."

"Our evening with Madame Blavatsky was hardly forgettable."

I told her about my father and Abigail White. She listened as solemnly as if I were discussing her own family, occasionally nodding and asking a question. When I finished, she drew herself even closer with such concerned affection that I nearly asked her once again to leave her father.

"I wonder if we ever know why we do things," she said, "Life is too short to be lived in ignorance."

"It is too long to be lived without illusion."

We stopped at the cornerstone inscription:

4th July, 1776
Declaration of Independence of the United States of America
4th July, 1848
This Cornerstone Laid, of a Monument, By the People of the United
States, to George Washington.

"This country is full of money," said Kate scornfully. "Millions are yearly expended on extravagance. A little more genuine reverence for General Washington would relieve the nation from the ridiculous position in which this incomplete structure places it."

"A finished monument would not be much of an honor if the nation that he created does not remain a nation."

Kate did not take her eyes off the inscription. "That is what we must talk about."

We took refuge from the cold in her carriage, seating ourselves opposite one another. She was quite knowledgeable. "Father said that Justice Wayne told Congressman Ashley that the Supreme Court could settle the slavery question for all time to come with a unanimous opinion. Wayne is saying the same thing in the conferences."

"I understand from Montgomery Blair that McLean and Curtis told him, in the strongest possible terms, that such a result, instead of putting an end to agitation in the North, would only increase it."

"They are right." She sighed. "Ellen says that her father comes home after the conferences absolutely fatigued."

Everything I had read in the newspapers and heard from Blair, now confirmed by Kate, suggested a divided Court which could not even agree on jurisdiction.

"Nelson drafted an opinion," said Kate, "that decided the case on narrow grounds." Startled, I began questioning her but she held up her hand. "Ellen doesn't know how his opinion ruled, only that it did not address the Missouri Compromise. Then something happened and Nelson's opinion was discarded. Ellen thinks that Justice Wayne became convinced that McLean and Curtis were determined to write a defense of the Compromise."

"Why on earth would they dissent on an issue about which the other Justices are silent?"

"McLean is still ambitious and Curtis will retire someday to Boston. His law practice will prosper if he strikes an antislavery blow."

"Nonsense. McLean is too old to run again and a former Supreme Court Justice from one of New England's oldest families will hardly struggle to build a law practice in Boston."

"Perhaps." She seemed to be making a calculation. "Still, Ellen says that when her father speaks of the possibility of a dissent he is in a state of rage. Then he falls into such exhaustion that she fears for his sanity, if not his life."

"Has she told you how her father intends to vote?"

Kate did not answer but instead said, "When they discussed the Compromise they only grew even more angry with one another. They have disagreed before, but never like this."

Something in her hesitant expression caused me to ask, "Why are you telling me all this?"

She looked away. "Montgomery would never do it. However the Court rules, he and the Republicans will win. But you could do it."

"Do what?"

She seemed finally to make up her mind. "This slave. Tell him— convince him to dismiss this accursed case."

"Dismiss it?"

"Do whatever you must to end it."

"That is an impossibility."

"Arba, scarcely a senator or representative enters the Capitol building without a firearm. The country is a tinderbox and the Supreme Court is about to strike a match. We fear disaster."

"For whom?"

"I fear for you. If you lose this case, it will be a disaster for your legal career. You will have no future in the North, where you will be blamed, or in Missouri or anywhere in the South, where you are known as a slave lawyer."

"I cannot imagine that concern is shared by your father."

"Father is concerned about—he believes in leaving well enough alone. He is furious that Buchanan plans to predict in his inaugural speech that the Supreme Court will soon settle the territorial issue. It will only draw more attention to a case in which a Southern victory can only enrage the North. And help the Republicans." She put her hand on mine. "I am concerned about you." Her eyes fell on the log cabin pattern on Harriet's scarf, which seemed to trouble her.

"You talk as though this were a vote in Congress. Your knowledge of politics does you credit, Kate, but it fails to compensate for ignorance of the law."

She drew back. "Is there a difference between the two?"

"We shall soon see." I asked, "How do you suggest I explain your proposal to my client who faces disaster unless he wins this case?"

"Your client is the least of it. I have never understood this devotion of yours."

"You were once devoted to a slave."

A very long silence followed.

"Persuade the Sanford people to free the Scott family," I said. "That would end the case."

"We tried."

"Was it your father's idea that you would approach me? Or yours?"

"Oh, Arba. I came out of concern for you. My father certainly would not have approved my coming."

For the first time since I had known her, Kate Fox's words were unfaithful to the truth.

"I am unafraid for my legal career. But I am going to win this case. Isn't that what you are really afraid of?"

"You don't believe what I am saying."

"We see the case differently."

"No, no." She shook her head. "Don't you believe me when I say I am concerned for you?"

"No, Kate. I don't in the least." In the uncomfortable aftermath of my cold words, I added, "You have never been able to separate yourself from your father and your—other loyalties. The case will not be dismissed."

"You don't trust me." I did not dispute her. "We trusted each other in St. Louis," she said, as though she needed to remind herself. "We loved each other."

She had been staring at Washington's column as she spoke. She turned towards me, her eyes moist, and put her arms around my shoulders. Once again, I felt Kate Fox's tears on my cheeks. For a moment, I forgot about Dred and his case and the Supreme Court, and embraced her just as I had dreamed of doing all these years since the night in her bedroom in the Blow mansion.

But just as that night abruptly had ended with the dawn, so did this moment end, only this time because the horses, startled by another carriage pulling alongside, stepped forward slightly, rocking our carriage. I could hear Ben pulling on the reins to quiet the horses and the passengers from the neighboring carriage exclaiming at the monument.

We slowly drew back from each other. She dabbed at her eyes with a handkerchief.

Speaking more to myself, I said, "I never understood the ties that bind you."

She put away the handkerchief, having dried her tears.

I could not fend away a lurking suspicion. "Ellen Taney never told you how the Chief Justice intends to vote, did she?"

She touched her fingers to her forehead, a gesture I had once found charming. Her mouth tightened. "No, she has not. I don't think she knows."

"How can you be so sure that we are going to lose?"

Her face was flushed.

"It really doesn't matter to you and your father," I said. "Does it? However the Court decides, you are afraid for the South." She nodded reluctantly. "You came because your father asked you to. You didn't come here out of concern for me."

She smiled wanly and said dreamily, "The ties that bind us are breaking one by one."

I could not tell whether she meant the two of us or the country or both.

"Do we have anything left to say to each other?"

She slowly shook her head. We sat encased in silence, neither looking at the other. I had to leave and I wanted to stay but the fire finally had been doused. I stepped out of the carriage without saying a word, and closed the door after a last look at Kate Fox, sitting in elegant sorrow, eyes averted from me, as still as the stone column.

Chapter 27

On the day of our final appearance in the Supreme Court in the matter of *Scott v. Sandford*, the weather was crisp and clear, but little of the cheerful sunlight penetrated the courtroom, which was so packed that many had been turned away. Precisely at eleven o'clock the black-robed Justices filed into view accompanied by an expectant murmur from the spectators. Blair and I stood together at our counsel table watching as each Justice appeared for signs of how the case had been decided, but their expressions gave no hint of their decision. Most looked impassively around the courtroom and then seated themselves and studied their opinions. As we were to learn that day, nine Justices had authored almost as many opinions.

As we sat down, I was rigid with tension and Blair clasped his hands together until the knuckles turned white. I looked at our final brief, which lay on the table open to the argument on the Missouri Compromise, and reread it as though it were not too late to make a new one. At the Sanford counsel table, Henry Geyer and Reverdy Johnson sat as erect as soldiers commanded to attention by a superior, staring at a point in space in the vicinity of the Chief Justice, who waited for his colleagues to finish arranging themselves and for the Clerk to call the last case on the last day of the Court's term.

"Case number 7, Dred Scott, a colored man, versus John F.A. Sandford," intoned the Clerk.

A hush fell such that had a piece of paper slipped to the carpeted floor it would have echoed through the courtroom. It seemed dangerous even to breathe without disturbing the delicate balance on which too much had come to rest in too small a space.

The Chief Justice held papers in hands that visibly trembled as he read aloud in a voice so soft and weak that every person in the courtroom, even Justices sitting at the ends of the bench, strained to hear.

> This case has been twice argued. After the argument at the last term, differences of opinion were found to exist among the members of the Court; and as the questions in controversy are of the highest importance, it was deemed advisable to continue the case, and direct a reargument on some of the points . . .

Night after night in the curtained office in the small apartment over a candy store on Pennsylvania Avenue, Taney had labored until late, writing and rewriting American history. As I listened and, like the rest of those present, tried with incomplete success to follow the labyrinth of his reasoning, the convoluted detours of his analysis, and the resentful tone of his conclusions, I came to believe that he had convinced himself that it was his purpose and duty to put an end forever to the slavery controversy. When had he assumed the burden that Justice Wayne had so relentlessly urged on him? Perhaps it was when Lawrence, Kansas was sacked or when Sumner was beaten or when John Brown dragged five men from their homes and murdered them. Perhaps it was when he thought that no matter how narrowly the Court ruled, McLean and Curtis would write an antislavery polemic, a possibility he could not abide on behalf of his native region to whose bosom he now committed himself for eternity with pen and paper. I was sure that late one night, when his eyes could barely stay open and his hand trembled too much to continue writing, Taney had allowed his thoughts to dwell on his dead daughter. Was his decision to write a vast, sweeping opinion affected by how hard his heart had hardened against the North as a barrier to unendurable confession that it was his very resentment of the North that had sent his daughter to her death? Even his iron discipline, forged and tempered by nearly sixty years of exacting legal labor, could not completely have banished such thoughts, although he would never concede that her death could play a role in his judgment on a legal case.

With bitterness beyond words, I could now see everything in my dream that had eluded me then. For a slave who did not meekly and with gratitude accept his enslavement, there was no expression of benevolent affection on Roger Taney's face or deed of emancipation in his hand. Free negroes could not be citizens in their own country:

> They had for more than a century before been regarded as beings of an inferior order, and altogether unfit to associate with the white race, either in social or political relations; and, so far inferior, that they had no rights which the white man was bound to respect . . .

I leaned over to Blair and whispered while trying to hear the beginning of Taney's holding on the citizenship issue, although I knew what it would be. "Did he say they 'have' no rights?" Blair whispered back, "I thought he said 'had.'" I shook my head, but whispered back, "Isn't it the same thing?"

For a moment the Chief Justice, distracted by our whispers, paused and looked in our direction. Our eyes met briefly and, despite my unyielding anger at what I had been hearing, I had to look away from the two dark, sunken wells of bottomless fatigue and endless defiance.

... Dred Scott was not a citizen of Missouri within the meaning of the Constitution of the United States, and not entitled as such to sue in its courts ...

How quickly hope can vanish and be replaced by despair. Once again I would have to explain to Dred Scott why apostles of justice decided he must remain a slave. I recalled my father's skepticism but knew that he would be almost as dismayed by the decision as I was. I wondered why I had ever thought I could win this case, even though, when I had woken that morning, the possibility of doing so had been as real and as tangible as any dream I had ever had. I drank deeply from the cup of bitter truth that a slave had no hope in this Court and that, in thinking differently, I had been a fool. At least, I had gotten Eliza and Lizzie out of Missouri.

Blair, assuming that Taney had finished, began tidying up his papers. I motioned to him to stop because, astonishingly, Taney, although ruling that the Supreme Court had no power to rule on the merits of the case, now began reading from his ruling on the merits. Blair calmly put down his papers. The spectators stirred with anticipation, and indistinct whispers floated through the courtroom, as Taney pointed out that Dred Scott's claim to freedom by virtue of residence at Fort Snelling was based on the act of Congress of March 6, 1820, which prohibited slavery in that part of the Louisiana territory north of thirty-six degrees thirty minutes.

The difficulty which meets us at the threshold is, whether Congress was authorized to pass this law under any of the powers granted to it by the Constitution ...

I found it hard to concentrate on the rambling and repetitious review of the history and purpose of the Territory Clause, from which Taney drew the conclusion that Congress had no right to interfere with property rights protected by the Due Process Clause, including slavery in the territories.

. . . the right of property in a slave is distinctly and expressly affirmed in the Constitution. The right to traffic in it, like an ordinary article of merchandise and property, was guaranteed to the citizens of the United States, in every State that might desire it, for twenty years. And the Government in express terms is pledged to protect it in all future time, if the slave escapes from his owner. This is done in plain words—too plain to be misunderstood.

Taney paused for a drink of water from a pitcher. I angrily whispered, not caring about Taney, "Constitution doesn't say that. Slave trade is only permitted, not guaranteed. Fugitive slave clause concerns only state obligations." Blair signaled his agreement.

Taney either did not hear or ignored me. He drew on some inner well of strength and his voice, for once, was easily heard. The packed hordes of journalists, public officials, and ordinary onlookers froze in a tableau of breathless expectation.

Upon these considerations, it is the opinion of the Court that the act of Congress which prohibited a citizen from holding and owning property of this kind in the territory of the United States north of the line therein mentioned, is not warranted by the Constitution, and is therefore void; and that neither Dred Scott himself, nor any of his family, were made free by being carried into this territory; even if they had been carried there by the owner, with the intention of becoming a permanent resident.

In a form of exhalation, the journalists scratched with their pens and the spectators whispered more loudly than at any time since Taney began reading his opinion. Here I saw triumphant smiles and nods and there disconsolate, grim expressions. Henry Geyer and Reverdy Johnson barely contained their delight. I thought of the great men— Benton, Clay, Webster, and others—who had sacrificed their political ambitions and even their health to fashion compromises that might save the country. Awe partly displaced my anger because these aging jurists, with a few pen strokes, had swept away all such compromises, now and forever. I could not fathom what consequences might flow from this sweeping ruling. I only knew with damning certainty that I shared responsibility. I had told Dred that he had a claim and persuaded Mr. Field to bring the case. Had I not done so, none of this would have happened.

Only one issue remained for Taney, the one that had first caught my attention one late, lonely night in Mr. Field's office when I had only the slave Dred Scott for company. It had originated with Dr. Emerson's orders sending him to Rock Island in Illinois and his decision to take Dred with him. It had been the original basis for our lawsuit and the heartbreaking and hateful reversal of Dred's trial victory by the Missouri Supreme Court. It was the issue I had been more certain about than any other, but Taney was equally sure.

> As Scott was a slave when taken into the State of Illinois by his owner, and was there held as such, and brought back in that character, his status, as free or slave, depended on the law of Missouri, and not of Illinois.

Taney then devoted time to criticizing the decision of Dred Scott's lawyers to file a new suit in the federal circuit court instead of directly appealing the ruling in *Scott v. Emerson,* of which he plainly approved, while stating at the same time that the Supreme Court would have had no jurisdiction to directly review the Missouri Supreme Court's ruling. I was well past the stage of caring about such criticism. Taney concluded,

> Upon the whole, therefore, it is the judgment of this Court, that it appears by the record before us that the plaintiff-in-error is not a citizen of Missouri, in the sense in which that word is used in the Constitution; and that the Circuit Court of the United States, for that reason, had no jurisdiction in the case, and could give no judgment in it. Its judgment

for the defendant must, consequently, be reversed, and a mandate issued, directing the suit to be dismissed for want of jurisdiction.

Taney finished, looking utterly spent. One after another, the other Justices read from their opinions. Blair, dividing a piece of paper into horizontal lines for each Justice and vertical columns for each issue, tried to keep track of how each Justice voted on the separate issues of whether the plea in abatement was before the Court, citizenship, the constitutionality of the Missouri Compromise, and Dred's claim to freedom based on residence in Illinois.

Justice Wayne, his work done, read from a brief opinion that concurred with Taney. New York's Justice Nelson was next and also delivered a short concurring opinion that could have been as comfortably read by any of the slave-state justices. Near the end, he offered a thought that no one in the courtroom seemed disturbed by but which astonished me.

A question has been alluded to, on the argument, namely: the right of the master with his slave of transit into or through a free State, on business or commercial pursuits, or in the exercise of a Federal right, or the discharge of a Federal duty, being a citizen of the United States, which is not before us. This question depends upon different considerations and principles from the one in hand, and turns upon the rights and privileges secured to a common citizen of the republic under the Constitution of the United States. When the question arises, we shall be prepared to decide it.

I penned a note to Blair, "He is inviting a lawsuit to establish that slave ownership is a constitutional right and that no state can forbid it, not even the free ones." Blair nodded with a tightly triumphant smile that barely suggested the political windfall he expected the Republican Party to gain in the North from the decision.

Pennsylvania's Grier read a brief opinion concurring with Taney. The three Southern Justices, Daniel of Virginia, Campbell of Alabama, and Catron of Tennessee, one after another concurred with Taney's ruling but not his reasoning. Only Daniel agreed with Taney that citizenship was properly before the Court, Campbell ignored the issue altogether, and Catron flatly disagreed. All three, for different reasons, agreed that the Compromise was unconstitutional. As the opinions were read, Blair's sheet filled with yes's and no's in such a crazy quilt pattern that it might have been a game played by madmen.

Finally, McLean and Curtis read from dissents nearly as lengthy as all the opinions previously read. McLean denounced the majority for ruling on the Compromise after declaring that the Court had no power to hear the case:

> The question of jurisdiction, being before the Court, was decided by them authoritatively, but nothing beyond that question.

The last opinion was delivered by Justice Curtis, who, sounding like a law professor lecturing his students, reprimanded the majority for ruling on the merits after denying jurisdiction. Curtis, finding that at least some negroes could be citizens, declared that the Court had jurisdiction and masterfully, to my exhausted impression, demonstrated that Congress had unequivocal power to legislate over the territories regarding slavery. As Curtis read his opinion, Justice Wayne grimaced as though he had been forced to listen to an abolitionist lecture and whispered first to Justice Daniel and then to the Chief Justice, both of whom nodded. Curtis paused and look impatiently at his three colleagues, who stopped whispering.

Finally, after six hours of reading opinions, they were done. The nine men filed out and the dazed audience milled about, slowly coalescing into small clusters whose expressions left no doubt as to regional loyalty.

James Harvey pushed his way through a group of celebrating Southern congressmen and joined us.

"Well, gentlemen," he said with an air of finality, "this morning slavery was a local institution and freedom was national. This afternoon, it's the other way around."

Blair, looking at his notes, said, "I agree, James, although I suppose we shall have to read the written opinion to be sure. Just on the issue of whether the plea in abatement was properly before the Court, four judges are of one opinion, two of the opposite, two will give no opinion, and one is divided."

"The American public will not read the opinions before they read in my newspaper that some things are clear. Congress has no power to exclude slavery from the territories and negroes in bondage are property."

I said, "One other thing is clear."

Harvey and Blair looked at me as much from curiosity at the bitterness in my voice as for whatever clarity I might contribute to the day's events.

"Dred and Harriet Scott and their children are still slaves."

The demands of custom required the Scott lawyers to shake hands with the Sanford lawyers, as though we had just completed a game of billiards.

"Montgomery," said Henry Geyer, gleaming with victory, "Southern opinion on the subject of slavery is now the supreme law of the land. Tell your Republican friends that resistance is treason."

Blair, who had scarcely seemed upset by the Court's ruling, smiled.

"Congratulations, Henry. But I don't think the Republican party is going out of business. Far from it."

Chapter 28

The news of the ruling preceded my return to St. Louis by many days. When I met with Dred, he had already absorbed the news and there was nothing more I could offer him but my sorrow and helplessness. He had no future other than to wait for whoever owned the Scott family to reclaim their property. But John Sanford's lawyers, sated by their triumph, were uninterested in an insane man's claim to a worn-out slave; and so, at least for the time being, Dred and Harriet had continued their existence in the half-lit world between freedom and slavery.

"If more time passes without legal action by the Sanford lawyers," I said to him, "Reverend Anderson could send for Eliza and Lizzie." Dred still had not asked where his children lived in Iowa.

"They stay where they is," he said. "Harriet, she pretty undone over this, but she also say we gonna leave our children in the free state."

"You are not undone?"

"Well, that's a whole lot of fuss they making about me. We just going to have to see what happens next."

For a moment I hesitated to speak and then I said what had been on my mind the entire desolate journey from Washington City. "Do you understand that I did my best, that I did everything I could?" It seemed terribly important at the time that he understand.

"Mr. Crane, I know you do your best for us since the day we met."

The "fuss" went on without end. I was pleased to hear from my father that the Vermont legislature, like those of many other Northern states, passed a resolution denouncing the decision. To emphasize its defiance of the Supreme Court, the legislature even enacted a law declaring that no person in the state should be considered as property, and that every slave who came into the state, voluntarily or involuntarily, was free. My father mentioned in his letter that he had urged his friends in the legislature to vote for the law.

Angry Northern editorials condemned the opinion and its *dicta*, calling it no better than what might be obtained in a Washington City barroom fight. The abolitionist ministers preached resistance to the decision, saying that obedience to it was disobedience to God. For the first time, Northern anger was not directed only at the expansion of slavery but at the South.

Sanctimonious Southern editors called the decision right and unanswerable and reminded the North that the Supreme Court interprets the Constitution and, once it does, patriotic citizens are duty-bound to acquiesce. In Southern opinion, the decisions covered every question regarding slavery, including the inferior status of negroes, and settled it in favor of the South. Southerners warned that the opinion must be accepted by the North or there would be disunion.

For a time there was considerable debate over just what Justice Taney had said in his ruling, because he refused for two months to publish it despite Justice Curtis's repeated letters to the Supreme Court Clerk, who had been ordered by Taney not to give a copy to

Curtis. Taney was in the meanwhile rewriting sections of his opinion to respond to the overwhelming cascade of Northern anger that had descended on the Supreme Court. When he finally allowed it to be published, reporters who had attended the Court's ruling noted that parts of the published opinion did not correspond to their notes and, if read aloud at the same pace as Taney's delivery, appeared to be more than a third longer. At the end of the following term, Justice Curtis resigned from the Supreme Court.

I received news a year after the decision of my father's debilitating injury from a fall on Newfane Hill. I had no choice but to return to Vermont to care for him and my mother, knowing that I would not come back to St. Louis. I had final, difficult farewells, and took leave of my youth.

From Newfane, where late each summer I climbed Newfane Hill to help scythe the Commons, I followed events in the newspapers, first with foreboding and then alarm, as the ripples from the stone that had been dropped into the water grew larger and larger.

I read avidly the accounts of the cool and overcast day in Freeport in northern Illinois where, amid banners and bunting, 15,000 gathered around a vacant lot with a crude platform like a pyramid of lumber. They listened first to a brass band thump merry tunes and then to a tall, gaunt Republican lawyer dressed in ill-fitting black broadcloth debate the short, burly Democratic Senator Douglas, who wore a tailored linen suit and black patent-leather shoes. The debate was mostly about the implications of the Supreme Court's *Dred Scott* decision for Senator Douglas's cherished platform of popular sovereignty and the Republican lawyer's opposition to slavery in the territories. According to the detailed and lengthy accounts in the newspapers, each politician was frequently interrupted by applause or jeers from the audience.

Each tried to demonstrate that *Dred Scott* could not be reconciled with the other's political position on slavery. The lawyer asked whether, in view of *Dred Scott*, Senator Douglas thought the residents of a territory could in any lawful way exclude slavery from its limits. Senator Douglas, impaled on the barbed choice between appeasing the Northern wing of his party and losing the Southern, or appeasing the Southern wing and losing the Northern, answered with gusto but not logic. However the Supreme Court ruled, he declaimed, the people would decide for themselves whether their territory would be free or slave.

Not long after John Brown's suicidal raid on Harpers Ferry, I had a final glimpse of Roger Taney at the Harvard Law School, when his portrait by Emanuel Leutze was unveiled two years after the decision. The Chief Justice wore his black robes for the portrait and the painter chose to seat him in a shadowed red armchair. His left hand rested on a pad of paper while his right hand hung limply, almost lifelessly, against the right arm of the chair. He sat looking straight at me, the way he had when the decision was read, except that the defiance then in his eyes had been replaced by profound sadness, the look of a man who had seen into the ruinous future that he had wrought but had not intended and could never undo.

I lingered for an entire afternoon before the painting. Various observers, law school professors, students, and lawyers, came and went. Few stayed more than a minute or two, their attention easily distracted by acquaintances, appointments or pleasures. Almost no one appeared especially moved or impressed by the painting.

One man, with a pinched New England manner, however, appeared as riveted to the portrait as I. He had aged much since the last time I saw him, when he read his dissent in *Scott v. Sandford*. I did not disturb former Supreme Court Justice Curtis until the light had faded and Roger Taney was deep in shadows. Then I approached him.

"Why did he do it?"

Justice Curtis looked at me without recognition at first, struggled for memory, and then almost imperceptibly narrowed his eyes when he realized who I was. He ignored me, and returned his attention to the portrait. Together, side by side, we stared at the ruined Chief Justice.

"Why did he do it?"

I had no intention of moving from his side without an answer. "He could have ruled on narrow grounds and left matters the way they were. Why did he write such a sweeping opinion?"

"Young man," said Justice Curtis, "that is a question I have been asked repeatedly. I have yet to answer it."

"He resented the North, he once owned slaves, and he could not abide the possibility that you and Justice McLean would write an antislavery dissent even if he ruled only on the jurisdictional issue."

Justice Curtis was silent.

"I am the lawyer who persuaded Dred Scott to bring the lawsuit. I am as responsible as anyone for its consequences."

After a long time, Justice Curtis said quietly, "Come closer." He walked a few paces toward the painting until his face was only an arm's length from the Chief Justice's. He glanced around to assure that no one was in hearing distance and returned to gaze at the Chief Justice, who stared bleakly back. I moved to Justice Curtis's side. He spoke without taking his eyes off the Chief Justice.

"Until I saw this painting, I did not think he could grow any older. But how he has aged, even so. And that look in his eyes, it is the look of the damned. Young man, what you said is true but that is not the explanation."

"Then—"

"He forgot that he was mortal." I stared at him. "Only God knows the consequences of what He does. The Justices of the Supreme Court are not Gods. They are mortals, they are fallible, they can never know the consequences that may flow from the use of their powers, and they must be humble in their use of them. The Chief Justice thought he would end the slavery controversy for all time. Instead, he made the madness worse, and has come to understand that." He peered at the painting and then drew back. "Look at his eyes. Look at them. He stares into an abyss, the abyss into which he has plunged us all."

Abruptly, Justice Curtis turned his back on Roger Taney and walked away. He did not say goodbye, only, "God help you. God help us all."

>⧽⧼⧽

Like the rest of the country, I read the breathless reports of the Democratic Party convention of 1860, where the Republican lawyer's skillful use of *Scott v. Sandford* bore fruit. The Democratic Party shattered over the Southern wing's anger at Senator Douglas's refusal to abide by the South's great victory in *Scott v. Sandford* and at the Northern wing's rejection of a national slave code based on the same decision. Southern delegates, believing that they were being cheated of their victory in the Supreme Court, marched out of the convention. The convention turned into a rehearsal for disunion.

I voted for the Republican candidate in a presidential election shaped by free-state disgust at Douglas's unwillingness to repudiate *Scott v. Sandford* and by the split in the Democratic vote between Douglas and the candidate of infuriated Southern Democrats, who felt he had not embraced it enough. The Republican candidate, Abraham Lincoln, won with a majority of the electoral vote but a minority of the popular vote.

I had planned to attend the inauguration, where Lincoln, who had asked the question at Freeport, would be sworn in as President by the man who elected him, Chief Justice Roger Taney. But I could not go because my mother died unexpectedly. I read in the newspapers how, in his inaugural speech, the new President spoke of the better angels of our nature. No one appeared to be listening as the slave states continued to leave the Union and raise armies.

>⧽⧼⧽

I pinned a snip of evergreen to my cap, as the other Vermont men in my company were doing, and began the journey on foot and by train to the South. I smelled the aroma of pine forests, peach orchards, and wheat fields. I heard the crackling and crashing of hundreds of fear-crazed deer driven through underbrush by long lines of advancing men whose gray clothes had been ripped to tatters by thorns and branches. I became versed in the different shades of blood, from the bright satiny red of the lining of the Devil's tunic to a decaying reddish-brown and finally the black of cooled lava.

At night, by the glow of a U.S. Army lantern, I read letters from Mr. Field telling how German newspaper editor Henry Boernstein, whom I had met at Taylor Blow's, and Montgomery Blair's brother, Frank, had kept Missouri in the Union; the death of Samuel O'Fallon fighting for the South; and the news that Kate Fox and her father had been driven from their Louisiana plantation by federal troops and had fled with no possessions other than the clothes on their backs.

That was the last I heard of Kate Fox, but not a day passed afterward when I did not think of her.

Chapter 29

After finishing the letter to my father, I lie on my hospital bed, exhausted from the effort. I have been moved to a ward reserved for the mortally wounded men. They lie patiently, listening to the sands of their lives rushing out of the glass. They ask for water when a nurse enters but stir only slightly when a properly sorrowful man of faith prays for them, and not at all when a blue-uniformed and gold-buttoned officer, beaming with sympathy and pride, lays on their sheets medals that they have no use for. At the end of each day, orderlies unceremoniously remove several bodies and our ranks dwindle as though, once again, we have been cut down on the battlefield.

They are beyond the help of doctors and certainly a lawyer has nothing to offer them. The legal arts shape the future by excavating the past but these men have only a past, no future. Even so, I have tried to comfort them by explaining that the battle they just fought at Gettysburg now appears likely to reverse the decision of the United

States Supreme Court in *Scott v. Sandford.* They looked at me in a haze of pain and desolation, mystified by my words, too weak even to ask for an explanation, let alone understand one.

On my bedside table sits a cracked and splitting volume of *Howard's Reports of Cases Argued and Adjudged in the Supreme Court of the United States,* which I asked for because I wanted to read again the opinion that was intended to put an end to the slavery controversy for all time.

When I was young, I loved the reassuring smell of volumes like these—their leather, their comforting weight, their finely printed and civilized pages. I drew strength from them and even a delicious sense of sharing a special secret. Once, these law books and I had been on intimate terms. We had a special understanding. If I contributed appreciation, devotion, and respect, they would yield up logic, certainty, and justice.

The doctors who examined me are all in agreement that the gangrene has advanced too far for amputation, which I had resisted when it might have saved my life. Dred Scott once said that I had more lives than a cat. Indeed, I have escaped death many times, but I, of all the men who lie here, am the least deserving of another escape from it. None of these broken and maimed men can hold himself responsible for any other man's fate, not even his own. The same cannot be said of me. But I have no regrets and nothing to atone for and no fear at the prospect of departing this mortal domain. My affairs are in order, including a will that my father will find when he opens my last letter to him. In it, I request burial on Newfane Hill, as near as possible to the site of the whipping of Abigail White.

I lie still, like the silent forms on the other beds, and let the memories wash over me, like waves breaking on a shore. One memory above all I cherish. I save it for last because of the comfort it brings as I contemplate the night of oblivion.

It begins a few months after the Supreme Court's decision when I received a letter from my father, which I opened in Mr. Field's office. The letter enclosed a Massachusetts newspaper, the *Springfield Argus*, and a note from my father that said only that I would find it of interest. Puzzled, I read the newspaper until I came to an article about a prominent abolitionist Congressman from Massachusetts. I read it and, not knowing whether to laugh or cry, showed the newspaper to Mr. Field. He put on his reading glasses, read the article and then, with a bemused look at me, put it down. "That is the unpredictable way of litigation." I proposed that we send at once for Taylor Blow, who arrived at the office later that day.

We showed Taylor the newspaper article, held a short discussion in which we quickly reached agreement on how to proceed, and the next day, after preparing legal documents and a letter to the Congressman and obtaining a bank draft from Taylor, I was on my way to Massachusetts. I bought newspapers in each major city and, in all, read the same story that appeared in the *Springfield Argus*.

I found a hotel in Springfield and left the letter at the Congressman's office along with a note as to where I was staying. A day later, his secretary came to my hotel and requested that I come to the Congressman's home.

I arrived at his spacious house and was escorted by a maid to a sitting room. The Congressman and his wife walked into the room. The Congressman, who had been a doctor before taking up a career as an antislavery politician, was a serious-looking, formal man. He eyed me with distrust and then introduced me to his wife.

"You look familiar, Mr. Crane," she said. "Have we met before?"

"We have."

She scrutinized me and then shook her head.

"We first met in St. Louis some years ago at a party at Taylor Blow's home."

She recalled who I was. Her eyes glared.

"Of course, you were Irene Emerson then."

We sat down on well-stuffed sofas. Congressman Chaffee and his wife sat far apart on their sofa and appeared not to acknowledge each other's presence. Their smiles were forced and their words uttered cautiously.

Congressman Chaffee cleared his throat. "I must take exception, Mr. Crane, to certain representations in your letter. John Sanford was and is the only person who had or has any power in this matter. Neither myself nor"—he nodded slightly towards his wife without taking his eyes off me—"any member of my family was consulted in relation to, or even knew of, the case in the Supreme Court until we learned of it in an accidental way."

Mrs. Chaffee vigorously nodded her head. She was somewhat heavier than I remembered and wore fashionable clothes, expensive jewelry, and poorly applied makeup. I declined to agree with Congressman Chaffee's contention, which almost word for word had been his statement to the newspapers, who had described the Congressman as, among other things, a free-soil hypocrite.

"Mrs. Chaffee," I asked, "can you confirm that your brother is in a mental asylum and that you are in charge of his affairs?" Her lips were so tightly pursed that they were white.

"You may not be aware, Mr. Crane, but my brother died last month."

"Oh, I see. I am sorry. That may, however, make it easier for us to conclude our business."

Congressman Chaffee was impatient. "Yes, your letter mentioned a proposal. Well?"

"Perhaps you might look over these documents." I handed over the legal documents, which the Congressman studied with distaste and then passed to his wife. Her face paled as she read.

The Congressman's face had grown red. "I have already explained to you that neither I nor my wife have any control in this matter. My wife has no legal authority to execute these documents."

"I beg to differ. The death of your brother, Mrs. Chaffee, puts you in charge of his estate. You have every right and authority to dispose of his—property."

Irene gave me a look that could have set fire to a stone. Her husband stood. "This is an outrage."

"Actually, Congressman, it's the country that is outraged. Not every abolitionist Congressman is married to the most famous slave owner in America."

Before he could answer, Irene all but shouted at me, "I do not own him!"

Congressman Chaffee silenced his wife with an angry gesture. "Mr. Crane, I would like to speak with my wife."

I waited on the porch. The clear, brilliant day had given way to a chilly spring evening. Clouds were gathering, some lighter, others more dark, hinting of an evening storm. I thought I heard the rumble of thunder but, as I listened more carefully I could only hear the quiet of the streets of Springfield, which, like so much of America, was innocent and undisturbed, a place where people led peaceful lives and only the newspapers told of unhappiness. How firm and solid were the footings of Springfield and how impossible it seemed that anything could mar its tranquility. Irene had finally found her husband, and from the security of this house, Dred and Harriet were only a distant memory from another life. She had no reason to tell her new husband and every reason not to. I tried to imagine how Irene had explained her past when it finally caught up with her, the look of distaste on her face when she was forced to even mention Dred and Harriet's names, tearful protestations that these were her late husband's slaves, and assurances that she had never even been aware of the case in the Supreme Court or that her brother, before he drifted into incoherent ravings, had ever confided in her. For a brief moment, I felt pity for the Congressman who awoke one morning to find that the woman he had married now stood for all that he publicly deplored.

I was summoned to the sitting room. Irene sat quietly, her hands in her lap, and eyes downcast. Her husband stood at a desk, where the documents had been spread out. His voice was slightly hoarse, as though he had strained it. "Please examine these, Mr. Crane."

I went over to the desk and studied the quitclaims, which Irene had signed in tiny, forced handwriting, and the other documents, which she had refused to sign. "I need Mrs. Chaffee's signature on the deeds of conveyance. It's a matter of Missouri law."

The Congressman looked impatiently at his wife, who refused to look at either of us.

"Mrs. Chaffee," I said, "under Missouri law emancipation must be performed by a Missouri citizen, which you no longer are. All the deeds do is convey title to Taylor Blow." I picked up a pen and held it out to her.

She sat for a while in the painful light of her husband's glare but then stiffly rose and walked over to the desk. Her dead husband's promise, Taylor Blow's pleas, the years of litigation in four courts, the Supreme Court degraded, and a country torn asunder had not been enough to compel Irene Chaffee to sign the final document, but the wrath of her second husband, who now turned fiercely towards her, finally brought honor to Dr. Emerson's assurance to his slave of freedom.

She took the pen from my hand without once looking at me, bent over, and quickly scratched out her signature. I removed Taylor's bank draft from my pocket and placed it on the desk. She ignored it and, staring straight ahead, left the room. I quickly shook hands with the Congressman, whose expression spoke volumes about the state of his marital happiness, and went to the telegraph office, where I sent two telegrams, one to Mr. Field and the other to the Reverend Anderson.

A few years afterward, a friend sent me a newspaper article in which Irene Chaffee claimed that she "was always in sympathy with the cause of the negro" and that it was she, and not her husband, who had made the decision to free them.

In a quietly pleasing ceremony in Mr. Field's office, Taylor Blow signed the emancipation papers that freed the slaves conveyed to him by Irene Chaffee. We walked to Judge Hamilton's court to file the documents. The court record, happily entered by Judge Hamilton, states:

Taylor Blow, who is personally Known to the Court, and acknowledges the execution by him of a Deed of Emancipation to his slaves, Dred Scott, of full negro blood and color, and Harriet Scott, wife of said Dred, also of full negro blood and color, and Eliza Scott and Lizzie Scott, daughters of said Dred and Harriet, also of full negro blood and color.

We went in Taylor's carriage to the Second Baptist African Church. The Reverend Anderson greeted us and introduced two girls, who had grown so much that I almost did not recognize them. The Reverend said, "Eliza, Lizzie, you remember Mr. Crane?" They nodded vigorously and curtsied.

"Hello, Mr. Crane, we sure be happy to see you," said Eliza, who appeared more adult than child. Lizzie's face still had the mischievous look that I had so adored. They came to me, each took one of my hands, and the three of us stood together as Dred and Harriet walked into the church.

The Reverend had not informed the parents of the purpose of their presence. Harriet stared at her daughters and staggered slightly. Dred reached out a hand to steady his wife, looked at his daughters, at the Reverend, and at me. He studied our faces and then he smiled broadly as his eyes filled with tears.

Lizzie and Eliza let go of my hands and ran gracefully in their white dresses down the aisle into the embrace of their parents, who hugged their children with a fierce, hard-won love that Roger Taney and Irene Emerson Chaffee could never understand.

Mr. Field and I managed to glance briefly at each other. Then we had to look away.

Late that afternoon, carrying the emancipation papers, I went to the Scotts' room in the negro quarter. I heard Eliza's voice through the door, singing softly. I lingered for a while, listening to the happy sound, and then knocked. The singing stopped, Eliza opened the door, and, seeing me, gave me a hug, and shouted, "Mr. Crane, he here." Harriet and Lizzie rushed to the door and hugged me. Harriet seemed unable to speak while Lizzie asked, "Mr. Crane, remember how I use to ask if you got any sweets? Well?"

I pulled from my pocket a small bag of candies, and handed them to Lizzie. She ate the candies happily, enjoying them like the little girl that she once had been, pushing away Eliza's hand until their mother commanded her to share the candies with her sister. A travel-worn inkwell and sander was on the table, along with sheets of paper filled with even, neat writing.

Dred had been standing near the stove when I entered the room, no less shabby than on my first visit after the great fire: the same bed boards, the clothes hanging from hooks, a plain table and stove, a few utensils, all the worldly possessions of the Scott family. But the air was different, and the people in the room were different. Something oppressive had been removed, an intruder had been banished, it was easier to breathe, and everything felt lighter and looked brighter.

Dred shook his head in disbelief as though he were still not certain whether he was awake or dreaming, and stared at me for a long time.

I handed him the emancipation papers. He had earned the right to be triumphant but he had only a patient, satisfied look. I thought of our conversations on the lonely nights in Mr. Field's office, and of our friendship.

The papers were much less important to him than hearing what his lawyer had to say.

"Well, Dred," I said, "you and your family are free."

AUTHOR'S NOTE

Several years ago, I read a scholarly work on the *Dred Scott* case. A footnote quoted a February 15, 1907, letter from a St. Louis lawyer, John F. Lee, to Miss Mary Louise Dalton, the librarian of the Missouri Historical Society (the letter is in the Society's Dred Scott Collection). Lee suggested to Dalton that "the following facts in relation to that [the Dred Scott] case may be of interest to you." He then recounted that Arba Crane had "told me that one night when he was sitting in Field's office (he was then a bachelor and had no home ties) Dred Scott, who had charge of cleaning the office, came into it to perform his duties. Crane entered into conversation with Dred Scott, and learning Scott's history, came to the conclusion that Scott was entitled to his freedom, and he informed Scott of this."

After I read that footnote I decided to write this book; indeed, I had to write it. At the beginning of my own legal career, like many young lawyers, I had worked late. Such nights are long and lonely and an excuse for conversation is welcome—you make friends with the janitor. I had an almost overpowering sense of recognition of how a bond had developed between the young Vermont lawyer and the illiterate slave. I was enchanted by their friendship and by the premise that the Civil War might have begun in a law office in St. Louis.

In fact, the historical Arba Crane was a former Harvard Law School student from an old Vermont family (some historians describe Crane as a Harvard Law School graduate; others as having only attended). He came to St. Louis to work in the law office of Roswell Field. Lee's letter describes him as "a man of very exceptional legal learning. He was also a man of wide reading in other lines, and was considered a very responsible, truth-telling man." Lee also mentions that, at least at one time in his life, Crane "drank rather heavily."

Crane's story of how he initiated the case has been rejected by some historians on the basis that he arrived in St. Louis in 1856, after Dred

Scott's federal court lawsuit had been filed (e.g., *The Dred Scott Case—Its Significance in American Law and Politics,* by Don E. Fehrenbacher, Oxford University Press, 1978, and *Dred Scott's Advocate—A Biography of Roswell M. Field,* by Kenneth C. Kaufman, University of Missouri Press, 1996.)

Fehrenbacher and Kaufman are leading historians of the Dred Scott case. They rely principally on memorial tributes and obituary notices at the time of Crane's death in 1904. According to these, Crane arrived in St. Louis in 1856, although the source of this date is not apparent from these documents, nor is it clear if the memorial speakers had first hand knowledge of Crane's arrival. Fehrenbacher noted that "Crane's story has been accepted by a number of historians . . ." citing *Dred Scott's Case* by V.C. Hopkins (Atheneum, 1951). One of those historians, a Columbia University professor, John W. Burgess, wrote in his book *The Middle Period* (Charles Scribner's Sons, 1901) that "Mr. Crane was, at the time that the [Dred Scott] case was brought in the Circuit Court of the United States, a clerk in the law office of the great lawyer who espoused Dred Scott's case."

In doing research for this book I came across an intriguing letter from Roswell Field's son, Roswell, to the same Mary Louise Dalton, dated February 13, 1907—two days earlier than the Lee letter. Apparently, Miss Dalton was seeking information about the Dred Scott case and had written to Field's son (Roswell Field had died many years earlier).

He responded to her request by suggesting that she contact John F. Lee. He wrote that "[w]hen I was in St. Louis two years ago Mr. John Lee talked of this case with me at the club . . ." Undoubtedly, in their talk two years earlier, Lee had told the younger Roswell Field the same story of Arba Crane's role that he later set out in the letter to Miss Dalton. Surely, among other things, he would have said to Field (quoting from Lee's February 15 letter to Dalton), "I think it quite remarkable that this case which produced such tremendous results in the history of America, was started because a young lawyer with nothing to do learned facts which he thought made an interesting case, and had to persuade the victim of slavery to bring a suit for his freedom . . ." It is hard to believe that Roswell Field's son would have mentioned his talk with Lee—especially if Lee had given so much credit to Crane at the expense of Roswell Field—in the letter to Miss Dalton if he had doubts about the source of Lee's account, namely, the recollection of Arba Crane.

In any event, what is not in dispute is that, regardless of whether he initiated the case, Arba Crane played an important role in the lawsuit and developed a friendship with Dred Scott. In 1857, Frank Leslie's *Illustrated Newspaper,* the *Life Magazine* of its day, featured an article about Dred Scott. The article identifies Crane as "Scott's lawyer." Dred Scott is quoted as saying that he would do anything Crane asked, because "he was his friend." Scott does not mention Roswell Field.

So this book, imagined as Arba Crane's recollection, depicts the undeniable bond between men who could not have come from more different backgrounds.

Dred Scott probably was born on the farm owned by Captain Peter Blow in Southampton County, Virginia, the same county where Nat Turner, the leader of the most famous slave revolt in American history, was born. The Blow family moved first to Alabama and then to St. Louis, where it became prominent and where Dred Scott later was sold to a U.S. Army doctor named John Emerson. Dred Scott was taken by Dr. Emerson first to Rock Island and then to Fort Snelling. There, as recounted in Major Taliaferro's journal in the collection of the Minnesota Historical Society, he met and married Taliaferro's slave girl, Harriet Robinson. During this period, Dr. Emerson married Irene Sanford of St. Louis.

The Scotts' first child, Eliza, was born on the steamboat *Gypsy* on the Mississippi in free territory; their second child, Lizzie, was born in St. Louis. Following the ruling by the Missouri Supreme Court in *Scott v. Emerson,* reversing the jury's verdict freeing Dred Scott, Eliza and Lizzie disappeared from St. Louis. They reappeared only after Dred Scott had been freed.

Roswell Field practiced law in Newfane, Vermont, where he attained prominence. After he failed to persuade the Vermont Supreme

Court to recognize the validity of his marriage to Mary Almira Clark, he left Vermont for St. Louis. He established a law practice successful enough to require Arba Crane's assistance, paid Irene Emerson to have the slave Dred Scott clean his office, and lost his first office to the Great Fire of 1849 and his wife and four of his children to cholera or similar diseases.

The slavery scenes in this book are based on historical sources. Charles van Ravenswaay's *Saint Louis: An Informal History of the City and its People, 1764–1865* describes an auction in St. Louis of a "remarkably beautiful octoroon" who had been lashed fifty times. The same book describes a slave business "run by a woman living at Morgan and Garrison Avenues, who bought up infants at the slave markets and raised them to sell." Lynch's Slave Pen was an active and profitable St. Louis business until the Civil War.

Kate Fox is a fictional character. The anguished feelings about slavery of many Southern women, the most conflicted women in American history, are not fictional, nor is the fact that most chose to resolve their conflict in favor of comfort and loyalty to their native region.

The legal proceedings described in this book are matters of historical record and the excerpts from various pleadings, briefs, court decisions, and the Scotts' emancipation papers are as they appear in the original documents.

Abigail White was tied to the Newfane post and given thirty-nine lashes for counterfeiting.

The slave Diana Cephas filed a lawsuit in St. Louis for her freedom on the ground that she had lived in Illinois, a free state—and won it against Roswell Field's client Murry McConnell.

The extraordinary, years-long proceedings in *Clark v. Field* and the underlying events, which led to Roswell Field's departure from Vermont, occurred as recounted here.

Dred Scott initially won his freedom in a trial in what is now known in St. Louis as the Old Courthouse. On appeal, the Missouri Supreme Court reversed and, in doing so, repudiated numerous of its own decisions that had been the basis for his lawsuit. When

Irene Emerson's attorneys moved to reclaim the Scott family, Judge Hamilton, in a courageous act, denied Emerson's motion even though he had no legal grounds for doing so. The court's docket states, "Said motion be overruled."

In the federal circuit court in St. Louis, where Scott filed his second lawsuit on the basis of diversity jurisdiction, Judge Robert Wells ruled that the court had jurisdiction on the grounds that Dred Scott was a citizen of one state suing a citizen of another but that the Missouri Supreme Court's ruling in *Scott v. Emerson* was controlling on the issue of whether Dred Scott lost his freedom when he returned to Missouri. He so instructed the jury, which returned a verdict in favor of John Sanford. This verdict was appealed by Dred Scott to the United States Supreme Court.

The case of *Scott v. Sandford* (Sanford's name was misspelled by the Court) was argued twice in the Supreme Court in 1856. The arguments made by both sides in this book are based on the Supreme Court's opinion, the legal briefs and contemporaneous newspaper accounts. The case was argued by Missouri Senator Henry S. Geyer and Reverdy Johnson for the defendant John Sanford and, in the first argument, by Montgomery Blair for the plaintiff-in-error, Dred Scott. In the second argument Blair was joined by George Curtis, the brother of Supreme Court Justice Benjamin Curtis. The arguments likely did not involve questioning of the attorneys by the Supreme Court Justices; the give and take of contemporary Supreme Court oral argument is a more recent development. The quotes from the Supreme Court's decision (declaring, *inter alia,* the Missouri Compromise unconstitutional because Congress had no power to bar slavery in the territories and negroes in bondage to be property) are verbatim.

The description of Congressman Butler's beating of Senator Charles Sumner on the floor of the United States Senate is based on contemporaneous accounts, including Sumner's recollection before he lost consciousness. Following the beating, Sumner recuperated at the home of Francis Blair in Silver Spring, Maryland.

The events in the life of Chief Justice Roger Taney, his defense of the abolitionist minister Jacob Gruber, his vote to free the *Amistad* slaves, his freeing of his own slaves, and the circumstances of his wife and daughter's death, including his unhappiness with his daughter's desire to vacation in Newport, Rhode Island, are recounted in his biographies.

In 1858, Justice Curtis resigned from the Supreme Court, denying that he did so because of *Scott v. Sandford*. That same year, on August 27 in Freeport, Illinois, Republican Senatorial candidate Abraham Lincoln posed the famous Second Freeport Question to Democratic Senator Stephen A. Douglas about the *Dred Scott* case, "Can the people of a United States Territory, in any lawful way, against the wishes of any citizen of the United States, exclude slavery from its limits prior to the formation of a State Constitution?" Douglas answered that "the people have the lawful means to introduce or exclude it as they please," and won the election for United States Senator from Illinois. Abraham Lincoln became a national figure.

At the 1860 Democratic convention, as stated in Don E. Fehrenbacher's *The Dred Scott Case*, "the Democratic Party came to its breaking point over the issue of slavery in the territories—as affected by the Dred Scott decision." When their request for adoption in the party platform of a national slave code based on the *Dred Scott* decision was rejected, the states that would later secede from the Union after Lincoln's election walked out of the convention. Abraham Lincoln ran as the sole Republican candidate for President against a badly fractured Democratic Party that produced two candidates, one being Stephen A. Douglas.

In one of the most ironic moments in American history, Chief Justice Roger Taney swore in Abraham Lincoln as President in 1861. Historian Charles Warren later wrote in *The Supreme Court in United States History* that Chief Justice Taney "elected Abraham Lincoln to the Presidency."

Shortly after, the Civil War, America's defining moment, began.

Fehrenbacher's *The Dred Scott Case* concludes that Justice Taney's opinion "was a conspicuous and perhaps an integral part of a configuration of events and conditions that did produce enough changes of allegiance to make a political revolution and enough intensity of feeling to make that revolution violent." Or, as Alexis de Tocqueville predicted in *Democracy in America* years before the Supreme Court's decision in *Scott v. Sandford*, "if the Supreme Court is ever composed of imprudent or bad men, the Union may be plunged into anarchy or civil war."

Taney remained on the Court during the Civil War until his death in 1864. President Lincoln refused to follow the Supreme Court's *habeas corpus* rulings, and the Chief Justice was reduced to mailing the Court's *habeas corpus* opinions to the White House in the hope that they might at least be read even if not enforced. He was described by a diarist of the time as one of the "sadder" figures in Washington.

Emanuel Leutze's 1859 painting of Roger Taney still hangs at the Harvard Law School. The scene with former Justice Curtis was inspired by Supreme Court Justice Antonin Scalia's vivid description of the ruined Chief Justice in the Luetze painting in *Planned Parenthood v. Casey*.

The astonishing story of how Dred Scott and his family ultimately gained their freedom occurred as described here, although Arba Crane's visit to Congressman Chaffee's home is not documented.

Sometime after she lost the trial in *Scott v. Emerson*, Irene Emerson married Dr. Calvin Chaffee, a Massachusetts Congressman and an outspoken abolitionist. After the Supreme Court's decision and the discovery of Irene Emerson's whereabouts and remarriage, a Massachusetts newspaper, the *Springfield Argus* (to cite just one example), wrote: "All the long years of servitude through which this [Scott] family has been doomed to labor . . . has this hypocrite [Chaffee] kept their ownership by his family from the public, while he had profited, not only by [the Scotts'] labor, but on the other hand by his extraordinary professions of love for the poor Negro."

After being forced by outraged public opinion to free (or cause his wife to free) Dred Scott, Dr. Chaffee did not run for reelection in

1858. Irene Chaffee later claimed to a newspaper reporter that she "was always in sympathy with the cause of the negro."

Arba Crane drew up the legal papers that ultimately emancipated Dred Scott and his family.

Dred Scott died on September 17, 1858, a free man.

CHAPTER
HISTORICAL NOTES

Chapter One

An English traveler, Henry Bright, recounted a journey like Arba Crane's in the early 1850s in *Happy Country This America, The Travel Diary of Henry Arthur Bright,* by H.A. Bright (Ohio University Press, 1978). Bright crossed the Blue Ridge Mountains by stagecoach at five miles per hour, experiencing the "excruciating shake" that "pitches you against your next companion," and reached the Ohio River. He boarded a steamboat, which journeyed down the Ohio River, and then up the Mississippi to St. Louis. He stayed in the Planters' House, which he described as a "capital Hotel" (id., pp. 179 & 218–60).

In the 1850s, Frederick Law Olmsted, later to gain fame as the landscape architect of New York's Central Park, traveled through the South as a special correspondent for the *New York Times.* In a series of letters that were published by the newspaper and later became a book, *The Cotton Kingdom, A Traveller's Observations on Cotton and Slavery in the American Slave States,* by Frederick Law Olmsted (Alfred A. Knopf, 1962), Olmsted describes a journey on the Mississippi that is the basis for the description of Arba Crane's steamboat, the *Sarah* (id., pp. 270–77). Olmsted also recounts how he came across a gang of female slaves ("forty of the largest and strongest women I ever saw together") (id., p. 407), which inspired the scene on the hurricane deck of the *Kimball.*

The St. Louis levee was described by Henry Bright, who was approached by an old man who "begged me to buy a gun-cleaner and a girl [who] offered me a watermelon" (*Happy Country This America,* pp. 261). See *Saint Louis: An Informal History of the City and its People, 1764–1865,* by Charles van Ravenswaay, p. 330 (Missouri Historical Society Press, 1991).

The Joker's Budget was a "scurrilous gossip sheet filled with ethnic and racial stereotypes in tune with the prejudices of the time . . ." ("Yankee Colonizers and the Making of Antebellum St. Louis," by Jeffrey S. Adler, p. 12; *Gateway Heritage,* Vol. 12, No. 3; Missouri Historical Society, Winter 1992).

Construction on the "New Courthouse," as it was then known, was begun on October 21, 1839 ("Glimpses of the Past, The Old Courthouse," by Stella M. Drumm and Charles van Ravenswaay; *Missouri Historical Society,* Vol. VII, p. 4, January–June 1940).

By the early 1850s, when Arba Crane arrives in St. Louis, the east wing of the courthouse was unfinished (it was finally completed in 1856) (id., p. 37). See "If Walls Could Talk: A Courtroom's Story," by Tom Richter (*Westward,* Vol. 1, No. 1, Jefferson National Expansion Memorial Historical Association). The painting on the cover of this book, "The Last Sale of the Slaves, 1860," by Thomas Satterwhite Noble, depicts a slave auction on the steps of the "New Courthouse."

Chapter Two

As described in *Dred Scott's Advocate, A Biography of Roswell M. Field,* by Kenneth C. Kaufman, pp. 6 n. 1, 11, 154 (University of Missouri Press, 1996), Roswell Field's two law offices were on Chestnut Street. The first was destroyed by fire in the late 1840s. The second, at 36 Chestnut Street, near what is now the north leg of the Gateway Arch, is where Dred Scott worked as a janitor.

The descriptions of Newfane in the early 1850s are drawn from *A Walk Through Historic Newfane Village* (Moore Free Library, 1985); *Dred Scott's Advocate,* pp. 35–36; and the author's visit to the town, one of the most charming in Vermont, where the Windham County Courthouse (where Roswell Field's portrait hangs) and the Union Church (now called Union Hall) are preserved much as they were in the mid-19th century. The ruins on Newfane Hill are accessible by car (most of the route up the hill is on a dirt road) and signs mark the site of the former town buildings. I have also relied on the following sources for the descriptions of Vermont life: *Brattleboro, Early History with Biographical Sketches of Some of Its Citizens,* by Henry Burnham (D. Leonard, 1880); *Hands on the Land, A History of the Vermont Landscape,* by Jan Albers (MIT Press, 2000); *Vermont Voices, 1609 Through the 1990s,* ed. J. Kevin Graffagnino, Samuel B. Hand & Gene Sessions (Vermont Historical Society, 1999); *Five Dollars and a Jug of Rum, The History of Grafton,* Vermont 1754–2000 (Grafton Historical Society, 1999); *The Growing Edge: Vermont Villages, 1840–80,* by T.D. Seymour Bassett (Vermont Historical Society, 1992); and *Releasing Rebecca, An Exploration of Life, Death and Gravestone Art in Early Vermont* (Grafton Historical Society, 1998).

The account of the legal proceedings leading to the whipping of Abigail White for counterfeiting is based on "News & Views From The Historical Society of Windham County," Newfane, Vermont (Winter 1998–99).

Arba Crane's father and mother, as depicted in *Two Men Before the Storm,* are fictionalized and did not live in Newfane (Crane's father did serve as the town clerk of Danville, Vermont). Arba Crane's name appears in a newspaper in Danville, Vermont, where he may have grown up. (Email dated November 13, 2003, from Marjorie Strong, Assistant Librarian, Vermont Historical Society.)

On November 7, 1837, the Reverend Elijah P. Lovejoy, an abolitionist minister and publisher in Alton, Illinois, was killed by an anti-abolitionist mob. The event riveted the nation (*They Have No Rights,* by Walter Erlich, p. 37, Greenwood Press, 1979; *The Civil War in St. Louis,* by William C. Winter, pp. 155–56, Missouri Historical Society Press, 1994).

Chapter Three

Both *Cutter v. Waddingham,* 22 Mo. 206 (1855) and *Cephas v. McConnell* are actual cases in which Roswell Field appeared as an attorney. *Winny v. Whitesides,* 1 Mo. 472 (1824) was followed by the Supreme Court of Missouri until its decision in *Scott (a man of color) v. Emerson,* 15 Mo. 576 (1852). E.g., *Milly (a woman of color) v. Smith,* 2 Mo. 36 (1828); *Vincent (a man of color) v. Duncan,* 2 Mo. 214 (1830); *Ralph (a man of color) v. Duncan,* 3 Mo. 194 (1833); *Julia (a woman of color) v. McKinney,* 3 Mo. 270 (1833); *Nat (a man of color) v. Ruddle,* 3 Mo. 400 (1834); *Rachael (a woman of color) v. Walker,* 4 Mo. 350 (1836); *Wilson (a man of color) v. Melvin,* 4 Mo. 592 (1837).

I have not attempted to replicate slave dialect, with two exceptions. The first is termed "left dislocation," in which "a noun or noun phrase comes at the beginning of a sentence or clause and is replaced by a pronoun in the sentence itself . . . (e.g., my mother, she . . .)" (*The Emergence of Black English,* ed. Guy Bailey, Natalie Maynor and Patricia Cukor-Avila, p. 178, John Benjamins Publishing Company, 1991). The second is the general tendency of the slaves who recorded their histories as part of the New Deal's Ex-Slave Narratives project to speak in the present tense (id., p. 275 et seq).

In describing slaves and slavery I have drawn on a number of sources, including *Remembering Slavery: African Americans Talk About Their Personal Experiences of Slavery and Emancipation,* ed. Ira Berlin, Marc Favreau, and Steven F. Miller (The New Press, 1998); *Incidents in the Life of a Slave Girl,* by Harriet Jacobs (Oxford University Press, 1988); *The Cotton Kingdom: Runaway Slaves, Rebels on the Plantation,* by John Hope Franklin and Loren Schweninger (Oxford University Press, 1999); and *Soul by Soul: Life Inside the Antebellum Slave Market* by Walter Johnson (Harvard University Press, 1999).

Chapter Four

Dred Scott was born a slave on the Virginia plantation of Captain Peter Blow, who moved first to a farm near Huntsville, Alabama, and then in 1830 to St. Louis. As recounted in *Saint Louis: An Informal History of the City and its People,* p. 406, "the Blow children were unusually able, and most became important in St. Louis . . . in a single generation, the Blows became connected with many of the city's most important families." See "The Blow Family and Their Slave Dred Scott," by John A. Bryan (*Missouri Historical Society*, Vol. IV no. 4, July 1948).

As stated, Kate Fox and her father are fictional characters. I relied principally on the following sources of information about Southern women before and during the Civil War: *A Belle of the Fifties: Memoirs of Mrs. Clay of Alabama, by Virginia Clay-Copton* (University of Alabama Press, 1999); *Brokenburn: The Journal of Kate Stone, 1861–68,* ed. John Q. Anderson (Louisiana State University Press, 1995); *Fanny Kemble's Civil Wars,* by Catherine Clinton (Simon & Schuster, 2000); *Mary Chesnut's Civil War,* ed. C. Vann Woodward (Yale University Press, 1981); and *Mothers of Invention: Women of the Slaveholding South in the Civil War,* by Drew Gilpin Faust (University of North Carolina Press, 1996). The descriptions of Kate Fox's evening dress and other clothes come principally from *Mr. Godey's Ladies: Being A Mosaic of Fashions and Fancies,* ed. Robert Kunciov (Bonanza Books, 1971). *Mothers of Invention,* pp. 223–24, provides a particularly insightful description of hoop skirts.

Samuel O'Fallon is a fictional character but his father, Colonel John O'Fallon, is not. Colonel O'Fallon was a prominent St. Louisian and a president of the Anti-Abolitionist Society (*Dred Scott's Advocate,* p. 144).

Thomas R.R. Cobb was, in fact, a prominent lawyer and slavery "apologist" who specialized in slave law. He wrote a well known treatise on slave law (L. VanderVelde and S. Subramanian, "Mrs. Dred Scott," 106 *Yale Law Journal* 1033, 1106, 1997). A New York case that upheld a Methodist minister's right to beat his wife with a horsewhip to ensure obedience was described in *Star-Spangled Eden,* by James C. Simmons, p. 68 (Carroll & Graf, 2000).

Chapter Five

There have been many descriptions of slave auctions, including those in the books on slaves and slavery cited in the sources to Chapter Three. I have drawn on all of those sources in describing the slave auction that shocked Arba Crane. One of the most sensational accounts of the time was an 1859 article by a New York *Tribune* reporter who observed a slave auction in Savannah, Georgia ("What became of the slaves on a Georgia plantation?: Great auction sale of slaves, at Savannah, Georgia, March 2d & 3d, 1859," by Mortimer Thomson, byline: Q.K. Philander Doesticks; originally published by the New York *Tribune,* March 9, 1859, and later in pamphlet form). Mortimer's account provides details unavailable in the other accounts, and I have used it to create scenes at the auction, including the slave Daphney and her infant, and the wrenching separation of Jeffrey and Dorcas.

In *Dred Scott's Advocate,* Kenneth C. Kaufman wrote that, "Harriet [Scott] would also have been aware of the woman who lived at the corner of Morgan and Garrison Streets and who brought up infants at the slave market and raised them to sell" (internal quotation marks omitted) (id., p. 141). See *Saint Louis: An Informal History of the City and its People,* p. 401. In *Soul by Soul: Life Inside the Antebellum Slave Market,* p. 163, Walter Johnson quoted from a contemporary account of "the image of slaves forced to dance to a merry fiddle while their cheeks were wet with tears" (internal quotation marks omitted).

In the same book, Walter Johnson described how "[i]n the interstices of the slave-pen routine there were ways for slaves to gather and spread knowledge about the traders and the buyers. As the traders instructed them in how to represent themselves as salable, the slaves learned about slaveholders' system of slave-buying signs; as the buyers looked them over and asked them questions, the slaves looked back and came to their own conclusion about the prospects held by a given sale" (id., p. 171).

Chapter Six

In *Memoirs of a Nobody: The Missouri Years of an Austrian Radical,* 1849–1866, by Henry Boernstein, p. 91 (Missouri Historical Society Press, 1997), the author, a first-generation immigrant who settled in St. Louis in the 1850s and later became a prominent newspaper publisher, rented horses from a livery stable in St. Louis, crossed the Meremac River and "[t]hen we rode on, ever farther and deeper into the country . . ." My researcher, Coralee Paull of St. Louis, found a reference in the Missouri Historical Society's Hull Papers from 1842, in which a traveler journeyed 25 miles to reach one stretch of prairie outside St. Louis (letter from Coralee Paull to author, dated March 11, 2002).

The description of the slave coffle is based on the 1843 account of the English traveler G.W. Featherstonhaugh, who came across such a bivouac: "It was a camp of Negro slave drivers, just packing up to start; they had about three hundred slaves with them who had bivouacked the previous night *in chains* in the woods . . ."), quoted in *Soul by Soul,* p. 49 (emphasis in the original).

When Arba Crane remarked, "I never would have expected that a slave owner could lose a case to a slave before a proslavery judge in a slave state," he quite accurately described *Cephas v. McConnell.* As recounted in *Dred Scott's Advocate,* pp. 103–09, the slave Diana Cephas filed a lawsuit in 1840 in St. Louis County Circuit Court against her owner, Murry McConnell. She claimed that her residence in Illinois freed her under the authority of the Missouri Supreme Court's decision in *Winny v. Whitesides.* Roswell Field, then a member of the law firm of Leslie & Field, and his partner represented McConnell. The case came to trial before one of the most proslavery judges in Missouri, Judge Luke E. Lawless (id., p. 104). Kenneth C. Kaufman noted Judge Lawless's "judicial leniency toward violent proslavery groups, such as the mob that had broken into the St. Louis jail, taken hold of a free black prisoner named Francis McIntosh, and burned him alive on a vacant lot on Chestnut Street" (id.). See discussion of the McIntosh case below. However, in *Cephas v. McConnell* Judge Lawless followed

Winny v. Whitesides and issued rulings consistently in favor of Diana Cephas and eventually a jury found that she was free (id., p. 108).

Dred Scott's account of his near immolation is not simply a dramatic device. The 1836 burning of Francis McIntosh was a gruesome event in St. Louis history. As told in a memoir of a St. Louis mayor, McIntosh, a steamboat steward, had been arrested for fighting. On the way to jail, a deputy-sheriff joked that he might be hung for his offense. McIntosh went berserk, stabbed the deputy-sheriff to death with a knife, and ran off. He was apprehended and taken to jail but the news spread and a mob of between 500 and 1,000 persons surrounded the jail and dragged him out. He was tied to a tree, kindling piled up at his feet, and set on fire: "The Negro was burned to death in an incredibly short time . . ." (*Personal Recollections of Many Prominent People Whom I Have Known,* by John Darby, pp. 237–41, G.I. Jones and Company, 1880).

The patrollers who caught Dred Scott were white men, "often nonslaveholders" who "captured and punished slaves who ran away . . ." (*Remembering Slavery,* pp. 54–55).

Slave marriages had no legal recognition. Nonetheless, they were of great importance to slaves. "Jumping the broom" was part of the ceremony at a slave marriage (id., pp. 122, 125).

Chapter Seven

In the late 1840s, throughout the 1850s, and especially after the appalling numbers of deaths in the Civil War, in the 1860s, a spiritualism craze swept America. It began in northern New York State near Rochester one winter night when two bored, adolescent girls discovered that they could make rapping sounds first with their fingers and then by "cracking their toe-joints against any surface which would conduct sound" (*The Spiritualists,* by Ruth Brandon, p. 2, Alfred A. Knopf, 1983). Their parents assumed they were in the presence of spirits when one sister summoned up rapping sounds from the other, who was hidden from sight. Neighbors besieged their home and the sisters' fame spread.

They became national celebrities, touring the country, and few were the wiser until they confessed to their fraud forty years later (id). Even so, their followers still came to see them perform séances, refusing to believe their confessions ("Across the Great Divide," *Time* magazine, Cover, p. 116, Oct. 25, 1999). As recounted in *The Spiritualists*, p. 44, "Madame Blavatsky founded the Theosophical Society in New York in 1881. It was an amalgam of eastern esotericism and spiritualism. She had, until that date, been active as a spiritualist medium." I have borrowed Madame Blavatsky from another era since she did not arrive in the United States until after the 1850s. The atmosphere of the séance attended by Arba Crane and Kate Fox is based on accounts of Blavatsky's performances and séances, e.g., "A Spirited Story of the Psychic and the Colonel," by Edward Hower (*The Smithsonian*, Vol. 26, no 2, p. 110; May 1995) ("Madame Blavatsky herself began to call forth spirits from the ether. Among them was her family's former footman, who wore a tall fez and sang folk songs, and her late uncle, a Russian judge wearing lugubrious, black robes"). The words Madame Blavatsky speaks at the beginning of the séance in this chapter are from her writings. *Isis Unveiled*, by Helena P. Blavatsky (The Theosophical Publishing House, 1972).

Chapter Eight

Don E. Fehrenbacher, in *The Dred Scott Case*, pp. 242–44, described Dred Scott's travels with his owner, U.S. Army doctor John Emerson (and Dr. Emerson's many ailments, marriage to Irene Sanford, and his death and will). In addition, I have relied on the following sources for details of life at Fort Snelling: *The Auto-Biography of Maj. Lawrence Taliaferro* (written in 1864) in 6 Collections of the Minn. Historical Society 189 (Pioneer Press, 1894); "Mrs. Dred Scott," 106 *Yale Law Journal*, pp. 1070–71 (regarding the importance of stoves at Fort Snelling in the winter); and *Historic Fort Snelling* (pamphlet publication of the Minnesota Historical Society describing the fort in the 19th century).

John Sanford, whose name is part of the caption (albeit misspelled) of the most consequential legal case in American history, is an obscure figure. As recounted here, he married into the prominent Chouteau family (*The Dred Scott Case*, p. 248), became an agent of the American Fur Company, relocated to New York—a move of enormous legal significance to the case and, ultimately, the nation—and eventually went insane (*Dred Scott's Advocate*, pp. 169–70 & 225).

Remarkably, few historians have devoted significant attention to Irene Emerson. Kenneth C. Kaufman suggested that she was motivated by profit from hiring the Scotts out and "family dignity" (id., p. 118). If "family dignity" is a euphemism for vanity, then Irene Emerson's vanity may have changed the course of American history.

Chapter Nine

Major Taliaferro was the Indian agent at Fort Snelling from April 1819 to January 1840. The description of Major Taliaferro and Fort Snelling, including the tragic fate of Tash-u-no-ta, are mainly from *The Auto-Biography of Maj. Lawrence Taliaferro*, pp. 233–34 (describing how in 1826 a group of Sioux Indians were stranded on the prairie by a snowstorm and the ensuing cannibalism). In it, Major Taliaferro generally, but not always, referred to himself in the third person, as in: "In order to enforce morality as far as practicable, being the highest officer at the post, he induced many traders with growing Indian families to legitimize their children by marriage. There being no minister in the country, he officiated as a justice of the peace and united many . . . closing with the union of Dred Scott with Harriet Robinson—my servant girl, which I gave him" (id., 234–35).

Because "[o]nly fragments of Harriet Robinson Scott's life have survived in the historical record," ("Mrs. Dred Scott," 106 *Yale Law Journal*, p. 1042), I have made assumptions about the circumstances of her acquisition by Major Taliaferro since historians cannot agree on whether he inherited Harriet or bought her. Based on Major Taliaferro's description of the many acts of bribery and attempted bribery of American officials by the American Fur Company (e.g., *The Auto-Biography of Maj. Lawrence Taliaferro*, p. 202, recounting baseless allegations against Major Taliaferro that he had accepted such a bribe), it is plausible if speculative that Harriet was offered as a bribe. That an otherwise upright American in those days would regard as immoral a bribe but not the purchase of a human being, however, struck me as all too historically accurate.

Chapter Ten

The Clerk of the Circuit Court in St. Louis, John Ruland, wrote out the summons for Harriet's petition and in doing so, started to write "Scott" after her first name, then crossed it out and wrote "a woman of color" (summons to Irene Emerson dated April 6, 1846, *Harriet, a woman of color v. Emerson*, St. Louis County Circuit Court).

The Reverend John Anderson was "a free black and towering man of more than two hundred pounds" whose mother had come west from Virginia to St. Louis (*Dred Scott's Advocate*, p. 142). As a young man the Reverend Anderson worked for the Reverend Lovejoy in Alton, Illinois. He was "in Alton the night proslavery mobs broke into Lovejoy's print shop, murdered the young editor and destroyed his printing press" (id). He returned to St. Louis where he became the minister of the Second African Baptist Church and helped slaves escape to freedom.

Fear of slaves was a recurring theme of antebellum life. The murder of Mrs. Middlespoon is based on an account in *Mary Chesnut's Civil War*, pp. 209–212.

Judge William Scott was the Chief Judge of the Missouri Supreme Court. In those days, a Missouri law license could be granted only by one of the Supreme Court judges "and then only by a personal examination of the applicant by the judge himself" (*Reminiscences of the Bench and Bar of Missouri,* by W.V.N. Bay, pp. 32–33, F.H. Thomas and Company, 1878). Billy Hart was a "fine looking and intelligent mulatto who, as janitor served the [Missouri Supreme Court] faithfully for a quarter of a century . . . and could personate . . . the judges in voice, language, and manner" (id., p. 328).

Senator Thomas Hart Benton, an outspoken opponent of the expansion of slavery, represented Missouri in the United States Senate for three decades. He was colorful (he gained public attention in part because of his success in fighting duels), powerful (he was at the center of the pitched political battles over the Bank of the United States in the 1830s and slavery in the 1850s), and eloquent (like so many of his Senate contemporaries, especially Calhoun, Clay, and Webster). He lost his Senatorial seat in January 1851 after 13 days of balloting at the state capitol in Jefferson City (*Old Bullion Benton—Senator from the New West,* by William Nisbet Chambers, pp. 374–75, Atlantic Monthly Press, 1956). The victor in that election was attorney Henry S. Geyer who, while a United States Senator, argued *Scott v. Sandford* in the United States Supreme Court for the defendant. In those days, United States Senators were elected by state legislatures.

Chapter Eleven

Scott v. Emerson was tried twice in what is now the "Old Courthouse" in St. Louis. Dred and Harriet Scott's petitions were filed in Missouri state court on April 6, 1846. The first trial was in 1847 and the second was in 1850. Both were presided over by Judge Alexander Hamilton, an antislavery Pennsylvanian and a relatively new appointee to the Missouri bench (*The Dred Scott Case,* pp. 250–57).

To meet the needs of a dramatic narrative, I condensed the two trials into one but kept the essential events. At the first trial, in which the Scotts were probably represented by Samuel Mansfield Bay and Irene Emerson by George Goode, witness Samuel Russell testified on cross-examination that he had no knowledge of Irene Emerson's ownership of the Scotts, other than what he had learned from his wife. As a result the jury returned a verdict for Irene Emerson. As Don E. Fehrenbacher wrote, "The decision produced the absurd effect of allowing Mrs. Emerson to keep her slaves simply because no one had proved that they *were* her slaves." (id., p. 254, emphasis in the original). The Scotts' attorneys moved for a new trial, "arguing that Russell's testimony had been a surprise and that the facts in question could readily be established" (id.). Judge Hamilton granted the motion for retrial.

At the second trial, the Scotts' new attorneys, Alexander P. Field and David N. Hall, corrected this mistake (id.). The testimony of Mrs. Russell established that Irene Emerson was the owner of the Scotts. The "decisive moment came when Judge Hamilton complied with a request that he instruct the jury in terms highly favorable to the plaintiff" (id., pp. 256–57). The jury found in favor of Dred Scott. Emerson's new counsel, Hugh A. Garland and Lyman D. Norris, appealed the case to the Missouri Supreme Court.

The testimony of Mr. and Mrs. Russell, as well as the other witnesses, and parts of the summations, are based on the typescript copies of the court proceedings from the Dred Scott Collection at the Missouri Historical Society, the court records in the files of the St. Louis County Circuit Court, and *American State Trials,* John D. Lawson, ed., Vol. XIII, p. 220–55 (F.H. Thomas & Co., 1914–36).

Mrs. Russell's inability to make up her mind whether she wanted a girl slave or a boy slave is based on accounts of similar first-time buyers in *Soul by Soul,* pp. 82–83 and 90–91 (quoting from a young Louisiana farmer's letter to a slave trader: "You will think we do not know our mind exactly as we have now concluded that it will be best to have a girl instead of a boy").

Arba Crane's encounter with the tough in the wilds outside of St. Louis is, of course, fictionalized. However, the Anti-Abolitionist Society existed, having been formed in 1846, and campaigned to have free negroes jailed if they failed to carry a license and to enact stronger prohibitions against African-American churches (*Dred Scott's Advocate,* pp. 144–45).

Chapter Twelve

The rage of wives at husbands who sexually violated their slaves knew no bounds. C. Vann Woodward wrote in the introduction to *Mary Chesnut's Civil War* that the feature of slavery "that most offended her was the sexual abuse of the slave women" and "[w]hat outraged her beyond endurance was the hypocrisy of the stern puritanical code these libertarian patriarchs imposed on their womenfolk and children" (id., p. li, "Of Heresy and Paradox"). But because of this code such rage was generally not directed toward the husbands but instead at helpless slave women, who were the real victims. As John Hope Franklin wrote, "[s]laveholding wives could be vicious toward black women they suspected of having relationships with their husbands" (*Runaway Slaves*, p. 24).

Chapter Thirteen

As Charles van Ravenswaay wrote, "[t]he year 1849 brought St. Louis the twin calamities of fire and plague" (*Saint Louis: An Informal History of the City and its People*, p. 383). I have incorporated both events into the narrative, albeit placing them at a time later than they actually occurred. The Great Fire began when a steamboat caught fire and its mooring lines were cut by firemen, which turned out to be a mistake. The steamboat drifted against other steamboats and the levee and soon the fire was on shore, where winds spread it to riverfront warehouses and beyond. More than a thousand firemen tried unsuccessfully to control the blaze. The city was saved by a fire company captain, Thomas B. Targee, who conceived the plan to blow up buildings in the path of the flames and was killed while setting a charge in a music store. Nearly fifteen blocks of commercial and residential buildings were destroyed, along with twenty-three steamboats (id., pp. 383–88). Roswell Field's law office on Chestnut Street was in one of the buildings consumed by the fire (*Dred Scott's Advocate*, pp. 153–54).

Most Americans' image of slavery is a plantation with slaves toiling in the cotton fields, such as Tara Plantation in *Gone With the Wind*. As one historian wrote, "[t]he [Southern] city had created its own kind of world, with a pace, sophistication, and environment that separated it from rural modes. In the process it transformed Negro no less than white, slave no less than free man" (*Slavery in the Cities: The South 1820–1860,* by Richard C. Wade, p. 27, Oxford University Press, 1964).

While many slaves lived with their owners, generally in separate quarters placed close to, but sealed off from, the owner's home or building (id., p. 59), others were both "hired out" and allowed to "live out." Under the hiring-out system, owners with more slaves than they had chores for hired some to employers with both short- and long-term needs (id., p. 38). Sometimes, slaves were allowed to hire "their own time," that is, find a job, negotiate wages, pay an agreed amount to their owners, and keep the rest (id., p. 48). Slaveholders also found it convenient, if not profitable, to allow slaves to find their own housing, an arrangement called "living out"—"finding a room here, renting a house there, and in other cases simply disappearing into remote sections of town" (id., p. 62).

In St. Louis, as in other Southern cities, the slaves "living out" generally found abodes in the free black quarter. In 1854, St. Louis had a population of 77,860, of whom 4,054 were blacks. Of these, 2,656 were slaves and the remaining 1,398 were free (*Dred Scott's Advocate,* p. 8). A very small number of the free blacks formed a black aristocracy, whose "wealth and position protected it from much of the restrictive abuse directed toward free black persons" (id., p. 147 n. 42).

Most urban slaves did domestic work, including caring for ill whites. Sick Southern women had "three or four female slaves . . . sleep on the floor of their sick room" (*Slavery in the Cities,* pp. 30–31, citation omitted). Young children, like Eliza Scott, did chores as well (id., p. 31–32).

Chapter Fourteen

Nothing in the experience of living Americans approaches the catastrophic epidemics that periodically afflicted American cities in the mid-19th century. For sixteen years, St. Louis had avoided serious outbreaks of cholera. But 1849, the year of the Great Fire, also became "The Year of the Cholera" ("Glimpses of the Past—The Year of the Cholera," *Missouri Historical Society,* Vol. III, No. 3, pp. 56–57, March 1936). Cemetery records show that 4,547 victims of cholera were buried between January and July 30, 1849, or approximately 7% of the population. In the last week in July, just before the epidemic subsided, 722 persons died. A third of the deaths were children (id., pp. 57, 64). The descriptions of cholera symptoms, the measures taken by the Committee of Public Health, the fake cures and the more effective treatments, the funeral processions, and the flight of wealthy citizens are drawn from *Glimpses of the Past—The Year of the Cholera* and *Saint Louis: An Informal History of the City and its People,* pp. 388–91.

Roswell Field lost four children—Frances Victoria, Theodore French, William Bradley, and Charles James—apparently either to cholera or similar diseases at very young ages, although these deaths occurred during epidemics after 1849 (*Dred Scott's Advocate,* pp. 153–55, 165, 213–14). According to a surviving son, Field's wife also died of cholera (id., p. 213. But see id. n. 21) (at the time of her death, in 1856, cholera was not active in St. Louis). He buried his wife and children at Bellefontaine Cemetery (id., p. 214).

Chapter Fifteen

At one point, antislavery lecturers met a hostile reception in Vermont. The Reverend E.R. Taylor's experience in Brattleboro is based on an account in *Brattleboro, Early History with Biographical Sketches of Some of Its Citizens,* p. 44.

The description of the Emerson brief to the Missouri Supreme Court is based on quotes from the brief in *They have No Rights,* pp. 55–62.

Chapter Sixteen

The Vermont Supreme Court's opinion in *Clark v. Field* can be found at 13 Vt. 460 (1841). The source of the basic events of the case are the opinion, the legal pleadings, and Kenneth Kaufman's fine narrative in *Dred Scott's Advocate,* pp. 56–70, including the details of their courtship (the rosebush leaf, the chess game), the elopement, the letter from Mary Almira refusing to see him again, the Windsor meeting, Roswell Field's quest for justice in the Vermont courts, his final loss in the Vermont Supreme Court, and his self-imposed exile from Vermont to St. Louis.

As to Mary Almira Phelps's visit to St. Louis, the following appears in *Reminiscences of the Bench and Bar of Missouri,* p. 239:

This incident in the life of Mr. Field had a marked effect upon his character, and almost made him a cynic. For years he withdrew from society, and scarcely ever mingled with the people. He ultimately married a Miss Frances Reed, of St. Louis, and after her death Mrs. Clark, whose husband had also died, visited St. Louis with the intention and desire of bringing about a reconciliation between herself and Mr. Field; but he declined an interview, and she returned to Vermont.

Chapter Seventeen

The Missouri Supreme Court's decision in *Scott (a man of color) v. Emerson* can be found at 15 Mo. 576 (1852). Had Dred Scott's case reached the Missouri Supreme Court a few years earlier than it did, the outcome might have been different, as Roswell Field suggests. But by 1852, the spirit of comity between slave and free states on slavery issues was gone. The "climate of opinion no longer encouraged and scarcely permitted a bias in favor of freedom . . ." (*The Dred Scott Case*, p. 262). By now, as well, a "siege mentality" was settling into Southern minds and with it a corresponding fear and hatred for Northern abolitionists (*War To The Knife: Bleeding Kansas 1854–61*, by Thomas Goodrich, p. 7, Stackpole Books, 1998). The outburst of resentment at the North in the majority's opinion is an illuminating example of the developing "siege mentality."

Chapter Eighteen

On June 29, 1852, Judge Alexander Hamilton denied the Emerson attorneys' motion to terminate the sheriff's custody of the Scott family and thereby restore Irene Emerson's ownership rights (*The Dred Scott Case*, p. 267). I found this to be one of the most remarkable expressions of conscience and courage in the entire case. Denying the motion was a violation of his judicial oath and without legal authority. Given the ever-increasing anger in Missouri at antislavery advocates ("Bleeding Kansas" was about to erupt), it likely was an act not without personal risk. Yet he obviously was moved by, and sympathetic to, the Scotts' plight, and he kept their hopes alive. There can be little doubt that his relationship with Roswell Field played a role in Judge Hamilton's handling of the case. See *Dred Scott's Advocate*, p. 111 ("Judge Hamilton was also to become [by 1852] a close personal friend of Roswell Field"). Don E. Fehrenbacher suggested that "[t]he only satisfactory explanation of Judge Hamilton's action . . . is that he had already been privately informed of an intention to carry Dred Scott's cause to the federal Supreme Court" (*The Dred Scott Case*, p. 267). If so, he undoubtedly was informed by his close friend, Roswell Field.

Chapter Nineteen

The Kansas-Nebraska Act of 1854 largely repealed the Missouri Compromise of 1820 and established the doctrine of popular sovereignty as the basis for determining whether the vast Nebraska Territory would be free or slave. Don E. Fehrenbacher wrote that, "[t]he two major consequences were a revolution in the party system and a civil war in Kansas" (*The Dred Scott Case*, p. 187). Its sponsor, Illinois Senator Stephen A. Douglas, was pilloried by opponents of slavery, who coalesced into the Republican Party largely as a result of the Act.

The first test of popular sovereignty was in Kansas. Opponents of slavery, mainly from New England, and proslavery men, many from western Missouri, converged on Kansas. Arba Crane encountered a band of the latter, the so-called "border ruffians," on his way to Iowa. These were rough men from a frontier population "that included teamsters, trappers, and hunters . . . ," (*War to the Knife*, p. 99) looking as much for a fight as they were to bring Kansas into the Union as a slave state.

During the litigation, Eliza and Lizzie Scott disappeared from St. Louis. After the United States Supreme Court's decision, the *St. Louis Daily Evening News* reported on May 26, 1857, that "[t]heir whereabouts have been kept a secret, though no effort has been and none probably would have been, made to recover them. Their father knew where they were and could bring them back at any moment," quoted in *Dred Scott's Advocate*, p. 227 & n. 68. No record exists as to how the two children fled, where they hid, or who helped them.

The description of the quilt is based on *Stitched from the Soul: Slave Quilts from the Antebellum South*, by Gladys-Marie Fry, pp. 52–53 (Dutton Studio Books, 1990).

Chapter Twenty

A Mississippi River sandbar, the scene of famous and not so famous duels, became known as Bloody Island. In those days, "[b]loody arguments often started casually" (*Saint Louis: An Informal History of the City and its People*, pp. 190–91). One duel started when two U.S. Army officers on a Mississippi River steamboat got into an argument over whether a tree in the river was a "snag" or a "sawyer" (a fixed or movable obstruction). Both missed (id., p. 191). By the 1850s, duels had been outlawed in Missouri but were still being fought (id., p. 434).

Scott v. Sandford was tried in federal court—the Circuit Court of the United States for the district of Missouri. The trial judge was Robert W. Wells, a Virginian who had been attorney general of Missouri. The legal significance of the new case was that it raised new issues not presented by *Scott v. Emerson*—Dred Scott's citizenship and (after the case reached the Supreme Court) the constitutionality of the Missouri Compromise's restriction on slavery. The case came to trial on May 15, 1854. Scott was represented by Roswell Field and Sanford by Hugh Garland. The jury's verdict, in view of the charge by Judge Wells that reflected the ruling by the Missouri Supreme Court in *Scott v. Emerson,* was foregone (*The Dred Scott Case,* pp. 276–80). Two years after the trial, Judge Wells told Montgomery Blair, "I may say to you, however, that my feelings were deeply interested in favor of the poor fellow, and I wish the law was in favor of his freedom" (letter from Robert Wells to Montgomery Blair, dated February 12, 1856, courtesy Missouri Historical Society).

Following the trial, as described in this chapter, Field wrote Montgomery Blair asking whether, in the "cause of humanity," Blair would argue the case in the Supreme Court. Blair accepted (without charging a fee), writing also that "in the Southern states, almost every lawyer feels bound to give his services when asked in such a case arising in the community in which he belongs" (letters from Field to Blair dated December 24, 1854 and from Blair to Field dated December 30, 1854, courtesy Missouri Historical Society). The pamphlet quoted in this chapter (dated July 4, 1854) is of unknown authorship. The pamphlet "was almost certain to have rankled Southerners who read it, not only in Missouri but elsewhere" (*Dred Scott's Advocate*, p. 197).

Chapter Twenty-One

In the 19th century, the Blair family was second only to the Adams family for its influence on American politics (*The Francis Preston Blair Family*, by William Ernest Smith, p. vii, The Macmillan Company, 1933).

At the time of the *Dred Scott* arguments, the Supreme Court was housed in a room below the United States Senate. The description of Washington and its outskirts in the mid-1850s, the Supreme Court, and the Justices are drawn from the following sources: *The Supreme Court in United States History*, by Charles Warren (Little, Brown, & Company, 1922); *The Sights and Secrets of the National Capitol: A Work Descriptive of Washington City*, by Dr. John B. Ellis (U.S. Publishing Co., 1870); and *Thirty Years in Washington or Life and Scenes in Our National Capital*, edited by Mrs. John A. Logan (A.D. Worthington & Co., 1901). The sketches of individual Justices are based on: *A Memoir of Benjamin Robbins Curtis, LL.D. with Some of His Professional and Miscellaneous Writings*, by Benjamin R. Curtis (Little Brown & Company, 1879); *The Life of John McLean: A Politician on the United States Supreme Court*, by Francis P. Weisenburger (Da Capo Press, 1971); *James Moore Wayne: Southern Unionist*, by Alexander A. Lawrence (University of North Carolina Press, 1943); and *John Archibald Campbell: Southern Moderate, 1811–89*, by Robert Saunders, Jr. (University of Alabama Press, 1997).

As to Chief Justice Roger Taney, the events depicted here—his defense of the abolitionist minister Jacob Gruber, the freeing of his slaves, his refusal to let his daughter vacation in Newport, Rhode Island, and the subsequent death of that daughter as well as his wife—are described in *Roger B. Taney*, by Carl Brent Swisher (Archon Books,

1961) and *Memoir of Roger Brooke Taney,* by Samuel Tyler (John Murphy & Co., 1872).

James Harvey of the New York *Tribune* wrote about the *Dred Scott* case from the abolitionist perspective. His pungent comments on many of the Justices can be found in *The Supreme Court in American History,* Vol. 3, Chap. 26, pp. 39–41.

In those days, the Supreme Court did not make a record of its oral arguments. I constructed the oral arguments on the basis of the surviving briefs, newspaper accounts and the Court's decision. In particular, *The Dred Scott Case* and *They Have No Rights* provided a helpful analysis of the arguments and the appellate strategies of the two sides.

Chapter Twenty-Two

Old Point Comfort is near Norfolk, Virginia. Taney's harsh words of rejection of Alice's request to vacation in Newport, Rhode Island, are verbatim from the letter he wrote to Alice's brother-in-law, dated June 26, 1855 (*Roger B. Taney*, p. 466 & n. 34). Three months later, while vacationing in Old Point Comfort, Alice died of cholera and her mother died from a stroke, a few hours apart. Taney, then 78 years old, had begun writing his autobiography at Old Point Comfort. As Carl Brent Swisher wrote, "[t]he broken-hearted family boarded a boat for Baltimore. Taney was leaving Old Point, the scene of many happy summers and of one terrible tragedy, never to return, and the writing of the story of his life, which had begun there, was never to be resumed" (id., p. 469).

Did the tragedy affect the outcome of the Dred Scott case? We can never know, but one historian suggested: "It is possible that the death of his wife and daughter and the breaking up of his home deprived him of the emotional reserves necessary to preserve the judicial balance for which he had hitherto received credit and led to the taking of more and more extreme positions" ("The Taney Period, 1836–1864", by

Carl B. Swisher, Vol. V of Oliver Wendell Holmes Devise, *History of the Supreme Court of the United States*, p. 722, quoted in *The Dred Scott Case*, p. 559).

Chapter Twenty-Three

Abigail White did scream. Roswell Field's brother, Charles, wrote that "[t]he High Sheriff applied a certain number of stripes, and the balance were allotted to his Deputies, some seven in number, and some of whom applied the blows with great vigor. Near the close of the whipping her back became raw, and she suffered excessive pain and she shrieked and screamed terribly in her agony" (*Centennial Proceedings and Other Historical Facts and Incidents Relating to Newfane*, by D. Leonard, p. 33, Steam Job Printer, 1877; quoted in *Dred Scott's Advocate*, p. 21).

The incident on the *Polar Star* happened as related by Roswell Field in his letter to Arba Crane (*War to the Knife*, p. 97–98).

Chapter Twenty-Four

Between the first and second oral arguments in the *Dred Scott* case, Americans began to debate slavery with more than just words. On May 21, 1856, border ruffians sacked the free-state town of Lawrence, Kansas. The next day, in Washington, D.C., Charles Sumner was beaten half to death on the floor of the United States Senate. Three days after that, John Brown, who, one of his sons remembered, went "crazy" at the news of the beating, led a raid near Pottawatomie Creek, Kansas, killing five proslavery men (*War to the Knife*, p. 123).

The account of the beating of Charles Sumner is based on *Charles Sumner*, by David Herbert Donald, pp. 282–322 (Da Capo Press, 1996).

Sumner recuperated at Francis Blair's Silver Spring home, whose description is based on *The Francis Preston Blair Family*, pp. 185–88 and 190–91. It was more than three years after the beating before Sumner could resume regular duties as a Senator (*Charles Sumner*, p. 312).

Chapter Twenty-Five

In November 1856, Democrat James Buchanan won the Presidential election, beating the Republican Party's candidate John Frémont (whose principal opponent for the Party's nomination had been Supreme Court Justice McLean). When the *Dred Scott* case was argued for a second time, on December 15, 1856, "[e]very one of the nine justices must have realized by this time that the Court had an explosive package on its hands . . . Many more people were now aware of what might be at stake in one Negro's suit for freedom" (*The Dred Scott Case*, p. 293).

In a brief filed on December 2, 1856, the Sanford attorneys forcefully argued against the constitutionality of the Missouri Compromise (*They Have No Rights*, pp. 112–13). In challenging the authority of Congress to limit the expansion of slavery, the Sanford attorneys struck at the foundation of legislative compromises that many had credited with saving the Union.

Chapter Twenty-Six

According to newspaper accounts and the memoirs and biographers of several of the Justices, the Supreme Court, at least initially, was divided over whether to resolve the case on narrow procedural grounds or on the merits. A draft opinion addressing only the former was written by Justice Nelson, but was then discarded in favor of a sweeping opinion on the merits that would declare the Missouri Compromise unconstitutional (*The Dred Scott Case*, pp. 307–309). At the suggestion of Justice Wayne, the author would be Chief Justice Taney, who "[b]ehind his mask of judicial propriety" had become privately "a bitter sectionalist, seething with anger at Northern insult and Northern aggression" (id., p. 311, internal quotation marks omitted).

On February 19, 1857, Justice Catron wrote to President-elect Buchanan, urging him to press Pennsylvania's Justice Grier to join a majority opinion. Buchanan wrote to Justice Grier, who wrote back that he had agreed to "concur" with the Chief Justice (id., p. 311–12). Buchanan, now privy to the forthcoming ruling, declared at his inauguration on March 4, 1857, that the Supreme Court would soon settle the issue of "when the people of a Territory shall decide this question [slavery] for themselves" (id., p. 313). By today's standards, and perhaps even by the then prevailing ones, such communications are a flagrant breach of judicial ethics.

Chapter Twenty-Seven

On March 6, 1857, the Supreme Court was filled to capacity, and many were turned away. For two hours, Chief Justice Taney read from his opinion in a low voice that was difficult to hear. Nelson and Catron then read brief concurring opinions. McLean and Curtis, the two dissenters, read their opinions the next day, taking about five hours. The remaining Justices filed their opinions and did not read them in the courtroom (*The Dred Scott Case*, p. 315). By all accounts, the atmosphere in the courtroom was serious and tense (*They Have No Rights*, p. 137). Several newspapers reported that, when Taney read his opinion, he used the phrase "they have no rights," instead of "they had no rights," which caused "perhaps the most acrimonious reaction associated with the opinion" (id., pp. 142–43). Given the historical context of this section of his opinion, it appears more likely that Taney used the past tense. But whatever the tense, his opinion, in effect, established that, in 1857, they still had no rights that "the white man was bound to respect." In any event, all quotes in this chapter are from the opinion as it finally was published by the Supreme Court.

Chapter Twenty-Eight

The Vermont legislature's resolution, the Northern and Southern newspaper editorials, Chief Justice Taney's refusal to publish his opinion (and his rewriting of it), and Justice Curtis's resignation are recounted in *The Dred Scott Case*, pp. 417–28 and 449–50 and *Vermont Voices*, p. 167–68.

As to the importance of the decision to the Lincoln-Douglas debates, "[i]t would not be far wrong to say that the meaning of the Dred Scott decision became the heart of the matter in the famous debates of 1858" (*The Dred Scott Case*, p. 443). See *Crisis of the House Divided: An Interpretation of the Issues in the Lincoln-Douglas Debates*, by Harry V. Jaffa (University of Chicago Press, 1959). See Author's Note for a description of the Democratic Convention of 1860.

Congressman Frank Blair, Montgomery Blair's brother, Heinrich Boernstein, and Roswell Field, among others, played important roles in keeping Missouri in the Union (*Dred Scott's Advocate*, pp. 230–32 and *Memoirs of a Nobody*, pp. 272–81).

Chapter Twenty-Nine

The emancipation of Dred Scott on May 26, 1857, made headlines in newspapers throughout the nation. See Author's Note for a description of the events leading to Scott's emancipation. Dred Scott found a job as a porter at Barnum's Hotel in St. Louis, where guests regarded him as a celebrity. Following his death on September 17, 1858, he was buried in Wesleyan Cemetery (*Dred Scott's Advocate*, p. 228 & n. 72). On November 27, 1867, Taylor Blow moved Dred Scott's grave to Calvary

Cemetery. Until 1957, the grave was unmarked and unnoticed. That year, the 100th anniversary of the Dred Scott decision, the grave was discovered and a stone placed on it "by a granddaughter of Taylor Blow, along with a bronze grave plaque by St. Louis African Americans" (id., p. 238 & n. 32).

ABOUT THE AUTHOR

Gregory J. Wallance is a prominent lawyer in New York City. He is the author of the acclaimed *Papa's Game*, a finalist for the Edgar Allen Poe award. He lectures and writes on a variety of legal subjects and has written articles for the *New York Times*, *Wall Street Journal*, *Newsweek*, *Village Voice*, *Newsday*, and *Miami Herald*, among others. His academic article on the Dred Scott case will be published by the *Civil War Times*.

"Colorful . . . [written] with considerable skill . . . the veracity adds so much to the interest and excitement of *Papa's Game*."

—*New York Times Book Review* on *Papa's Game*